GOOD JUNK

Also by Ed Kovacs

Storm Damage

GOOD JUNK

A Cliff St. James Novel

ED KOVACS

Minotaur Books ♏ New York

GOOD JUNK. Copyright © 2012 by Ed Kovacs. All rights reserved. Printed in the United States of America. For information, address St. Martin's Press, 175 Fifth Avenue, New York, N.Y. 10010.

www.minotaurbooks.com

ISBN 978-0-312-60089-1 (hardcover)
ISBN 978-1-250-01605-8 (e-book)

First Edition: December 2012

10 9 8 7 6 5 4 3 2 1

*For Mileena Amika, who wasn't afraid to
roll the dice for one more go-round*

AUTHOR'S NOTE

Thanks in advance to my readers for understanding that while most locations in this book are real and worth a visit, others are purely fictional.

Please excuse my taking liberties with certain procedures of the New Orleans Police Department. Those officers have a tough job that few of us would want. I have nothing but good wishes for police officers in the city of New Orleans.

ACKNOWLEDGMENTS

How fortunate I am to have encountered teachers and mentors and purveyors of encouragement along the long and sometimes lonely road of the author.

Thank you, Mr. Gurley, Miss Johnson, Doug Hobbie, Danny Simon, Jackie Kahane, April Smith, Steven Whitney, Saraswati Smith-Stegman, Randall Fitzgerald, David Tseklenis, and all of the many others who gifted me with sparks of light as I navigated my way.

In the days before PCs and iMacs, my salt-of-the-earth sister, Judith Cline, gave me an electric typewriter for graduation. My father, who so badly wanted me to follow in his business footsteps, broke ranks with his hopes and instead turned to his heart and bought me a dictionary. And years ago, Lisa and Maggie Chan gave me time to write when my world was a dark place.

What possible repayment could I render for their investments of blind faith but to continue putting words to the blank page? It seems to be a horribly meager dividend, but I pray it stands as hard evidence of my heartfelt thanks, love, and gratitude.

More specific thanks go to Michael Homler, Jeanne-Marie, Hector, Cassie, Rafal, Kate, and all the rest of the hardworking folks at St. Martin's Press who have treated me and my books so kindly.

ACKNOWLEDGMENTS

I'm lucky that Carl Scholl, Tony Ritzman, and Dave Roy are still looking out for me. Hats off to Richard Curtis. Chris Graham did yeoman's service on my Web site that shall not go unsung. As for Ed Stackler, he is simply terrific; thanks once again, Ed, and keep sticking to your guns when we cross pens.

Police Chief Robert Hecker, Harbor Police, Port of New Orleans, was of great help and was one of the true heroes to emerge during the chaos of Hurricane Katrina. Jorge Young of Fontai Metal and Equipment Company in Southern California kindly shared his expertise regarding the scrap business.

Captain Eric Morton made for a hell of a detective. He has a generous spirit and can cook a mean pork butt; there's a connection there, somewhere. Blue skies, partner.

Detective Myron Gaudet of the Jefferson Parish Sheriff's Office could be a tough-guy Hollywood action star, but he wouldn't be acting. I still owe you, brother.

Neungreuthai Chanphonsean is, hands down, the coolest customer around and gets the nod for Biggest Thanks of All.

CHAPTER ONE

Funny, that a concerned friend would ask me to come and look at a couple of dead bodies in an effort to cheer me up. Maybe not cheer me up, exactly; maybe Honey wanted to distract me, get my mind engaged in something other than bruising guilt over having recently killed a guy in my fight-cage ring. That it had been unintended, during what was supposed to have been a friendly sparring session, was of no solace to the dead fighter. But unlike my dead mixed-martial-arts opponent, the two dead men here in a grubby parking lot surrounded by CSI techs and crime-scene tape were both very intentionally dead, most likely at the hands of a third party, despite New Orleans Police Homicide Detective Honey Baybee's assertion that this was a probable murder/suicide.

The black guy, the one in the high-gloss white Mercedes S550 with fancy rims, was thirty-ish and had the kind of *GQ* looks that suggested a certain pampering, and I'm not talking about by Mama.

"Pretty Boy here was definitely killed in the car," I told my friend Honey. "Nice manicure."

"Ty Parks," said Honey, wearing latex gloves as she rifled through the guy's wallet. "Same address as the other victim. Gay lovers, I figure."

I'd seen bloodier car interiors, but I wouldn't want the cleanup job. "Plays havoc with the resale value."

"What?"

"New headliner, new seats. Pull the pieces of skull out of the leather trim. Still, you run a CARFAX on this vehicle, what will come up? 'Never been in an accident, but a guy got his brains blown out in the passenger seat.' Is that a selling point?"

Honey knew how to ignore me better than most. I think she took comfort from the fact that I was being my usual wiseass self. Since I didn't want her worrying, I worked hard to generate my customary patter and mask my deep funk while pretending nothing was wrong with me. But there was a lot wrong with me, and it was only partially due to the fact that my adopted city was still largely in ruins, one year after a Cat 5 hurricane had nearly wiped us out.

"They both worked at Michoud. Both stiffs."

"Security clearances?" I asked.

"Not sure. They do secret stuff at Michoud?"

"It's a federal facility, part of NASA. They're known as being the external tank people for the space shuttles, not exactly hush-hush work, but who knows what all goes on out there." I checked out Ty's gold diamond ring, thick gold chain bracelet, Kenneth Cole brogues. "This guy is pretty tricked out for a civil servant punching a clock."

"So is his buddy. Del Breaux. Fifty-three years old."

I'd been leaning into the front-seat area and backed off to straighten up. "Sugar daddy, you think?" I used the sleeve of my Polo shirt to mop the sweat that had beaded up on my forehead. At 8:19 in the morning it was already ninety degrees with a humidity to match. It's why the smart tourists stayed away in summer; tourists staying away was maybe the only good thing about August in the Delta. We were still shaded here in the parking lot, otherwise the corpses might be puffier than Paul Prudhomme after a night of binge drinking tequila shooters.

"Breaux has some sort of business downtown. On Poydras." Honey read from a business card extracted from a second wallet. Breaux's personal effects—keys, cell phone, cigarette case—were secured in plastic evidence bags. "Breaux Enterprises. One Shell Square. Forty-ninth floor."

I glanced over at Breaux, an older white male sprawled supine about twenty-five feet away, getting photographed by a squirrelly crime-scene tech who kept whispering, "Say cheese," before each snap.

"Forty-ninth floor is almost the penthouse. That's some pricey high-rise real estate." I circled the car, checking for abnormalities. "This is a brand-new, hundred-thousand-dollar ride. Let me guess; it's registered to Breaux Enterprises."

Honey nodded. "Leased."

"Luxury, fine German engineering, and a look that says to everybody else, 'I've got it, you don't, so kiss my ass.'" I checked out the Michoud decal on the driver's side of the windshield. "So Mister Breaux works at Michoud, but he's also a business tycoon?"

"Does anyone in New Orleans not have a scam on the side?"

"Speaking of that . . . you sure the chief okayed me being here?" Chief Pointer and I had a long history, none of it good, dating back to when I had been an NOPD cop. I'd been doing pretty well as a private investigator since resigning from the department almost exactly a year ago, but I couldn't imagine the chief wanted any part of me.

"He agreed you act as an unpaid consultant. Attached to the Homicide Section. To me, specifically. I made him put it in writing. Said you'd never believe me if he didn't." Honey handed me a signed sheet on the chief's letterhead.

I scanned the document authorizing me to assist Honey. "This from the guy who'd like to sauté my liver with some onions?"

"You read the papers. He's fighting for his job. We're the murder capital of the planet. He's the scapegoat. He knows you're good. And he loves the nice headlines I've brought the department. We deliver a couple of high-profile arrests? He might make it to the end of the year. Keep the letter. You'll need it."

"I can't believe you went all the way to Pointer to get me aboard," I said, crossing toward the body of Del Breaux.

"The average homicide dick is working twenty-three cases. I'm lucky. I only have seventeen murders on my plate," she said, following, as she made a notation in her pocket notebook.

Honey wasn't the kind of friend who ever asked for much, so when she called me this morning and asked for my help, almost pleading with me, there was no way I could refuse her. I'd assumed she was pretending to need my assistance because she felt concerned about me. But now, as I looked at the corpses, I couldn't be sure about that; this was a rather sophisticated crime scene. Ultimately, it didn't matter. I simply had to spring myself from a self-imposed isolation and come out to help her if I could, regardless of her motivations. That was fine, even though I would prefer to be buried in my couch, feeling sorry for myself and avoiding all contact with the outside world.

Actually, I'd do just about anything for Honey, but since Chief Pointer had personally derailed my career as an NOPD cop, solving murders to help prolong his reign was almost too much to bear. Especially on a brutally hot hurricane season morning, with Del Breaux lying in a thickening pool of blood and other fluids, the flies already starting to tuck in.

"Well, detective, I'll give you my best shot. Maybe we can grab some good press. The gay angle will help. And you got a double murder here; this is no murder/suicide. *The Times-Picayune* gives double murders more ink."

"How d'you figure this for a two-bagger?"

"If this was murder/suicide, then it'd be a crime of passion. Rich old Mister Del here is not going to drive his high-priced ride over to Shit Street for a love-life meltdown. And I don't buy the idea that he shoots his squeeze in the car then gets out and walks over here. To do what, deliver a soliloquy to the wall? To get a better cell signal? And look around; I don't see much in the way of lights or security cams here."

"That's not unusual in this city."

"Granted, but this would make a good place for a secret meet," I said, slipping on a pair of latex gloves. "We're surrounded by two-story brick walls with no windows."

The bodies had been found by two location scouts on contract to a Hollywood film production. I hadn't asked, but I wondered if the movie script had called for a gritty place to shoot a drug buy. We stood on crumbling black asphalt in a boxed-in rear parking lot to a defunct bakery warehouse in a neighborhood where it was easier to find crack than a loaf of bread.

The city was full of such locales, but this parking lot could make a list of Top Ten Scuzzy Places: rusted-out car bodies sat useless with nothing valuable left to strip; rats rooted through piles of stale and fresh garbage; a bloodstained mattress soggy from recent rains smelled of mildew and worse; thousands of broken glass shards from cheap booze bottles speckled the faded blacktop; third-rate, busted-up furniture teetered in piles where it had been arbitrarily dumped; and the caustic stench of urine insistently impinged on the sense of smell like an itch that wouldn't go away.

If those film boys hadn't stumbled on the crime scene and called it in to PD, I figured the friendly locals would have already helped themselves to little things like the car, wallets, cell phones, jewelry, and maybe even the shoes of the deceased.

"Crack dealers work the corner, but I don't think we're looking at a drug buy gone bad," I told Honey. "These boys weren't crackheads; they were too in love with themselves for that."

"I had uniforms talk to those dealers. But you know how that goes."

" 'Don't know nuthin'; ummm, didn't see nuthin','" I said, using my best thug impression, then squatted down next to the second corpse, who had a better blond dye job than a lot of Uptown ladies I'd known carnally. A 9mm Steyr M9 sat inches from the outstretched right hand. Like Ty Parks—the stiff in the car—Del Breaux's appearance just screamed well-heeled metrosexual: his IWC watch had to be worth close to ten grand. Its gold face matched the gold color of his hand-made linen shirt, and I doubted that was an accident. He probably had expensive watches with different face colors to match different outfits. I checked his Armani belt, Mizani raw silk slacks. I gingerly checked out the Bally loafers, then moved up the body. Breaux's hands were soft; skin maybe a little too tight around the eyes for a guy in his fifties, unless you've been under the scalpel. Whatever the case, Breaux and Parks were simply immaculately dressed, in what I guess they call "casual chic."

For me casual chic was a pair of pressed, khaki-colored 5.11 Tactical pants with hidden, inside-the-waist pouches for black anodized handcuffs, my subcompact Glock 36, and an extra magazine. Not to mention the extra cargo pockets to accommodate the knives I always carried, plus all the electronic gadgets. I was a gadget guy, pure and simple. I liked tools and having them handy.

Which meant my concealed digital video cam was recording everything I said, saw, and heard. I'd found memory to be too fallible and impeachable, especially in court.

Hunches stand on shaky legal footing as well, but I'd come to honor them. And I suddenly had the nagging suspicion that a guy like Del Breaux wouldn't own a scratched-up, Steyr M9, kind of a clunky-looking, poor man's Glock. The Steyr is a perfectly fine weapon, mind you, sold at a nice price point; I'd shot one at a range. But the M9 didn't strike me as being fancy enough for this guy. He'd have some pricey SIG SAUER or HK or any number of other semiauto handguns that cost three or more times what the Steyr went for, and that held a haughtier cachet. Again, just a hunch, but since I'd already concluded

Mr. Del was murdered, the gun probably would prove to be untraceable.

Honey bowed her head slightly as she rubbed her eyes. Murder/suicide was a neat and tidy package, but now, if I were correct, she was looking at having nineteen homicides on her plate. She looked tired most of the time since leaving the joy of eight-hour shifts as a patrol officer and joining homicide, where she was on call 24/7. Eighteen-hour days were now the rule, not that she could get any kind of a normal night's sleep. Her thirty-year-old baby blue eyes had lost some sparkle, and her freckly skin was paler than normal. But she still had the sexiest blond French braid in the state—she wore it that way in case she got called out for a SWAT op—and kept the same slightly muscular but still feminine physique. I was happy for her because her career was taking off, but I missed all the time we used to spend together.

"Not sure I see this as a double murder," she said. "You saw the temple entry wound? Triangular tears to the skin. Soot. Seared skin. He shoved the barrel right against his head."

"To me it means the killers were smart enough to fake the suicide right."

"That's pretty up close and personal."

"Exactly. But have you studied our victims, the way they're put together?"

"They're well dressed."

"It's a little bit more than that. They're meticulous about their looks. A guy with a two-hundred-dollar dye job, monogrammed custom-made shirt, silver cigarette case, and designer socks is not going to leave the homestead wearing badly scuffed Swiss loafers. Freshly scuffed, I might add. On the heels. I'll bet you forensics will find microscopic pieces of black asphalt from this parking lot embedded in the abrasions."

Honey bent down and checked out the heels of his shoes. "How did I miss that?"

"You would have caught it. I'm just a second brain, that's all. Breaux died right on this spot. He either stepped out of the car or they pulled him out. Then they dragged him over here, scraping his shoes along the way. The shooters wanted to separate him and Ty Parks."

"More than one shooter, huh?"

"Got to be. Breaux has soft hands, but he's a big guy. And buff. Probably a workout fanatic. Got to look good for the young lover."

"So you think two, maybe three killers?"

"Probably."

"Breaux's house is over in Broadmoor. But something tells me we should check his office first. After I finish up with the coroner."

"This is your case," I said, pulling off the latex gloves that made my hands sweat even worse than the rest of me, "so you have to attend the autopsies. But do you want me to beat the bushes in the meantime?"

She ripped a page from her pocket spiral notebook and handed it to me.

"Your to-do list. Check in at the main gate at Michoud. You'll be meeting with the head of security and Breaux's supervisor."

I raised my eyebrows. "They work on the weekend?"

"Government types? Hell no. They're coming in 'cause they're worried about something."

"Maybe Mister Breaux knew some big secrets. What's this phone number written here?"

"Somebody at that number called Breaux's cell at twelve fifteen this morning. The last call he ever got."

I studied the number with interest.

"I'll call you when the coroner has finished filleting our victims. And don't forget to call Kendall."

I flashed a look of complete confusion.

"We were supposed to go to his birthday party."

"Right." Kendall Bullard had worked for me on a few cases and had proven to be a shrewd operator and a great street source. An

MMA fighter I had coached for many years, Kendall had successfully made the jump to the UFC, the Ultimate Fighting Championship. Partly because Kendall had become one of the most popular athletes in the city, a number of other serious fighters had asked me to coach them, and the mixed-martial-arts classes I'd been teaching for years at my dojo in the Lower Garden District were now all wait-listed.

"What's he doing having a brunch party, anyway? Why not have it at night, when people get off work, so it's easier for them to come?"

Honey gave me a pitying look. "Today is Sunday."

"Oh. Yeah."

"You would have caught it. I'm just a second brain, that's all."

Honey turned away and went back to work.

She was right to worry about me.

CHAPTER TWO

I'd forgotten Kendall's birthday party because I hadn't intended to go. Kendall was a good friend, and under normal circumstances you couldn't have kept me away. But I felt far from normal. I could fake it, like I'd just done with Honey. I could mouth off, crack jokes, deduce a scenario from a collection of facts, and generally stand around looking like I was okay. But I wasn't.

The emotional roller coaster was a rough one, especially at night. And especially when I was alone, which was most of the time, since I didn't hold a regular job. I'd stopped working out, arranged for others to teach my classes at the dojo, taken a hiatus from coaching, turned down any new PI work, started hitting the sauce pretty hard, and virtually abandoned my daily run. People might call it "reevaluating" or "taking stock of one's life," but I knew it to be a cancerous malaise that nibbled all around my edges.

Since unintentionally killing Bobby Perdue, I'd withdrawn from most social intercourse and had become the Frozen Man. I'd just sit in my loft for hours upon hours feeling like a heavy gray mass weighed upon me. I knew I needed to do something to help myself, but I'm not a guy who will pop a Prozac or start seeing a shrink. I'd tough it out somehow, because that's the way I operated.

My main form of therapy was telling myself repeatedly that I hadn't meant to kill the kid. It was a horribly tragic accident, and I felt awful for twenty-year-old Bobby Perdue and his family. The whole thing had messed with me in a way nothing else ever had before, not even the deaths of my father and brother. Plenty of fighters have died in the ring, but damn it, he died in *my* ring. I couldn't stop thinking about why this had to happen. What had I done to deserve being drafted against my will as the kid's executioner? As a result, I not only felt depressed, I also brimmed with anger. Righteously pissed off didn't come close to describing my prime sentiment. An undirected rage that I barely controlled ran right below my surface interactions, one reason I had largely avoided people for the last month. I was running on a super-short fuse as I feigned normalcy, and that might mean trouble.

I tried to blink thoughts of the kid from my consciousness as I sat in my 1986 Bronco and gave Kendall a quick call, apologizing for missing his birthday party. I had a different party in mind, so I drove the Bronco around the corner from the murder scene and jacked up two crack dealers.

New Orleans thugs were universally amoral parasites who weren't worth the powder it would take to blow them to hell. They absolutely hated the NOPD. They would never help us, ever. After stealing a car, trashing it for no reason, and then abandoning it, they would often use indelible markers to scrawl obscene messages on the dashboard— not that they could spell or construct a grammatical sentence—directed at NOPD. Of course, if you ever read a police report, you'd know that not all coppers graduated at the top of their English class, either. But our hoodlums were absolute scum. On the West Bank, in the days after the Storm, thugs had tried to shoot repairmen off cell-phone towers in Algiers. People who had come in to help fix the city, they tried to kill. You would think the hoods would have wanted their cell phones working to aid their larceny back then, but no one ever accused them of being anything approaching smart. In the chaos of the Storm, after looting scores of restaurants and bars (note to the apologists: a big-screen TV is not a necessary item for survival), the grateful thugs would leave their calling card by defecating into a cash register. That's the kind of human garbage I now stared at.

Sharp, powerful thunderclaps from a storm cell rolling in from the Gulf punctuated the tension between me and the two men in their late teens who stood about five feet from me. They wore the gangsta regalia of sagging jeans, oversized white T-shirts, and askew baseball caps.

I had no street cred with these guys and didn't feel like wasting time trying to establish any; I had too much to do.

"You guys can make it easy or hard on yourselves: your choice. What do you know about the murders of the two men in the Benz over in that parking lot? What do you know; what have you heard? Sooner you help me out, sooner PD is out of here and you can get back to your dope deals."

They both had longish chee-wee-type dreads. Neither would make eye contact. One just scratched his chin looking bored, using his other hand to hold up his five-times-too-big-sized pants; the second dealer shot a quick glance in my direction, then turned to the side and spit.

"Don't know nuthin'," said the spitter.

I lunged forward, yanked the pants down on Mr. Chin Scratcher so they fell around his knees, and then knocked him on his ass. I spun the spitter around and slammed him against the side of the Bronco.

"Don't you look at me and spit, you piece of shit."

I wrenched the spitter's arm up behind him, and he yelled in pain. I looked down at the chin scratcher. "Hands behind your head, or I will break your fucking face." The chin scratcher stoically complied.

I wore an Alpha Hornet loosely on my right hand. The superlightweight Hornet, made of a reinforced polymer, looked like an elongated, visionary take on a set of brass knuckles, but it wasn't used for straight punches. It was a compliance tool. Not authorized NOPD carry, but then again, I wasn't NOPD. A blunt tang protruded from each end; I now turned my right hand so a tang pressed down on a pressure point on the spitter's wrist, and he screamed.

"You got a name, shitbag?"

"Yeah." He pronounced it "yeh-ya," with two syllables.

"Well, what is it?"

"Marvonne."

"What's taking you so long to apologize to me, Marvonne?"

He didn't speak quickly enough, so I pressed down with the Hornet. He screamed and then blurted out, "I sorry!"

I didn't have any particular ax to grind against these two leeches, or drug dealers in general, as long as they were nonviolent, because without users, there wouldn't be suppliers. But our local crack dealers sold to kids. I'd seen it dozens of times when I worked patrol. That's where I drew the line, so to hell with these two.

"What do you know about those dead guys?"

I started with the pressure, but he talked quick. "We work dis corner daytime. Umm, night we be at, umm, Earhart and Galvez."

"Did I ask about your work habits, or did I ask you about some murders?"

I dug the tang into his wrist. His knees buckled and he yelped like a scalded Chihuahua.

"Two SUVs, I hear." The words shot out fast; he wanted this over. "Dark color. Pull out da lot after couple, three gunshots. 'Bout two dis mornin'."

I made a mental note: *Two SUVs, 2:00 A.M.*

Then I released Marvonne with a shove and let him fall hard to the ground. For a long moment I stood over both men, silently begging them to mouth off or make a move. The rage that had been below the surface since accidentally killing Bobby Perdue now coursed through my system with a vengeance.

The thugs were smart enough not to look at me or make a sound, and I was smart enough to let it go, take a silent deep breath, get into the Bronco, and drive off.

The phone number Honey had scribbled down for me had to be a land line, because it would ring and ring and not go to cell-phone voice mail. I didn't want to call my inside guy at Bell South so early on a Sunday morning, so I kept calling the number, and the fifth time I called and after the thirtieth ring, a very polite female answered, screaming, "What do you want, asshole? You're driving me crazy!"

Whiskey-and-cigarettes voice, funky blues playing in the background, what sounded like baseball on TV, and the *ping ping ping* of a video poker machine. Had to be a bar.

"I think I left my keys there. What's your address?"

"Banks and South Alexander."

"You the bartender?"

"Who wants to know?"

"A very big tipper."

"Sandi's the name. Come by for a drink and I'll look for your keys."

She hung up. It wasn't much of an invitation, but a Bloody might take a little of my edge off.

It was easy to spot Sandi since she had her name tattooed on her neck in one-inch Algerian-font script. I wondered what she'd think of that tattoo once she hit her sixties, or once she sobered up, whichever came first. She'd been pretty maybe ten years ago, needed to see a dentist, and a couple of hundred sit-ups a day would nicely tighten up her slight beer pouch.

A half dozen beer-swilling guys and one old black lady with a cocktail in a plastic cup and glued to a poker machine were sitting around getting hammered in the cool, colorful confines of Banks Street Bar. I spotted one security cam above the bar pointed at the cash register, reminding me that, damn it, it's your employees that you have to watch more than your customers. The pay phone was in a corner and maybe not covered by a security cam.

The sandwich-type chalkboard on the sidewalk next to the front door hadn't been changed yet, so I knew that Walter "Wolfman" Washington had played last night, meaning they probably had 200 people crammed in here, even though city code for the joint was 110 bodies. So I doubted any employee would remember someone using the pay phone at 12:15 A.M. It would come down to video.

I told Sandi I found my keys, bought us both a Bloody Mary, and tipped her twenty bucks. She really liked that and warmed right up to me. I gave her my PI business card.

"Sandi, I'm working with NOPD on a homicide. I need to check your security video from last night. How many cams you got in this place?"

"Two outside, two inside, but you need to come back when Junior is here, maybe seven tonight."

"Can we make it happen now, sweetie?"

I showed her the letter from Chief Pointer and put two more twenties on the bar. She reached for the bills as she read the letter, but I held them in place.

"The two dead guys aren't in a hurry anymore, but I am."

She sized me up. A gal who has been around the block a few times can get good at that.

"Follow me," she said, and winked, scooping up the money.

The video results were not as accommodating to the investigation as Sandi had been. The dark footage looked inconclusive at best, but still, I copied the video onto a thumb drive. As I sped toward New Orleans East and the NASA Michoud Assembly Facility, I sucked on a couple of menthol lozenges, lest the suits I was about to meet object to the notion of an investigator imbibing while on duty.

"I can't stress enough how important it is that Del Breaux's Department of Defense–issued laptop computer be located immediately and returned to us here."

Ralph Salerno was ex-FBI and Chief of Security at Michoud. Short, beer gut straining at his belt, crew-cut brown hair going gray, and the wrinkles around his mouth didn't suggest he smiled a lot. This was the third time he had mentioned the laptop.

"I understand your concern. You'll be the first to hear about it when we find it," I said. That was bullshit and Salerno probably knew it.

"I still can't believe Del is dead. And Ty Parks too." Harold Klenis, a silver-haired man in his seventies, sat erect behind his desk in his third-floor office. Salerno had made a big deal out of keeping me in the hallway outside while he insured that Klenis had left no sensitive documents out in the open for prying eyes to see before letting me enter. If he'd known I was wired for video and audio, we'd probably be having this meeting out in the parking lot.

I'd already seen Breaux's desk here at Michoud, set up in a project room with about seven other desks. I'd found little at his workstation and nothing of a personal nature at all. He must have kept everything he needed in his missing laptop.

I'd also seen the small office of Ty Parks, just off the shipping docks. Parks's office had been heavily decorated with framed family photos, whimsical mementos, tchotchkes, and Post-it notes. Salerno refused to let me check Park's computer but said he'd provide NOPD copies of any files not of a proprietary nature. I spent thirty minutes carefully going over the place before we went up to Klenis's office.

"How did Breaux get along with the other members of his team?" I asked Klenis.

"Just fine. Del was meticulous and held himself and everyone else to the highest standards. He was a highly experienced metallurgical engineer. A respected figure. People knew he had worked at Skunk Works on the Stealth—"

"Harold, let's don't go there," interrupted Salerno, acting like he was running the interview. He was one of those ex-FBI types who had put in his twenty and now earned a healthy six figures in his second career pretending he knew everything there was to know about securing a sensitive facility and the secrets therein. I didn't like him and I figured the feeling was mutual.

I stared at Salerno. "The thing is, while you kept me waiting in the lobby for twenty-five minutes after I signed in, I used my cell phone to do a simple Internet search, and what do I find but a *Who's Who in Science and Engineering* article stating that Del Breaux worked on the Stealth program. That means, Mister Salerno, that we definitely can and will 'go there.' If either of you gentlemen hold back on me, here's what's going to happen: NOPD units with lights flashing will roll up in front of your homes and you will be paraded out past your wives and kids and neighbors for a ride down to Broad Street and an un-friendly interrogation in a murder investigation."

I let that hang in the air as I stared down both men.

"I'm sure that won't be necessary, Mister Saint James. Please excuse my colleague, but as you can imagine, his job is to be obsessed with security."

I ignored Klenis and stared hard at Salerno. "His job today is to cooperate." *That's right, Fido, you're not the biggest dog in the room anymore.* "Save the whitewash job for some rookie."

Salerno met my gaze but not in a challenging way. He tried to use a look that I had perfected; he tried to look at me like I wasn't impor-tant, but he couldn't pull it off and finally looked away.

"Just to clarify, yes, Del Breaux worked at Skunk Works back in the late eighties. He worked on many other black projects, which, I'm sorry, but I'm not cleared to discuss with you," said Klenis.

"You mentioned he had very high standards. Did that cause any friction?"

"Not really. Everyone knew up front that if you were going to show something to Del, it had better be right."

"So he was here nine to five?"

"He was only consulting. Came in two days a week, ten or fifteen hours a week."

"So as far as you know, none of his coworkers had it in for him, no resentment, couldn't stand him for some reason?"

"Well there's always office politics. We all have to work with people we don't particularly like, but as far as I know, there was nothing of an ugly nature, if that's what you mean."

"Were Breaux and Parks gay? Did they see any of their coworkers outside of work?"

Both men shifted in their seats. "I'm not sure it's appropriate to discuss that," said Salerno. "Federal regulations prohibit—"

"Screw the regulations; I got two dead guys in a parking lot. Gay, straight, bi, asexual—I could care less. But I need facts. Facts help solve murders."

"Yes, they were gay, and they were a couple. They made no secret of that, and that is the best policy for people in sensitive work, I think," said Klenis.

"It eliminates the blackmail potential," said Salerno, deciding to go along with Klenis.

"The funny thing is, you never would have known it. There was nothing about Del's manner or behavior that indicated he was a homosexual. As to off-hours socializing, I'd have to say no. Del wasn't friendly with any employees other than Parks."

"Tell me, since your work is so hush-hush here; did he have some information that might have gotten him killed?"

"Like what? What are you suggesting?" asked Salerno.

"You know exactly what I'm asking. Since you can't tell me what your secret program is here, is it possible Breaux was killed for his laptop? For what was inside it?"

Klenis looked uncomfortable merely considering the question. I guess he didn't want to believe that maybe it could happen to him, too. I expected that Salerno would be handling these kinds of questions and that he'd most likely stonewall me.

"Well, I suppose you'll be finding that out and telling us," said Salerno.

The subtext of Salerno's response told me that this was a super-secret program of the highest order. But I wanted somebody to say it.

"I thought I made it clear we weren't doing those kinds of non-answer answers. I'm not here to debate the merits of how things get classified, and I'm not asking you to compromise national security. But there's secret work and then there's the kind of secret work that a foreign government will do just about anything to get its hands on. Was Breaux working on the former or the latter?"

"The latter," said Klenis, matter-of-fact.

"Thank you, that's helpful. What kind of security clearance did Breaux hold?"

Klenis looked to Salerno, who looked like he was in some kind of retreat as he tried to decide how to answer. He was now the bottom head on a three-man totem pole. "A Top Secret SCI clearance with a polygraph."

"I'd rather not get into the exact nature of his clearance compartmentalization, if that's all right with you," said Klenis. "That information going into a police report could become public, and coupled with Breaux's résumé, a foreign intelligence agency might deduce what we're working on here."

"Okay. What about Parks?"

"He had a Secret clearance when he was in the air force. But he didn't have an active clearance. His work as the shipping manager wasn't of a sensitive nature," said Salerno.

"And how did Parks get along with his coworkers?"

"Are you kidding? There will probably be two hundred employees from Michoud at his funeral. He was a great guy, knew how to manage staff, never had a complaint. Incredibly well-liked."

"Were Breaux or Parks being investigated for anything? Were they under any suspicion? I mean, the red flags are pretty obvious. Ultra-expensive luxury vehicle. Pricey jewelry, accessories, clothes . . ."

"Breaux's income as a government consultant was substantial, and his trading company did very well. He submitted yearly financials. The fact that he legitimately earned so much made him less of a risk. He passed every security evaluation he'd ever taken with flying colors," said Salerno.

"So neither of them were being investigated or looked at, officially or unofficially?"

"I didn't say that." Salerno looked at me evenly. "It's like painting the Golden Gate Bridge. It takes something like three years. When the painters finish it, they go back to the beginning and start all over again. That's how I run my shop here. The investigations never stop. But the details of all that are classified."

How interesting. Salerno had just refused to go on record stating that Del Breaux and Ty Parks *were not* being investigated.

"So, other than the laptop, is anything missing, Mister Klenis?"

"Such as?"

"Documents, files, equipment—"

"A full inventory and a security review will begin tomorrow, as a matter of policy. I'm sure Mister Salerno will let you know how that develops."

Now I was the one getting the bullshit. I smiled and nodded.

I stepped out of the Michoud administration building into the furnace of the afternoon. Moisture condensed on my sunglasses so heavily that I couldn't see. As I wiped my glasses clean I figured I was in a race with the Feds to find Breaux's laptop; maybe with local FBI, maybe special agents flying in from DC. Either way, I wanted to find it first. Breaux's computer would contain the most pertinent clues to any work-related motives for his murder, and I wanted those clues for myself.

I was halfway to the Broadmoor District—I remembered Breaux's home address from his driver's license—before the air-con in my classic, midnight-blue-and-white Ford Bronco sufficiently cooled the vehicle to the point I could stop sweating. I preferred biking whenever possible, but it often wasn't practical since the Storm, nor that much fun when the pavement felt like the surface of Venus.

The Bronco functioned as a good PI work truck, outfitted not only with hidden compartments, but with racks of locking compartments as well. I stocked weapons and ammo, surveillance and tracking electronics that I might need to plant, night vision and other optics, lock picking and burglary tools, disguises and changes of clothing, an evidence-gathering kit, a well-stocked combat first aid kit, MREs, a case of water, and other supplies. I had a computer built into the dash and could project a heads-up display on the windshield. She had exterior high-resolution video cameras providing 360-degree coverage, so I could use her as a surveillance vehicle even when empty. Like I said, I liked tools. Mechanically, the Bronco was perfect. Like some middle-aged gals, she could use a little bodywork and desperately needed a paint job, but just as with people it was the inner guts that really counted. I kept the tires dirty but the tread deep. No need to make her attractive to the city's legion of car thieves, although often a thug would boost whatever was at hand simply because he was tired of walking and needed something to drive for a week or so. That's why I had a kill switch installed. Nobody would be stealing my Bronco. And I kept the bullet holes in the tailgate to remind me not to overestimate myself or to take my security for granted.

I had a second truck, a massive monster that I tried out of pure guilt not to drive. There was enough guilt shadowing my life. I didn't feel razor sharp but seemed to be focusing better now that my mind was engaged in the investigation. I'd surfaced from a dark gray malaise, and while I still felt emotionally raw, I wasn't thinking about the dead kid all the time. That was good; that was an answer to my prayers.

I called Honey, figuring she'd want a break from the stench of the autopsy room, even if it was just to take a phone call. I'd always spread a generous amount of Vicks VapoRub under my nose as a masking agent before going in to witness the procedure, but Honey had told me she wanted to get used to the smell. We had agreed to disagree; one could get used to being tortured every day, but would you really want to?

"You sound like you're in a car," I said, surprised.

"Six murders last night in the great city of New Orleans. Plus five dead from car accidents. A couple of suicides."

"So the bodies are stacked in the temporary morgue like chips on a roulette table."

"And the coroner is still short of staff. He'll give me a heads-up in a few hours. I'll go in then," said Honey. "What happened at Michoud?"

"Breaux had a government laptop and the Feds want it back. We need to get it first."

"That might be a problem."

"Oh?" I asked.

"Just left Breaux's office on Poydras. Jammed over there after the coroner told me to chill."

"And? What did you find?"

"It's what we didn't find. The place had been sanitized."

"Sanitized?"

"Yeah, it looked like some kind of model office. That no one actually worked in. New computers but no digital files. No notes, papers, Rolodexes. Fax- and copy-machine memories had been wiped."

"Building security would have video," I said.

"I'll have it tomorrow. Security says a crew of guys with a work order and invoices came in overnight. At two twelve A.M. Delivered a bunch of new office equipment."

"Out with the old, in with the new. So maybe they got Breaux's laptop as well. Unless . . . are you thinking what I'm thinking?"

"Pretty sure so," said Honey. "Meet me at 9412 Derbigny Street."

Del Breaux's house.

"I'm just rolling up," she said. "Damn. Looks like these boys didn't do anything small."

CHAPTER THREE

The big thunder boomers of earlier had been somewhat anticlimactic, and a gentle rain began caressing the city as I hung a right on Napoleon, past dozens of corrugated plastic signs stuck into the ground at the corner, as they were all over the city, advertising the services of roofers, contractors, stump grinders, plumbers, electricians, landscapers, and reopened restaurants. The post-Storm recovery boomed, and at the very least, the person selling the plastic signs was making some money.

Yes, things were getting fixed, but it was taking so damn long. One year after the Storm and the police academy was still in trailers, as were any number of district station houses, post offices, banks, and half the population. The city morgue had yet to be fully cleaned out, so the coroner operated out of yet another temporary facility. Huge sections of New Orleans still stood in ugly ruins. And in nice neighborhoods like the one I currently traversed, parking remained at a premium due to all the pickup trucks and repair vehicles driven by mostly out-of-town contractors getting fat on our misery.

I made a quick left and found Breaux's house. But to call it a mere house didn't do the structure justice. One could find exquisite southern mansions all over New Orleans, not just in Uptown on St. Charles

Avenue. Six massive pilasters supported the deep overhang of the lavishly maintained Greek Revival, double-galleried, clapboard-sided townhouse. The second-floor gallery, faced with a fine wrought-iron railing design, wrapped the front. A massive teak and leaded-glass door centered the ground floor, bookended by lesser entryways, which I realized belonged to separate apartments. Excellent! Living below Breaux and Parks were renters who might prove to be nice sources of info.

I jogged up the wet walkway and logged in with a uniform at the front door. I figured the renters had already been interviewed, so I bounded up the oak stairs in the narrow entryway to the second floor to be greeted by oversized rooms painted in bold color schemes, polished hardwood floors, large statuary, art pieces, and expensive Oriental rugs. The place looked like a private museum.

I found Honey on the third floor in a massive bedroom. She had a CSI team with her, but there was a lot to cover in the house.

"Lifestyles of the rich and famous," I said, looking around. "If the FBI wasn't keeping an eye on Breaux, they should have been."

"Exactly. And let me ask you. How much cash do you keep in your bedroom?" Honey popped open a leather Louis Vuitton carry-on bag on the bed. Full of crisp one-hundred-dollar bills. "The quick count is two point five million. Sequentially numbered."

"That should trace it. And my answer is maybe thirty bucks. In my bedroom."

"Looks like they lived up here on three. Entertained on two."

"And rented out one. You talked to the renters?" I asked.

"You mean the Guardians."

I looked at her funny.

"If it wasn't for those nosy renters downstairs? This house would have gotten the sanitation treatment, same as the office," said Honey.

"Don't tell me they stopped delivery guys trying to bring in new computers."

"Five men posing as FBI agents. Claiming to have a federal search warrant."

"How did they know it was bogus?" I asked.

"Five guys picking the front door lock at four in the morning? The renters just kept a shotgun trained on them as they called nine-one-one. The perps left saying they'd return with NOPD backup. They didn't. But we got them on video. Breaux has an extensive CCTV setup."

"Quality good enough for an ID?"

"Night footage isn't great. I'll have it enhanced," said Honey.

"So if the bad guys were here at four in the morning, what time did Breaux and Parks leave?"

"The fat guy downstairs said about one A.M. They got in at midnight. Left at one. Never came back."

"Those crack dealers said gunshots were heard from the murder scene sometime around two."

"And the bad guys showed up at Breaux's office just after two. Came here at four."

"Right after they cleaned out Breaux's office. They can't be happy they didn't get the two point five mil."

"You think?"

"Were they driving dark SUVs?"

"The fat guy didn't see their ride. A rental truck was used to deliver the computers to Breaux's office. I ran the plate. Truck was stolen."

I picked up one of the bundles of money, and then my attention shifted to the Louis Vuitton bag itself. "This bag's a fake."

"What do you mean?"

"Look at the stitching. This is some cheap Chinese knockoff. It's not even a good fake, like you can get in Bangkok or Singapore."

"Okay."

"So I don't think it belongs to Breaux or Parks, but to whoever gave them the money."

"We'll give the bag a good going-over."

"But speaking of the mountain of cash. Were they killed for the money? If so, why hit the office?"

"Maybe they thought the dough was in the office," said Honey.

"So why replace the computers and clean out the place? And take the risk building security would ask too many questions and maybe bring in PD. The killers had to be removing incriminating or sensitive information. Something they wanted badly. Maybe something related to Breaux's black-projects work."

"Black projects?"

I nodded. "The Stealth program and a long career in secret engineering projects of the first order, including whatever he was doing out at Michoud."

As I stepped into a walk-in master closet, my eyes riveted on a couple of military uniforms hanging in clear plastic dry cleaner's bags: U.S. Navy dress whites. "Was Breaux ex-navy?" I asked.

"He's ex-everything now." Honey joined me in the closet.

"Parks had been air force, according to the security guy at Michoud."

"Military service didn't come up for Breaux," said Honey.

"So what's with the navy uniforms?"

"This is New Orleans," she said, like speaking to a particularly dense pupil. "You know anybody who *doesn't* have costumes in the closet?"

Once again, Detective Honey Baybee was thinking better than me. "Costumes or skeletons."

She shrugged. "Why don't you take the second floor?"

The second floor featured four large high-ceilinged rooms, two bathrooms, a couple of smaller rooms, closets, and a kitchen. One large room functioned as an art gallery, another as a drawing room, the third I'd call a media room, and the biggest I simply thought of as the party room.

The party room had a well-stocked wet bar, felt-topped card table and chairs, pool table, a small raised stage complete with a brass stripper's pole and stage lights, karaoke machine, sofas, machine-age-design aluminum lounge chairs, and a big circular bed. Screens discreetly partitioned an area with thick pillows on the floor. A goldfish bowl on the bar sat full of condoms in colorful packaging.

I'd brought my backpack with evidence-collection materials inside, so I methodically worked the second floor. After an hour and a half, I'd carefully examined the kitchen, art gallery, drawing room, and media room and I'd found a few things out of the ordinary: a Fabergé egg, which might be downright pedestrian to an art collector like Del Breaux, and two sophisticated listening devices that had been hardwired into lamps in the drawing room. Had Breaux planted the bugs himself, perhaps to eavesdrop on business guests when he was out of the room? Maybe, but the high-end nature of the technology baffled me; the units weren't products on the commercial market, which led to a whole different kind of speculation.

And then there was something else I found that might lead to some insight. Like other antique collectors, Breaux taped the invoice for the piece to the item itself, but out of view. Each of his nineteenth-century Swiss-carved Black Forest side chairs, for instance, had a paper receipt taped on the seat bottom. This way Breaux could easily check to see where he bought the antique, when, and how much he paid. I found receipts from a number of dealers, including an acquaintance of mine, Barry Morrison, who owns an antique shop across from my dojo in the Lower Garden District. I'd be giving Barry a call.

The last room I checked on the second floor was a bathroom, and that's where I found it: the edge of Breaux's laptop jutting out from under a magazine on a small wooden table. A sticker on the laptop's battery compartment identified it as being property of the Department of Defense.

Breaux must have been sitting on the "pot," using the laptop before he and Parks went out for the last ride of their lives.

I tried to boot up the computer but naturally it was password-protected. This case was quickly shaping up to be the biggest I'd ever worked on. The presence of the real FBI, or whatever three-letter agency should be responding to the murders, had to be imminent. Meaning Honey and I would get dumped from the investigation and the laptop would disappear from scrutiny once the Feds got their hands on it.

Unless I didn't tell Honey I found it.

There was another reason not to tell Honey, not just yet, anyway: the NOPD Crime Lab. Demolished by the Storm, they were working their way back, but they had a huge backlog, were understaffed, and I wouldn't trust them with something this sensitive.

Actually, there was a lot I wouldn't trust them with. On the other hand, I knew exactly whom I could trust.

I instinctively knew the laptop to be a major key to unlocking the case. If I was going to help Honey solve these murders, I needed to throw the rule book out the window and keep the laptop under wraps until I could divine its secrets. It's a risk Honey could never take, because she had a career with the department; I, however, didn't have too much to lose. At worst I figured I could get arrested for tampering with evidence or theft or whatever charge the Feds would want to nail me with. If I got caught. And getting caught wouldn't be good for Honey, since she had brought me in, but her career would survive. I could take the heat if it came to that; it was worth the risk.

I simply had to make sure I didn't get caught.

And if there was damning evidence in the laptop necessary to prove some malfeasance in a future prosecution, then I'd have to fudge the chain-of-evidence issue. Once I'd obtained the secrets within, I could return and plant the computer elsewhere in the house. I could use the excuse of needing to look for more listening devices, magically recover the laptop from an as-yet-to-be-determined hiding place, and log it into evidence control. And then if the Feds grabbed it, so what?

It was all a bit devious, but that was nothing new to my MO. The plan would work.

A loud rapping on the restroom door snapped me out of my ruminations.

"Saint James, you in there?"

It was Honey.

"There are nine bathrooms in this house. Can't a guy get a little privacy?" I silently slipped Del Breaux's US Government–issued laptop into my backpack. There would be no going back now. I took a final look in the mirror before opening the door, hoping I had made the right choice.

The gut check hit me as soon as I opened the door. Two men in dark gray suits stood bookending Honey looking like they'd just been informed their wives had given them a dose of the clap.

"Saint James. Special Agents Gibbs and Minniear. From DC Counterintelligence," said Honey with a distinct lack of warmth. They were both big men in their late thirties and drilled me with the kind of stares loss-prevention agents give to shoplifters. They didn't offer to shake hands, so I just nodded.

"What about the laptop?" asked Gibbs, who seemed to be in charge.

Did he know? How could he?

"I give up. What about it?"

"Did it turn up here on the second floor?" Minniear practically snapped.

My gut eased a bit. "Seems to me it must have either been in Breaux's office or his car. Makes sense that whoever capped him grabbed the laptop. I'm thinking he was killed specifically for the computer."

Looking even less pleased, Agent Gibbs fished out his cell phone and walked off as he dialed a call, followed by Agent Minniear. Honey and I exchanged glances and waited until they were out of earshot.

"Have they taken over the case?" I asked.

"No. Just looking over our shoulders. For now." She glanced over to them and then looked back to me. "Anything turn up?"

"It's a big house; let's keep looking."

I stuck around for a couple more hours helping search the house. Once the FBI boys left, I used an excuse to bug out that startled Honey and left her speechless: I told her I needed to go to a church service.

And I wasn't lying.

The Divine Trinity Church of Blessed Union on St. Claude had been making a steady comeback since the Storm had damaged the structure and sent much of the congregation into Hurricane Exile. In the immediate bleak months after the killer hurricane, the pastor had delivered his sermons from under the roll-out awning of a borrowed RV in the parking lot as attendees sat in lawn chairs, on milk crates, or in their cars with the doors open and windows down as they fanned themselves. The churchgoers had formed working groups, and in every second of spare time they labored to bring each other's homes into livable condition while at the same time facilitating repairs to the church itself. If you were looking for some folks with indomitable spirits, this was a pretty good place to start.

Tonight the parking lot stood half full as testament to the city's greatly reduced population; before the Storm, overflow parking filled nearby empty lots. I knew that about two-thirds of the way through the service the deacons would meet up in the foyer just before they passed the donation plates. So I stood in the dimly lit vestibule next to a table where four donation plates were stacked on top of one another, and listened as the small choir backed by a four-piece band finished a rocking gospel number. The pastor then picked up the thread of this evening's theme: forgiveness. He said we needed to forgive the government for failing us, to forgive our neighbors for stealing from us, to forgive God for sending the Storm, and most important, to forgive ourselves, for surely we must have done something to deserve having gotten into such a tough pickle. The pastor was asking a lot.

I watched as three men—deacons—rose from the pews and quietly made their way back toward the foyer. I removed a lucky two-dollar bill decorated with a red Magic Marker from my wallet and placed it in the top donation plate, then faded into the shadows. The greenback had been the only money I'd had on me the night Kerry Broussard and I first met, and we'd since used it as a secret signaling device. As head deacon, Kerry would be picking up that top plate.

Halfway through my second mini cigarillo, as heat lightning stabbed a charcoal ash sky and muted chords from the church organ hung in the air, Kerry found me in the parking lot. He was an old friend and maybe the best crime-lab tech in the state. We'd been fishing buddies for years, and he had unofficially helped me countless times with lab results on sensitive evidence. I felt a little bad about ambushing him during an early evening church service, but I knew he wouldn't mind.

"Cliff . . ." He'd come up behind me, and as I turned he put a big hand on my shoulder. "How's it going? You okay?"

He was asking about Bobby Perdue.

"I'm trying to stay busy."

"Why don't you come in for the rest of the service? If you want, have a chat with the pastor afterward. Then over to the house for late supper. You haven't seen the kids in a while now. Charlene was asking me about you the other night, said we needed to have you over."

"Please give me a rain check. I'm on a murder case, Kerry. That's why I'm here. Sorry to interrupt like this, but time is working against me."

"You know I'll do whatever I can."

"Don't say that too quick; you may not want to do this one. But if you agree, this has to stay secret. I mean, you can't let anyone know you're working on this. Period."

"Okay."

"Maybe they won't figure out the past connection between you and me."

"Who is 'they'?"

I wondered that myself. "I'm not sure. Bad people."

I gently guided Kerry over to his minivan, where we stood out of view.

"You're in trouble," he said, looking me over.

"Not yet. But I figure soon."

Kerry broke out in a big toothy smile and shook his head. "Cliff, Cliff, Cliff. When you gonna learn?"

"You know how it is."

"Don't I, though. You being watched?"

"No. Right now I'm just being careful. I don't know how things might play out. It's why I didn't call you and why you can't call me for the foreseeable future. I'm now having second thoughts about even giving this to you."

"You're trying to solve a murder?"

"Double murder. Powerful forces might be involved." I showed him the DOD laptop. "Password-protected. I need the password. You'd have to do it in a way that couldn't be traced to you."

Kerry took a breath and exhaled slowly. "Then we do it on the down-low, same as we always do." He took the laptop, opened the side door of the van, and slipped it under the rear seat.

"Maybe a lot lower than we always do. How long do you need?"

"I'm swamped with work right now. I'll need to take extra precautions. . . . Better give me two days."

I checked my TechnoMarine chronograph. "Let's call it seven A.M., Wednesday morning. Puccino's out on Vets in Metairie. Caramel macchiatos on me."

Kerry nodded.

"You haven't seen me and we haven't spoken. And if for some reason I don't show up for coffee, don't try to contact me. Hide the laptop somewhere, but not at your home or office. It'll probably be nothing, just a sign that things are getting sticky."

Thanks to the continuing post-Storm real estate bubble that applied to undamaged structures, I'd sold my French Quarter condo for a small fortune, allowing me to buy a fixer-upper three-story brick building in the Warehouse Arts District a couple doors down from Ernst Café. It's a good thing the second floor was already livable, since I hadn't done much in the way of fixing up. In fact, I hadn't even unpacked, really, since move-in day had been the day after I killed Bobby Perdue. The only work I had done was all security related and I'd contracted it out: expensive alarms and video surveillance got installed, a safe room and hidden storage constructed, a secret entry/exit passage secured, and extra-heavy-duty locks put in. I'd made the place impregnable as possible but with a covert way out if I had to turn tail. I tried not to think about how the psychology behind those renovations reflected upon my mental state.

So my open-plan loft, which should have served as a cool bachelor hang to impress females like Honey, instead resembled a trashed-out stockroom with a few sticks of furniture thrown in. But there was streaming jazz on my laptop and Grey Goose in the Sub-Zero freezer. Honey had dropped in moments ago at 11 P.M. after finishing up with the autopsies, and she pretended not to notice we were drinking out of paper cups because I hadn't unpacked my kitchen stuff yet.

"Nice place," she said, looking around as she took a healthy taste.

This was the first time Honey had seen the new digs. Nobody had seen it since I hadn't been in the mood for company.

"Thanks, I . . . I need to get this stuff unpacked, I guess. I had a key made for you; it's around here somewhere." I sat on the leather couch and she joined me.

Honey and I had an unusual relationship; we possessed an intimacy that had never gone sexual, but we often flirted with doing so. We loved each other and were best friends but were both damaged goods, possibly damaged beyond repair to any kind of normalcy.

"Our time line is good. Coroner figures time of death at about two in the morning."

"Any revelations?"

She shook her head. "Have to see if toxicology comes back with anything."

"That will take awhile."

"Yeah. And the chief wants the case wrapped yesterday," said Honey.

"What I can't figure is the two and a half million. Even the super-rich don't keep that kind of cash on hand."

"If he was selling the laptop secrets? And was killed during the exchange? How did the money get in his house?" asked Honey.

"Could he have had more than one thing to sell? He's worked in black projects for decades. Maybe he recently sold something for the bag of cash, then last night he was going to sell something else, but the deal went bad."

"Aside from murder, we're talking espionage. Foreign-intelligence-agents kind of thing," Honey said, frowning. The last thing she needed was a twisted, complex case full of pitfalls, politics, and jurisdictional issues.

"Yes we are. Remember, that bug in Breaux's house didn't turn out to be his own. Somebody *was* spying on Breaux. And Salerno, the Michoud security guy, pretty much hinted that Breaux and Parks were being investigated."

"Think the bug was planted by Salerno?"

"Possibly."

"So whatever Salerno's investigating Breaux and Parks for ends up killing them?" Honey took another sip of vodka. "Or was it related to Breaux's trading company work?"

"We need to learn more about Breaux's company," I said. "Any other workers at Breaux Enterprises, or was Breaux a one-man band?"

"One personal assistant." Honey fished a pocket notebook from her purse. "Guy named Peter Danforth. Security kind of hinted that he was light in the loafers, too."

"So where is Peter Danforth?"

"That will have to wait. Until tomorrow." Honey threw back her drink, scooted over on the sofa, wrapped her arms around me, and held me close like she had a hundred times before. But this time I think she wasn't doing it for her, she was doing it for me. "Will you teach me kickboxing?" she murmured, just above a whisper.

Nothing like getting cozy with a beautiful woman who then brings up a super-violent pastime, but it was one of the reasons I loved Honey. And I loved her even more because I knew she was baiting me into getting back on the horse. I had offered many times to teach her kickboxing, but now that I was avoiding my dojo, she suddenly wanted to learn.

What could I do but turn the tables? "Tomorrow. Let's talk about it tomorrow."

She searched my eyes in a way that made me feel like she was evaluating my inner condition and forming a silent diagnosis as to my mental state. I did my best to hold her gaze.

"Everything is so different now. I've hardly seen you the last couple months."

"You're a rising star in the department. I'm really proud of you," I said earnestly.

"Other things are more important than that."

I laced the fingers of my right hand through hers. "Yes they are. I . . ." My eyes lowered to our interlocked hands. I wanted to tell her how I really felt, to talk about the demons I currently wrestled with, to let her know how I missed our games of chess and the quiet moments we'd shared together, how I missed holding her at night and the narcotic scent of her perfume carrying me to other worlds that gave me peace and comfort. I wanted her to understand that I would climb out of this mental sinkhole and be the old St. James again, that if she could just give me some time, I would make her laugh again and carp at me with her clipped banter that rang as a focused counterpoint to my more unbridled thought processes. I wanted to tell her that my heart hurt and that I needed her. But all I could manage was, "I have your favorite shampoo in the shower."

Maybe she understood. She squeezed my hand, laid her head on my chest. I held on to her like a good thought, one I didn't want to fade from my consciousness. I held her as if she were the fleeting answer to expunging the misery of my guilt and suffering. The fact that I was allowing her into my space at all made me realize what a fool I'd been in keeping her at arm's length since the death of Bobby Perdue.

CHAPTER FOUR

At first light I jogged over to the St. Charles Avenue neutral grounds—the wide, grassy median strip between the traffic lanes—on the other side of Calliope Street, pronounced "KAL-ee-ope" not "Ka-LIE-o-pee," because people down here did things differently, so get used to it. This section wasn't even officially named Calliope Street anymore; the city council had changed it for no good reason back in the 1990s, and I figured in another thirty years locals might start using the new name, whatever it was. Like most folks around here, I'd simply ignored the name change.

I currently had been ignoring a lot of things, and presently was half-assing it; instead of what used to be my serious, mega-mile run on asphalt at Audubon Park, I'd be trotting on damp grass as I leisurely headed uptown and stopped for cross traffic. I could try and fool myself into thinking I was starting to get my act together, but really I'd simply been unable to sleep after Honey left at 5 A.M. I got tired of staring at all the unpacked boxes in my loft, so I forced myself to attempt a return to my usual routine. Maybe this jog, Mickey Mouse though it be, was still a step in the right direction, and I deeply inhaled the dew-fresh dampness of the lush greenery as I trotted.

The city's neutral grounds on streets such as St. Charles, Esplanade,

Carrollton and Napoleon, were finally getting back to pre-Storm shape, largely thanks to ad hoc groups of local volunteers who got tired of waiting for the city to do what cities are supposed to do, and took it upon themselves to remove trash and debris and downed tree limbs from the green expanses. As bad as things still were, it would be hard to imagine the condition greater New Orleans would be in were it not for the volunteers, some local but mostly from out of state—church organizations, student groups, sister-city programs—who continued to flood the Gulf Coast bestowing goodwill and hard work.

The mayor and his administration tried to take credit for all the progress, but they possibly ranked as the most inept and inefficient group of spoiled egotists who ever held power. FEMA waited to disperse tens of millions of dollars to the city for myriad recovery projects, but the mayor and his staff acted like they couldn't be bothered to present the properly written proposals that would get the money released. The mayor simply wanted it handed to him, so he screamed and whined, playing the blame game in TV sound bites, pointing his finger at the governor, the Feds, the president—anyone but himself and his incompetent lackeys. So The People, as usual, were the ones who suffered thanks to the city/FEMA standoff.

There was no love lost between me and the FEMA buffoons, but I couldn't blame them for being unwilling to hand over tens of millions of dollars to the city, carte blanche. Odd how poorly monitored recovery funds could just somehow evaporate.

As I jogged along dodging the occasional wine bottle and pile of dog droppings, my thoughts shifted from my broken city to Del Breaux and Ty Parks. A double murder meant to look like a murder/suicide was an unusual crime in NOLA, and the killers had done a pretty good job staging it. Even if they realized they'd scuffed Breaux's shoes, what could they have done short of breaking into his house and getting a different pair? Such sophistication in a crime suggested a fairly high level of criminal mind. Then throw in the facts that both victims worked at a federal facility that held deep secrets, had been living the good life, had all that cash on hand, and that Breaux's office had been sanitized and an illegal entry into his home thwarted, and . . . well, it stunk to high heaven.

As I paused at MLK Boulevard for an old pickup truck to cross St. Charles, I felt a familiar emotion—anger—rise up within me, but this time it had a new source. People were driving around my adopted town in dark SUVs thinking they could get away with a double murder. It didn't matter who had done it or why. It pissed me off. I realized with a start that this kind of normally toxic anger, focused on the Breaux case, acted more like a badly needed elixir. Tracking those killers down and bringing them to justice, I hoped, would balance the scales of guilt that had been weighing me down.

"I'm about to meet with those FBI boys in the chief's office. The counterintelligence guys from DC."

Honey had called my cell just as I stepped into Pravda.

"Keep us on the case if you can," I said.

"I'll do my best. Meanwhile, try and track down Peter Danforth."

"I'll get right on it. And hey . . . it was really great seeing you last night."

Silence on Honey's end, then, "So invite me back." She terminated the call.

I smiled, feeling better. I settled in at my permanently reserved table in the back corner at Pravda, a funky extrapolation of a Russian revolutionary salon on Decatur Street that, thankfully, the tourists didn't get. Any bar with a Van Gogh take on a portrait of Rasputin hanging on the wall is a place where I want to spend time. This was my little rented corner of the Quarter and functioned as my office. I removed my laptop from a steel-reinforced faux-neoclassical antique cabinet and logged on to the Internet to do some checking. I exhaled bluish smoke from a Partagas mini cigarillo, *hecho en Habana, Cuba.* A Cuban-American woman I'd tried but failed to date had taught me that cigars go best not with Scotch, but with good strong coffee; hence, I was brewing up a pot of Pakxong Lao Classic Robusta, using beans grown in the mountains of Southeast Asia.

Pravda didn't open till 7 P.M., but the front door was often unlocked, since Michelle, the Goth chick owner or one of her minions usually lurked around to take deliveries and restock, clean up, and, more important, fix me a proper cocktail, if need be. Lately there had been a lot of need.

On my laptop I rechecked the dark video clip from Banks Street Bar, tweaking the zoom and contrast in an effort to try to ID the pay-phone caller. A guy in a baseball cap was as close as I could guess, and I couldn't be 100 percent sure about the guy part.

I was just beginning my effort to locate Breaux's assistant Peter Danforth when a familiar voice interrupted me.

"Saint James, you got a minute?"

I'd been so focused I hadn't seen or heard the pretty brunette in her late twenties enter the bar.

"Agent Harding, it's been awhile." My mind was spinning. *Harding? Coming to see me here?* I stood.

"That coffee smells good. Mind if I join you?"

"Cups are behind the bar. Help yourself."

Special Agent Harding operated out of the New Orleans FBI office. She had worked briefly with Honey and me on a high-profile case that had ended well for all concerned. Except the dead bad guy. I watched her as she fixed us each a coffee. The blond dye job I remembered so fondly was gone; actually, Harding looked better in her natural color. She wore a nicely tailored dark blue business suit—blazer and skirt. This was the first time I'd seen her legs, and it occurred to me I'd like to see more. The fact that she felt secure enough to wear a skirt and not try to hide her femininity in a male-dominated arena impressed me. Smart, ambitious as hell, and very thorough, Harding could be a good ally, as long as it benefited her. But I'd never count on her in the clutch to have my back.

"Must be nice having your office in a bar," she said, crossing over to join me.

"Del Breaux and Ty Parks," I said, taking a cup and saucer of java from her. I usually wasn't much for chitchat. Harding had never been here before, and there could only be one reason why she was here now. I'd said it before she'd even had a chance to sit down, and she looked a little resentful that I had gotten right to the point. "Tell me about the agents from Washington about to meet with Chief Pointer," I said.

"Please put your recording equipment on the table and turn it off."

Now I was intrigued. I removed my mini audio and video digital recorders from a pocket and set them down. "They weren't turned on."

She checked them nonetheless. "Never met those agents. They're CI-3, counterintelligence folks." She took a sip of the dark brew, and we just looked at each other.

"You're obviously working the case, so what can I do for you?"

"I'm not working the case at all. I'm not even here. You and I aren't having this conversation. Okay?"

I nodded slightly. "Fair enough."

"I don't know with certainty who killed Breaux and Parks. I know a little bit about some things they were up to."

"Black-project-secret selling?"

"Not to my knowledge," she said, somewhat surprised. "You have proof of that?"

"No, but it seems a logical possibility."

"Be careful with those kinds of assumptions."

"Good advice. So you are here because . . . ?"

"I was working an investigation. It's classified; I can't discuss it. Breaux came on my radar screen. I was unofficially ordered to cease and desist, so I did. If I had a smoking gun, I wouldn't have backed down so easily. But . . ." She shrugged.

"But what?"

"I came to realize that the original source of my investigation was an unstable individual. He had some kind of personal vendetta. He was obsessed with . . . let's just say I heard him say numerous times how he wanted to kill Del Breaux and certain other people."

"And you think it's possible that he did."

"That's why I'm here, in a completely unofficial capacity. If he killed Breaux and Parks, then there's a long list of other murders just waiting to happen."

I didn't know Harding well, but she looked troubled. For her to come here like this and tell me these things was beyond unusual.

"So who is this guy? Where can I find him?"

"I don't know his real name. He goes by Decon." She pronounced it "DEE-con."

"You started a classified investigation based on information from a source and you didn't know who the person was?"

"We'll start an investigation based on an anonymous tip if the information is good. As far as I know, Decon is homeless. We put a lot of man hours in trying to track him down. All I can tell you is he used to work at a place called Scrap Brothers in the Ninth Ward. The owners weren't too impressed with an FBI badge. Maybe you can get further with them than I could."

That was a given.

"So you dropped in to give me a tip on a murder case?"

"No. The dead are already dead. It's the people on the list who are still alive that concern me."

Harding looked terribly serious.

"So why aren't you sharing this with the CI-3 agents?"

"Maybe you'll figure that out." She pushed the coffee away from her, stood up, and walked out the door.

As I watched her go I mentally replaced Peter Danforth with some homeless guy named Decon at the top of my to-do list.

A few scrapyards populate the blighted industrial area in the Ninth Ward over by the Galvez Street Wharf on the Inner Harbor Navigation Canal. Scrap Brothers sits on Kentucky Street. The neighborhood had been seriously swamped in the Storm and hadn't come back yet, except for a few businesses and residents here and there. The scrap businesses, however, had reopened quickly, because, let's be honest, when your inventory consists of piles of rusty junk no one wants except some guy with a smelter in Guangdong Province, being flooded with twelve feet of water for a couple of weeks doesn't exactly kill the resale value of your stock. Maybe a forklift or a welding unit got ruined, maybe a beat-up office computer or two. But the Storm also created a world of new scrap overnight, a tsunami of iron, steel, aluminum, brass, bronze, copper, and more exotic metals like nickel, chromium, cobalt, Monel, and titanium, all still being brought to the scrap dealers almost around the clock by industrious scavengers. Occasionally the matériel brought in wasn't even stolen.

The sun lasered me through a patchy sky as I entered the scrapyard; a couple of thunderheads signaled rain cells drifting in from the Gulf. I noticed that Scrap Brothers had a shredder. A black guy whose name patch on his blue work shirt said "Skip" nudged an old heavy steel filing cabinet onto an inclined conveyor belt that carried the four-drawer unit up about ten feet into the throat of a feed hopper. The cabinet then dropped onto 36mm-wide blades spinning on four powerful shafts. The screeching whine as the super-sturdy filing cabinet was torn to pieces didn't last long at all, and petals of shiny metal snowed out of the grinding compartment and into an open-topped Dumpster. The shredder was one of the few machines you could throw a monkey wrench into and the monkey wrench would lose.

Skip threw more metal junk onto the conveyor belt, so I figured I'd nose around the yard until somebody stopped me. I skirted an overheated Doberman chained to a steel pole in front of two locked forty-foot, oceangoing cargo containers—one painted green, the other silver. The nice doggy made it a point to display his impressive incisors for my consideration.

The place was filthy, like all scrapyards, and piles of haphazardly separated metal stood piled everywhere. I spotted a massive pile of railroad rail partially covered by tarps over in a corner. A guy on a forklift loaded palletized scrap into a cargo container in an open area where roll-off trucks would back into and then literally winch the containers onto their frames and deliver them to the Port of New Orleans.

I was looking for some shade in the already-hundred-degree heat, when I saw another guy pour gasoline onto coils of insulated wire, then set them on fire. This was a legal no-no, and I sensed an advantageous opening as I crossed to him. He was stripping copper wires the lazyman's way. All kinds of toxins were being released, which is why it's usually done in China, not the States.

"You're violating about fifteen federal, state, and city statutes there, partner."

"No kidding?" he said mock-sweetly, looking up at me. "Well the Feds, the state, and the city can go suck on a razor blade. Who the hell you be, anyhow? You with the EPA? Stupid regulations are killin' small bid'ness in dis here country. So go stick a jagged rubber hose up your ass, douche bag." He turned back to his illegal work at hand.

I had to suppress a smile. Potty Mouth used the direct approach, like I usually did. "I'm not a Fed; I'm looking for guy named Decon."

"Don't know nobody named Decon."

"Yes you do, Pops. Call all your people in. I'm dragging you all down to Broad Street and throwing you in the drunk tank for forty-eight hours with a bunch of guys covered in vomit and lice. Maybe that will refresh your memories." I couldn't help it; I still had the cop look, vibe, and feel. Sometimes you didn't need to show a badge.

The man, whose blue work shirt also had a name patch that said "Skip," same as the guy on the conveyor belt, whistled a shrill alert that might have been heard in Dallas. The Doberman winced. But the other two guys looked up, and we convened a powwow in the office.

The old window air-con unit didn't look like much, but it put out an icy breeze. Leroy and Jimmy Jefferson, the Scrap Brothers, were the two men wearing "Skip" shirts. I didn't ask. They were both short and stocky with thick forearms covered with scars from a lifetime of handling sharp metal objects. They made me feel as welcome as a herpes outbreak. Their employee, Herbert, who had been running the forklift, practically inhaled a cold can of Coke, then told me he'd only worked there a couple of months and never met anyone named Decon. I gestured that he could go back to work, and he went outside as a pickup truck pulled up with a load of tire rims that looked suspiciously new.

"Who you be?" asked Jimmy. He had a yellowish left eye, was missing any number of teeth, and generally looked like he'd disassembled one old transformer full of PCBs too many.

"We're not here to talk about me. We're going to have a little talk about your future."

I glanced around the dirty office, which looked like it had been furnished from a military surplus auction—heavy gunmetal-gray desks, creaky uncomfortable office chairs, a grimy old-fashioned steel Rolodex with dog-eared name cards. Since I'm a lock guy, I recognized a steel government-issue file-cabinet safe with a digital combination lock that will lock you out if you get the combo wrong three times in a row. Then the safe can't be opened without having some higher-up come out and reset it. But there were no higher-ups now, there were only Jimmy and Leroy Jefferson, and they were wasting my time.

I picked up a length of lead pipe that had been leaning against a desk and slapped one end into my palm a few times.

"I mean, you're basically crooks and have been all your life. You're fences for stolen scrap items, or just plain stolen goods, like those car rims outside. You have an all-cash business, so you report, what, twenty percent of your action to the tax man? You made a small—no, check that—large fortune since the Storm, so now you're fat, dumb, and happy. And those piece-of-shit vehicles I see parked out there that you drive to work every day, that's just to play the 'poor man' role. You can't let Herbert out on the forklift or any of your customers see what you really drive. You have new Caddies or Lincolns parked in the drive-way at home, right? A nice spread in the burbs out on the West Bank, or maybe a big piece of land in Mississippi, past Slidell. You both rake in a solid six figures a year, probably around a quarter mil, almost all tax free. And you think you're untouchable because you've been doing it so long. You think in a place like Louisiana the gravy train will never stop. Hell, it's a federal offense to scrap steel rail, but you've got tons of it sitting out in the yard."

"We storing it; we ain't scrapping it," said Leroy.

Jimmy stood up from a broken office chair and took a step toward me. "You get the hell out. We got friends downtown, too."

I slammed the pipe onto the top of the nearest desk, demolishing a dirty beige phone handset. Jimmy stopped in his tracks. "Cockroach," I said, by way of explanation. "There's a few in here." I gently placed the end of the pipe onto Jimmy's chest and guided him back onto the office chair. "You called me a douche bag, Jimmy." I said it in a way that suggested Jimmy was in line for some payback.

Jimmy settled down quick, but Leroy had the look of a man who was thinking about going for a gun. I figured he had one in the desk drawer next to him.

"I wouldn't, if I were you." I gave him a look I used sparingly. It was a look that suggested he had better cooperate. No, actually, it was a look that suggested I was considering ripping out his heart.

Of course, it was all an act on my part. In order to get results, sometimes you have to cajole and sweet-talk, sometimes you simply have to politely ask, sometimes a bribe is enough, sometimes you need to raise your voice and get angry. Other times, you might threaten legal action, and sometimes you have no choice but to crack some heads. Or threaten to. And sometimes it's a combination of all of the above.

I sounded pissed, I looked lethal, but strangely the raw anger that for weeks had been underpinning my every thought, word, and deed was in sleep mode. For some reason, I felt strangely calm with the Jeffersons.

I placed a call on my phone and put it on speaker. A husky male voice boomed, "Sergeant McCarty."

"Dice, it's Saint James. I have a lead on those expensive rims that got stolen from Kirby Ladue the other night."

Leroy and Jimmy glanced out the window at the wheel rims Herbert was unloading from the truck, then looked at each other.

"Oh, yeah?" An NOPD detective now in auto theft, Dice McCarty and I were old enemies, but we had settled into an uneasy truce. "I figure the thief hasn't been able to fence them, they're so hot. You don't steal from Kirby if you have half a brain," said Dice.

"Half a brain is what these two guys have between them. The wheels are aluminum, right?"

"Yeah, top of the line. Listen, save me some paperwork and just call Kirby. He'll send his boys to get the rims and kill whoever took them. And give you a nice spiff for the info."

"Sounds good."

Before I could even hang up, Jimmy started waving at me. "You know, I rememba' now. I think I know why you came here."

We stood sweating in an outdoor stall where mostly brass and bronze items were stored. I spotted a long brass staircase railing that I could have sworn I'd seen once upon a time in the public library. Brass fittings that had to have come off ships were piled in a corner. A crack of thunder ripped the sky with an intensity that rattled my bones and vibrated some of the stacked metal.

"Here 'tis."

Jimmy reached into a heap of flat items and hefted up a bronze plaque, a cornerstone marker that *The Times-Picayune* reported had been stolen from the exterior of a historic building in the Central Business District.

"Your boy Decon brought this in. Maybe two, three day ago."

"He used to work for us, for a little minute. Before Herbert," said Leroy. "Brings small crap in from time to time."

"What's his last name?"

"Hell, we don't know. Ask him when you find him."

"C'mon, you must know; you gave him a payroll check."

"We look like we issue payroll checks?"

They had me there. "Describe him."

"Skinny-assed white boy with blue eyes and long black hair. Short beard. 'Bout tall as you. Lot of tattoos. And an egghead too. He know some shit."

"Where can I find him?"

"He crazy; always be hangin' out in cemeteries."

I gave each of them an impatient, skeptical look.

"Don't know where he live, but know where he drink at night," said Jimmy. "You know dat minimall off Clearview on the river side a' I-Ten? Out in Metairie?"

"I'll find it."

"He drink in them bars there. Always has."

"You takin' it or no?" asked Jimmy, still holding the bronze plaque.

"Somebody else will come by for it."

Leroy's eyes narrowed to venomous slits. "Let's see your badge."

"Never said I had a badge."

I turned away, and they followed me out of the stall past the Dober-man and the two locked cargo containers.

"What's in the containers?" I asked.

"Ain't none a your bid'ness if you ain't police," barked Jimmy.

"You trespassin'!"

I turned to see Leroy with a revolver pointed at my chest, a little Smith & Wesson .38 snubby. But they can make big holes. I'd gotten a bit too lackadaisical with the Jefferson brothers. Leroy had the piece in his pants pocket all along. Over Leroy's shoulder I saw Herbert tossing the shiny aluminum wheels onto the conveyor belt for the ride into the shredder. And with them went my leverage.

"Go ahead and make your call. Them rims be gone in a few min-utes," said Jimmy, regaining his piss and vinegar now that his brother had the drop on me. "Now git!"

The fact that I had the evidence of Kirby Ladue's stolen rims all recorded on my hidden video cam was moot. I'd gotten a nice boost toward tracking down a guy that the local FBI office had been unable to locate, a guy Agent Harding suspected might be involved in the deaths of Breaux and Parks. But as I left, I felt most curious why the Jeffersons had a Doberman guarding a green and a silver cargo container—and why Leroy had only drawn his pistol when I asked to see what was inside them.

CHAPTER FIVE

The address the DMV and Bell South had on Peter Danforth was a Creole cottage in Mid-City that must have been nice before the Storm, but now it looked like an eyesore that needed to be bulldozed. Looters had stripped away the wrought-iron fence and all the architectural detail. Part of the roof was gone, a wall seemed to be in a super-slow-motion collapse, and most of the windows were broken out. I called Honey with an update from what used to be Danforth's front yard.

"I found Danforth's house, but it's vacant. Nobody's here but the rats."

"So keep looking."

"Does that mean we're still on the case?" I asked, practically holding my breath.

"Yeah. I have to report daily to the FBI CI-3 assholes. They get possession of all evidence we turn up."

I exhaled with relief. "So we do the heavy lifting, but they suck up all the hard proof."

"They want the two point five million, too."

"Oh?"

"And the chief ain't giving it to them. They didn't like it that I had checked those sequential serial numbers. The money came from the Bank of China in Beijing."

"Really?"

"But when you called me earlier? You said Harding didn't think Breaux was selling secrets," stated Honey.

"I didn't tell her about the money," I said.

"She's FBI. She must know we recovered the cash."

"I don't think the local office is dialed into this, Honey."

"The FBI boys I met looked stressed. Like they got a lot on their plate."

"I'm beginning to think Breaux and Parks were merely appetizers at an all-you-can-eat buffet."

Honey and I made plans to meet up later tonight and try to track down the homeless guy named Decon. Meanwhile, we followed up different leads, meaning I was going to talk to a guy about a chair.

Jack Dempsey's Restaurant occupied a remodeled double-shotgun house over in the Bywater, across the street from the East Bank element of Naval Support Activity, and just a couple of minutes from Scrap Brothers. Barry Morrison, the antiques dealer acquaintance of mine, had agreed to meet for a very late lunch, or maybe it was early supper, although I hadn't told him what I wanted to discuss.

Jack Dempsey's featured huge portions and waitresses to match. Barry, a salad kind of guy who had searched the menu for something healthy to eat, settled on a chicken salad, which arrived with nine pounds of fried chicken sitting on three leafs of iceberg lettuce and could feed a family of five. He tried not to look aghast. I knew better than to try to order healthy in Dempsey's. The condiment caddy on the red vinyl tablecloth included both Tabasco and Crystal hot sauce and thirty-two-ounce squeeze bottles of homemade Ranch dressing and tartar sauce, 642 grams of fat per half-teaspoon serving, give or take. Old R&B played on the jukebox, but the main reason I liked the place was that they weren't chintzy with where they set the thermostat on a searing hot day.

As much as I hated chitchat, Barry was the kind of guy you had to schmooze a little. And since he had helped me out once when bad guys were trying to kill me, I indulged his idle gossip, pretending to be interested. It wasn't until the entrées came that I got down to business.

"I'm working with NOPD on that double murder case—Del Breaux and Ty Parks."

Barry lit up like the Steamboat Natchez on a dinner cruise. "You're kidding! I couldn't believe it when I read that in the paper. They were clients of mine!"

Barry wasn't the tricky type and hadn't figured out that I already knew that.

"How well did you know them?"

"My partner and I went to a few parties at their house. We weren't close friends, but Del bought a number of very expensive pieces from me."

"How expensive?"

"A couple of them went for over fifty thousand dollars."

"Pricey. How did he pay?"

"What do you mean?"

"Check, credit card . . . ?"

"Cash, now that you mention it. Del always had a fat roll in his wallet. And he didn't just buy from me. He bought from practically every high-end dealer in town."

"He had a company called Breaux Enterprises. What kind of business was that?"

"He said it was international trading," said Barry, moving chicken around on his plate in a vain search for something green.

"Trading of what?"

"Commodities, I assume. I don't really know."

I hated euphemisms like "commodities." You could be talking about heroin, whoopee cushions, or barrels of beer.

"I need a straight answer here. Did Del Breaux do drugs?"

"Sure. Viagra, Cialis, Levitra . . ."

"Got it. What about Ty Parks?"

"His drug was yoga. They were big drinkers, but I never heard any chatter that they used drugs."

"You know if either of them owned a gun?"

"They were anti-gun. But then, they've never been robbed or mugged, like I have." Barry smiled and patted his attaché case, suggesting he had a firearm concealed inside. Barry's anti-gun comment confirmed my suspicion that the Steyr M9 would not be traced to the victims.

"So how did you meet Breaux and Parks?"

"Through an acquaintance. Peter Danforth."

Bingo.

"I heard that a guy named Peter Danforth worked for Breaux."

"Yes, he's been working for Del. And he did consulting work for him as an interior designer." Barry took a sip of water. "Of course, maybe there were some other things going on, but I don't like to gossip."

Barry loved to gossip; just don't call it that. Now his pump was not only primed, it was gushing.

"Look," I said, "we're not gossiping here; this is a murder investigation. And you're being a huge help."

"Well, Peter has exquisite taste. Some people have—I don't know if it's breeding or what—they just have an instinct for color and arrangement and composition, design, fabrics and materials, everything. Peter is handsome and smart and utterly sophisticated."

"Okay."

"Anyway, the whispers were that he and Del were having . . . an indiscretion."

"Recently?"

"No, no, no. This is history. From just after the Storm."

"So Danforth was sleeping with the guy he was working for."

"Yes. Then maybe six months ago certain tongues started wagging about Peter and *Ty*."

"You're suggesting that this Danforth guy gets around."

"To say the least. He's had an off-and-on-again boyfriend for years— Joey Bales—but Peter is a player."

"So these affairs caused problems for Breaux and Park's relationship?"

"Not at all. They had an understanding, as many gay couples do, especially when there's a younger partner involved. Certain freedoms granted, if you get my drift. They threw big parties and liked to . . . have fun."

"But what about the sometimes boyfriend, this Joey Bales guy? Could he have been jealous of Danforth and Breaux being an item?"

"You mean like jealous enough to kill? I think not, otherwise, half the gay population in New Orleans would be deceased."

"I need to find Peter Danforth. Right away. Can you track him down for me?"

"I should think so," he said, pulling out his cell phone. "But I want a favor for it. Find out if Del has any heirs. They may want me to broker the sale of those pieces he bought."

Barry was a sensitive-enough guy but seldom missed a chance to make a buck.

As I worked on my fried redfish plate, he made a couple of calls and actually got Peter Danforth on the line. He rang off, removed a leather-bound pocket notebook from his attaché case, scribbled out an address onto monogrammed stationery, and handed it to me.

"He'll see you at seven tonight."

Del Breaux's mother in Pascagoula was still alive, and I relayed that information and a phone number to Barry Morrison after grabbing a shower in my loft and doing some Internet research. I drove the Bronco to the meeting with Danforth, who was apparently running scared and holed up in a gay gentlemen's club called the Academy, which took up an entire three-story former warehouse over by the old Falstaff brewery. Honey was swamped checking out Breaux's and Park's financial records and gave me the go-ahead to meet Danforth alone; I guess she really did need my help.

I hadn't been aware of any place called the Academy, but a number of new restaurants, bars, and clubs had opened since the Storm. Optimistic entrepreneurs rolling the dice on doing business in a city still in ruins were either bold visionaries or patently insane. In a sense I was one of those entrepreneurs, and on any given day I wondered if I wasn't half nuts to remain in the ravaged city suffering from fractured infrastructure, decades of corrupt neglect, and the mostly laissez-faire attitude of a citizenry that tolerated it all. Of course, my business thrived upon the problems of others, and there were plenty of problems to go around in New Orleans.

The Academy stood in a neighborhood that had been crappy before the Storm made everything crappier. Trashed and abandoned buildings sat hobbled, corpses of past industrial might long gone; broken glass littered empty lots where no vehicles cared to park, anyway; street signs, when present, tilted askew at crazy angles implying a lack of care on the part of either the city or its workers.

There didn't seem to be much recovery going on in this neighborhood. Yet big money flowed into New Orleans from around the world; it had to be going somewhere.

If one didn't take into consideration the tragic loss of life, maybe at the end of the day, the Storm would be a good thing. Maybe the millions pumping into the area would mean change for the better, providing funds that heretofore had been lacking, and inspiring a renaissance of thought, word, and deed. Maybe the potholes would finally get fixed; maybe the citywide free Internet plan would reach fruition; maybe the water pressure would get fixed; maybe the pumping stations would get fixed; maybe the levees would get built right; maybe some of the blight could get eradicated; maybe a new city Master Plan would actually have some common sense and not just be a load of feel-good Utopian bunk; maybe there would be money to pay police and firefighters a decent wage; maybe principals and teachers and custodians wouldn't steal what was meant for the students; maybe local business owners and restaurateurs would pay their workers better and stop gouging their customers; maybe the politicians and bureaucrats would steal less and instead funnel cash into projects that put people to work; maybe some of the intergenerational on-the-dole lazy louts of every color would get off their asses and take one of the legion of job offers that went begging; maybe subsidence would subside and the city could stop sinking; maybe what little industry we had left would stop its flight to more sensible locales.

Maybe a new New Orleans could rise from the rubble to reclaim past glory and be anointed as the belle of the South, as a city that mattered, as a city on the move to the future.

Maybe.

But probably not.

In place of any signage at my destination, armed guards protected the entrance to the gated private parking area of a solid old brick building that looked as imposing as a fortress. What does it say about our city that this new private club appeared more secure than Fort Knox? The guards checked my name against a list before letting me pull in. If Danforth truly feared for his life, this might not be a bad place to be.

But it wasn't a good place for a guy out of uniform, as I discovered at the front desk.

"I'm here for an interrogation; I'm not joining."

"Sir, all guests are required to be in dress uniform to enter the premises during the dinner hour, which is now."

I flashed on the navy whites in Breaux's and Parks's closet. *Had they been Academy members?* Peter Danforth would probably clear that one up, but between him and me stood two doormen dressed as U.S. Navy MPs with nightsticks on their duty belts and semiautos in their leather holsters. They were big beefy guys, and this was a private club with its own set of rules.

"I wasn't informed about the uniform rule."

"Sir, we have a small wardrobe room right over there."

I was there on official police business, but my letter from the chief didn't convince them. I could just go along with their program and pay twenty-five dollars to rent a set of ensign's dress whites. I liked Halloween and enjoyed a good costume party as much as anyone, but I wasn't much for dress-up games with a bunch of weak-kneed wannabes whom I figured never served in the military. It wasn't as if they were doing some kind of historical reenactment, or even a WWII-era dinner-dance replete with an orchestra playing Glenn Miller music; no, these guys—civilians—dressed in military uniforms every time they came to dinner at their expensive members-only club. I didn't like it at all and decided it was *they* who were going to go along with *my* program.

"If you want to see uniforms," I told the fake MP at the desk, "I can arrange to have about twenty of 'em here in ten minutes. They'll be wearing blue, be heavily armed, and I will help them shove those nightsticks on your belts up your asses. You have ninety seconds to clear me to come in, or I make the call and take Peter Danforth into police custody."

"So NOPD is outsourcing its homicide investigations now. What a joke," said Peter Danforth as he disdainfully handed the chief's letter back to me. He lit another cigarette, forgetting he still had one burning in the ashtray.

We sat in overstuffed leather club chairs in the library. A massive oak conference table in the center of the room could seat twenty. Newspapers from around the world dangled from wooden racks. Other than a couple of husky guys standing guard at the door, we had the place to ourselves. It had been strange to see over thirty men in uniform eating in the main dining hall with Bette Midler on the sound system when I first entered. Even in the bizarre world of New Orleans, having to be in uniform to gain entrance to a place for dinner kind of boggled my mind.

I lit a cigarillo and sipped a glass of Buffalo Trace Kentucky bourbon poured neat.

"Nice place. Breaux and Parks were members here, weren't they?"

"Yes, but they didn't come often. Usually only when there was a special event."

"How did you meet them?"

"In the bars. I met Ty maybe five years ago. I didn't meet Del until after they got together. I did some design work on their house and consulted Del on purchases for his art collection."

"So you became better friends with them over time."

"That's right."

"How would you describe your relationship with them at the time of their deaths? Were you close friends, best friends . . . ?"

"Close friends." Using very formal mannerisms, he took a sip of mineral water. But his hand shook slightly; he was nervous. He wore two stars on his dress whites, the navy rank of rear admiral. Awarding himself flag rank clearly indicated he thought highly of himself. Pale with soft features for a thirty-year-old, he didn't strike me as an outdoorsman. His hands told me he'd never done a day of manual labor in his life.

"What do you know about Breaux's work at Michoud?"

"He consulted on some classified project. He certainly never struck me as being a scientist dealing in secrets. I mean, engineers are usually a certain kind of personality type. Del didn't fit that mold. Of course, I met him after he came out of the closet. I heard he was different way back when he was closeted."

"He tell you any specifics?"

"Never. And asking didn't elicit the nicest of responses. He would go to Michoud maybe twice a week for half a day. What he did, I have no idea."

"So you sometimes worked for Breaux as a consultant, but then you started working as his personal assistant, right?"

"When the Storm hit, I got wiped out like a lot of people. Del needed an executive assistant, I needed money, so I took the job."

"You had keys to the office on Poydras?"

"Of course."

"When's the last time you were there?"

"Thursday afternoon when I left work."

"What kind of business was Breaux Enterprises?"

"Whatever Del was into at the time."

"And what has that been recently?"

"You don't know?" he asked incredulously.

"I'm asking you."

"Have you been to the offices yet?"

"I can't reveal details of the investigation."

"Investigation," he said mockingly as he shook his head. "There won't be an investigation, don't you get that? Anytime now, the word will come down, NOPD will back off, and that will be the end of that."

"Please answer the question. What kind of business was Breaux doing?"

"You have to have been to the office by now. How can you not know what the company did?"

"I want to hear it from you."

"Sorry, I abhor redundancy."

Peter Danforth was a real smart-ass. An equivocating, smart-mouthed bastard. He acted like he could simply blow off the police and it wouldn't amount to a hill of beans. I felt tempted to smack the information out of him, but we had witnesses watching.

"Are you in possession of any office files?"

"No."

"Which financial institutions did Breaux use for his business transactions?"

"You won't get that from me." He took a long drag and gave me his best "screw you" look.

"Don't play cute, Mister Danforth. There's a lot of evidence in play that puts you right in the middle of things."

"If you say so."

"When is the last time you had sex with either Breaux or Parks?"

Danforth flushed. "What has that got to do with Del's and Ty's murders?"

"Maybe everything. Jealously is the oldest motive for killing known to mankind. Your old boyfriend Joey Bales the jealous type?"

Danforth snorted. "Joey? The only thing Joey would be jealous of is that he didn't get to join us for a threesome."

"Where can I find him?"

"Somewhere in the bars on the gay end of Bourbon Street, I imagine. I'm not in contact with him anymore."

"Where were you the night Del Breaux and Ty Parks were killed?"

I studied Danforth carefully, waiting to analyze his body language. I'd already asked him a few questions I'd known the answers to and had watched him carefully as he answered. He certainly looked nervous, but then he'd pretty much been a nervous, chain-smoking wreck since the moment I'd walked in. Still, I had an idea of what to look for in case he lied.

"Atlanta. When it made the news, I flew back here." He looked me straight in the eyes.

"Have proof?"

"I bought plane tickets, I have boarding passes. Stayed at the Hilton, ordered a lot of room service. You could probably get their security video if you needed visual proof I was there." His lips didn't tighten; he wasn't pointing a finger or making demonstrative gestures. I guessed he'd told the truth.

"I'll do that. So we can establish an ironclad alibi in terms of you not being present at the crime scene." Of course, he might have hired the killers, for all I knew.

"I'm not worried about establishing my alibi. No offense, but the only reason I'm speaking to you is because Barry Morrison is an old friend."

"You thought you wouldn't have to speak to the police after your boss was murdered?"

"You're not really the police, but even if you were, I don't think you will get very far with this."

"What's that supposed to mean?"

Danforth just shook his closely cropped head of streaked blond hair, then templed his fingers together and put them to his lips in a worried gaze. "It's kind of pathetic how clueless you are." He gestured to the guys at the door, and one of them disappeared. "No reason to talk to you since I can't count on NOPD for help."

"Are you suggesting there is some kind of grand conspiracy at play?"

"It doesn't matter what I tell you. You *can't* help me. That's why I need a high-priced DC attorney to get me into a federal witness-protection program. I'm guessing the only reason I'm alive is because, A, I was out of town and, B, I came here immediately, to the Academy, when I got back from Atlanta. There are armed men here who will do everything they can to protect me, but that isn't nearly enough to keep me alive, considering what I'm up against."

"Why would your life be in danger?" I flashed on Harding and her warning that more murders were imminent.

"Loose ends."

"Related to Breaux Enterprises."

"I should think so."

"You need to tell me what kind of business Breaux was up to."

"It would be healthier for me if I didn't."

"You only say that because you haven't seen me pissed off." I looked him right in the eyes. He stared back blankly, and I took a slow sip of fine bourbon, never breaking my gaze. "Ever heard of a guy named Decon?" I asked.

"Decon? No."

"So who wanted to kill Breaux and Parks?"

"They had to have been after Del."

"Who's 'they'?"

"Someone in the Buyer's Club, I imagine."

"The Buyer's Club?"

"They all had their reasons."

"How about some names?"

Peter Danforth gazed down at the reddish Oriental carpet, scowling.

"Do you really think I can't take you down to Broad Street head-quarters right now? There won't be any safe houses or around-the-clock security details there. You're a suspect in a murder investigation, asshole. I'll throw you in a fucking holding cell with thirty guys who would cap your ass for fifteen bucks. Now give me some names!"

Danforth looked at me evenly. "Like I said, it's pointless, you'll be off the case before the day is out. But here's a name you can chase: Clayton Brandt. Add Del Breaux and three other men and you have the Buyer's Club."

"Give me the other names."

"No. I give you Brandt. He's the scariest, which is saying some-thing."

"And what did the Buyer's Club buy? Drugs? People? Secrets? Are you looking for immunity, is that why you want witness protection?"

The guy at the door who had disappeared returned with four more men. So six guys, all looking like gym regulars, crowded into the room near the door. Danforth stood and motioned them forward as he backed away.

"Look, we both know that I don't have to tell you or any other detective a thing. You want to arrest me? Go ahead. But this is a waste of my time. The fact that you're going to be pulled from the case may just save your life. Until then, be careful. Give those people the slightest reason and they will simply eradicate you. Cop"—he gave me a derisive look—"or not."

Back at my loft by nine, I ran Clayton Brandt's name through some online databases. The only likely candidate to emerge was a retired air force general, but the details were sketchy. Honey could run him through LE, law enforcement databases, and I could probably wheedle Harding for a deeper background check. If Breaux had been on her radar screen, chances were that Clayton Brandt had been, too.

I replayed the Danforth interview using a cheap waterproof digital music player as I showered, alternating from hot to cold. The thing that bothered me was that he identified Brandt as the likeliest of the likely killers, but then said, "Give those people the slightest reason and they will simply eradicate you." "They" had to refer to the Buyer's Club as a group. Or did it? And what kind of group acts with the kind of impunity that doesn't think twice about killing police officers? The only thing that made sense was the Mexican drug cartels. New Orleans had not had much of a Mexican population until the Storm hit. The Hispanic community was mostly comprised of Hondurans, a population firmly entrenched here. But Mexican illegals flooded NOLA by the tens of thousands to work as laborers in the hurricane's wake, and with them came the cartels and gang graffiti, something else we never had. The damage the Storm had wrought was bad enough; the Mexican gang graffiti uglied things up even worse. Maybe I'd been wrong initially, maybe Del Breaux and Ty Parks *were* killed over drugs—drugs on a major scale. That would certainly explain the $2.5 million in cash. And might explain why the local FBI had been investigating, even though it seemed more like DEA turf.

Danforth had wanted federal witness protection and was convinced Honey and I would be pulled from the case. That suggested an extreme sensitivity as to the nature of the conspiracy, yet Harding emphatically denied being aware of any connection between Breaux and the selling of secrets.

It occurred to me I should pull the body armor out of my closet. It occurred to me, but I didn't because it was so damn hot. I opted for a second pistol—a reconditioned 1911A .45—and extra mags instead. I'd replaced the sights and grips, added a Picatinny rail in case I wanted to pop on a laser, and had a trigger job done to ease the pull. I wore the big pistol and mags in plastic paddle carriers hidden by my long shirt-tails; I still kept the Glock 36 tucked in to my rear waistband.

I also stuck a stainless steel Japanese-made karambit in my front waistband to function as a last-chance knife that I could use with my weak-side hand if I were struggling for my weapon. Karambits have a hole in the handle/frame to insert your index finger into as you grip the knife. Mine has a short, sharply curved, razorlike blade that folds into the handle and works well at slicing and dicing. I'd attached a plastic flex cuff to the second, smaller hole in the blade, then snipped off the plastic excess. That left a small knob protruding from the blade's blunt edge, so that when I pulled the knife from my pants, the plastic nub caught on my waistband and automatically opened the blade as I pulled the knife clear. It was a nasty knife that deployed into fighting mode faster than any other knife I owned, and I wore it sparingly, usually when expecting extreme trouble.

I'd just added about five pounds of gear to my waistband and, for no terribly good reason, I found that comforting.

Weird that I geared up, but I didn't exactly know what I was up against. Thoughts of Bobby Perdue got exiled by the encroaching sense that I was about to step on a hornet's nest.

I stopped for a frozen granita with two extra shots of espresso at the PJ's not far from my place, since the rest of the evening in my mental day planner had the name *Decon* written all over it, and I figured it would be a long, hot night.

CHAPTER SIX

Leave it to Greater New Orleans to have a strip mall comprised of nothing but bars, taverns, lounges, saloons, pubs, and a drive-in daiquiri stand. That left no doubt as to why people pulled off the Interstate 10 frontage road into the parking lot; they were thirsty. And I guess that was the big attraction here: Plenty of Free Parking! Freeway Close! In that regard, it sure beat the Quarter.

But only in that regard.

At a daiquiri stand you can buy cocktails to go, handed to you though your car window, like getting burgers at McDonald's. Just don't insert the straw, because that would be drinking and driving. What was to prevent someone from lifting the lid and taking a sip as they cruised our safe streets, I'm not sure, but then this was Louisiana.

Honey had parked her unmarked unit a couple of blocks away, and we pulled into the grubby strip mall lot together in the Bronco as I finished debriefing her on the meet with Peter Danforth.

"I have to bring him in for questioning. All of the money from Del Breaux's business and personal bank accounts was transferred into some offshore account the night he was killed."

"Traceable?"

"If I had unlimited resources. Even a good financial forensics person? It might take months."

"I'm guessing Danforth was up to his eyeballs in some dirty business with Breaux."

"And we'll need to confirm his story about Atlanta," said Honey.

"Sorry I'm not much of a partner. I can't do the small things for you like running checks on Clayton Brandt and requesting security video from a hotel."

"You're helping me. Don't worry."

"Danforth's tone was like . . . resigned. Nervous, but resigned. He thinks our investigation is insignificant, that we'll be pulled from the case any minute, that NOPD is meaningless."

Honey shrugged. "I work for a department that had a bad reputation before the Storm. Now it's worse. A lot of people think we're a joke."

"I don't think he was putting down NOPD. He was alluding to the power of the opposition."

"Good," said my beautiful best friend, without a trace of irony in her voice. "The bigger they are, the harder they fall."

The pub was mostly empty, but a skinny drunk with a voice like a fork stuck in a garbage disposal told me Decon had been permanently 86'd months ago, for reasons he wouldn't elaborate on.

In the saloon, an overweight but pretty-faced blond bartender told me Decon owed her three hundred dollars so she never expected to see him again. Yet she insisted he was always around.

As Honey and I walked into the tavern, a guy with glassy eyes slammed his cell phone onto the bar, breaking it and sending his flat battery flying because his drug dealer wasn't answering. He told me Decon owed him thirty bucks, and could I give him the money and then collect it from Decon when I found him. Uh, that would be no.

In the lounge, when Honey brought up his name, we were met by a roomful of very unfriendly stares, firmly establishing that Decon wasn't the most popular guy in the minimall. A beefy guy told us Decon slept in a crypt at Greenwood Cemetery. I chalked that up to drunken bar talk, although it did remind me of the Jefferson brothers' contention that Decon hung out in cemeteries. Shrugging at each other, Honey and I moved on.

To me the drinking establishments felt interchangeable; slightly seedy workingman's joints with darts, video gaming, and pool tables. Lots of tattoos, trash talk, drug dealing, low energy, and way too many quarrelsome drunks.

I lit a mini cigarillo as Honey and I stepped back out into the sultry night, heat still radiating from the crumbling parking-lot pavement. "I wouldn't be surprised if he lives within walking distance," I said, looking over to the buildings on the other side of Interstate 10, no more than a few hundred yards away. "I don't buy that he sleeps in cemeteries in New Orleans but drinks every night out here in Metairie."

"Then let's take a walk," said Honey.

We circled around behind the minimall, surprised to see two more watering holes in a gravelly parking lot.

Different bars, same story. We soon found ourselves strolling into a so-so neighborhood of apartment buildings and multifamily dwellings.

"Check out those neon lights up ahead. Does that look like what I think it is?" Honey asked.

"Yep. Another bar. Wonder what the car insurance rates are in this neighborhood."

We picked up the pace a bit, and Honey took my hand. "Is there something you want to tell me?"

I stiffened. *Damn, does she know I pinched the laptop? How could she?* I searched her eyes for a clue. "Possibly."

She looked at me, waiting, then said, "Kind of strange, you coming out of Breaux's bathroom. Wearing your backpack."

She knew. "Then you know what I found. But it might be safer for all concerned if we kept that off the record."

"I know why you took it. I understand."

Did she really?

"What kind of problem do we have then?"

"None. Between you and me. But if you lied to me? If you told me you didn't take it? It wouldn't be good."

"I can plant the laptop back at Breaux's, introduce it into the chain of evidence—"

"What laptop? Just keep it safe for now. And let me know what's in it." She stopped, pulled me into her arms, and kissed me like a blissed-out lover on a hot date. And I kissed her back. It was the most intimate kiss Honey and I had ever shared. She broke off, smiling, then said, "Let's go get lucky."

Millie's Lounge was a stand-alone joint on a mixed-use-zoned unremarkable suburban street. About half a dozen customers seemed to be behaving themselves, although someone had dialed up a run of acid rock on the jukebox that made it hard to hear. Maybe that's why the skinny guy with long black hair and a goatee didn't seem to notice us enter.

Millie's looked like a quantum leap up in class from every other bar we'd been in so far. They even had an old-fashioned absinthe fountain set up, and the bartender had just started the water drip onto a sugar cube set over a glass of the magic juice. Classy, but looks can be deceiving.

The guy matching Decon's description sat angled away from the front door, his nose buried into a video screen. Honey remained near the front as I casually circled around, approaching him from behind.

Still unaware of our presence, Decon, who'd already had a few, looked over to the bartender, and said, "I like mine strong, so if the last one was three to one, make this one two to one." He smiled and announced to no one in particular, "I'll be chasing the green fairy all night tonight."

He looked back to the video screen and began a new game where you compared two seemingly identical photos—in this case, a partially clothed woman provocatively posed in exotic surroundings—and had to quickly mark and identify the differences between the photos.

I closed in behind him and leaned in over his shoulder. "She's missing a nipple ring; there's two coconuts in the tree instead of one. . . ."

He checked out my reflection in the video screen. "Good eye, friend," he said cautiously.

"And then there's that bronze cornerstone plaque missing from the building in the CBD."

His eyes went wide with white showing all around, telling me he was about to bolt, or slug me. He quickly pivoted but was unsteady on the bar stool. I grabbed his right hand, put him into a wrist lock, and applied pressure. Well-executed wrist locks cause a binding-type pain that is pretty scary initially as your balance gets displaced, usually accompanied by a takedown that is quickly overshadowed by your head hitting the concrete. Which is what happened to Decon in about 1.5 seconds.

Honey moved in to back me up as I changed to a wrist lock known as *Kote Mawashi,* also called a gooseneck lock. I wasn't shy about applying pressure to his joint, and he yelped in pain as I stood him up and guided him toward the front door like a puppet on my string.

"Damn, man, you don't have to torture me!"

He resisted, so I increased the pressure a bit, and he relaxed.

All of the customers watched, but no one said a thing or seemed remotely surprised or concerned that he was being escorted out against his will. That's what friends are for. Only the bartender expressed an objection.

"He owes for this drink! Fifteen bucks!" called out the bartender.

"Just hold the drink for me, Billy, I'll be right back."

"Yeah, he'll get out in a couple years, I'm sure he'll pay up then." I reapplied some pressure.

"There's no need to get physical here, officer; I'm not resisting; I'm prepared to fully cooperate with the proper authorities if—"

"Keep talking; I like that. You're going to do a lot more of that."

Honey had my back as I took him outside, bent him over the hood of a car, then cuffed him.

"Am I under arrest?"

I ignored the question, and a quick pat-down revealed a 4-inch folder, handcuff key in a back pocket, a tiny screwdriver, and forty-two dollars in crumpled bills.

"No cell phone, keys, wallet, or ID."

"My own personal protest against the encroachment by governments and corporations against our constitutionally guaranteed privacy. My lack of keys are a repudiation of—"

"Shut the hell up!"

"You said you wanted me talking."

"I'll cue you when I want your mouth to run," I said.

"Nothing like a jailhouse philosopher," said Honey.

"The unexamined life is not worth living, if you know what I mean. And as a matter of fact, yes, it was during a period of incarceration, but not by law enforcement—I prefer to refer to myself as being a political prisoner of conscience—that I began to espouse a—"

"What's your real name?" I asked.

He seemed confused by the question. "Danny Doakes."

"Your full legal name," said Honey. "The way it is on your birth certificate."

"Daniel Hawthorne Doakes. You didn't know?" He seemed disappointed.

"Why they call you Decon?"

"It's short for 'Deconstruct.' Are you familiar with the French philosopher Jacques Derrida?"

"Want to know what I'm familiar with? I'll show you."

I kept a tight grip on him as I pushed him around back, where it was much darker, with little chance of being observed.

"Hey, this is not kosher! Police brutality!" Decon yelled.

Honey held him by the cuffs and wrenched them just a tad, enough to quiet him down, as I performed a more-thorough search.

"Decon Danny Doakes. I'm gonna shorten that to Three-D," I said.

"I'm not sure I like my name being reduced to some kind of pop culture shorthand, if you understand what I'm saying."

"I thought you were all about deconstructing things?" I held up a key to show Honey. "In his pants cuff. Looks like a house key."

"It's a gate key, and you clearly fail to grasp basic deconstructionist tenets."

"That's probably true. I'm still trying to wrap my brain around nihilism." Decon had a slim jim vehicle door lockout tool tucked into his sock going up his calf. I tossed it on the cement. "Crap, we may have to strip-search this guy."

"Body cavity search behind a building? Not without latex gloves and a privacy screen."

"Who said body cavity search? Wishful thinking, Decon?" asked Honey.

"You know, I asked if I was under arrest. And you haven't identified yourselves."

"How much did you get for the stolen bronze piece?"

"That's a loaded question; it's like saying, 'How often do you molest choir boys?'"

I looked him over carefully. Skinny as a rail, maybe five feet eleven, he couldn't weigh more than 130 pounds at best, but I didn't get a meth or crackhead vibe. Probably an ex-junkie, though. Jet black, shiny, shoulder-length hair; black goatee with a few flecks of gray; pale white skin; deep-set ocean blue eyes that suggested a soulfulness, intelligence, and sadness all at the same time.

"You think we found you based on lack of evidence, counselor? We found you because we have enough to convict your ass," I said.

"You didn't even know my name. Which pains me greatly. Partly," he said to Honey, "because you are possibly the most beautiful woman in the city. But allow me to humor the both of you for a moment, if you can appreciate the situation. Assuming a person did do what you say, what are they looking at? Petty theft?"

"Do you understand how pissed off people are at looters right now? You stole a plaque off a historic building. You'll do serious time."

"And not for petty theft. Try felony looting. Carrying a concealed weapon. Possession of burglary tools. Resisting arrest." Honey was running out of fingers counting the statutes.

"What arrest? And what burglary tools?"

"The slim jim and the screwdriver, Einstein. But I know you're just an upstanding citizen, that's why you had a handcuff key in your back pocket," I said.

Honey removed a police radio from her purse. "Dispatch, Detective Baybee, Homicide. I need you to run a wants and warrants on a Daniel Hawthorne Doakes, aka Decon, spelled D-David, E-echo, C-Charlie, O-ocean, N-Nancy."

"Standby, detective," said dispatch.

"Homicide? Look, be reasonable," pleaded Decon.

I pulled him a few steps away from Honey and turned his back to her. "You have two options and time is running out. Option one is to keep being a prick, get arrested, and go to jail."

"Your partner is really hot. I mean, holy cow, check out that ass, if you know where I'm going."

The guy had more non sequiturs than a coked-up millionaire socialite. Honey was actively engaged with the dispatcher, going back and forth, but I tuned it out, giving Decon my complete attention, as you would a gifted but disturbed child.

"You know they're holding a drink for me in there. An absinthe. Do you know much about absinthe?" Decon asked. "We could have a drink; you could tell me about my second option."

A part of me wanted to snap his spine on the spot, but Honey functioned as a governing device on my rage. If I were alone I would have right then pressed down on a pressure point, and he would have screamed in agony and then told me what I needed to know.

I didn't like absinthe since I hate licorice, but Mr. Decon Danny Hawthorne Doakes was driving me to drink. Mercifully, Honey rejoined us.

"That's not his real name. That name is clean, not even a traffic ticket."

"Yeah, sorry, it's not my real name. But I kind of like it. Danny Doakes. Sounds like I'm from around here, you know what I'm saying?"

Honey and I looked at each other. "I have a fingerprint kit in the Bronco." Honey knew I wanted to run his prints without taking him into a station. She nodded, and I kept a tight hold as I pushed him forward.

"Where is your Bronco parked?" he asked.

"In front of a bar where a couple dozen people would like to see you dead."

"Then let's don't go there. My prints will come back same as my name. There won't be anything. Unknown, if you understand my point."

"We'll see about that."

"You know, detective," Decon said, turning to Honey, "what are you doing in police work? Because you are absolutely stunning. When all this gets cleared up—"

I jerked Decon to stop. "White Mercedes S550. Sunday morning, two A.M. Del Breaux and Ty Parks."

"The two dead guys? I read about it in the paper today."

"Where were you Sunday at two in the morning?"

"Probably committing a misdemeanor somewhere."

"You saying you didn't have anything to do with it?"

"Please. Do I look like a killer?"

"Killers don't have any particular look. You didn't know Breaux or Parks?"

"I never met them."

"You never met Breaux, but you wanted to kill him, right? You talked openly about wanting to kill Del Breaux, and now he's dead."

Decon's eyes widened. "Oh, so you're not really here for the looting charge, you're following up on death threats. I said some things, but it was just trash talking, if you get what I'm saying. Kind of an unfortunate coincidence, really."

"What about all the other people you trash-talked about killing? Got some names for me?"

"I was quoted out of context. I'm not a violent person."

"Is that so?"

I uncuffed Decon and had him put his arms around a live oak that was just the right size. I recuffed him so he was embracing the tree and wouldn't be going anywhere soon unless he had a chainsaw handy.

"I like trees, but I'm not a tree hugger, if you understand my point. Hey, there are ants on this tree!"

Honey and I walked off out of earshot but never took our eyes off of him.

"This guy is just a fast-talking, third-rate, drunken crook," said Honey.

"Harding said he was unbalanced, and that's an understatement. But he knows something. And who's to say he couldn't pull a trigger?"

"Let's take him in. Book him as a John Doe on the looting charge."

I nodded. "You can pick up the bronze plate tomorrow at the scrapyard. He's homeless, so better if we stick him behind bars for the theft, then we'll know where to find him if it looks like he was involved in the Breaux case."

We crossed to Decon, I released him from the tree and recuffed his hands behind his back.

"I'm ready for a cocktail," said Honey, sighing.

I jerked our prisoner forward, and we moved along at a brisk pace toward the boozy strip mall.

"Mind if I join you for that drink?" asked Decon.

We ignored him.

"How much did the Jefferson brothers sell me out for?"

We ignored him.

"I don't want to go to jail. I want to deal. And I have a lot of chips. Big chips. Maybe too big for NOPD."

We slowed him down a little bit.

"What's that supposed to mean?" I asked.

"What I can give you is way out of your jurisdiction. You'd both be in way over your heads."

Echoes of Peter Danforth. I stopped him in his tracks.

"So give it to us," said Honey.

"You need to keep me out of this," insisted Decon.

"That shouldn't be too hard since we don't know who the hell you are."

"It's the feckless leaders, the corrupt bureaucrats who are bringing this country down."

"Not guys like you, huh?"

"Come on, I'm chump change. But I have prayed to act as an instrument of karma, if you can entertain that concept. I don't do what I do for great personal gain. You think I couldn't score big if I wanted to with my background?"

"What background?" Honey asked.

But Decon kept his rant going. "I'm not greedy like the boys and girls selling off America's secrets, selling our most sensitive military technologies to our enemies, if you know what I mean."

"Who's doing that?"

"Well, the very people who sold me out to you are part of it; I can tell you that."

More echoes of the Breaux case. He definitely had my attention now.

"I'm trying to do the right thing. And my calling now is to act as a force for justice. This must be done, if you can appreciate my motivation."

"Talk straight or the next stop is Fifth District Station," said Honey impatiently.

"High-end weaponry. Super-small drones, prototype mines with advanced high explosive signatures, advanced avionics, nuclear-sub electronics, grenade launchers that look like they're from the future, exploding cell phones . . ."

Honey gave me a look like she wasn't having any of it.

"Crates and crates of the stuff over the last months," said Decon, speaking quickly now, as if racing to get it all out. "Rockets, odd-looking guns, none of it had standard military designation stamps or data plates; that's why I assume they were prototypes, and—"

"Whoa," I said. "Where exactly did you see this fantastic arsenal?"

"In a green cargo container protected by a Doberman pinscher at Scrap Brothers in the Ninth Ward."

CHAPTER SEVEN

We all sat at a rear corner table back in Millie's Lounge. On the juke-box Sade sang one of her eighties' hits about a smooth operator, which seemed appropriate considering the guy Honey and I sat across from. As Decon relished his absinthe, Honey and I knocked back Crown and Cokes.

"If you don't work at Scrap Brothers anymore, how would you know there's weaponry in the green container there right now?"

"I'm no longer employed there, but I'm a regular visitor."

"And the Jefferson brothers just let you look around?" I asked.

"Are you kidding? I'd probably be dead if they knew."

"So the weapons are in both of those containers where the dog is?"

"No, only the green container. The silver container is welded shut. I have no idea what's in that one."

Honey didn't make much of an attempt to hide her exasperation. And she was tired and getting bored. She didn't buy his story, and maybe even Decon sensed this.

"Look, I go in late at night, on a pretty regular basis, if you under-stand what I'm saying. Not just Scrap Brothers, but a lot of the yards. I make small change selling scrap. So if I need some scrap to sell, what better place to get it than at another scrap yard? I first found out about the military equipment in the container when I worked for Leroy and Jimmy. I've checked it regularly ever since."

"Why?"

"Information is power. Power is money. I like to make money."

"What about the Doberman?"

"I'm an ex-junkie. The dog is still hooked."

"You dose the dog?"

"Ten minutes, he's out. I lift the stuff from a vet's office."

Honey shook her head scornfully.

"You told FBI Agent Harding about these weapons and she didn't get a search warrant?" I asked.

"I never told her the location of the weapons. I told her the names of some individuals committing federal crimes. And, yeah, Breaux was on the list. But not the other guy, Parks."

"Why didn't you give her the weapons location?"

"I was testing her and she failed."

"Testing her?" asked Honey.

"I didn't know if the FBI was part of the plot or not. They are. She dropped the whole thing."

"What other names are on your list?"

"Take a look at the weapons first. Then I'll give you the names."

"The names of the people you want dead," I stated.

"I want what they're doing stopped. I don't want them dead, although I'm not sure it would be any great loss to the human race if they expired."

Honey shot me a look confirming that she was thinking what I was thinking: the guy was a whack job. That had been my knee-jerk reaction. And yet Harding had told me she'd been unofficially ordered to drop the investigation initially spurred by Decon. Why? Breaux had been up to no good, there was no denying that, and maybe futuristic weapons were being developed out at Michoud. Were some of them now stored in a container at the scrapyard? Leroy Jefferson had pulled a pistol on me in front of those locked containers after I had inquired about the contents.

"If you're wasting our time, if there's nothing revealing in that cargo container—"

"You'll book me for looting. I understand. And as much as I would like to have another absinthe, I suggest we go to Scrap Brothers right now. I have a couple of doses for the dog in the false heel of my shoe; you missed it during your search."

I looked at Decon and couldn't help but smile, then I turned to Honey. "You should go home and get some sleep."

"No. I'm curious what he'll look like when you finish with him."

The brothers only kept the Doberman chained during business hours, and he now sprawled unconscious by the office door. Honey watched as I picked the hockey-puck-style padlock on the green cargo container at Scrap Brothers. I'd picked the padlock on the front gates and left Decon handcuffed to the exterior driver's-side door handle of the Bronco parked out on the street in front of Honey's unmarked unit.

I wrenched up the dual levers, jerked them to the right, and pulled open the heavy steel right-side door. The wooden-floored container looked empty, but there was something way in the back. I turned on my SureFire flashlight, and Honey and I entered the long steel box that felt many degrees warmer than outside. At the far end I shined light on a wooden pallet. A single piece of metal, about twelve inches by eighteen inches, rested securely in a frame, like the kind of frames that hold auto windshields or panes of glass. The whole pallet was shrink-wrapped with clear plastic.

"What do you make of this?"

"Sheet of some kind of metal," said Honey.

"Valuable, whatever it is, to get such special care."

"Breaux was an exotic-materials specialist. Could this be some kind of sample?"

"If Breaux stole it from Michoud, maybe that would be what Salerno's investigation was about." I swung the beam over to several large ultra-modern locked crates. "Ever seen crates like this?"

"Can't say I have."

The crates looked to be constructed of some kind of material like graphite or boron or some composite matrix. Bar codes were stenciled onto the cases, but there were no other identifiers. Each locked case had an electric cipher lock with a row of lights above it, all glowing red.

"Decon said the combo was eight-one-eight-nine."

"How would he know?" asked Honey.

"How would he know there were crates inside? The guy is a freak of nature."

Honey reached over and entered Decon's combination. A whirring sound was followed by the lights sequentially blinking to green as hidden pins retracted with a loud click. I slid open latches and lifted the case lid.

I heard Honey inhale sharply.

A shoulder-fired weapon lay perfectly nestled in custom-fitted foam padding. It looked like a futuristic take on the South African–made, handheld 40mm grenade launcher with a rotating chamber. But any 40mm grenade I've ever seen came in a brass shell. These grenades, if that's what they were, were caseless: there was no metal cartridge holding the primer, propellant, and explosive projectile together. Instead, a solid block of propellant seemed to encase the primer and the explosive round. And although the diameter looked to be about 40mm, each round had to be close to 100mm in length.

Twenty rounds sat nicely tucked into cutout foam, and I picked one up.

"Be careful."

"Caseless ammo. Very light. I figure this is some kind of high-explosive round."

"What kind of damage you think it could do?"

"Probably bring down Breaux's house without too much trouble."

"Our military field anything like this?"

"Not to my knowledge." I looked at Honey. "Someone is up to some serious no good."

"It would seem so. Unless this is all legit."

"Legit? Futuristic weapons sitting in a scrapyard?"

"Maybe these are props for the movies. Maybe they're de-milled. Maybe Scrap Brothers has a Federal Firearms License. Maybe they're working with some three-letter agency. Arms dealing is nothing new. You remember that captain who retired and moved to San Diego? He became an arms dealer. Sells everything from boots to bullets. To every Third World slime hole you never heard of."

"Well this might shed some light on the subject." I retrieved a DVD in a clear plastic case that had been tucked between the foam padding and the side of the crate. The disk was labeled: GL,SF-X-02. There was no other writing or information of any kind. "We'll have to copy this."

I put the weapon and ammo back the way I found it, then took some cell-phone snaps. "You might be right that this is all legit. But you haven't had the pleasure of meeting Leroy and Jimmy. So for now, I'm assuming the worst."

"That son of a bitch!"

It looked worse the closer we got to the Bronco. The driver's door was open, and there was no sign of Decon. The door panel had been completely disassembled from the inside. The exterior door handle sat neatly on my front seat, along with a cold Browning .380 I kept in a hidden compartment in that door.

"Looks like Decon deconstructed your door."

"If he could do this, why didn't he just pick the handcuff key lock?"

"He was showing off," said Honey, gingerly holding up the chromed door handle by its ends. "I'll have the lab check it for prints."

"That little prick."

"He's some kind of something."

"Yeah, and he booked before giving us the rest of the names on his list." I glanced at my watch; there was enough time. "You should go, but I'm heading back inside."

She rubbed her eyes wearily. "I'm coming, so let's get it over with."

Honey copied the DVD from the weapons crate using my Bronco's in-dash computer while I grabbed gear out of locked compartments in the back. We reentered the yard. I returned the DVD and we planted GPS tracking units in a couple of the weapons crates inside the cargo container and on the roof of the green container itself.

In the scrapyard office, Honey copied the brothers' computer hard drive onto an external drive while I tapped the phone lines. I planted a sophisticated listening device on top of a tall steel filing cabinet covered with years of dust. The battery-powered ghost transmitter would record all sound in the office—a week's worth—and store it on a flash drive. The unit had a SIM card, so I could simply dial a number and the digitally encrypted data would be sent via burst transmission to a receiver in my Bronco, as long as I was within a quarter-mile radius. Whatever the brothers were up to, I was going to find out.

Honey noticed that one of the brothers used a desktop ink blotter like a day planner, with the notes being in some kind of shorthand code, so we photographed every large page of the blotter, one huge page for every month of the year. Then, as she was photographing every card in the old Rolodex, Honey abruptly stopped.

"Here we go."

I went over and looked at the card listing the name Breaux Enterprises along with several phone numbers.

"Nice piece of hard evidence linking our victim here."

It's called a second wind, and we both suddenly caught one. A bit more alert, we took a final look around. I noticed a bottle of brandy standing next to an out-of-date phone book. But what caught my eye was the edge of a piece of paper sticking out from the middle of the phone book. I retrieved the single sheet of typing paper, shocked to see that it listed all of the Jefferson brothers' user names and passwords for e-mail and bank accounts, plus every kind of Web site imaginable. I also saw what had to be a combination that I figured went to the government-issue file-cabinet safe. I'd found the Keys to the Kingdom. We'd already been there two hours, as I photographed the password sheet.

"We're pushing our luck, let's get out of here," said Honey.

As if to emphasize her point, we heard the Doberman stirring outside, sounding like a monster clearing his throat.

"If this is the combination, it'll just take a second to open the safe and take a peek."

"What about the dog outside?"

"Maybe he's got a hangover."

I spun the dial to the right several times, causing the digital display to light up. I stopped at sixty-seven. One spin to the left, to thirty-three, then one spin right to seventeen. I waited a few seconds, saw the OPEN code, then turned the heavy lever and opened the top file drawer.

"The scrap business must be pretty good."

"Kind of reminds me of Del Breaux's carry-on luggage," I said.

Bundles of hundred-dollar bills were stacked deep in the first two drawers. A money-counting machine and a couple of pistols sat in the third drawer. "Wish I needed a money-counting machine. It's always the dirtbags that need them. You notice that? This looks like about half a mil to me."

"Just hurry up," said Honey.

As I reached for the bottom drawer, the Doberman made some

otherworldly guttural sounds. Maybe he was licking his chops. Maybe he knew dinner was standing inside the office.

Inside the bottom drawer was a cigar box full of identical sleek black ballpoint pens with gold pocket clips and trim.

"Designer pens?"

I picked one up and examined it closely. "No markings, just a serial number." As I went to unscrew the cap—

"Saint James . . . let's go."

I looked up at her; the dark circles under her eyes were the worst I'd ever seen on her. I nodded, replaced the pen, and relocked the safe. We locked up the office, and as we skirted the dopey dog, I showed him my incisors, for his consideration.

The hands on my watch pushed at 4 A.M. Honey wanted me to crash at her place, only minutes away, but I refused to park my truck on the street in the Bywater without being able to lock it. So she followed me into the Warehouse District. I was able to park both of my trucks inside my building on the ground floor. She parked her unit in a small space I had in the back.

I'd just made us a couple of Grey Goose Sevens when she came into the kitchen wearing only a red bra and panties, her tramp-stamp tattoo of crossed lightning bolts visible just above her buttocks. She took her drink from my hand and took a sip.

"I can't give this info to the department since I was never there."

"I know."

"But I can pay the Scrap Brothers a visit to pick up the bronze plaque," said Honey. "Get a look at the Rolodex. Legally establish Del Breaux's number being in there."

"Take some uniforms with you. Maybe find a bunch of code violations. Sweat them."

Honey nodded, then, "So it looks like they're developing weapons systems at Michoud."

"They're doing something secret. Maybe Breaux and Klenis work for DARPA."

"I can't keep track of all the federal agencies."

"Defense Advanced Research Projects Agency. Black-projects scientists and engineers. They come up with all kinds of gadgets and gizmos."

"That might make sense. The shuttle program is in the toilet. Michoud is a big facility. Looking for a mission."

"You think it's a safe bet Breaux was selling stuff out the back door at Michoud?"

"I think I'm too tired to think anymore. And I have to be in court at eight A.M. on another case."

But my mind was in overdrive and hadn't downshifted yet. "Honey, it might be a good idea to call Eighth District, ask for some uniforms to work the Quarter, see if they can turn up Joey Bales, Danforth's ex-boyfriend."

"You considering a jealousy angle? Knowing what we know now?"

"Not doing that bit me in the ass on another murder investigation, didn't it?"

"You're right about that."

We tossed back our drinks. She took my hand and led me to bed. We'd slept together many times but never had sex, so this was nothing new to me. It didn't matter; I was tired, pissed at Decon Danny Hawthorne Doakes, and more aware than ever that murky water was rising fast all around me. The only good things were that I had the sexiest cuddle-buddy in town and thoughts of Bobby Perdue had been sidelined.

"So how was it seeing Blond Ambition again?" Honey asked me, climbing into bed.

"Who?"

"Harding."

I sat on the edge of the bed and took off my shoes. "She's a brunette now, and Harding and I have a pretty testy relationship."

"Unrequited lust," said Honey, with more than a tinge of jealousy. Basically Honey was jealous of any woman in my life, except Mom. And even then, I wasn't completely sure.

"The only unrequited lust I have is for you."

I'd said it matter-of-factly, and she looked at me as if I'd just shot her dog. She didn't like me relating to her as a sexual object, yet she interjected more and more sexuality into our relationship as time went by. It was she who had to control the sexual content in our relationship, to an extent, reducing me to the object.

But I wasn't looking for a fight. "Honey, you know I love being with you, just the way you are. Just the way we are. No strings attached, no preconditions."

Her look softened. "You sure about that?"

"Have I ever pressured you otherwise?"

She looked down, then put her hand on mine.

"We don't ever have to become lovers," I said, then paused. "You think it would screw up our relationship if we did?"

After a long pause, she said, "Maybe."

I nodded. "I mean, you don't want to do that, right?"

"Screw up our friendship?"

"No, I'm talking about . . ." But I let it trail off. We were waltzing around the topic of becoming lovers. I'd figured our fatigue might make it easier to talk about this, so I'd thrown out the bait, but once again, Honey didn't take it.

"You mean a lot to me. More than you know." I took her hand, kissed it, and got up from bed. "I have to get the lights, set the alarms, text Kendall to meet me here first thing in the morning."

I was back in three minutes and Honey lay fast asleep. I stripped to my T-shirt and boxers and climbed in next to her. There was a lot to do tomorrow, including examine all the evidence from Scrap Brothers. Then I'd have to track down Decon and get the other names on his list. And this time, I might just snap his spine. After a moment I exiled those thoughts and gently spooned with Honey.

Perhaps she was right to keep sex between us out of the picture. Maybe what we both needed more than anything was a true friend practicing unconditional love. Life was hard enough; why complicate it more?

Even though Perdue and I had agreed to pace it light in round one, just to see how it went, then pick it up later if we needed to, he came at me hard as the ring timer rang in the first round. I didn't quite know what to make of the fact that we'd just spoken about beginning in a controlled way, yet here he was throwing a hyperaggressive attack strategy at me. There's a reason there are weight classes; he had a good fifty pounds on me, three-inch height advantage, and fifteen years less time walking the planet.

Was it because his girlfriend was watching or his buddy was videotaping? Big Bob, an ex-felon and old friend of mine who had a gym out in Fat City, acted as the ref, and I could see in his eyes he was surprised the kid was coming at me so hard.

The kid hammered me with his long jabs, then followed up with a wild series of body and head hooks. Then he'd clench, applying his weight advantage to try to wear me out.

At the end of the first round, I realized I was in a fight, not the sparring session we had agreed on. I could have just ended it, I could have climbed down from the cage. I could have spoken to him, told him he needed to dial it way down. But I didn't do any of that. I just went to my corner and considered what his weaknesses might be. I strategized how I was going to win this fight.

It wasn't like the kid was some white belt who didn't know his own power or how to control it. He was an experienced fighter and knew exactly what he was doing. And his goal was clearly to kick my ass. So naturally, I decided then and there that I would kick his instead and teach him a little lesson.

What a stupid decision on my part. What was it in me that needed to go into competition with the kid? To prove I still had it? To assuage my ego? Was it because the session was being videotaped, because the kid's girl was watching—was that why I didn't back down? Were the kid and I somehow motivated by exactly the same immature reasons? And why did I have to be the guy to teach him a lesson?

I'd slept for about an hour before waking again and being flooded with thoughts of that day with Bobby Perdue. As I lay next to Honey, staring at the ceiling and listening to the quiet whir of the air-conditioning, she rolled over and draped her pale arm around me. I smelled vanilla and citrus, and her caress helped me to focus on something good. Even though she slept deeply, she gave me strength, and I closed my eyes and drifted to a sweeter place.

CHAPTER EIGHT

Honey left at six thirty just as Kendall Bullard arrived. Quite the babe magnet, Kendall functioned like a UN ambassador to women; his many girlfriends came in every size, shape, and color, sometimes in triplicate. So there was no way he would understand my relationship with Honey—not that I did, either—and I let my old student assume whatever he cared to. But when you see a girl leaving a guy's place early in the morning, there's usually only one conclusion to arrive at.

Kendall stood next to me in the kitchen as I fished a set of truck keys out of a utility drawer. His curly peroxide-blond hair was getting shaggy, and his sweat-damp forearms glistened, making his cheap, monocolored tattoos—the ones he got before he had money—look better than they should. He had blue fiberglass casts on his hand and foot, which seemed to just disappear thanks to his ease of movement. The casts were a result of his last UFC fight; "The Killer Creole" had broken both his right hand and his right foot in the second round. Tough as nails, he'd kept fighting for two more rounds after the breaks and won the fight with a knockout using his left hand.

"How's the rehab going?" I asked.

"Good. You be the one I worried 'bout." Kendall and other local pro fighters knew I'd been having a rough time dealing with Perdue's death. They had all graciously been teaching my classes at the dojo for the last month.

"You know what?" I said, looking at him. "I'm actually feeling a little better."

Kendall nodded, satisfied, then listened to the special assignment I had planned for him. I gave him the keys and sent him to stake out Scrap Brothers in one of my specially equipped surveillance vans. I wanted footage of whomever went into or came out of that cargo container. The brown stakeout van looked like crap, so it wouldn't stand out in that neighborhood. But it bristled with all the latest bells and whistles and even had a small toilet and well-stocked kitchen. The tires could deflate and reinflate at the touch of a button. Flat tires worked wonders in keeping the local thugs from trying to jack the ride, and Leroy and Jimmy, if they eyed it, would think it had been stolen and abandoned. I owned two such vans and rented them out to other PIs in town when I wasn't using them. For this gig I'd be paying Kendall out of my savings—a small price to pay for the sanity I was regaining by working the case.

I brewed a pot of 100 percent Kona coffee, cleared boxes from the dining table, and went to work examining the evidence collected from Scrap Brothers.

Big surprise—they kept little money in the bank. I ignored the porn Web sites they subscribed to, but logged on to their cell-phone account and downloaded their phone records. Who needs a subpoena? A number of Web sites revealed they actively bid on and sometimes won numbered lots of surplus government goods, much of it junk, all purchased from local facilities such as Naval Air Station Joint Reserve Base New Orleans out in Belle Chasse, Naval Support Activity, the New Orleans U.S. Coast Guard Station, Jackson Barracks, and . . . NASA's Michoud Facility. These were legal auctions, consolidated and run by a company called Government Liquidators. It made sense that scrap dealers would buy and bid on select lots at these types of auctions.

That's why the Scrap Brothers office was furnished in government-surplus chic.

What didn't make sense was the Jefferson brothers' code on the desk blotter. Every Saturday night there were notations for late-night appointments with TDF Shipping, a freight-forwarding company. Cargo came in during off hours on a regular basis. One would almost think they were up to something.

I viewed the GL,SF-X-02 user's manual DVD from the weapon's case. I understood the code to mean: Grenade Launcher, Shoulder-Fired-Experimental. Zero-two probably meant second generation. The video guide was useful and chock-full of helpful information, demonstrated by a man in fatigues with no insignia, but speaking American English. I'd been wrong about the HE rounds for the gun: they wouldn't just take down a small building; one round could take out half of a city block. The explosives were of a magnitude far beyond what the public had been made aware existed.

A few hours after he'd left, Kendall called with an update.

"The green container has left the yard?" I asked, surprised.

"Ten minutes back. Soon's they open this mornin' start loading all kinds of rusty-assed pallets into it. Truck came from TDF and took it away."

"What's the location now?"

"Look like they headed to the port. I'm 'bout two minutes behind."

"You won't be able to enter the port. You can park somewhere on Tchoupitoulas. I already have the container number, but did you get the truck's license plate?"

"I'll text it."

"Good work, Kendall."

I called Honey, but her cell went straight to voice mail. Damn, she was in court and had her phone turned off. I knew that outbound containers sometimes would sit at the port, but sometimes they got put right on a cargo ship. Honey could probably get the container stopped, claiming it contained evidence related to Breaux's murder investigation, but all I had was a piece of paper from the chief authorizing me to assist Honey. I doubted I could even gain entrance to the port, much less intercept a shipment, with only the chief's letter in my pocket.

So I called Harding on my encrypted cell and got her on a secure line. I gave her the CliffsNotes about the weapons from Scrap Brothers now heading to the port.

She actually said, "Whew."

"You told me before you were unofficially ordered off the investigation and that you didn't have a smoking gun. Is this the kind of hard proof you're looking for?"

"Do you own a nice suit?" she asked.

"A suit?" I wasn't really a suit kind of guy, but I always kept some handy for funerals. I hadn't attended Bobby Perdue's service, figuring the family wouldn't want their son's killer to attend.

"Yes, a suit," she said. "Like a business suit, nothing flashy, preferably in dark blue, gray . . ."

"Black okay?"

"Fine. I'll pick you up in thirty minutes."

Twenty-five minutes later I was riding in a silver Crown Vic Interceptor with Harding as we hotfooted it to the port. We'd learned the container was getting fast-tracked right onto a Chinese freighter. One call to Customs and Border Protection stopped that, and another call to Chief Carl Ritzman of the Harbor Police resulted in a cordon of officers securing the train-car-sized steel box.

"You haven't explained why you wanted me to come with you," I said, after she put her cell phone away.

"You're familiar with the container and what's inside."

That sounded lame; she didn't need me for that. "We can't tip off to anybody that I've been in that container."

"We won't."

I felt less and less comfortable about doing this with her, but I was damn well intent on busting this case wide open. Plus, I was never one to shy away from being on the front lines of stirring up some shit.

"Why the suit?" I asked.

"Don't represent yourself as being with the Bureau or some other federal agency, but if they assume that, I wouldn't mind."

As I wrestled with that one, we cruised past the Walmart on Tchoupitoulas, where Kendall sat parked.

"Has Gunderson signed off on this?" Special Agent-in-Charge Gunderson was Harding's supervisor and ran the New Orleans FBI office. He knew me, but I wasn't sure that he was a fan.

"So far."

Harding turned into the Felicity Street entrance to the Port of New Orleans. We signed in at the big guard shack on the Clarence Henry Truckway, drove under the trestle of cameras and other kinds of sensing equipment, and in a minute and a half pulled into TDF Shipping's staging yard on the Jackson Avenue Wharf, where the green container, still sitting on the roll-off truck, was surrounded by Harbor Police.

Harding and I got out of the car, and she flashed her badge, announcing, "FBI," to all concerned.

A green-uniformed CBP agent approached and stuck out his hand. "Terry Blanchard. I'm the inspector who oversees the inspection of outbound cargo."

"I'm Harding, that's Saint James. We have reason to believe there might be some contraband in this container."

Blanchard looked uncomfortable. He stepped in closer to us and spoke softly so no one else could hear. "Did I get something wrong? Has there been a change in plans?"

To our credit, Harding and I managed to keep our poker faces intact. *U.S. Customs was in on this?* I could only imagine what kind of maelstrom we were about to be thrown into.

"There's been a mistake," I said, quickly, before Harding had a chance to speak.

"Okay. So you what, want this one scanned?"

"Right," said Harding, going along. "How does that work?"

"I can have the VACIS truck come right here, and scan the container in no time."

"Let's do that," said Harding.

While Blanchard made a call, Harding and I spoke quietly as I fired up a cigarillo.

"Change in plans? What do you make of that?" she asked me.

"You're not in Kansas anymore, Dorothy. I think our only play is to balls this through and see how the dust settles. I say we sweat Blanchard before the muckety-mucks get here and screw the lid down tight. Which might happen pretty damn quick."

"You're joking? You think CBP is in on arms smuggling? Blanchard has to have gone bad and he's on the take."

"From guys posing as FBI? He assumed *we* were in on whatever he's up to."

"Maybe there's a rogue FBI agent in town," she said.

Blanchard finished his call and Harding waved him over.

"VACIS truck will be here in a couple of minutes."

"Who was it who told you not to check this container?" I asked.

Blanchard looked like the wheels were spinning inside his head. "Why are you asking me this?"

"Because J. Edgar Hoover is dead and I got Terry Blanchard standing here instead. Now answer the question."

"Look, I've done everything you guys asked."

"Who asked?" Harding barked.

"The FBI! I know what FBI identification looks like."

"You got names?"

"Maybe."

"Let me guess what they 'asked' you. To look the other way, make sure certain containers don't get any attention on their way out of the country," I said.

"You're acting like you don't know about this."

"You might be in some trouble, Terry. Just answer the questions," said Harding.

"Trouble! Son of a— you think I *wanted* to do any of this? An FBI badge is great, but I wanted proof these guys were for real, so they showed me copies of my personnel file, my military two-zero-one file, results of lie detector tests I took when I was with Border Patrol. If they're not FBI, how they gonna get all that?"

"You weren't suspicious?"

"My job is to be suspicious. But I also know when to obey orders and keep my mouth shut."

"Okay, look. The rules have changed. From now on, every container you're not supposed to check, we need to know about it," I said.

Blanchard shook his head. "I want to go to my superiors about this. My union rep. You're trying to put me in the middle of something."

"You're already in the middle," I said, without a note of sympathy. "You got in the middle when you agreed to do some shady shit outside your SOP and without written authorization or orders from your chain of command. You don't take orders from somebody just because they have a copy of your two-zero-one file."

"Oh, my God . . ."

"Play ball with me." Harding instinctively slipped into the good-cop role. "I'll keep you out of the fallout; you'll keep your career."

"You're putting me in deeper!"

"Buddy," I said, "you're in so far over your head already, you have no idea. Now what's it going to be? You want to get cuffed right now, or you want to fix what you screwed up?"

Blanchard looked like he was going to be sick. "What do I have to do?"

"How often these shipments come through?" I asked.

"All the time. At least five or ten every week. From different shippers to different destinations."

I surreptitiously handed Blanchard a sterile cell phone that I kept handy for working witnesses in all kinds of investigations. "This phone is only to be used to call me and vice versa. Use the auto redial— mine's the only number in it. You will keep me informed. Always call from outdoors. Keep turning around in case you're being watched."

An all-white ten-wheeler that at first blush resembled a mobile crane pulled up and parked. VACIS stood for Vehicle and Cargo Inspection System, and was a mobile gamma-ray imagining system. Using a high-energy X-ray source, the unit can penetrate more than a foot of steel. Harding and Blanchard entered the boxy control room behind the cab as the L-shaped boom arm swung out and deployed perpendicular to the truck, creating what looked like a large door frame. Before I could finish another cigarillo, the TDF Shipping roll-off truck started up and slowly drove through the "frame" alongside the VACIS truck, then stopped.

Harding and Blanchard emerged from the truck's control room.

"Get it unloaded; we have an irregularity in the container," announced Harding as she made a beeline toward me.

Blanchard shouted some commands, and the TDF Shipping roll-off truck deposited the green cargo container on the concrete. Then he started making a series of cell calls out of earshot.

"I got a call from Gunderson while I was in the control room," whispered Harding. "Some FBI CI-3 agent from DC was bent out of shape, asking what the hell we thought we were doing and telling us to cease and desist."

"Gunderson order you to back off?"

"No; exactly the opposite. Gunderson's close to retirement, and he knows where plenty of bodies are buried—dirty little bureau secrets. He told the guy to send his order in writing. That's not going to happen."

"But Gunderson will get notified through his chain of command to back off?"

"I don't know. What I do know is that Blanchard wasn't lying. Somebody in the FBI wants these containers to leave unnoticed."

"It's going to be interesting to see who shows up here or who makes themselves known in the next hour or so, Agent Harding."

She nodded tensely.

We looked over to see a forklift arrive along with more CBP vehicles and Chief Ritzman's souped-up Harbor Police unit.

"Let the show begin," I said.

Within seconds, pallets of scrap started getting hauled out of the container and placed on the concrete. A very tall CBP agent carrying a Samsung tablet computer approached us.

"Doug Simms, Senior Special Agent, Office of Investigations, U.S. Customs."

"Harding and Saint James," said Harding, keeping up the charade, for whatever reason, that I was there in an official capacity. She didn't bother with showing Simms any ID.

"So we got some goodies in this container here, Agent Harding?"

"According to your fancy machine, we do."

"Just so you know, if we find any military goods, I'm going to have to open up a National Security Investigation."

"Good."

"How does it work here, Agent Simms, with outgoing cargo getting checked?" I asked.

"All outgoing containers get scanned for radiation as soon as the trucks pull into the port. In terms of image scanning or spot checks, the focus is on what's coming in. For outgoing cargo, we'll consider the manifest, where the cargo is heading. We pay more attention to shipments that aren't regularly sent. But we don't check every outgoing container. We're just not able to. A bad guess might be that sixty percent of what leaves gets checked."

"What do your records say about this container?"

Simms checked his tablet computer. "Scrap metal heading to Shenzhen, China. Frequent shipper. Nothing unusual about this at all."

Harding looked over at the container, where the forklift pivoted with the weapons cases resting on its tines. "Those cases," she said, "sure look unusual to me."

CHAPTER NINE

Harding used the lock combination I'd given her earlier to open the cases with the cipher locks. Doug Simms stood at a loss for words as he gazed at the weaponry. He began madly taking photos with a big Nikon digital camera to document the scene, and then made a quick call to a higher-up. From his reaction, I didn't take him to be part of the smuggling scheme.

Chief Ritzman walked up and got a long look at the goods. "Damn. I need to call HAZMAT in on this, and maybe the bomb squad."

"Do what you need to do, Chief," I said.

I casually looked around and spotted the shrink-wrapped pallet with the single sheet of material held safely in a frame. It had been on its way to China, so it didn't take a genius to connect the dots. Del Breaux had sold it out the backdoor at Michoud for $2.5 million in cash to the Chinese. How it tied in to the weapons, I could only speculate. But Peter Danforth's fear of the power of "them" (as well as Decon's seconding of the motion) was starting to make more sense.

As the chief made his calls, a black stretch limo stopped at the police cordon. A lanky gentleman in a bone-colored linen suit and an open necked shirt got out of the limo. A buzz cut masked the fact that his hair had gone silver, and his hawkish eyes narrowed as he scanned the scene. "Chief Ritzman, Clayton Brandt!" the man called out, an unmistakable command of authority infusing his deep voice.

Hearing the name startled me, and I drilled him with my eyes, soaking up every detail. If Peter Danforth were to be believed, I was about to meet a ruthless killer.

Chief Ritzman gestured for an officer to allow Brandt to approach.

"Well, look who's here," said Harding, whispering to me.

"The Big Fix is about to be put in," I said. "How long has it been since you first called to stop the container from being loaded onto that Chinese freighter?"

"About two hours."

"Terry Blanchard must have given someone a heads-up as soon as you called to stop the shipment. Let me guess: Brandt was one of the people you were investigating along with Breaux, right?"

"That would be a big ten-four."

"Cocktails on me if you'll share later."

"My associate, Mister Tan Chu, is mortified that the laborer in the scrapyard commingled the two shipments," said Clayton Brandt. I didn't know if Brandt had ever practiced law, but if he had, he was the kind of cagey fox you wished you could afford if your ass ever got put into a sling.

We all stood in a circle in the TDF Shipping yard: Harding and myself, Customs Inspector Terry Blanchard, Chief Ritzman, Clayton Brandt, Senior Special Agent Doug Simms, and a couple of port honchos who had shown up. HAZMAT vehicles had started to arrive, and I noticed the limo's chauffeur now stood smoking outside the car: he was an Asian guy, unusual for New Orleans.

"As Customs and Border Protection is well aware, Mister Chu has a long history of buying scrap metal from the area and shipping it to his smelter in China. There should have *only* been scrap in the container, obviously. Mister Chu readily admits that he legally purchased the weapons and ammunition in those cases for export. I have copies of the receipts right here."

Brandt distributed copies to Harding, Simms, and anyone else who wanted one.

"China is an embargoed country, according to the State Department. It's illegal to ship weapons there from the United States," said Harding. "Right Simms?"

"ITAR, International Traffic in Arms Regulations rules are fairly complex, but generally, you're correct," said Doug Simms.

"Yes, absolutely," said Brandt. "These weapons were bound for Peru and would have gone out in a container tomorrow—I believe Customs will have a record of that scheduled outgoing shipment in your logs—if the worker hadn't made this egregious error."

Simms worked his tablet computer to check Brandt's contention. "Yes, I see the bill of lading for a scheduled shipment to Peru."

"That is ludicrous to say the weapons would have gone to Peru. They didn't. They were a hundred yards from going onto a Chinese ship." Harding was getting worked up, which only made her sexier to me.

"I also have here copies of a signed and notarized affidavit from Leroy and James Jefferson, owners of Scrap Brothers, attesting to our contention that the weapons were mistakenly included in the shipment of scrap as a result of miscommunication between them and their employee, Herbert Rondell." Brandt distributed more copies.

"Mister Chu is ultimately responsible—"

"Mister Chu could have legally shipped these weapons to China if he wanted to, Agent Harding," interrupted Brandt.

"What?"

"Congress passed a very specific law, a little-known waiver for the Space Station Freedom program. The law allows embargoed technology to be shipped from the United States to countries that participated in the building of the space station. China was a participant in that program." Brandt was handing out more paper than a guy hyping a pizza-delivery joint.

This time I reached for a handout. I wanted a closer look at the silver ring Brandt wore on his right hand, which looked like some kind of class ring with a pale blue stone in the center. I caught a quick look, confirming my suspicions.

"You're telling me that these weapons are part of the space station program?" asked Harding.

"No, I'm just telling you that Mister Chu could have legally shipped them to China if he so chose. But as I said, they were being sent to Peru. In lieu of these facts, I would suggest that at most what we have here is an unfortunate case of mislabeling perfectly legal, exportable goods."

Time to punt. Everyone examined Brandt's documents and took a step back to make cell calls, including Harding. I noticed the Asian driver crush out his cigarette and glance into the backseat of the limo, and I just knew that the mysterious Mister Chu was sitting behind the opaque tinted glass. If Brandt were such a terror, who was this guy Chu he fronted for?

I pulled Chief Ritzman aside.

"Chief, everyone in that limo should have signed in at the gate, right?"

"That's required, yes."

"Would you mind finding out who the occupants are?"

The chief turned away and dialed a call as Harding rejoined me.

"Here's a little morsel to chew on: Tan Chu is a Chinese intelligence agent."

It took a second for that statement to sink in. Chinese intelligence purchasing and shipping prototype weapons to China with the aid of the FBI, Customs and Border Protection, and maybe a dead guy named Del Breaux. And Chu's on-site rep, Clayton Brandt, wearing a U.S. Air Force Academy class ring, was a man Peter Danforth fingered as the deadliest person in the Buyer's Club, which had likely murdered Del Breaux and Ty Parks.

"Want to arrest Chu? If I'm not mistaken, he's sitting in the back of the limo."

"He has diplomatic immunity. Works out of the Chinese embassy in D.C. as a commercial attaché."

"Well, he's doing commerce, all right. But isn't his travel restricted?"

"Supposedly he can't go beyond fifty miles of Washington, D.C."

"So arrest him for that."

"His travel has been authorized. By FBI CI-3."

"The same counterintelligence people who are crawling up your boss Gunderson's ass."

"Exactly."

Just when I thought we might be stepping on the toes of some kind of FBI sting operation, Chief Ritzman quietly interrupted. "Two people signed in from the limo: Clayton Brandt and the driver, Ding Tong, a Chinese national."

"Chief, what do we do if there's someone in that limo who didn't sign in?" asked Harding, smiling.

"That's a security breach, and we take that very seriously around here, Agent Harding."

"Then let's take a walk."

As Harding and the chief crossed toward the black limo, I glanced at Brandt. A retired air force general shilling for a Chinese agent. Something felt surreal about the whole game. Clearly, regardless of what might happen this afternoon, this ultimately would be resolved in favor of Tan Chu and the forces that supported and abetted his actions, for whatever reasons. So I took a stroll over to the forklift driver, because I had a double murder to solve.

"Do me a favor." I palmed the guy a fifty without anyone noticing. "When you put all this scrap back into the container, load this one in last." I indicated the shrink-wrapped pallet with the single sheet.

"Done," said the forklift guy.

Just then, all heads turned, including mine, toward the limo, where Harding and Chief Ritzman faced off with the wiry driver, Ding Tong, who apparently had a short temper and was emphatically barring them from entering the rear of the limo. A couple of Harbor cops headed over to back up Chief Ritzman as I snaked my way around to the other side of the limo.

"You can no go in car!" shouted Tong.

"Who's in the backseat?" asked Harding.

"No one in backseat! You have search warrant? Huh? You have search warrant?"

"If there's someone in the backseat who didn't sign in, they have committed a crime," said Chief Ritzman calmly.

"No crime here; only stupid Americans think they can do anything they want. Show me search warrant, I let you in."

I had heard about enough from the Ding Dong Driver. I stood on the opposite side of the limo from all the action and was surprised to find the rear door unlocked, so I jerked it open. I looked into the face of a Chinese man in his forties, who could only be Tan Chu.

His appearance was unremarkable, perfect for an intelligence operative. He wore gray slacks and an inexpensive open-necked shirt. Thick black hair combed straight back but neatly trimmed. He calmly met my gaze through his cheap wire-rimmed glasses, his deep brown eyes showing not the slightest sign of unease.

"Mister Chu, please step out of the car, right now." I spoke the words with the kind of authority that left no option open for negotiation. Amazingly, he complied, quickly and without protest. Just as amazingly, as Mr. Chu and I stood there sizing each other up, a body came hurtling over the limo's trunk and slammed me to the ground.

I rolled clear and found my feet just in time to face my attacker. On pure instinct I blocked a combination of incredibly fast blows from Ding Tong. I vaguely heard shouts in the background. I couldn't even compute what martial-art modality he was using, but it sure felt strange fighting in one of my funeral suits.

I went offensive out of sheer desperation, wondering if any of the dozen cops watching might jump in and help me out. Then I realized I was pulling my punches. Why was I doing that in a fight with a guy trying to rip my head off? A couple of kicks, if I'd administered them full force, would have taken Tong down.

I flashed on Bobby Perdue's face at the same moment that Tong came at me with a blistering combination—man he had fast hands—that sent me to the pavement, flat on my back. I expected the ground game to begin, but thankfully, it never happened. As I lay bleeding and barely conscious, I tilted my head in time to see the Harbor cops shoot multiple Tasers into Tong's body, causing him to perform that kinetic, freaky mambo the perps always dance.

I dropped my head back on the blacktop blinking, thinking *Bobby Perdue strikes again.*

New Orleans has a lot of experience with cluster fucks, and it was right now getting some more. As EMS bandaged the cuts on my face and the back of my head, a tow truck winched up the limo for a ride to the impound yard. Clayton Brandt had been invited to use his prissy, overhyped and overpriced iPhone to call for a taxi. Tan Chu and Ding Tong stood handcuffed, but not under arrest. Turns out they *both* had diplomatic immunity, the arrogant assholes. They were being detained for questioning as witnesses to a number of possible crimes.

Doug Simms had ordered the cases of weapons loaded into a second container and stored in a secure Customs facility pending the outcome of the National Security Investigation. The scrap in the green container from Scrap Brothers would most likely be released in twenty-four hours, according to Simms, and would spend the night here in the TDF Shipping yard. I was happy to see that the last pallet back into that cargo container was the shrink-wrapped job I'd grown attached to.

"Harding, I could use a cold one."

"Me too, but I'm still on duty. I can't be seen drinking."

"What, you haven't been kicked off the case yet?"

"In a manner of speaking, I have, but I can't get into that right now. Anyway, while you were laid out, I got a call from some DC puke in CI-3. Before he could get started, I put the call on speaker and asked for the correct spelling of his name. Told him the *Times-Picayune* reporter next to me would want to spell it right. The line went dead."

"Don't you hate cell-phone dropout?"

She smiled, maybe the first time I ever saw her do that.

"Harding, there's a cold one at my place."

If I fell for another woman, it would cause problems in my unusual relationship with Honey. Having sex with another woman, however, caused no problems, as far as I was concerned, anyway. Honey was always accusing me of laying everything except the Atlantic cable, so I might as well be guilty once in a while. I never copped to anything, but women always seemed to know. Honey and I weren't lovers, we had no exclusivity agreements, and, hey, I'm a single heterosexual male with a healthy libido.

So it was that I had Harding spread-eagled on my dining table, her skirt up around her hips, as I banged the snot out of her. I think she was turned on by the cuts and bruises on my face. As for me, I was turned on by her business suit. Not the "take me seriously just like you would a man" jacket-and-pants thing, but a short skirt and matching blazer, white blouse, nylons, and heels—oh, yeah, the shoes had to stay on—it was a uniform of sorts. Women in uniform, except for Orleans Parish prison jumpsuits, turned me on big-time. I pined for the all-white nurse uniforms of old.

It was a short visit; Harding had to go. Sure we were attracted to each other, but the sex had been fast, furious, and perfunctory, a needed feel-good physical release absent of any true affection. There were no complaints on either of our parts, though, as she hurried off, and I fully expected that we might schedule similar conferences in the near future. I felt good. So good I had forgotten to ask Harding how she knew Tan Chu was Chinese intelligence. She'd only said that "in a manner of speaking" she was off the case. So it seemed like I had a good reason for a follow-up session with Harding.

After Harding left, it struck me that Tan Chu must be one of the remaining people in Danforth's Buyer's Club. I checked the copy of the weapons receipt Harding had gotten from Clayton Brandt, allegedly showing that Tan Chu had purchased the weapons legally for export. I'm not an ATF agent, and as Doug Simms had hinted, leafing through ITAR documents was like trying to find your way out of the Atchafalaya Swamp. The weapons seller was an outfit called Global Solutions Unlimited out of McLean, Virginia. Since Global Solutions possessed numerous State Department permits and current FFLs, including a Title 20, it seemed that Chu's purchase of the weapons for export was indeed legal. So the questions became: Who is Global Solutions, and where were they getting the weapons from? A quick Internet search revealed zip.

My next step was to call in a guy to pull a twelve-hour shift, replacing Kendall in the surveillance van still parked at the twenty-four-hour Walmart. I wanted to keep it close to the port, just in case.

I had intended to run down Decon tonight, but the wild events at the port necessitated another course of action. So I grabbed a few hours of sleep, then drove off in the Bronco wearing all black, since I was about to do some bad things.

I made short work of climbing the concrete flood wall, set back on the south side of Tchoupitoulas, and entering the port area. There was no traffic on the Clarence Henry Truckway, so my biggest worry was any long-range security cams that may or may not be monitored. I made it into the TDF Shipping yard; the security guy in the guard shack had his nose in a DVD player. Dozens of other cargo containers, including green ones, had arrived in the TDF yard today, but the GPS signal led me right to my target.

I picked the hockey-puck-type padlock. Generally, there is no quiet way to open a steel cargo container, but I sprayed WD-40 on the hinges and lever mechanisms and rotating tangs, and that helped. I think the movie soundtrack coming from the guard shack helped even more. Inside the container, I quickly cut through the shrink-wrap and extracted the materials sample, which felt incredibly lightweight. I secured it into my black Pacsafe backpack.

Twenty minutes later I cruised past Ms. Mae's bar on Napoleon, then hung a right and parked. Terry Blanchard lived in the house around the corner. I'd gotten the address from Honey, who got it from the DMV. She'd sent some uniforms to his neighbors, who stated that he was divorced and lived alone. Blanchard wouldn't be happy to see me, but I had a few questions.

He answered the door and I barged in past him, noting on my way through that the guy wore pajamas with rabbits on them.

"Hey, you can't just come into my house and—"

I put him into an arm bar. Customs agents don't usually have to get physical in the line of duty, and Blanchard was rusty with his defensive tactics.

"I'm in a hurry, okay?"

"You're assaulting a federal agent!"

"No, I'm assaulting a corrupt dirtbag. Now tell me who you called today!"

"What do you mean?"

"You know what I mean. The deal still holds: we'll protect your sorry ass, but you have to give it all to us, Terry. Who did you call to warn them, and how much are they paying you?" I applied more pressure, and it didn't take much to get him talking.

"I get a thousand a month in cash."

"How?"

"An envelope. Put in my mail slot in the front door."

"How are you told which containers to protect?"

"I log into an e-mail account. Check the Saved Drafts folder."

"Terrorists use that technique, Terry. Share the same log-in info and communicate via unsent e-mail messages. So who was it you called when the shipment got stopped?"

"I don't have a name. Male, American. If there are ever any issues on what's been previously arranged, I'm to call that number."

I released him with a shove. "Write the number down for me and the e-mail log-in info."

As he complied, I counted out ten one-hundred-dollar bills. He gave me the jotted-down information and I stuffed the Benjies into the chest pocket of his bunny pj's.

"Since you're for rent, I want a piece of you. You're on retainer. I wasn't joking earlier today. I'm expecting calls from you to inform me of any pertinent contact or event relating to all of this. And you keep our little arrangement to yourself. You got that?"

He lowered his head and nodded. The guy looked pathetic, repulsive, actually; I didn't bother to close the front door behind me.

Out on the street I fired up a cigarillo and dodged mud puddles as I angled toward the Bronco. I was coming up in the world; I had a Fed on my payroll.

As I drove off I decided Decon could wait until tomorrow. I felt hungry and thirsty. After making certain I wasn't followed, I stashed the stolen top-secret exotic-materials sample in an abandoned warehouse at Soraparu and Rousseau. It was the second piece of sensitive, U.S. government–owned technology I had illegally obtained in as many days. Maybe I'm not the smartest guy in the room, but at least I'm curious.

The kitchen was open late at the Bulldog on Magazine so I stopped in for a beer and a burger. I sat at the end of the bar, lost in thoughts of recent events. After mentally prying myself away from a growing obsession with the case, I reflected on why I had pulled my punches with Tong. Something in me was afraid. Afraid that in an all-out fight, I might accidentally apply lethal force. Which meant I was questioning my skills, second-guessing myself in real time as to how I applied physical violence. Strange that at the same time I fought to control an unbridled rage over the whole Bobby Perdue mess, that same anger suddenly had a governing device placed on it when I got into a fight. No solution to the conundrum came to mind, so I sloughed it off, simply happy that I was no longer the frozen man. Not frozen, but maybe half-baked.

I'd killed six people in my life. I figured that didn't put me down there with Pol Pot but didn't put me up there with Mother Teresa, either. When you put on the badge, there's room for compassion, but not for pacifism, and that carried over to my work as a PI. You become an instrument of justice, and sometimes that justice is meted out quickly, on the street. The problem lay in administering that righteous street justice, instantly, under extreme stress and in life-or-death scenarios. I took the responsibility very seriously.

I never used lethal force except as a last-ditch defense in the face of extreme potentially terminal aggression, either directed at me or some innocent nearby person. I can remember very clearly the details of each of my prior killings, the where's, why's, who's, and how's. Little details like a blistering breeze blowing with a scent of magnolias, or the sizzle and smell of bacon from some nearby fry pan, are as real to me now as they were then.

I'm not an automaton. I had to deal with guilt and depression and second-guessing my actions in every instance. Even though I took down bad people who deserved to go, there was no escaping the feeling that you had somehow sullied yourself. *Why was it me who had to kill this person; why not another officer? Why are people thanking me when all I have done is take a human life?* The aftermath of a killing wasn't pleasant, but none had ever affected me the way killing Bobby Perdue had. Before, I had processed the emotions and moved on. I had acted responsibly, without malice in the spur of the moment to save a life or lives, including my own. I had slept pretty well at night.

The most abysmally stupid armed criminal understands the old credo "Live by the gun, die by the gun," even if they think it won't happen to them. Sometimes the world kills back.

And every mixed-martial artist, male or female, who stepped into the octagonal fight cage understood that things could go bad and they might not be breathing when all is said and done and the bell rings. But not because your opponent had been trying to kill you.

I understood all of this intellectually. But after I killed my sixth person about a month ago, I no longer slept well at all. Thoughts of Perdue were no longer all-consuming, but I had a long way to go to escape his clench.

CHAPTER TEN

The heavily armed security guards at the front gate of the FEMA trailer site at Independence Park didn't seem too surprised when the SWAT team and a convoy of vehicles pulled up at 6 A.M. But then I knew that FEMA site guards handled rapes, robberies, burglaries, assault, drug dealing, and shootings on an almost daily basis. The criminal dynamic that existed before the Storm now operated in the microcosms of the FEMA trailer parks, which often housed some of the most violent offenders. Ironic that taxpayer-funded security operators stood guard for the sleeping gangbangers, thugs, and killers mixed in with the good folks.

Honey had to spend yesterday morning in court testifying; today, thanks to the rarity of murder witnesses coming forward, she was about to arrest a quadruple murderer in a case she had been working for about ten days. Bleary-eyed TV news crews remained at the gate getting their equipment ready. At a pleasant seventy-eight degrees, the dead, humid night air didn't seem so oppressive. I turned around to look up the dark street outside the trailer park. The neutral grounds of St. Roch were in much better shape now, but garbage and fresh debris just never seemed to go away. As residents continued to trickle back from Hurricane Exile, they gutted their damaged homes, keeping the debris piles constantly replenished.

As we moved into the trailer park pointing flashlights down onto the black asphalt, I remembered the day six months or so ago when I found a female lady friend murdered in her trailer, just half a block away. I had always wanted to cry for Kiesha Taylor, but had never let myself do it. I had never let myself cry for anybody, ever, even when my father and younger brother passed away. Crying simply didn't seem like something a man should do, and it didn't change anything.

The soft sounds of rubber-soled boots on the pavement increased in frequency as the pace got picked up in anticipation. Even though she was SWAT, Honey wore plainclothes, since this was her case and she would be making the collar. She tracked along quietly, adrenaline overriding her fatigue. Then she stopped and motioned me over for a quick conference in the darkness as her SWAT buddies hurried ahead to take up positions.

I had already given her an extensive briefing about yesterday's events at the port. She'd been so tired she forgot to chide me for spending so much time with Harding.

"What's with the TV cameras?" I asked.

"Chief's orders."

"Good publicity. He'll be a happy guy. For a day."

"This bust I'm about to make will cut us some slack. Major bonus points with the chief."

"Decon's prints come back from my door handle?"

"He's not in the system."

"That doesn't make sense; he's got con written all over him," I said.

"He's like the joker in the deck. Be better if we brought him in."

"Sorry, I should have done that last night."

"Eighth District can't locate Danforth's boyfriend Joey Bales. He's got a rap sheet for burglary. Mostly art and jewel heists. Been in and out of drug rehab."

"Sounds like a winner," I said.

"Most importantly? We need to ID the other two members of the Buyer's Club."

I thought about my upcoming meeting with my old buddy and crime-lab tech Kerry Broussard. "I might have something on them in a couple of hours."

Honey gave me a knowing look. "The two FBI CI-3 agents hounded me yesterday about Breaux's laptop. They want it bad. And they mentioned a missing materials sample."

"They must be conferring with Ralph Salerno out at Michoud. Were CI-3 the ones who sanitized Breaux's office?" I asked.

"That's what I asked them. They glared at me."

"But they didn't answer."

"Of course not. But they suspect we might have the goods," said Honey.

"Think they're the same crew running the Customs inspector?"

"Whoever's doing that has to be rogue. These guys? I dunno. Maybe."

"I can log the laptop into evidence, like we discussed. Get those guys off your back. The sample I think we should keep."

"Hold off for now. Just ID the rest of the Buyer's Club."

The SWAT commander approached with a phone, and Honey began talking to the quadruple-murder suspect in the trailer. Fifteen minutes later he meekly surrendered. Honey cuffed him herself, then lead him out past the cameras. He'd shot four young men to death in front of their girlfriends as they sat on a front stoop in the Tremé. Miraculously, two of the girlfriends decided to cooperate with a very sincere female police detective.

It occurred to me the suspect must have thought the killing was a way to prove his manhood. He had a mostly clean record and wasn't a hard case. Eighteen years old. I assumed he'd never see another day of freedom in his life. He no doubt lacked good role models and probably didn't understand that shooting human beings down like animals isn't really a rite of passage to manhood; it just makes you a cold-hearted murderer.

I was now, as a matter of course, going to great lengths to ensure I wasn't being followed or tracked. I used a GPS jammer to defeat any GPS tracking device that might have been planted on the Bronco. And I used a broad-range radio-frequency jammer to block any kind of signal from a device similar to, say, LoJack. I kept my cell phone in a signal-blocking pouch when not in use so my position couldn't be triangulated.

I drove on I-10 out to Kenner, then turned around and headed back east. The heavy congestion on the freeway at Causeway was due to the never-ending road construction. The construction company knew how to stretch out a project to keep its guys working, just as they knew how to cheat The People by pouring less concrete than they were paid to pour. Miraculously they'd been caught and held accountable, meaning they had to tear up a newly formed stretch of roadway and do it all over again, doing it right this time and extending the massive road congestion by many weeks. Traffic jams created by the roadwork seemed to be more than many locals could bear, as evidenced by the large number of drivers who drove off the freeway onto the grass, then drove the wrong way against oncoming one-way traffic and used entrance ramps to exit. This was a certain Mississippi Delta behavior that today I mimicked. After all, the Louisiana State Police were spread thin, with many of them still assigned to work as street cops in New Orleans and not as ticket-writing machines on the highway. It was also a good way to check if I was being followed.

Kerry Broussard and I sat at separate tables at Puccino's on Veterans Boulevard and never made eye contact. We'd done surreptitious drops before, so Kerry knew the drill. The laptop sat on the chair next to him under a copy of *Gambit Weekly,* a free local paper that raised a lot of hell about local politics and also provided discount coupons for strip clubs, thus ensuring a healthy circulation. Kerry spoke sotto voce into the *Wall Street Journal* stock-price pages, which he held in front of him. My eyes constantly scanned the 7 A.M. Metairie coffee crowd that ebbed and flowed, looking for what didn't look right.

"Password's written on page three," said Kerry.

I wasn't a ventriloquist but did pretty well at talking without moving my lips much.

"Okay."

"I took a peek. Couldn't resist."

I wasn't happy to hear he'd looked at files after he'd doped out the password. "And?"

"Watch your ass. I mean it."

Kerry folded his newspaper, tucked it into his briefcase, and walked out with his macchiato. After sitting for twelve minutes alone in the shop, I nonchalantly gathered up the *Gambit Weekly,* a laptop, and a lucky two-dollar bill marked up with red.

After the laptop pickup I'd let myself into Pravda, not that I had a key. The bar wasn't alarmed and the front door locks weren't particularly consequential. I brewed up a pot of coffee and skimmed the depths of Del Breaux's Department of Defense–issued laptop. Perhaps because of the encryption—I couldn't say—but Breaux used the device as a repository for all of his personal affairs and business as well as his secret government work. The word "jackpot" didn't do justice to what I had in my hands. It would take days to examine all of it.

A few things quickly became clear. The secret materials project he had been working on at Michoud was called GIDEON, and its purpose was to insulate U.S. military and intelligence satellites from enemy attack by lasers or electromagnetic pulse weapons. GIDEON was in final testing, and, I assumed, the materials sample from Chu's green container had been purloined from Michoud and sold for $2.5 million. Cash that came directly from the Bank of China, according to Honey. The Chinese government had already demonstrated a willingness to shoot satellites out of the sky; they must have wanted the GIDEON material very badly.

The laptop also clearly showed that Breaux was *not* working in weapons development of any kind. There was no mention of DARPA or any kind of weapons program. And yet, the most shocking revelation in the computer was that Breaux was a weapons *broker*.

Del Breaux was an arms dealer, pure and simple. At least for the last year. I had all of Breaux Enterprises' books in the laptop. Spreadsheets showed what he bought, when, for how much, and who he subsequently sold and shipped to. Transportation and warehousing expenses were clearly delineated. He bought exclusively from Global Solutions. The laptop showed that on the night he died, Breaux bought a parcel of "nonlethal weaponry"—one dozen portable microwave crowd-dispersal generators—for $312,000. There was no indication that he had sold or shipped the nonlethal weapons.

There was a separate category for "Bribes." And Breaux's assistant Peter Danforth had been raking in 1 percent of the action.

Breaux's laptop did not indicate that weapons like the kind Decon had described seeing or the kind Honey and I uncovered in the cargo container were being developed or manufactured at Michoud. So were all of these armaments being manufactured by Global, or simply being acquired by them? For a federally licensed entity, Global Solutions Unlimited remained an enigma.

I began to wonder about Del Breaux's connection to Scrap Brothers. Could Leroy and Jimmy Jefferson be the front for Global? Had the Jeffersons somehow been buying weapons and equipment out the back doors at Jackson Barracks, Belle Chasse, Naval Support Activity, and the Coast Guard Station, doors that had been opened vis-à-vis the legitimate surplus auctions at those facilities? But if so, how could they legally sell to Breaux or other members of the Buyer's Club what they had illicitly purchased from U.S. facilities?

As a bonus, other laptop files revealed the identities, phone numbers, and local addresses of the Buyer's Club. Peter Danforth had told the truth: Clayton Brandt was a member. As was Tan Chu. Two men named Grigory Pelkov and Nassir Haddad rounded out the group, whoever they were. New Orleans was a corrupt place, but it made me mad that an association of businessmen seemed to be selling out America to our enemies—working hand in hand with them—probably aided by crooked Feds and military-base workers, all for the coin of the realm.

I'd been lost in the laptop for three hours when my encrypted cell phone rang with Harding on the other end. I had the phone out of the signal-blocking pouch, otherwise I couldn't make or receive calls or texts. I hadn't swept Pravda for bugs, so I moved behind the bar and turned on the sound system.

"What's up?"

"I'm off the case, officially and with finality. And I'm not supposed to have any contact with you."

"I'm sorry to hear that."

"Me too," said Harding, then after a pregnant pause, "I'd like to have another drink."

"I think that can be arranged."

"Go to the front door. A package has just been left for you. Burn everything after you read it. I'll explain more the next time we meet."

The line went dead.

Outside, I retrieved a large sealed manila envelope on the sidewalk. I relocked the door and was pleasantly surprised to find copies of FBI dossiers, complete with photos, on Clayton Brandt, Tan Chu, Grigory Pelkov, and Nassir Haddad. I recognized Haddad from a picture in Breaux's laptop that showed three men all cozy in navy dress whites: Ty Parks, Peter Danforth, and, apparently, Nassir Haddad.

Harding had just handed over to me the suspects in her investigation, which had been all about arms smuggling, not espionage. But why would CI-3 order her to stop? Interdivisional rivalry? Her orders had to have come officially, through channels.

Maybe even more troubling was how the hell did she know I was at Pravda? I could only surmise she had triangulated my cell-phone signal or was having me watched. Before I had a chance to read the dossiers, much less burn them, Honey called.

"You get your perp booked and all the paperwork in?" I asked. "Because I've got something you'll want to see."

"My something trumps yours."

"What you got?"

"Three bodies. Kind of."

CHAPTER ELEVEN

Leroy Jefferson didn't look happy. At least not the half of his body visible above the giant steel blades of the metal shredder. Jimmy Jefferson and Herbert Rondell were in even worse shape. Not that they had any shape to them anymore. Two and a half men had gone through the metal shredder. Only the flies were having fun.

I had logged in to the crime scene with a uniform at the front gate. The first thing I'd noticed was the dead Doberman, shot in the head and still chained to the post in front of where the cargo containers used to sit. The green container had been taken to the port, but now the silver container with the doors welded shut was also gone.

The crime-scene techs had arrived at the same time I did. There was no open-topped Dumpster under the grinding compartment, so the body matter had splattered all over the ground under the giant machine, and the wafting stink could knock a buzzard off a shit wagon.

Honey motioned me over to the office door as the techies got busy. The squirrelly tech with the camera took a look at the mess and said, "Kind of early in the day for a gumbo party."

Honey and I both put on purple latex gloves and entered the cool air-conditioned office. She closed the door behind us so we were alone.

"I finished my paperwork after booking the kid at headquarters this morning. Grabbed some uniforms. Came here to get the bronze plaque and brace the brothers. Gate was locked, I saw the dead dog. Climbed over the fence."

"Are you okay?" I asked. The mound of ground bones, meat, flesh, and organs stewing in blood and other liquids under the grinding compartment ranked as the most repulsive crime scene I'd ever come across.

"It gets more interesting," she said. "The locked filing cabinet is open. All the money you and I saw in there the other night—you figured it was about a half mil—is gone. But a package of what looks like a kilo of cocaine is in the top drawer."

"Five hundred Gs for a twenty-five-thousand-dollar kilo of coke. That's a nice trade for the killers."

"And makes it look like a drug hit."

"Why am I thinking Tan Chu didn't want the brothers around to maybe blow the whistle on him?" I asked as I crossed toward the tall cabinet where I had planted my listening device. "And he killed Del Breaux and Ty Parks because once he had the materials sample, he didn't need any witnesses to who bought what."

"Maybe. But if you have an inside man in black projects? Why take him out?"

"If he was a liability, I would. Can you get a search warrant for Chu's residence?"

"Based on what?"

"The recording I'm about to retrieve of the killers in this office."

I pushed a chair against the cabinet to stand on.

"The bug you planted is gone."

I looked at her in disbelief and then checked the top of the cabinet. Gone.

"That was a thousand-dollar device. How did they find it?"

Honey shrugged. "They swept for bugs."

"Most sweeps wouldn't turn up that bug."

"The computer is gone, too," she said.

I looked around the room. "And the desk blotter, the Rolodex . . . so now we can't legally establish the connection between Breaux and the Jefferson brothers."

"We'll have to see what the phone records turn up. This place was sanitized. Different than Breaux Enterprises, but still sanitized."

"Good thing we have copies of everything that was here."

"Which we need to recheck, privately," said Honey.

"You figure this happened when they opened this morning?"

"Probably. They open at seven. They're the only business on this block. No one lives around here since the Storm. I doubt we'll find a witness. But I got uniforms out canvassing."

"They would have needed a roll-off truck to haul that silver container out. Wish I'd put a GPS on it. We could track it right to the killers."

"We can do tire impressions. It's something, anyway. How many men to operate a roll-off truck?"

"Just one," I said.

"Footprints will be tough. Any given day they had a hundred people walking around the yard. Picking up or dropping off."

"We've brought a lot of unwanted attention to Chu's illicit dealings here. The more I think about it, the more likely it seems he took out the brothers to keep them from rolling over, in case the National Security Investigation actually went somewhere."

"But if the Big Fix is in like you told me? An NSI won't go nowhere."

"Then there's Decon to consider. He worked here. He knows I tracked him down, thanks to the Jeffersons. Leroy and Jimmy weren't in the Buyer's Club, but they were involved. And Harding was worried Decon would kill everyone connected to her investigation, which is turning out to be our investigation."

"Not sure Decon could have pulled this off. Unless he has friends and resources we don't know about."

"You're right. And if Decon's motive is to put the Buyer's Club out of business, he wouldn't bother trying to make it look like a drug hit."

"Generate a photo of Decon from your video. I want to put it out on the wire to bring him in as a person of interest."

"Okay."

"What about the laptop?" asked Honey quietly.

"It's the mother lode. The Buyer's Club is arms dealers, buying and selling weapons, pure and simple. Chu lives over in Harahan. If we can get something on him, maybe we couldn't prosecute him for capital murder because of his immunity, but we could arrest him with a lot of publicity, make a big stink. State Department would be forced to deport his ass. And we'd shine a light on this dirty business. I also have the other two—"

"Let's talk about this later. I have a lot to do."

I paused. "I'd like to get going on some of the Buyer's Club. Maybe drop in on one of them."

"Okay. But stay away from Chu for now."

I looked at her closely. She wasn't being herself. Something weighed on her, and it was more than simply the gruesomeness of the deaths. "You're bothered about something."

"We're barely hanging on to this case. We need solid evidence before we try to chase Chu up a tree."

"Those FBI guys have you spooked?"

Honey had been avoiding my gaze. She looked out the window, glancing at the CSI people. "While you and I were at the FEMA trailer park this morning? Two guys from CI-3 stopped by my mom's house. Pretending to look for me."

I felt my face flush.

"They told my mom to give me a message. The message was, 'Tell your daughter not to fuck with us. Bad things can happen to corrupt cops.'"

I crossed to her and put my hand on Honey's shoulder. I reeled in my anger because I didn't want her worrying more than she already was. I figured it was an empty threat, but right then I decided I'd spend money out of my own pocket and assign people to cover Honey's mom 24/7. I had strong motivation to solve this case, but I'd just added a good bit more.

"Maybe you should drop out of this," I told Honey. "I'll continue by myself. You have plenty of other cases to work."

"No way. Anybody who shoots dogs? And puts human beings through a metal shredder? They need to go down."

I gave her shoulder a gentle squeeze. FBI agents, real ones, had threatened my partner and best friend, and they did it through her mom. It was like being in some kind of peculiar upside-down world where nothing made sense. I'd just suggested to Honey that she back off the case, exactly the opposite of what I intended to do. I was about to shift into a higher gear and step on some toes.

"We'll wrap this case. I promise." I gave her the most reassuring look I could muster. "You okay?"

She nodded but said nothing.

"Then my first stop is to see a guy who's already gotten away with murder."

According to the dossier provided by Harding, Grigory Pelkov was a firmly established, midlevel international arms dealer from the Ukraine, not known for letting much get in his way. He was assumed to be an agent for the GRU, Russian military intelligence, the most closed and opaque of all Russian intelligence organizations. I knew the GRU to have retained its Soviet-era methodology; they were crude, rude, and lewd, and if they had an American-type motto it would be "Just do it." They took pride in not letting niceties stand in the way of achieving results.

From what I'd read in Breaux's computer and Harding's dossiers, Pelkov bought and sold everything from utensils to utility trucks, and handheld GPS units to hand grenades. His customers were dictators, warlords, Third World armies, shaky democracies. He spoke seven languages fluently, had no arrest record, and wasn't wanted by any LE agency. But he'd been detained by police in Cannes, France, last year, accused of knifing a homosexual in a bar who had made an unwanted advance. Even though the man died, charges were dropped and Pelkov quietly left the Côte d'Azur. An FBI psychological profile concluded Pelkov was a homophobe, which didn't seem to be much of a stretch, but it made a city like New Orleans, with an outrageous, openly gay population, an interesting choice for him to put down roots. He'd been in and out of NOLA for almost a year, mostly in, and seven months ago he rented a large house Uptown on St. Charles.

I decided on an approach that, even for me, was a bit unorthodox.

"Mr. Pelkov, please join me for a drink."

I sat in an easy chair in Pelkov's study holding a bottle of Russian Standard. A big ostentatious desk and oversized chairs set the design tone. Pelkov wore a silk paisley robe with slippers and looked like he'd had a rough night, even though it was midafternoon. He blinked wolfish gray eyes as he focused on me, looking only mildly startled as he ran stubby fingers through salt-and-pepper curly hair.

"Okay, but . . . I don't know you or how you get in my house."

He looked to be about five feet ten with a waistline that suggested he enjoyed the good things in life.

"Do you drink vodka?"

"You know Russian who doesn't?"

"You are Ukrainian."

"Words," he said, waving off the idea of international borders and nationalities. Those kinds of loyalties might get in the way of his global arms-dealing operations. "I give staff day off. Maybe not good idea." He checked his watch, touching the face as he moved his arm to bring the dial into focus. He casually sat across from me and gestured for me to pour.

I set to preparing our drinks, enjoying his consternation. I'd gotten in by jumping the fence and simply picking a lock on a side door. I'd expected to find assistants, bodyguards, but there weren't any.

"Your alarm wasn't set."

"Too complicated. Sasha do for me, Mister . . . ?"

"Saint James. I really expected a security detail." I handed him straight vodka over rocks and we clinked glasses. *"Za vas."*

"And to you." He took a healthy quaff. "If I hire men with gun to protect me, maybe they see my money and get other idea."

"I'm working with NOPD, looking into Del Breaux's and Ty Parks's murders."

"I won't miss that son of bitch Del Breaux. Asshole."

"Tell me about your association with him."

"We have same business. Middlemen. Sometime compete, sometime do joint venture, sometime help each other, sometime he cheat me. It called business."

"Buying and selling weapons."

"Matériel. I make more to sell trouser or flashlight than I make to sell gun. Rations, medical supply, truck part, computer, and software. I sometime do deal with not one bullet or gun in shipment."

"You make it sound harmless."

"I kill no one. A child can buy knife at hardware store and slit Mommy's throat. So is hardware clerk bad guy?"

"I hear you know something about knives. What was the dead man's name in France?"

Pelkov waved it off. "Just misunderstanding."

"Did you tell that to his family?" Pelkov didn't answer. "When did you last see Breaux alive?"

"Same night he die. At restaurant. Clayton Brandt can tell you. He was there. And others."

"What others?"

"Ask Clayton Brandt. He good with names."

"Fuck that, I'm asking you, shitbird," I snapped.

Pelkov had a hard face; he could be thinking about butterflies but still look like a brute. I wasn't exactly giving him the nicest of looks, either. Many seconds ticked by as he decided how to answer.

"Myself, Clayton Brandt, Del and Ty, Tan Chu, and Nassir Haddad."

"The Buyer's Club."

"Ty Parks just wife, not buyer."

"Where was this dinner?"

"Restaurant August. Nice food."

"So did you see him after you left the restaurant?"

"No."

"In your business, would it be common to have two and a half million dollars on hand in cash?"

"Not common, not smart. Most deal use international escrow account. Cash is like blood to bring shark. Not good."

"Then why did Breaux have all the cash in his house?"

"If he have big cash in house then he not smart."

"Maybe he sold something valuable to some shithead intelligence agent?"

"I don't know," said Pelkov frostily.

"Your masters in Moscow would pay with your blood if they could get their hands on Breaux's secrets, wouldn't they?"

"Only master I ever have is wife, who is now ex."

"What about your purchases here in New Orleans? You don't use cash?"

"Sometimes at grocery store, yes, I use cash."

"You know what I'm talking about."

"I use bank transfer to pay for my business purchase. I don't keep big cash money."

"So you won't miss the million dollars I found in the locked drawer," I said, gesturing toward the ornately carved wooden desk dominating the room. Pelkov froze, as if I'd taken his breath away. "And you're right; it's not too smart to have big cash on hand, Grigory."

Pelkov's eyes shifted to my backpack sitting at my feet. I casually lit a cigarillo.

"Relax," I said. "The money's still in your desk. I won't take it until you're dead."

He stared hard at me.

"You want kill me?"

"Somebody does. Not sure I blame them." I exhaled toward him. "Tell me about Global Solutions."

There are times when you wish you could read minds. Pelkov's face could have been carved from a quarry.

"Solution to what—climate change? If ice melt in Siberia, is okay with me."

"Hey, shitbag, you're a prime suspect in a murder investigation. That pretty little paisley robe you're wearing will go over real big with all the convicts when I throw your ass into Orleans Parish Prison. Now tell me about where you buy the weapons here, how you take delivery, make the payments."

"I tell you this. Breaux cheat me on few shipments to Africa. Shorted merchandise. Goods I can't supply to my customer, he have in stock. I lose face and I don't like that. And I lose money; I like that even less."

"Arms dealers don't keep stock on hand."

"Most don't. Breaux has capital to risk and he get lucky, he make many sale." Pelkov lit a cigarette. "I want ask you, why you care who kill two gay guys?"

"I don't know about the hole you climbed out of, but in America we actually arrest murderers and put them away."

"So why you not put away rapist like Del Breaux?"

I tried but failed to hide my surprise at the remark. "Rapist?"

Pelkov slowly freshened his drink, taking some pleasure in drawing out my interest and making me wait for his response. "He attack me in Nassir's hotel suite when he drunk. Like wild animal. Old man can't keep penis in his pants."

"I find that hard to believe."

He shrugged slightly. "Why would I lie about the dead? Ask others; they will tell you. Check hospital records, because when he come at me, I slam his head into wall. I think he wake up with bad headache. And memory not to fuck with Pelkov. He tried same thing with Nassir, but Nassir not do so well."

Damn, he might be telling the truth. "The same night?"

"No, different night. There was party at Breaux's house. I never go there, but I hear he get drunk, attack Nassir. Nassir want to put hit on Breaux after that. Tell me he will kill Breaux when time is better. Clayton Brandt had to give Nassir big present to make some peace."

"So Breaux raped Nassir Haddad?"

"Yes. So you see, Nassir hate him more than me."

If Pelkov was telling the truth, I needed to pay Nassir Haddad a visit, pronto.

"Have you been to Brandt's office?"

"Of course."

"Is his desk very neat like yours, or is it cluttered?"

"Strange question."

"Not really. It tells me a lot about someone's personality."

"Office is big and nice. Expensive furniture. Desk is messy, papers and junk every place."

"Where were you at two o'clock Sunday morning?"

"Right here."

"You can prove that?"

"I have many guests every Saturday night. Small party. Sing Russian song, drink. They can tell you."

A bullshit alibi; no reason to even ask for the names.

"This city very dangerous," Pelkov said. "I don't go out much. Never late at night. Why so many murder in your city?"

"Greed, of course. You might know something about greed."

"I know the greed of countries. Like U.S., Britain, France, Germany, Brazil, China, Russia, Iran. They make the weapon and sell them. I just middleman, like alcohol distributor." He held up the bottle of vodka. "More people die in U.S. every year from alcohol death than from gunshot death. So who is more bad, more greedy—man who sell gun, or man who sell alcohol? You don't like gun selling? Go talk to your generals and your president."

"I'm sure you're as pure as the tap water in Nigeria, but you didn't answer my question: tell me about how you buy the weapons here."

"Who say I buy something here?" he asked indignantly, shrugging his shoulders with his hands out, palms up. I noticed his ears start to redden as he pointed a stiff finger right at me. "My business is my business. I don't tell my secrets."

"You mean the GRU doesn't tell its secrets, right, Mister Russian Spy?"

I had casually slipped the Hornet onto my right hand. Pelkov reached for his glass on the table in front of us, and I grabbed his hand. "Let's get something straight," I growled. He was strong, but I was fast. I wrenched his wrist as I started to press the tang down onto a pressure point. "You're going to tell me everything I want to know."

Pelkov's eyes darted to the side at the sound of the front door flying open and rushing footsteps. Four armed men streamed into the foyer, spotted us in the study as they shouted in Russian then stormed into the room. I released Pelkov, and he angrily pulled his hand away from me and rubbed his wrist as he took deep breaths.

Pelkov had signaled them somehow, but I hadn't seen him touch anything since I'd surprised him . . . except his watch. He must have a wireless panic alarm built into his timepiece. Nice touch.

"No security detail, huh?"

Red faced, Pelkov's eyes riveted onto me with hate. "Sasha, Mister Saint James is leave now. Help him go." Sasha, a tall bald freak of nature with the kind of build that could make a UFC heavyweight appear small, approached me practically smacking his lips. "I don't think he see front door yet; please show to him. But check backpack. Make sure he not have my money."

As I stood up, Sasha grabbed my backpack and started rooting through it, finding nothing but burglary tools. I hadn't bothered bringing any listening devices and bugging the place. I'd figured that after this visit they'd be checking for bugs for the next three days.

"Three men were put through a metal shredder at a scrapyard this morning," I said quickly, holding Pelkov's gaze. "Their bodies now look like a large bowl of borscht. They were handling Tan Chu's shipments for him. You're right. New Orleans is a dangerous place. And people can get away with things . . . until events catch up with them. Tan Chu has diplomatic immunity. You don't, Pelkov. And one way or the other, I'm going to put your sorry ass down."

Sasha and the Russian bodyguards roughly hustled me to the front gate. By the time I got to the Bronco parked around the corner, I was fairly drenched with sweat. Clouds blew in fast from the Gulf, but I couldn't seem to catch any shade. Blistering sunlight kept finding me, and I decided to take that as a good omen.

CHAPTER TWELVE

I was taking side streets to cut from St. Charles to Tchoupitoulas, when Terry Blanchard, the compromised U.S. Customs inspector, called my sterile cell.

"Go ahead."

"The green container with the scrap left the TDF yard. About fifteen minutes ago."

"Onto a Chinese freighter?"

"Negative. A truck picked it up and took it out of the port."

"What about outbound shipments? I'm not seeing anything in that e-mail box."

"Me either. The shipments have stopped."

"Okay, good work."

The line went dead. The guy was earning his money. I called Kendall, who was on day-shift duty in the surveillance van.

"Kendall, can you get on the GPS tracer? Our green container has left the port."

"Done followed it. 'Bout to call you 'cause the container be piggyback on a truck. Just pull into a big building out in Harahan. Truck done dropped it quick, then booked out. They just now closing the door, so I can't see in."

As usual, Kendall was a step ahead of me. We compared addresses; the green container was at Chu's place. Chu's dossier noted that he and his entourage lived in an unmarked steel building with a large garage door that could accommodate big-rig trucks. Kendall had already set up an observation post in an abandoned building kitty-corner to Chu's building.

I imagined that Chu wasn't a happy camper right now, probably having just discovered that the stolen GIDEON sample was missing.

As I started to feel a little smug, reality set in. I had grown a tail. A professional one. Which meant maybe four or more vehicles using a technique called a "floating box." An advance vehicle drove about a block ahead of me, a tail vehicle a block behind. A vehicle paralleled me one street to my right, another vehicle one street to my left. And maybe there was an extra command vehicle somewhere. It was hard to break out of a floating box, if that was what I faced. If I turned right, the vehicle now to my right would become the advance vehicle, the vehicle now to my left would become the tail vehicle, and so on.

The best way to break out was to quickly hang a U-turn. If a vehicle behind you suddenly turned left, then that was the tail vehicle taking up a new position as the box tried to adjust.

The small side streets had given them away. I felt 90 percent sure. Then the 10 percent started to make me second-guess myself. Maybe I was creating some self-fulfilling paranoia. Either way, I needed to find out, so I executed a fast U-turn, and sure enough, a white van about a block back made a quick left turn.

I didn't try to outrun the box; I wanted to ID each vehicle. I had the white van made and recorded on video, so I leisurely drove over to I-10 and headed to New Orleans East, a largely obliterated, deserted area that had not even begun to recover from the killer Storm of one year ago.

I cruised past massive apartment complexes, abandoned and in ruins, then exited onto Read Boulevard. The shopping center, hospital, and high-rises there loomed as terminally wounded, empty hulks. No repairs or demolition, no mold remediation, no gutting. Nothing had commenced. Seventh District NOPD officers and National Guard MPs driving Humvees still operated out of makeshift headquarters—trailers—next to the obliterated station house on Read, but there weren't enough officers to adequately cover even half of Seventh District. Looters operated at will, stripping copper pipes and wire from homes; black gangs robbed isolated Mexican work crews of their daily cash payments and sometimes killed them. As a result, the illegal Mexicans had started to arm themselves.

The best you could say about the area was that the streets were cleared and a couple of gas stations, fast-food joints, and scattered home owners had returned to give it a go. Read had been a major thoroughfare before the Storm. It now lay virtually deserted, and, unless my shadows had an accompanying air unit, it should be easy to pick them up.

After darting through some residential neighborhoods that led me onto Chef Highway, hanging a left on Wright Road, and then snaking my way back to I-10, I had ID'd and recorded the images of four vehicles: a white van, blue Camry, white pickup, and a silver Ford coupe.

I had pending business with Honey, so I leisurely drove into the French Quarter and parked in the Omni Hotel parking garage. Knowing the service passageways well, I exited the building into a crowd on Royal, hailed a cab on St. Louis, and was clear.

A quartet worked out a swinging, jazzy blues number in Tommy's Wine Bar across from Emeril's, and the cat on the Hammond B3 organ made some lightning fast runs that almost made me forget about the deep kimchi I was in. I ordered a $110 bottle of Bordeaux, shattering my bar-tab budget, because, what the hell, life is short. I told Honey about the tail I'd just shaken.

"Think they were Feds?" she asked.

"Either Feds or they work for the Buyer's Club."

"I want to find out. I'll arrange something."

"I'm all for that. And here's a tidbit: Pelkov claimed Breaux raped Nassir Haddad, and that Haddad wanted to put out a contract on him."

"What a swell bunch of guys the Buyer's Club was."

"And I found a million bucks in the desk in Pelkov's study."

"Tell Chief Pointer that? He'd get us a warrant in about three seconds."

"Arms dealers almost never do deals with cash, but Breaux and Pelkov both had large sums on hand," I said. "Breaux sold the GIDEON sample to Chu. Could he have had something else to sell to Pelkov? Not weapons, but something from his black-projects work?"

"Maybe," said Honey as she laid out three listening devices on our private, corner table. "Found these in my house. They're disabled now. Recognize them?"

I examined the units closely and removed a SIM card from one. "SIM card transmitters. When the perpetrator sees you enter your home, they call the number associated with the SIM card. That activates the device, and they can eavesdrop on whatever you're doing. Made by a British company. Not for sale in the States, except to law enforcement."

"I don't like those FBI creeps going into my house."

The cocktail waitress returned and used a "waiter's," the handiest kind of corkscrew, to expertly open the bottle. I waved off the rest of the ritual and instructed her simply to pour.

"We're getting closer, so they're ramping up the pressure," I said, taking a quick glance at the waitress's ass as she sashayed off, hoping Honey didn't notice. "I'll take their spying on us as a good sign and a vote of confidence that we're on the verge of screwing up their game."

"And the next move in the game?"

"Nassir Haddad."

Honey nodded. "Let's put the squeeze on him. Soon as we leave here."

The waitress crossed in front of me again, and my eyes helplessly followed her.

"Stop checking out the waitress's butt and look at this video footage. I just got it from the security guys at Breaux's office building," she groused.

We used her laptop to watch the video from One Shell Square and compared it to the video from Del Breaux's home CCTV cameras. The same crew who sanitized his office had tried to get into his home. One of the perpetrators in both videos wore a green cloth bracelet on his right wrist.

"Be great if we could ID Mister Green Bracelet."

"How to do that?" asked Honey. "We need a task force. But there's just you and me."

We followed up the bottle of wine with triple espressos as we reviewed key items in Breaux's laptop, skimmed the dossiers of Buyer's Club members, and revisited the files from the Scrap Brothers' computer and office. I told her about my conversation with Blanchard, then Honey asked to listen to my recording of the talk I had with Grigory Pelkov.

Amazing how jazz musicians could take a tune like "Will You Still Love Me Tomorrow?" and turn it into a thumping bluesy groove that just made you want to snap your fingers. Honey shot me a look like I needed psychiatric help.

"Hey, hipster, did you catch that Pelkov said Breaux had his goods warehoused?"

I nodded. "And the spreadsheet in the laptop had a category for warehouse expenses. We should track down the location."

"We can get that from Peter Danforth. Tomorrow."

"Speaking of keeping goods warehoused, what was in the sealed silver container that disappeared from Scrap Brothers?" I asked. "Could Breaux have been keeping something in there? Maybe something Danforth didn't know about?" I asked.

"Decon said that container has been welded shut since forever."

"I'll track down Decon after we finish with Haddad." I took a healthy swig of the strong coffee. "This Global Solutions Unlimited, whoever they are, must have some incredible caches of weapons in the area. I mean, international arms dealers and intelligence agents like Chu and Pelkov have made NOLA home for the last year. And it's not because they like Shrimp Creole."

"Global has to be a front company controlled by Brandt. Don't you think?"

"The FBI dossiers don't clarify that. That's another reason I want to find Decon. He knows more than he's told us. He could know who Global is and where they're operating from."

"Brandt was acting as a fixer for Tan Chu at the port. He has to be part of Global."

"I'll ask Harding what she can find out about Global Solutions Unlimited," I said.

"Wait a second. Except for Breaux? They all showed up a year ago. Right after the Storm. The city was destroyed. Where could they have been operating from? How could they even find a hot meal? A hotel room?" asked Honey.

"Phone service didn't exist. The port was closed. The airport was out of commission for weeks to all but military and government flights," I added, picking up her line of thinking.

"Would've been tough to ship out anything they bought."

"And where could Global Solutions have gotten arms from? Jackson Barracks got flooded bad. Michoud did okay because it has its own levees. Belle Chasse wasn't in good shape, but it ran most of the helicopter rescue operations out of there."

"When the Eighty-second Airborne Division arrived? They camped out at Naval Support Activity on the West Bank. In the parking lot. That was a mess," said Honey.

"And the Coast Guard facilities got hit hard. Those folks were up to their eyeballs."

"We had all those U.S. Navy ships docked along the river. But they acted as housing for government workers. And brought in relief supplies, not weapons," said Honey.

"Doesn't make sense for Pelkov, Haddad, and Chu to be here then. Hell, we were under curfew, the city was closed. Residents weren't allowed to return till the end of September."

Honey and I looked at each other; it didn't make sense.

"What was it Decon said? That NOPD couldn't handle this case, that we'd be outclassed."

"Maybe he was right," said Honey.

"Or maybe we just need a lucky break. And where better to get lucky than at a casino?"

CHAPTER THIRTEEN

Harrah's New Orleans Casino reopened six months after the Storm. First responders had used the building as a staging area in the immediate wake of the disaster. Cops and firemen from out of town who had never been to New Orleans could see what the city was supposed to look like, because the interior of the casino was decorated to resemble a French Quarter street party. I found it odd that the casino was done up to replicate an area that was only a few blocks away. Last time I checked, there were no casinos in Las Vegas done up to look like Las Vegas.

Gamblers complained that since the Storm the slots were tighter than a spinster's ass. Since I'm not much of a gambler, I couldn't say, and Honey and I weren't here to play slots. We'd come because the FBI dossier had stated that Nassir Haddad gambled and partied at Harrah's almost every night of the week. Turns out the Feds were right.

We nursed lattes as we observed Haddad, an Egyptian, gambling in the private baccarat room. The young blonde on his arm must have had really good fake ID. The brunette I figured for a casino shill. A couple of young guys and another female rounded out his party.

"If the FBI has it right, Haddad should be retiring to his penthouse suite for his nightly party right about now."

"But he lives on his cargo ship, right?" asked Honey.

"Right. The casino penthouse is for partying. His ship is docked in Saint Rose. He commutes via helicopter to the New Orleans Downtown Heliport over at the Superdome, then takes a limo here. An armored limo."

"He has a helipad on the ship?"

"A big one that can accommodate two choppers."

"Business must be good," said Honey.

"In the history of the world, has there ever been a time armies haven't been attacking each other?"

"I'd like to think so. But probably not." Her phone beeped and she checked an incoming text. "SWAT exercise tomorrow."

"As if you're not busy enough."

"Maybe we can kill two birds with one stone."

Before I could ask her what she meant, Haddad stood up and casino security escorted him and his party to a private walkway that connected to the hotel tower.

Haddad's parties lasted for hours, meaning he would keep for a minute. We were both famished, so I treated Honey to overpriced sushi at Bambu in the casino lobby. I waited until we finished our salmon-skin roll to tell her something I thought might set her off, so I braced myself before I spoke.

"Listen, don't get mad, but . . . I assigned some guys to cover your mom, around the clock. They're in a blue van a couple doors down from her house. Let her know, but tell her not to take them coffee or anything. Just let her know they're there and they're watching her." I slid Honey a slip of paper. "If your mom has a problem, she can call this number and they'll come running."

Honey looked at me wide-eyed. I figured she was about to blow her top and lay into me, since she'd always taken her own and her family's personal safety to be exclusively her domain. Detective Baybee, as she had proven time and time again, was quite capable of taking care of herself; I was now stepping on her toes, so to speak, by getting in-volved in her family's protection, the inference being she couldn't handle it herself.

"I know you can take care of your mom on your own, but we're both just so busy. So I apologize for not checking with you first. It was a gut reaction; I just wanted to make sure she'd be okay." I was ex-plaining myself too much in hopes of mitigating her anger.

"The department isn't going to pay for this."

"The department has nothing to do with it," I said.

"You're paying for it? It was a gut reaction?"

I wasn't sure where she was going and couldn't read her thoughts. "Look, I'm sorry. If you want me to pull the coverage . . ."

She took my hand and squeezed it hard. Tears burst from her eyes and rolled down her creamy white cheeks dappled with freckles. For Honey to even hint at showing emotion was a huge thing. But to cry? I'd only seen her do it once, when we had found her grandpa's corpse after the Storm. I watched as she bit at her lip, and I averted my eyes. I didn't know what to say. So we just sat there.

After a minute or so, her vicelike grip loosened into more of a ca-ress as she used her free hand to daub her eyes with a celadon-colored linen napkin.

She stroked my hand and looked me in the eyes. I had horribly mis-judged her reaction; there was no anger, only deep gratitude. She had no words, so I struggled to find some. I wanted to tell her how much I cared for her, how I worried about her and thought of her and, I sup-pose, needed her.

"Honey, I . . ." was all that came out. I wished to clarify my relation-ship with her, but somehow this—sitting in a casino restaurant while on a murder investigation—didn't feel like the right time. But then, it never felt like the right time.

The green-tea ice cream arrived, we finished the meal in silence, then wordlessly headed up to the penthouse.

———

Maybe it was frustration in general, maybe it was the needlessly pro-fane hip-hop music coming from the penthouse door, maybe it was the idea that Haddad was a borderline pedophile, or maybe it was because people were tailing me and breaking into Honey's house and threaten-ing her mom. Maybe it was all of those things. But when two foreign members of Haddad's security detail refused to honor our being there on official police business and laid hands on us to stop our approach to the penthouse door, we simply demolished them. I gave my guy a quick pop to the chin. When he swung at me, I had him where I wanted and hit him in the diaphragm pretty hard. It was a carefully measured blow; I could have hit him much harder, but it still knocked the wind out of him, and he dropped to his knees with his eyes rolling back in his head. Perhaps I was getting my mojo back. I casually reached into his suit jacket and removed a Taurus 9mm and his key cards.

Honey had kicked her guy in the shin—she wore sensible shoes with steel toes, like mine—grabbed his arm, spun him around, and then used the bar-arm control to cut off his air passage and choke him unconscious. The public had a hard time understanding that choking out perps was much more humane than beating them senseless, I guess because it looked like you had just killed them.

"I haven't used that hold in a while. Good to get some practice in," she said, not even breaking a sweat, as she took his Springfield XD from a shoulder holster.

"I got it on video in case they file a complaint. They initiated first contact."

"They won't file a complaint. You heard the accent? They're not licensed to carry concealed while working here."

I swiped the key card in front of the lock, and the penthouse door clicked open.

"I feel like raining on Haddad's parade," said Honey.

"Sounds good to me."

We entered quickly. Nassir Haddad, an obviously devout Muslim, danced sex-sandwich-style with a guy and a girl as he swilled from a bottle of champagne. The sweet, sharp smell of hashish hung in the air. Maybe twenty people were scattered around the room, meaning a group had to have been up here partying while Haddad was downstairs gambling.

A few people gave us cursory glances as I scanned the room. Except for the guy smoking a small hash pipe, I saw no obvious signs of drug use, although a young half-dressed redhead stumbled around with glazed eyes in some kind of stupor.

"New Orleans Police Department! Everybody out!" shouted Honey, holding her sixty-dollar gold shield in the air. The department was so cheap, detectives had to pay for the badge themselves. The guy with the hash pipe dropped it but was too scared to exhale. "I said everybody out!" yelled Honey.

By the time I turned off the sound system, the more sober present were already exiting. Haddad hadn't said a thing. His beady eyes shifted between Honey and me as he edged toward another room.

"Nassir Haddad! Stop right there!" Honey lasered in on the short thin Egyptian in his forties with thick black hair.

Always keen on helping others, I lifted a couple of college-aged guys off the sofa by their shirts and shoved them toward the door. "The detective said everybody out!" I had a nastier tone than Honey, and the room cleared quickly.

Haddad darted into a bedroom and almost had the door closed when Honey reached in and pulled him out. She shoved him up against a wall and cuffed him. A pat-down revealed a small cloisonné-and-sterling-silver vial, which she tossed to me. She led him to a sofa, and he fell onto it, askew. He still hadn't said a word; in truth, he looked like he didn't believe Honey was a real cop and he expected instead to get a bullet to the head. Perhaps he felt that's what he deserved. I sat on the armrest near him as Honey sat across from us. I tapped out a tiny amount of white powder from the vial. "Hmmm, hard to say. Cocaine, China White, crystal meth . . ."

"Why was he trying to get into that bedroom?" asked Honey.

Haddad tensed as I stood and crossed to the bedroom. The young blonde who had to be underage that we'd seen with Haddad in the casino lay fully clothed on the bed, unconscious. A silk scarf was tied around her right bicep and her "outfit" dangled from the vein in her arm. She was zoned-out on heroin. I took a quick cell-phone snap.

I lit a cigarillo as I reentered the main room and sat on the sofa armrest. I exhaled into Haddad's face, then showed him the cell-phone photo of the girl. "His underage girlfriend in there is a skin-poppin' mama. She's geezed out. If we look around, wonder how much 'H' will turn up? In addition to this here." I held up the vial.

Tiny beads of perspiration formed a sheen on Haddad's upper lip. His eyes fluttered like his horizontal hold needed adjusting.

"I'll just MMS this photo to Judge Grenadine," I said to Honey. "You know, the judge whose daughter OD'd on smack. I figure it'll take about five seconds to get a search warrant for Mister Haddad's boat. Oh, sorry, it's an insult not to call it a 'ship,' isn't it? Be interesting to see what turns up, huh?" I exhaled again into Haddad's mug. "Did you know Detective Baybee was a member of the SWAT team? We'll bring them along when we go on board. Hopefully they won't break anything."

"You're bluffing," said Haddad. He spoke with a slight British accent; I pegged him for a moneyed Egyptian who'd gone to university in England.

"Read him his rights," I said to Honey. "We got him on contributing to the delinquency of a minor, possession of narcotics, resisting arrest, plus whatever we find on his garbage scow."

Honey stood and pulled Haddad to his feet. "You are under arrest. You have the right to remain silent—"

"Wait!" His small eyes shifted back and forth as he blinked faster. "What is it you really want? I know who you are. You want to talk about Del Breaux's murder. And arms dealing, yes? So let's talk, I have nothing to hide."

"Brother, you're in big trouble right now. You don't have diplomatic immunity. This heroin is no joke." I turned to Honey. "Let's just take him to the station and book him. And call the TV stations."

"Please! What do you want to know?"

"You had dinner with Del Breaux and Ty Parks the night they were murdered, didn't you?"

Haddad paused a moment. "Yes."

"And you saw them later that same night."

"I did but so did many others. We were in a group together."

"Where? Doing what?"

"What do you think? Buying weapons!"

"Where?" I practically yelled.

"In the city. Del and Ty left the group to go home. I didn't see them after that."

"What group? The Buyer's Club?"

"Not just the Buyer's Club; there were many others there. But Del and Ty left and I never saw them again. I *should* have killed Breaux, that son of a whore, that *yabn el wiskha*! Do you know what he did?" The veins on Haddad's face pulsed, engorged with blood. "He raped me! The thieving *yabn el mara el mitnaka* raped me! I'm not gay. Okay, maybe I take a young boy once in a while, but I'm not gay! I don't take it up the ass!"

"Interesting distinction," I remarked, trying not to sound too sarcastic.

"I'm glad he's dead. But I didn't kill him. And his lover Ty was a good person, though why he was with Del, I don't know. I swear to you, I would have killed Del if given a little time. Please find the killer so I can give him a bonus."

"Who sells the arms? Global Solutions?"

"Yes."

"And who are they? Who runs the sales? Who are the owners?"

"Are you trying to get me killed? Do you realize what you are asking?" Haddad was shaking.

"Answer the question!" said Honey, getting into his face. "If you hold back? If I think you're lying? You go to jail. Your ship gets raided. Tonight. The FBI can't stop me."

"It's your funeral, detective."

I grabbed Haddad by his shirt and lifted him off the couch. "Don't you threaten her. Sometimes prisoners have accidents on the way to booking. Fatal accidents."

"I'm not threatening her. Nor would I hurt her. There are forces in play that will kill you both."

"What forces? Chinese intelligence? The Russian GRU?"

"And they will kill me, too, if I say much more."

"Keep stalling me and they won't have to kill you; I might do it for them," I said, pushing him back onto the couch. "Breaux sold secrets to the Chinese. We traced the cash. Was he double-crossed? Were you in on it? Was Pelkov going to buy something from Breaux?"

"You have crossed a line that's . . . just arrest me for the drugs. You won't be alive to testify against me, and I have nothing to do with that, one way or the other. I didn't kill Del Breaux. I have an alibi. I can provide thirty witnesses to prove I was on my ship when he was killed. But as for these other questions, no, I won't answer. So either arrest me or get out of my room."

I lifted him to his feet, then slapped him hard with an open palm. He fell back on the couch and started to quietly whimper. He was terrified and that was too damned bad. I had no business hitting him, even if he was getting teens hooked on No. 4 Thai heroin, but I didn't care. And I didn't care that Honey was watching. My rage was taking over, and I quite simply was going to start beating answers out of him.

"Where did you and Chu and Pelkov stay when you came to New Orleans one year ago? Right after the hurricane hit. How could you even do business then?"

I lifted him back up. His eyes blinked so fast he could have sent an epileptic into a fit. I slapped him again. I wasn't seriously hurting him—yet. But I was getting his attention.

"Answer my question!"

"On board." It came out in a husky whisper.

"On board your ship?"

"No. A ship docked at Violet."

Then he did something odd. He fainted. I caught him and then gently laid him on the couch.

Honey was tugging at my shoulder. "Saint James . . . the ships that docked at Violet after the Storm? They were U.S. Navy."

CHAPTER FOURTEEN

"Honey, how could the Buyer's Club have been living on a navy ship after the Storm? Haddad is a lying weasel." I looked down at him, still passed out on the sofa. "You see the way his eyes were blinking? He lied through his teeth. Trying to scare us off. If the FBI wanted us to go away, they would have yanked the case from you. Claimed 'national security' and all that crap. And as I think about it, I don't think foreign spies are going to kill American cops with FBI counterintelligence agents running all over town. That's ludicrous."

"Haddad could be our guy. For the murders of Breaux and Parks, anyway. He had the motive. He's not shy about admitting it," said Honey.

"Any alibi would be bullshit, provided by his cronies. He could have used crew members from his ship to carry out the hit," I added.

Honey thought about that. "So what do you want to do?"

"Take a look at the girl on the bed in there and tell me you don't want to book his sorry ass."

"This wasn't a perfectly clean bust. The way we let ourselves in, I mean."

"What are you talking about? We knocked on the door and some drunk kid let us in thinking we were here to party. Anyway, who needs a conviction? We just need the arrest, the print reporters, and the TV cameras."

"And the search warrant for his ship? Who is Judge Grenadine?"

"You know grenadine—it goes well with tequila, lime juice, and club soda."

She gave me one of her looks, then radioed dispatch as I headed for the door.

"But try for a search warrant anyway. And make sure those lazy reporters get footage of the girl getting loaded into an ambulance. At least it's a poke in the eye of the Buyer's Club."

Picture perfect choreography and timing is a beautiful thing. First came the nodding-off blonde on a gurney getting loaded into the back of an EMS unit. Then the press pack scurried like rodents to document the perp walk. Honey escorted Haddad as he delivered one of the guiltiest slinks I'd ever seen a felon perform. The Fourth Estate had been front-loaded that he was a high-living international arms dealer, so the unanswered questions got shouted fast and furious. He was our very own Adnan Khashoggi.

I watched the spectacle from the shadows on South Peters Street. I decided to leave the Bronco sit tight for now in the Omni parking garage, tying up my tail, I hoped. I hailed a cab. My first stop would be the loft to retrieve a night-vision monocular in case I needed it, and then I'd head on to a place where some people chased the green fairy.

Decon wasn't at Millie's Lounge and hadn't been lately. He was nowhere to be found in the bars. I remembered that a bar patron had told Honey and I that he slept in a crypt at Greenwood Cemetery, and although I'd written it off at the time, I now scanned the cemetery with a Bushnell night-vision monocular. I'd taken a cab to Greenwood.

The cabbie was spooked to sit and wait for me in the dark, but the hundred bucks I gave him ameliorated his fear, like a talisman against the evil eye.

I scaled the wall, dropped into the cemetery, and waited. Probably just my imagination, but the night seemed to go incredibly still. I stopped to listen. I heard no barking dogs, just the muted rumble of occasional late-night traffic streaming along the I-10 only a block away, or a passing carload of drunken college kids, contractors, or thugs puttering along Canal. But those sounds were anomalies; the silent humid warm air hung like a dead physical thing that weighted me. With my vision adjusted to the absence of light, I carefully moved forward.

I stopped when I caught movement at the edge of a tomb to my right. I'd seen a momentary blur. Or had I? I rechecked the area with the night-vision monocular, but there was no sign of anything. Damn, I hated cemeteries at night. I cursed my luck and silently approached the crypt in question. I stopped when I heard low grunts, like someone being beaten was muffled, so I pounced around the tomb and shined my SureFire onto . . .

. . . some fat guy being ridden by a long-haired fake redhead with her breasts, also fake, hanging out.

"Hey!" she said in complaint, covering up.

I killed the light, and the fat guy rolled clear and scampered off as he pulled up his pants. I'd seen crazier things in cemeteries. Back when I was still in patrol, I spent three months working a "cemetery detail" to earn extra money. "Details" were essentially private security work that police officers did while off duty, but in uniform, to supplement their meager pay. I'd chased off dopers, drunks, Goths wanting to drink beer and howl at the moon, pseudo-voodoo practitioners who had shown up to attempt some kind of black rites, vandals, thieves, guys in Star Wars costumes dueling with light sabers, and teens who didn't have any place else to screw.

But "Scarlet" here was a professional lady of the evening, for sure.

"Turning tricks on a crypt?"

"Why not?" she said, standing as she adjusted her bustier. "It's frigging hot. The stone feels cool to lay on. And the dead are the only people in town who ain't overcharging. These are the dog days of summer, off season, but the cheapest motel in town is still eighty-five bucks for a room. So I put an ad on the Internet. Figured there would be some freaks who would want to do it in a cemetery. And I was right."

"How much?"

She gave me a look, thinking I might be soliciting. "One-fifty, short-time."

"You're right about everybody overcharging." Before she could figure out if that was an insult or not, I asked, "Know a guy named Decon?"

I peeled off a fifty, and she snatched it.

"Normally I wouldn't rat him out, but . . . he owes me one-fifty."

The tomb door didn't creak at all. Decon lay sprawled on a sleeping bag on the marble floor. A stone sepulcher took up the center of the room, but the rest of the place was furnished in homeless chic. Folding lawn chair, pop-top canned goods, empty liquor bottles, dozens of books, a boom box, candles everywhere, an out-of-date calendar, and an old cover of a *Maxim* magazine stuck somehow to the stone wall. Clothes were stuffed into paper shopping bags and black plastic garbage bags.

I kicked his foot. "Wake up."

He only stirred. So I kicked harder.

Decon screamed like a wedding-night virgin. I had killed the light, so he only saw a dark form looming over him. He scampered against the wall screaming and blabbering, then yelled, "Don't, I'm sorry, please forgive me!" He was so scared he started to sob and had a hard time catching his breath.

I turned on my flashlight. "Decon, get a grip. The Grim Reaper hasn't come for you just yet."

Two cigarettes later, his hands weren't shaking so bad.

"You bugged out the other night before giving me the rest of the names on your list."

"You cuffed me to your truck. I can't stand being restrained. That's why I can't go to jail, if you can appreciate that."

"You took apart my truck door. I see why they call you Decon."

"But see, I gave that name to myself, so it doesn't count. I'd like to have a real moniker."

"You mean, like, the Scrapyard Bandit?"

He motioned with his hand as if to say *Something like that.* He didn't want to demean my suggestion. "It's not easy for a criminal to earn a title. You have to work hard, be original. It's a mark of distinction, if you know what I'm saying."

"Like Tony 'the Ice Pick' Sorbello, or Jimmy 'the Fist'—"

"No, those guys named themselves, or their buddies did. It's gotta be a name the press or the cops give you, like John Gotti, 'the Dapper Don.'"

"Okay, so like the Night Stalker, the Freeway Rapist, the Nylon Stocking Rapist, the Zodiac Killer . . ."

"Those are unfortunate examples, if you understand what I'm saying."

"Decon . . . what are you doing sleeping in a tomb?"

"This is a rent-controlled unit adjusted to zero. I like that price. Sometimes I sleep on top. Fresh air, moonshine, nobody kicking me in the side telling me to move on. And let's face it: it's quiet, except when the weirdos show up."

"Where were you at about seven in the morning yesterday?" I asked.

"Thanks to the gods, I wasn't at Scrap Brothers. Saddam Hussein's sons put people though a shredder in Iraq, did you know that? If they really didn't like you, you went in feet first; more painful and took longer to die."

"Leroy went in feet first."

"I have to agree, Leroy was a prick. You think I killed them?"

"You talked about it."

"I talk about having sex with Miss Universe, too; but if she gets laid, I unfortunately wouldn't be at the top of the suspect list."

"So no alibi."

"I was here. Asleep. Don't think the ghosts are much for giving depositions to support that fact."

"Were Leroy's and Jimmy's names on the list you gave to Harding?"

"They were. But not the worker Herbert."

"Who else was on the list?"

"Clayton Brandt, Tan Chu, Grigory Pelkov, Nassir Haddad."

I nodded. "Our information seems to match. Where exactly are the arms coming from? Where's the operation located?"

"I don't have the whole picture. I only know that the weapons and fancy gear always came in from Michoud."

Michoud. "You sure about that?"

"Yeah."

"And that was always on a Saturday night."

"The weapons? Yeah. Other stuff—junk, mostly—came in the daytime from military or government surplus auctions from all over the state, but the weapons always came from Michoud. It's a NASA facility; they use special pallets, easy to identify."

"So weapons in crates would come in from Michoud to the scrapyard on Saturday night. And they'd get locked in a cargo container."

"Right."

"When did the stuff go out?"

"Within a couple of days usually."

"Were the Jefferson boys the buyers of the weapons, or just trans-shippers?"

"I asked myself that same question, seeing as how I'm so naturally curious. Leroy and Jimmy didn't know much about guns or weapons systems. They only knew about scrap. Seems to me they had to be working for somebody, or fronting, if you know what I mean."

I knew that the brothers paid for their legitimate auction purchases using the business bank account. So how to explain all the money in their safe, unless it was from years of skimming cash from the legitimate business proceeds? Maybe the money acted as the off-the-books slush fund to pay for illicit scrap purchases—like the stolen car rims. But five hundred thousand dollars was a lot to keep on hand for such purposes. Would Chu be paying such large amounts for the brothers' services?

"Sometimes weapons got mixed in with scrap going to China, sometimes not," said Decon. "I know because I ran the forklift and Jimmy had told me to do it. I say 'weapons,' but it was, like I said before, if you recall our earlier conversation, maybe sophisticated electronics, communications gear—"

"But not obsolete stuff."

"I don't think so. Even if it was, it's illegal to send it to China, even as scrap. Anything with a motherboard or circuit board, and Customs will spank your monkey, if you get my drift. I heard a few scrappers in California got popped and sent to Terminal Island."

"The freight forwarder was TDF, right?"

He nodded. "Three Dumb Fucks."

"What?"

"That's what TDF stands for. 'Three Dumb Fucks.' Except only one dumb fuck is still living, and he's not so dumb."

"Who would that be?" I asked.

"Eddie Liu."

"Chinese."

"Yeah. The drivers, too. Eddie's partners were a couple of Cajun boys. They both died in traffic accidents."

"How convenient for Eddie."

The NASA Michoud Assembly Facility was a huge place covering over eight hundred acres and comprised of hundreds of structures. Haddad said that after their final dinner he'd gone with the group to buy weapons. Had he gone to Michoud? And since Ty Parks had been the shipping manager at Michoud, had he somehow been covertly handling the outbound shipping? How could he have done that under the nose of Ralph Salerno and Michoud security?

"The TDF truck drivers would know exactly where they picked the stuff up," I mused aloud.

"I know some of those boys. Trust me, they won't tell you nothing about that," said Decon emphatically. "Compared to them, the Sphinx is chatty."

"Could be," I said with a smile. "But the paperwork in the TDF office might tell us everything."

CHAPTER FIFTEEN

Seen one trucking company lot and you've seen them all: rows of trac-
tors and trailers lined up on flat open land and a crummy-looking office
with a radio tower. This land on Almonaster had been under twenty
feet of water from the Storm; the office now was in a double-wide
trailer. TDF had no fence and no guard dog, but it had something
worse: a Chinese security guard patrolling the lot in an electric golf cart.

Decon and I reconnoitered the place from behind a clump of shrubby
rosemary bushes.

"A security guard in New Orleans working nightshift, and he's
awake? I need to take a photo and send it to *Ripley's Believe It or Not!*"
I said.

We watched the guard for an hour to time his movements; he was
utterly predictable, with a circuit around the yard every fifteen minutes. So Decon and I timed our approach, ran like hell to the back of
the trailer, and went to work.

We'd both brought our B&E kits. Before even thinking about the
lock or alarm, Decon used a modified multirange bug detector scanning in the 20–45 kHz range to check for any sensors inside the office.

"Ultrasonic area sensor alarm inside. Most likely will be in one of
the four corners."

"So we'll have thirty seconds once we get in to find it."

He nodded. "Should be a breeze."

Decon put away the bug detector and then used a tiny external magnet to maintain the circuit on the simple magnetic door switch alarm on the double-wide's door. I picked the locks in under five minutes and we were in, with the door closed behind us, as I hit the stopwatch function on my TechnoMarine chronograph. One alarm down, one to go.

Now we had thirty seconds, the delay time before the ultrasonic alarm would begin to screech. Since motion-sensing-type alarms were usually placed in corners. I had the two corners on the right, Decon, the two on the left. We moved quickly and came up empty.

"Look for something disguised as a speaker or a thick book with some generic bullshit title!" called Decon.

I spotted two speakers on a shelf. "I got speakers." But they were really speakers. "Negative as alarms," I said.

"Got it!"

I turned to watch as Decon grabbed a large book with two square lens covers on the binding. He simply flipped the unit over and powered it off.

"Two seconds to spare," I said, checking my watch.

"The owner is being sneaky."

"No doubt because he's got something to hide," I replied quietly.

We obviously couldn't turn on the lights, but within minutes I rifled through file folders containing hard copies of bills of lading, invoices, and other paperwork. I couldn't find a file for Breaux Enterprises, but Chu's FBI dossier stated he had an export company called Jade International. I found that folder and recent paperwork showing that a shipment had been picked up from Michoud and delivered to Scrap Brothers last Saturday. The pickup point was "Michoud J-19." I stuffed the single piece of paperwork in my pocket and replaced the file folder.

We waited for the golf-cart-riding guard to do another circuit. Decon returned the book-alarm to its shelf and activated it. That gave us thirty seconds to clear out. Outside the back door I relocked the locks. Decon removed the external magnet, and we melted into the darkness, no one the wiser.

The food arrived just as I came back from the men's room. Decon had ordered a beer and a club sandwich; I'd asked for an Original Tequila Sunrise and a cheeseburger. The Jimani Lounge in the Quarter was packed pretty tight. More than a few Bourbon Street strippers had just gotten off shift at 4 A.M. and were drinking with prospective johns they'd met earlier in their strip clubs.

"You didn't think I'd duck out while you were in the head?" Decon asked.

"No, now that we're working together and you're on my payroll."

"Wow. Yes, sir, boss."

I figured it was a safe bet Decon would be waiting for me. We'd just bonded by committing a burglary, after all.

"Not many people trust me. Maybe only you and one other."

"Yeah, who would that be?" I asked, not really caring, as I started to sample the fries.

"Maybe you know this person."

He smiled but he wasn't going to say the name. I let it slide; I was hungry.

"I gave you a hard time the other night," he went on. "You're probably having a tough enough time. There is redemption, you know. Maybe not for me, but for you, absolutely."

I took a huge bite of my cheeseburger and looked at him as I chewed. I finally asked, "What do you mean?"

"You know, the fighter you killed. At your gym. Accidentally," he said, casually lighting a cigarette.

I looked at him hard. I wasn't sure if he was trying to provoke me.

First, by suggesting someone I knew trusted him, and now this. "How would you know about that? I didn't see a TV in your crypt."

"I read the newspapers that people leave behind at the coffee joints. But if you're asking what I know about redemption, let's just say I'm a serious student of the concept due to my past behaviors. You and me might be more alike than you imagine."

"I doubt that."

"Wait and see. But don't wait to forgive yourself. The longer you wait to do that, the longer it'll take to get over this. Have you talked about what happened to anyone? Not a 'just the facts' conversation, but talking freely, from your heart."

I wasn't interested in Decon's pop psychology. "Thanks for the friendly advice, but let's discuss your work at Scrap Brothers. When did you leave there?"

He shook his head with a sad and knowing expression on his face. "You haven't. You're keeping it buttoned up inside, the strong alpha male. It's going to eat you up, man. Trust me, I know. Because you're not some stone killer, you haven't sold your soul, if you can appreciate my point. You can save yourself, but you have to face this sooner or later."

"When did you leave Scrap Brothers?" I repeated.

"Denial is not just a river in Egypt. But don't get me wrong, I'm not some armchair therapist. Or pacifist. Actually I'm a staunch proponent of righteous violence, to put it mildly."

"When—"

"I'll answer your questions posthaste; but first, I'd like to have a conversation with you, if you'd be so kind. See, I'm someone who is willing to sacrifice in order to serve a higher cause or ideal. It's not an easy step to take. The sacrifice is a physical one, but I'm also talking about sacrifice of an inner, personal nature."

Decon was off on a tangent, but what the hell, he wasn't going anywhere, and neither was I. And the last tangent he'd gone on had led me to the cargo container full of weapons. "You talking about compromising your morality or something?"

"I'm talking about being willing to chip off pieces of your soul as a result of having to do what needed to be done. Let's say, for example, that pretty girl at the next table was a terrorist asset who had the names of American agents in her purse. Names she was about to turn over to her terrorist handlers, resulting in the deaths of those American agents: men and women, people with spouses and kids and homes in the burbs, people who worked in dangerous conditions to serve their country for not-great pay. And if you don't put a bullet in her brain, grab her purse, and run out the door right now, those American agents will die. You can't arrest her, you can't call for backup, there is no other option; it's just you and her in the here and now. Get the picture? Would you do it? Would you make that sacrifice? And it is a sacrifice, because when you start to kill people who are posing no *immediate* threat, you're applying lethal force under a much broader set of parameters and it messes with you in a different way."

"Anyone who makes a jump to those kinds of killings has crossed a Rubicon of sorts."

"You are right," he exhaled.

"Pretty soon, it seems to me, you start to justify whacking bad guys simply because they are bad guys. No legitimate law-enforcement agency does that."

"Forget law enforcement. I gave you a specific example."

"Probably not, is my answer then."

"Good people would die."

"Good people die all the time."

"But you could prevent those good people from dying."

"There is no black and white, you know that. Only gray," I said.

"What if the people who were going to die were simply innocents, not agents?"

"I don't like these kinds of hypotheticals."

"What if children were going to die? What if one of those who absolutely was going to be killed was a friend of yours? Maybe Detective Baybee."

"Then I would be more inclined to act."

"Yes. It's all about gradations isn't it? And gradations are like the steps of the Great Pyramid at Giza. They begin to erode over time. And that's when redemption becomes more problematic."

Decon crushed out his cigarette in the ashtray.

"There's an old saying," he continued, "and I'm paraphrasing: 'Evil thrives when good men fail to act.' What should good men do, when taking action to oppose evil stands in opposition to existing social mores? Or to what has become standardized civilized behavior in our country? This reminds me that America can never win another war. Our rules of engagement are too civilized. It'd be better just to bring the boys home, you know? Why have them die for nothing if we are not willing to fight to win? War is a dirty, ugly thing, and if you are not willing to get dirty and ugly, don't fight, because you won't win."

"But you weren't talking about war before," I said.

"No, I wasn't."

I took a healthy drink, which was probably healthier than the cheeseburger that I pushed away from me, and then lit a cigarillo. "I think you know that I'm not a guy who always operates within the rules. But we still need the rules, because otherwise, where would that leave us? I'm not going to say that I never, for instance, planted dope on some abusive, ruthless, drug dealer to make the bust and get him off the street. I did. He ditched his stash the first time; I got him the second time using a little something I had in my pocket."

"Right," said Decon. "Then you made a sacrifice: You risked your career, your livelihood, your freedom—you could have gone to jail for doing that—to put a bad guy away. A guy you one hundred percent knew was bad. You broke the rules to oppose an evil, to serve a higher good."

"That's not the same as killing the pretty girl sitting over there and running out with her purse because somebody has told me it will save lives."

"Gradations," he said, staring off into nothing, maybe recounting a past memory. "Anyway, about four months ago is when I quit Scrap Brothers, to answer your question. I got tired of punching a clock, and a few other opportunities dropped into my lap."

"Del Breaux warehoused his merchandise in the city. Could it have been somewhere at Scrap Brothers?" I asked.

"Not unless it was in the welded cargo container. But if you weld the doors shut, you can't get to it. If you're in business and warehousing merchandise, you need access."

"You don't have any idea what was in that silver container?"

"It drove me crazy. I tried to figure how I could pop the welds, check inside, then mix paint in with putty to try and fake the seal. But I never did; they would have noticed."

"You know that container is gone. Taken during the murders."

It was the first time I saw Decon look genuinely surprised. "No, I didn't know that."

"So who killed Herbert and the Jefferson brothers?"

"Well, now you've got me wondering if they were killed for what was in that container."

Could the silver container have been full of secret materials Breaux had siphoned off from his black-projects work? If the container had only contained run-of-the-mill weapons, it didn't seem likely the Jeffersons would be killed in such a brutal way for it.

"You have a cell phone?" I asked.

"Fresh out."

I gave him a cheap one. One from which I could surreptitiously monitor all incoming and outgoing calls and texts.

"You remember that piece of metal that was shrink-wrapped on a pallet all by itself?"

"Next to the crates of weapons? Yeah, I couldn't figure that one out."

"Plant some seeds with those Chinese TDF drivers that you know. Tell them you stripped my Bronco in retaliation for me trying to arrest you for the stolen bronze plaque. Float the story that you found the sheet of metal with my notes on the Breaux murder, and put two and two together that it's worth money to the right buyer."

"You want to set up a sting? That's a good idea. And there are plenty of witnesses to you and Detective Baybee assaulting me in Metairie. That will lend credence to my righteous anger, if you know what I mean."

"We assaulted you?"

"A figure of speech. My credentials as a crooked character have been long established with a couple of those Chinese drivers. We did some off-the-truck specials together when I worked at Scrap Brothers, if you get my drift."

"You're a thief, I get it."

"Only in between regular jobs."

"I'm sure the chamber of commerce appreciates it."

I handed him a couple hundred bucks.

"So what is it about this piece of metal that's so valuable?" asked Decon.

"Take my advice and just stay dumb about that."

"This is exciting. I wanted those fuckers shut down, and now I get to be part of it."

"A guy like you, Decon. Why would you care that these guys are dealing in weapons?"

"I look forward to the day when we know each other well enough that you will understand the answer to that question before having to ask it. But I will tell you what I told Miss FBI: for a cup of coffee, a baguette, and two nickels I would kill each and every one of those leeches. Think of it as a cancer that needs to be cut out for the patient to survive. Lessons need to be relearned from time to time, and sometimes the lessons are harsh."

Decon wasn't making complete sense, but then I suspected that his brain was one tadpole short of being a swamp. Cheap trash talk about killing can come easily, and I had a hard time envisioning him as the guy who so far had whacked five local yokels. His passion, however, was unmistakably genuine; harnessing that in furtherance of my goals was the horse I had chosen to ride. When Decon got the word to a TDF driver about the GIDEON sample, it should get to Chu. And executing the right kind of sting on a master Chinese intelligence agent would be very satisfying indeed.

CHAPTER SIXTEEN

News of Nassir Haddad's bust was nowhere to be found in *The Times-Picayune* the next morning. Nor had it made any TV news reports. The FBI CI-3 boys must have had a busy night buttoning up the story in the interests of national security. This enhanced the great respect I had for the Buyer's Club's reach and influence. And Haddad was already out on bail, free as a bird. No judge would issue a search warrant for his ship.

I finished the last of my take-out coffee, tossed the newspaper on the floorboard, and considered the power of the forces I faced. *What in the world have I gotten Honey and myself into?* Before I could dwell on that too long, Ralph Salerno stepped out of his Metairie home. It was 8:10 A.M. I'd gotten two hours of sleep but didn't look as ragged as I felt. I sat parked half a block away, so I quickly pulled up behind Salerno's Ford Escape before he could drive off. He turned to face me as I approached.

"No flashing lights to embarrass me?"

"Just a friendly visit," I said.

"You have my cell-phone number. But this morning I have an early meeting with—"

"Did you plant the bugs in Del Breaux's house?"

The question took him aback. I handed him one of the listening devices I'd found at Breaux's; I'd only logged one into evidence control and kept the other.

"No," he said, examining it carefully. "If I could legally do that, my job would be a lot easier. This is a high-end unit."

"Someone was spying on him. How long have you suspected Breaux of selling secrets?"

He handed the unit back to me. "I had absolutely nothing on Del Breaux."

"Really? When did you discover the GIDEON sample had gone missing?"

"What sample are you—?"

"Cut the bullshit, Salerno. CI-3 is asking me and my partner about a missing sheet of material from the GIDEON project."

He shifted on his feet, deciding what to say. "Off the record?"

I nodded.

"About an hour after you left Michoud on Sunday is when we found it missing."

"Let's make this give and take, since CI-3 is probably keeping you out of the loop, and I imagine you don't like that. Breaux sold it for two and a half million to the Chinese. But they may not have possession of it." I left out the small detail that *I* had it.

He nodded, grimly. "No, they didn't tell me that."

"Is Michoud becoming some kind of weapons R-and-D and manufacturing facility?"

"Weapons? No. We're still part of NASA. Everything we do is space-based, but nothing that's weaponized."

"What else could Breaux have sold to foreign agents? Any hardware missing?"

"Only the one GIDEON piece. If what you say is true and he became a traitor, then what he had to sell were all the secrets he had from a lifetime in black projects."

"Computer files," I said.

Salerno nodded and looked troubled.

"My instinct tells me you had him under suspicion, even if you didn't have anything on him. Why?"

"I can't go there, even off the record."

"Let me help you then. Global Solutions Unlimited."

Salerno flashed me a look and an almost imperceptible nod.

"You and I are on the same side, you know. Just trying to get rid of some bad apples." Salerno remained silent, so I tried another tact. "If you're willing to confirm something I say, scratch your elbow," I whispered, just loud enough for him to hear me.

I was somewhat surprised to see him scratch his elbow.

"You knew Breaux was an arms dealer?"

He scratched his elbow.

"Okay, that explains your concern. You had a guy working on a super-secret program at your facility who also, as a side business, started running guns about a year ago after General Clayton Brandt showed up. I'd be concerned, too."

He scratched his elbow.

"Let me guess: Global is a stand-alone operation that got dumped in your lap, and your orders were to keep hands off."

He scratched his elbow.

"In Building J-19."

He scratched his elbow. "Sorry I couldn't be of any help to you today, but I really have to get going," he said loudly. Never know when someone might be listening.

I nodded and watched as he eased his bulk into his small SUV.

"Salerno . . ." He lowered his window. "If it should work out that NOPD recovers certain items, I'll make sure they get returned to you."

We locked eyes for a moment, then I turned away. Sometimes guys you fight with turn out to be your best friends. Salerno was a tough SOB who took his job very seriously. And while we hadn't physically fought, we'd crossed swords. I imagined he was behind the eight ball due to the fresh espionage at Michoud. Maybe CI-3 was setting him up for the fall. Either way, it felt good to have enlisted a new ally, because I needed all the help I could get.

I had an Omni Hotel parking garage attendant deliver the Bronco to me at the foot of Canal Street where I met Honey just before 10 A.M. I filled her in regarding events with Decon and showed her the TDF receipt indicating that Building J-19 out at Michoud was where all the action was.

"We need to drop in there," said Honey.

"I'm working on a plan for an unannounced visit."

"You trust Decon? I like the sting idea with the GIDEON sample, but—"

"Decon has the right street cred and contacts to pull it off. We don't."

Honey nodded and then told me the chief was not a happy guy. He had no qualms with the Haddad bust, would have loved the headlines, but had to field a lot of heat from the FBI and the mayor. Since he was already fighting to keep his job, Pointer didn't appreciate the extra heat, but he still backed us. For now.

Which meant our radical morning plan was a go.

Clayton Brandt stood out as the nexus of the Buyer's Club. We had the layout for his offices on the twenty-fourth floor of One Canal Place; we knew he had a messy desk; we knew where his staff sat; and we coordinated our moves.

"Detective Baybee, Homicide, I need to speak with Clayton Brandt, right now."

"Do you have an appointment, detective?" The secretary casually pressed a button on her desk.

"I don't need one. Mister Brandt is a person of interest in a homicide investigation."

The office suite consisted of four rooms: the outer office where we now stood and where Brandt's secretary's desk sat, a security team office, a staff office, and Brandt's private office.

"If you would wait just a moment . . ."

Honey didn't. I followed her lead. We could see into the room where two staffers at computer workstations gave us wide-eyed looks. But we didn't get much farther as six big, husky guys in suits piled out of the security office. They looked like the Saints' first-string defensive line and they planted themselves between us and further encroachment.

"Officers, Mister Brandt wants to fully cooperate with your investigation, but he wants his lawyer to be present. Would you mind if he met you at police headquarters later today?"

The leader was a well-spoken guy with a bulge that told me his concealed carry wasn't that concealed.

"I'll be happy to discuss that with Mister Brandt right now," said Honey.

"Mister Brandt is occupied."

"Step out of the way," ordered Honey.

"He wants to fully cooperate—"

"Step aside or you're under arrest for impeding an investigation."

"I'm simply trying to—"

"All of you are now under arrest," said Honey.

Honey hit squelch on her police radio, tuned to a certain frequency, and one second later the hallway door flung open and ten members of the NOPD SWAT team in tactical-ops gear not yet pointing their weapons stormed into the room.

Honey and I pushed past the goons who opted not to resist in the face of the men in black carrying HK-MP5A submachine guns and Benelli semiautomatic shotguns.

We rounded the corner that led to Brandt's office and ran smack into my good friend Ding Tong.

"Well, look who's here. It's Ding Dong the witch is dead. He carries the luggage for Mister Chu," I said.

"Move aside," said Honey.

"You may not enter."

"Oh, yeah?"

Honey tried to push past Tong. He grabbed her arm, and then it was on. I jumped in and we both began grappling with him. Tong displayed incredible strength and balance for such a small-framed man. Before I could think of what move to use, a large hand reached in and pulled him to the side, as a crushing black-leather-gloved fist demolished his face, knocked out two of his teeth, and dropped the Chinese agent onto the floor.

As he cuffed Tong, the SWAT team commander looked up at Honey and said, "No problem, I got him."

I had hesitated again in a fight when it counted, when Honey was under attack. I should have taken Tong easily, especially with Honey's help. I hated myself for being so ineffective, but there was no time to think about that now, as we barged into Brandt's large office.

Clayton Brandt and Tan Chu sat in chrome and leather Eames chairs set at right angles in a corner of the plushly appointed room. They didn't get up as we entered, nor was there any attempt to shake hands. There were no papers, files, folders, notes, cell phones, laptops, or data of any kind out in the open in front of them. They'd had enough time to prepare for our coming through the door.

"You couldn't be polite and wait until I came downtown, could you? You two have no clue," said Brandt.

Honey and I remained standing, but I leaned against his massive, heavy desk and crossed my arms in a gesture that suggested he was insignificant.

"Well, we have a little bit of a clue," I said. "But why not explain why you're sitting next to a Chinese intelligence agent and why you facilitated his purchase of weapons to the People's Republic of China and other nations unfriendly to the United States?"

"Because it's legal! Because the Pentagon wants the weapons and other goods sold! Did you somehow miss that the United States is the largest manufacturer and seller of arms and military matériel in the world? The country is broke, and we're getting some money back for the taxpayers. I am the Pentagon's point man; I broker the sale of weapons and equipment that our defense contractors have built. If the military or other federal agencies choose not to deploy these items, they become surplus and are sold to the highest bidder. Those grenade launchers that were in that shipment you stopped at the port cost about ten million dollars to develop and manufacture. A decision was subsequently made that they were too lethal to use. So they are auctioned off for maybe ten cents on the dollar, putting a million dollars back into the coffers, which is better than locking them up in a warehouse to rust."

I was surprised he was speaking to us and not "lawyering up," but I was floored by his assertion that this was a sanctioned Pentagon operation. Backdoor, illicit dealing from military bases or even sensitive installations was to be expected. It's what Honey and I thought had been happening. But sanctioned selling? With a wink and a nod to embargoed countries? The merchandise was leaving through the *front door,* with the blessings of the Joint Chiefs.

This was big stuff. I glanced at Honey, and she seemed to be having a similarly difficult time wrapping her head around it.

If Brandt weren't lying, then the FBI CI-3 agents were probably acting under orders as the security arm of the operation. That meant Terry Blanchard was working for them, although the under-the-table payment couldn't have been legal. The guilty always maintain their innocence, but perhaps Pelkov and Haddad had told the truth: perhaps their dealings were legitimate. Maybe. But I wondered how Americans would feel if they knew state-of-the-art weaponry and technology our defense contractors developed with taxpayer dollars was being sold to our enemies for pennies on the dollar to possibly be used against us someday. To me it felt wrong through and through.

It had previously occurred to Honey and me that we might have stumbled on an FBI sting operation, but the only sting in all of this was that our so-called protectors were selling us out. If this had been some kind of counterintelligence op that sold technology that was bogus or useless, that would have been sweet. But the Pentagon was selling the real thing to the highest bidder.

I tried not to let this rattle me and kept my poker face in place.

"If this is above board, why are you upset that you have to discuss it?"

"Just because it's legal doesn't mean it's not classified. This is done on the QT for obvious reasons, not the least of which is public safety."

"Please, General, I grew up on a farm and I know what bullshit smells like. Global Solutions Unlimited, the company that provided Tan Chu a receipt for the weapons—who controls it? Where are they operating out of?"

"If either of you held an active security clearance of Top Secret with the right compartmentalization, I might answer that question."

"We don't need a security clearance to investigate the murders of local citizens. Are you saying the Feds made a decision to let Mister Chu get away with murder?"

"You think Chu killed that coon-ass Del Breaux? Breaux was the biggest shyster in all of Louisiana, and that's saying something. I mean, he had become an embarrassment, a liability. I deeply regret ever letting him come into the group. But my policy was that if a qualified individual showed up with cash, they were welcome."

"How egalitarian of you."

Brandt ignored the remark. "Breaux would steal everything that wasn't bolted down. He shoplifted, for heaven's sake, right in front of me, over at the Windsor Court Hotel gift shop. He'd walk out of a busy restaurant without paying a check because he knew he could get away with it. To say he felt like the world owed him a free ride is an understatement."

"Why did you let him remain in the Buyer's Club?"

"I didn't. I put him on notice. Gave him sixty days, so he could make a little money to put aside. After that, he would be expelled."

"When did you give him the notice?"

"About three weeks ago."

"General, you said you were the Pentagon's point man to get the matériel sold. But I heard you were also a buyer."

"That's correct. I'm a licensed arms dealer. I deal with very reputable organizations, many of which you would recognize, all over the world."

"So you are very familiar with all of the items that have come up for auction through Global?"

"Yes, very."

"Then can you tell me what this is?"

I showed Brandt a couple of eight-by-tens of the stolen GIDEON sample.

"Some piece of metal. Hard to say."

"Was this part of the auctions you described to me, General? Is this something Global Solutions Unlimited was selling?"

"No."

"Del Breaux worked on Project GIDEON. Surely you're aware of that."

For the first time, Brandt looked uncomfortable. "That's highly classified and shouldn't be discussed in the presence of Mister Chu."

"Does that mean Mister Chu here shouldn't have had this materials sample carefully packed next to the grenade launchers in that green container of 'scrap' going to China? Would you and FBI CI-3 really want to facilitate Del Breaux selling the secrets of the GIDEON program?"

Clayton Brandt's lips tightened and his jaw tensed.

"You created this situation, General. You baptized Breaux as a buyer and seller of American high-tech weaponry; he was buying from Global with your blessing and then selling to every murderous dictator on the planet. Didn't it occur to you he might become tempted to sell some of his scientific secrets as well? Secrets he accumulated over a lifetime of engineering work. When he learned you were dumping him from the group, the facts suggest he decided to take that small step— small for someone with the integrity of an arms trader—to sell a little something else to China. *You* made it easy for him to become a traitor, throwing around your papers, talking about congressional waivers allowing dual-use technology to be shipped to those communist bastards. We found two point five million in cash in his house, and the bills were sequentially numbered, traced to the Bank of China. Does that sound right, General Brandt? Maybe your little arms bazaar here is on the up-and-up, I don't know. But I do know it's a real bitch to wake up and realize you're on the wrong side and that the fingers will be pointing back to you."

Brandt wouldn't make eye contact with me. If he clamped his jaw any tighter his teeth were going to shatter.

"Why are you persecuting me?" It was the first time I had heard Chu speak, and his words were carefully measured, his tone even and calm. "You make offensive accusations without presenting proof. I have committed no crimes. I am in your country legally. Are you racist? You don't like Asians?"

"I like everyone except the people who want me dead, lie to me, steal from me, hustle or disrespect me. I don't like people who think I owe them simply because I have something that they don't have, even though I worked for it and they didn't. I also don't like the rude, selfish, inconsiderate, or mean-spirited. Nor do I like hypocrites, phonies, or smug elitists with a superiority complex, which would probably include most politicians. I don't like crooks, murderers, and rapists. I don't like waiters who want to be actors and give me service in a restaurant that is all about them and not about me. I dislike bartenders who won't give me a healthy pour or ever buy me a round. And I really don't care for pushy old women who wear too much cheap perfume and elbow me aside in line at the supermarket. I figure that means I dislike about half the people on the planet.

"And regardless of what the asswipe politicians, State Department bureaucrats, sell-out lobbyists, the news media, pointy-headed think-tank intelligence-analyst schmucks, defense-industry salespeople, and corrupt retired flag officers would like us to believe, the Chinese government, your employer, is *not* our friend. We fought Chinese soldiers in Korea, we fought them in Vietnam, and will fight them again probably sooner rather than later. Your state-sponsored hackers have been cyber-attacking us for years, stealing our most precious secrets with impunity, and we're too chickenshit to do anything about it. You're an intelligence agent for a government that does not allow freedom of speech, freedom of the press, freedom of religion, freedom of dissent. Your government puts its critics in front of a firing squad, shoots them down like animals, and then sends the bill for the bullets to their families. Regardless of all that, as an investigator, I just have a nose for duplicitous psychopaths capable of great evil. But to try and play the race card, Mister Chu? You can do better than that."

On cue, Honey crossed in front of Chu's and Brandt's sightlines to retrieve the eight-by-tens. In that spilt second I slipped a listening device that looked like an ink pen between stacks of folders on Brandt's cluttered desk.

"Saint James, why don't you wait outside and cool off?" asked Honey. As I pretended to leave in a huff, I heard her say, "Just a few more questions about the murders, General Brandt, and then we're done here."

I closed the office door behind me. SWAT had removed Brandt's security detail and all staff from the suite of offices and were questioning them downstairs, as had been prearranged with the SWAT commander. I knew he had a crush on Honey. She had come onto the team and established herself right off the bat in a weapons-retention exercise. One at a time, she had taken the sidearm away from eight two-hundred-plus-pound operators, including the SWAT defensive tactics instructor, using a technique I had taught her. She had established some bona fides with the boys. And since they were running a training exercise this morning anyway, Honey asked if they would play supporting players for us. Nice to have them waiting right outside in the twenty-fourth-floor hallway exactly when we needed them.

It took me ninety seconds to locate and download Brandt's appointment book from his secretary's PC. I then made a beeline to the office where Brandt's two key support staffers worked. I installed fast-loading keystroke, screenshot, and eavesdropping software onto their PCs as I copied their hard drives. They hadn't had a chance to log out of their computers when SWAT stormed in. The eavesdropping software would allow me to listen to the staffers remotely via the Internet by turning their computer speakers into microphones.

I texted Honey and the SWAT commander "CODE 4," then took the stairs down to the twenty-third floor and dialed in the bug I'd placed on Brandt's desk.

From the sound of things, Honey and Chu had left his office and Brandt was now alone, talking on the phone. He sounded unsettled, not thinking straight, as he made calls on what I assumed was an encrypted line. All part of my plan to come on strong and shake his cage.

"We hold the auction as scheduled, but it will be the last one in New Orleans," Brandt said. *"We'll have to move the whole operation. So I want every last crate we have down here moved into J-19 immediately. It'll be a closeout sale."*

Brandt hung up and dialed another number.

"It's me. My guy call you about those cops coming here? Well, they've figured out too damn much and they're on a high horse about that queer's death. We need to initiate Plan B, now! And we have to rethink how to handle Chu."

Honey joined me, and as I recorded the transmission we listened using earbuds. The small battery-operated ink-pen device would only transmit a hundred feet, so we stood in the hallway one floor below Brandt for one hour and eleven minutes, until the bug was discovered by Brandt's security guys, who had returned and conducted an electronic sweep.

"Even if the arms dealing is legal? We still have murders to solve," said Honey.

"Why don't you and your mom move in with me? You guys take the bedroom, I'll take the couch. My place has better security so I won't have to worry so much," I said insistently.

Honey pursed her lips. "I'm not afraid, but . . . I'll do it for Mom's sake. We'll make the move tonight. Feel better now?"

"I'd feel better if I knew what Brandt's Plan B was."

CHAPTER SEVENTEEN

Brandt wasn't the only person with a plan. Honey and I also had something up our sleeves. As I followed her unmarked unit up Canal, I spotted the blue Camry tail vehicle. The day's fun and games were just beginning.

It was time to see Peter Danforth and learn where Del Breaux warehoused his weapons. Honey and I also needed to review the files from Clayton Brandt's office computers. And there were about ten other things I should do immediately if not sooner, like run Brandt's spiel by Agent Harding, update Kendall's assignment, thank Barry Morrison and Chief Ritzman, and call an NOFD captain buddy of mine for the exact GPS coordinates of Building J-19 at Michoud, which I planned to visit later tonight.

As I drove I rewound the confrontation with Ding Tong in my mind. I could have head-butted him, kicked him, tackled him. There were a hundred things I could have done, moves I have made thousands of times. But instead I had stood there flat-footed, wrestling around like I was going to cuff him or something. Honey could have been hurt if the SWAT commander hadn't stepped in. That was another thank-you call I had to make.

With no answers, just questions, I booted up the in-dash computer, engaged the heads-up display on the windshield, and eavesdropped on Claytons Brandt's staff as I followed Honey all the way to the fairgrounds.

Honey had made a lot of friends in the department in the last year. It didn't hurt that she was beautiful. Hence, unmarked detective units rolled up all four of our tail vehicles simultaneously, freeing us up to go where we wished, unseen.

Based on the detective's traffic stops, we'd soon know who was so interested in us. Meanwhile, Peter Danforth had some explaining to do.

"I should have a lawyer present," said Peter Danforth, wiping sweat from his forehead.

"Okay," said Honey. "I'll take you downtown right now. Park you in an interrogation room. When your suit shows up, we'll talk."

"And I'll text Brandt, Chu, Haddad, and Pelkov to give them your location," I said. "Who knows, maybe it was one of them that put the Jefferson brothers through that metal shredder over at Scrap Brothers."

"Go ahead and get your lawyer. It will skyrocket you to the top of our suspect list," said Honey.

"Suspect?" Danforth blew air in frustration. "That's not why I want a lawyer. Like I said before, I need witness protection. The federal program."

"Then call the Feds," I said. "Tell them where you are. Then *everybody* will know."

Danforth didn't look happy. He looked good: six-pack abs, chiseled features, blond-streaked hair. But he looked far from content as he wiped his face again with a workout towel.

He'd been on a treadmill in the Academy's cardio room when we bulldozed our way in.

"Did you check out Clayton Brandt?" he asked me.

"Yes, and the other Buyer's Club members. Why not start by telling us how Breaux got into the arms business?"

Danforth looked us up and down as if gauging how much contempt he should show us. Finally he threw the towel on the ground. I knew what it meant to throw in the towel.

"Ty Parks opened the door."

We just looked at him.

"Ty was the main logistics and shipping guy at Michoud. And he's ex–air force. Clayton Brandt is a former air force general, and Ty helped out in the early days after the Storm to get the general's operation set up at a remote part of the facility. Nuts-and-bolts stuff, like providing forklifts, helping with loading-dock repairs, things like that."

"So Ty Parks was helping Clayton Brandt's civilian staff out at Michoud?" I asked.

"Brandt has a small group of air force personnel who are assigned TDY, temporary duty, to Belle Chase. But they spend most of their time at Michoud."

"How many air force people?" asked Honey.

"Maybe a half-dozen. Mostly they handle the warehousing duties. They stay in the Hilton, drive rental cars."

"So when Parks figured out the nature of Brandt's project, he told Del Breaux about it."

"Exactly," said Danforth. "Del had money, a security clearance, and a trading company; he wanted in on the action. So Ty went to the general on his lover's behalf, and Brandt said okay. Del became the last member of the Buyer's Club. Del didn't know the first thing about arms dealing, but he knew there was money in it and he learned fast."

"How could Brandt be the Pentagon's point man but also be a member of the Buyer's Club?" I asked.

"The greedy bastard did both, and the Pentagon let him. He got paid to run the sales operation for Global. So that meant he was also a facilitator working to make sure that the whole thing ran smoothly and stayed off the radar screens."

"He came to Tan Chu's rescue at the port," said Honey.

Danforth shrugged. "He would have done it for any buyer. His job is to make sure the goods get sold and leave the country quietly."

"Since Brandt is running the operation for the Pentagon, does that make Global Solutions Unlimited one of his companies?"

"Not at all. Brandt buys weapons from Global and sells them on the world market, just like the other members of the Buyer's Club. Global Solutions is some kind of Pentagon cutout, but sometimes it's best not to ask too much."

"So the Buyer's Club was the exclusive purchaser of all this exotic material?"

"No. Buyers from all over the world fly in every week. They stay at the Windsor Court—Germans, Iranians, Swiss, South Americans. Sometimes they show up in uniform."

"Iranians?" asked Honey, surprised.

"Yes. Iranian military. And Syrians too. In uniform. Buying weapons from America. Come one, come all."

Honey and I glanced at each other; sometimes it was hard to keep the poker face going.

"So they come every week because . . . there's a weekly auction?"

"That's right. The Buyer's Club was just a euphemism for the dealers who stayed local. Pelkov, Haddad, and Chu were buying so much, the ongoing sales became so important to them, they essentially relocated here. Brandt was here to run the operation, but Del was the only truly local arms dealer."

"Why did this kick off right after the Storm? Conditions were terrible," I said.

"The move to New Orleans had happened a week before the Storm hit. Brandt doesn't let much get in his way of making money, even a killer hurricane. And he was right; in the chaos of the Storm, it was even easier to conduct business and get things done. No one paid attention."

"So after the Storm, buyers were housed on navy ships docked on the river?"

"That's what I heard. Brandt has tremendous pull, as you can imagine."

"Have you been out to Building J-Nineteen at Michoud for one of the auctions?" I asked.

Danforth nodded cautiously. "A couple of times."

"You told me before that all of the members of the Buyer's Club had their reasons for wanting Del Breaux dead. Haddad and Pelkov, I understand. And I think I have a good idea about Chu. But why would General Clayton Brandt want him dead?"

"Because he suspected him of leaking to the FBI," said Danforth matter-of-factly.

"I thought the FBI was the security arm giving you guys cover," said Honey.

"A unit from Washington does that, yeah. But somebody started talking to a local agent, who opened up an investigation. It created a lot of fear and suspicion until the boys in DC put the kibosh on it."

Harding. He was talking about Agent Harding's investigation.

"Why did Clayton Brandt think Breaux was leaking?"

"Petty revenge. He was kicking him out."

"But Breaux wasn't the leaker, was he?" I figured the leaker had to be Decon.

"No way. Del was a greedy, corrupt horse's ass. He wouldn't blow the whistle on a gravy train, especially since he had a plan to worm his way back in."

"If he was that unscrupulous, would he have sold out his country? Would he have sold some secret-something from his scientific work at

Michoud? Something separate from the buying and selling of arms he was doing?"

"Well, when he saw that the government was willing to sell sophisticated weapons and equipment to our enemies, his thinking definitely changed. I can't say I ever saw him do anything treasonous, but I wouldn't put it past him."

"You handled billing?" asked Honey.

"There was no billing. The goods never shipped until a buyer transferred money into an escrow account. Del did keep money in a small company account that I wrote checks on to pay the rent, utilities, incidentals. But at any one time there was never more than seven or eight thousand in that account."

"So why did Breaux have two point five million in cash in his house?" I asked.

"I don't know."

Danforth's response was too quick, the voice tighter. He was good, but we'd struck a nerve.

"Sure you do."

"I don't. Del always knew how to make money. Lots of it."

"We have the serial numbers from the cash in his house, so don't bullshit me."

"Good for you, but I don't know what you're talking about. Del didn't trust me with the money end. He wouldn't have trusted anyone, not even Ty. I was a well-paid assistant, but the money part he handled himself. I don't know anything about a bag of money in his house."

"You mean you didn't drain his bank accounts the night he died?" asked Honey.

"Hey, I got screwed out of my last paycheck, including one percent of a four-million-dollar sale to Liberia."

I glanced at Honey, who looked back at me. Danforth's statement about his commission fit Breaux's laptop records precisely.

"Since you made a small fortune—one percent of the weapons sales—where's your money?" I asked.

"I sink every dollar into real estate. I'm in it for the long term. I'm rich on paper but cash poor. Fixing up demolished properties isn't exactly free."

"What business did Breaux have with that scrapyard over in the Ninth Ward?"

"The first few weeks after he joined the Buyer's Club, he kept his stock there. All the guys in the Buyer's Club did at one time or another, because Tan Chu had an established relationship with them buying scrap. Once anyone bought merchandise at auction, it had to leave Michoud the same night—Brandt's orders. But Del didn't trust people, and he sure didn't trust the Jefferson brothers, so about ten months ago he found another location to warehouse his stock."

"What location?" I demanded.

Danforth waited a beat before answering. "Right here."

Peter Danforth unlocked a large padlock, swung out the hasp, and heaved open a heavy old wooden door oily and darkened with age. The room felt cool as we stepped in. Wooden cases of 7.62mm ammo stacked six high. Barrels, bundles, boxes, crates, and canisters brimmed with war matériel, much of it Soviet-bloc manufacture.

"This building used to be a warehouse. The owner offered Del a good deal to rent this space, so he took it."

Honey and I did a quick walk-through, appraising the inventory.

"So everything Breaux bought from Global Solutions came here first. Before he shipped it to a buyer somewhere in the world?"

"Yes. Toward the end, items would ship out a day or two after they arrived here. Del had the Midas touch, and business was taking off."

"Who had access to this room?" asked Honey.

"Del, myself, the security guys."

"This is all Soviet manufacture. None of this came from the auctions at Michoud," I said pointedly.

"Del bartered for these goods. With the other guys in the Buyer's Club."

"So where are the nonlethal weapons units he bought the night he died? Microwave crowd-dispersal generators."

Danforth glanced around the room. "Good question. I'll have to get back to you on that."

Honey and I worked our cell phones as we walked to our vehicles, then conferred, as fat rain droplets fell sparingly from a partly cloudy sky, sizzling partially to steam as they hit the hot pavement.

"Two operators in each tail vehicle," Honey said, relaying the info about our tails from the detectives who'd helped us out. "Six men, two women. All carrying concealed, but they have valid permits. High-end comms. No law-enforcement ID. All flew into town two days ago from around the country. Rented the vehicles from Avis out on Airline Highway. Staying at the Sheraton." Honey stopped. She had more to tell me, but looked worried.

"Okay. Any sniper rifles or heavy artillery?"

"They had extra sets of keys to vehicles unknown. Maybe a gun truck."

I nodded. "Where are they now?"

"Detained. No arrests yet. Each group of two is being held at a different district station house. Fred Gaudet will make sure they're held overnight."

Detective Fred Gaudet was an old buddy of mine; we'd gone through the police academy together. "To get their latent prints, I bet. He can't print them since they're not under arrest, but they have to eat, go to the toilet, drink something. He'll get their prints from what they touch, then maybe we'll know more," I speculated.

"We know a little more already. Each vehicle had an identical notebook computer. Three were password-locked. The fourth, we got lucky. There were files inside. Photos of your dojo, your trucks, you riding your bike, your place in the warehouse district. Photos of my house, rooms inside my house, my mom's house, me driving my unit. Text files of our dossiers. Routines, habits, places we frequent."

"So *they* planted the bugs in your house, not the FBI."

She shrugged. "I just want my mom left out of it. Fred's assigning two uniforms to Mom, to supplant your guys."

"Good. Fred's a good man to do that. Once we get you and your mom moved into my building, you can breathe a little easier."

"Get this," said Honey, cracking a smile. "Fred called a thug in the Iberville Projects. Told him the locations of the four tail cars. Said NOPD would like the vehicles to disappear forever. No questions asked."

I smiled for the first time today. "Excellent. We need to keep poking our opponent in the eyes."

"We're not the most effective police department. But we know how to screw with people who screw with us," said Honey.

"Indeed. If I know Fred, their cell phones will be returned after being accidentally dropped into a bucket of water, he'll leave no shoelaces in their shoes, he'll report their credit cards as stolen, check them out of their hotel rooms. Little things mean a lot. Especially to an out-of-town crew."

All of this held some small solace, but Honey looked frustrated. "So who are they working for?"

"Clandestine operators don't carry badges. Could be from any number of government agencies. We've been stepping on some toes here. Or maybe they're freelancers working for somebody in the Buyer's Club." I wanted to put Honey's mind at ease. "If they were going to take us out, they could have easily done it already. The photos prove that."

"I'm not a rookie. We both know that with these high stakes, there's no telling what they might do next. Or to whom. Like maybe to one of our family members. To send us a message."

She was right. I'd already decided to fly two guys to St. Louis to look after my mom.

"I talked to Kendall," I said. "The FBI showed up in force at Chu's warehouse in Harahan."

"A raid? Looking for the GIDEON sample?"

"I would hope so."

"Local FBI?" asked Honey.

"No, a Special Response Team. They must have already been in the city. Maybe showing Brandt the pictures had an effect." I lit a cigarillo and looked up at the sky, trying to tell which way the wind was blowing. "So what did you think of our boy inside?"

"He lied a few times. Probably could have drained Breaux's bank accounts."

"Did you notice he referred to the cash at Del's house as being in a bag? We never said that. It might have been in a safe, in a box, on a shelf."

"'Bag of money' is a common term. If you had that kind of money at your place? Where would you keep it?"

"In a bag," I admitted. "But that storage room just now? Pelkov and Haddad both complained that Del cheated them on shipments, shorted customers of theirs that he was supplying. Maybe Danforth was the guy doing the shorting. Creating his own little stash. That could be what he just showed us."

"So Breaux's actual storage room could be elsewhere in the building," said Honey.

"With the nonlethal weapons system and who knows what else. Can you get a search warrant?"

"No. We need more evidence."

"Then we keep digging."

"Danforth could have whacked Breaux and Parks. Emptied the bank accounts. Then went after the two and a half million."

I shrugged. "Would he also be the one who sanitized Breaux's office? Who would be helping him?"

"He has his own small army in there," Honey said. "But why kill the Jefferson brothers?"

"Good point," I admitted. "There doesn't seem to be a connection. I'm heading back to my place. I need to go over the files we got from Brandt's office."

"All right. I'm paying a visit to TDF Trucking. Getting a search warrant. I want to legally establish J-Nineteen as the origin of the weapons. And see what else might turn up."

"I'll go with you," I offered.

"I can handle it."

I looked at Honey. She wielded an edginess that she couldn't quite conceal. "Is there something else you want me to do?"

"I want you to be the old you. I want you to be brilliant and solve this."

She turned, got into her unit, and drove away.

I'd never thought I was brilliant, just bullheaded. And obviously I was a selfish son of a bitch, because my need to have the distraction of this investigation, to help me forget about Bobby Perdue, had ended up endangering the lives of people I cared for. This case needed to go down *yesterday,* but I only had multiple guesses as to who staged a murder/suicide and then brutally, heinously killed three others, all as part of an effort, it seemed, to keep an illicit cash cow rolling along.

The scent of a cigarette stopped me cold. No, check that, not of a cigarette, but of a heavy smoker. It didn't smell like someone had lit up in my loft; that was a very distinct aroma. It smelled like the stink of smoke on someone's clothing. I stood in my kitchen, polo shirt soaked with sweat, about to reach for a bottle of water in the fridge. I'm a cigar smoker, but never in my home. A cigarette smoker leaves a distinctly different airborne marker. And since I don't run the air-conditioning in the huge loft when I'm out, no air currents had disturbed the wafting aroma. I had a very good nose. A smoker was in my house.

I pulled my big semiauto. I carried the 1911A cocked and locked, so I eased off the safety to condition zero.

Since I wasn't sure if Fred Gaudet and the other detectives had rolled up the entire surveillance team, and since the bad guys had already cased my place, I hadn't wanted to publicly announce my return home. So I'd parked a few blocks away, then gone into Ernst Café. I had a key for the door to the stairway that led to the roof, a key I'd made myself after disassembling the lock early one morning when no one was around. With an iced sweet tea in hand and no one looking, I had easily unlocked the door on the first floor of Ernst, entered the stairway, and emerged on the rooftop.

Unless my loft was under surveillance from some high vantage point, which I doubted, I wouldn't be spotted. In less than sixty seconds I had made it to my roof and unlocked my heavy-duty, alarmed, steel rooftop door.

That was moments ago, and now I stood perfectly still, .45 in one hand, smart phone in the other, as I logged on to the Internet, where I accessed the security system in my house. Using the phone, I was able to perform a fast rewind of the digital video that had been recorded by the interior and exterior security cameras. The cell-phone screen showed a lone male figure dressed as a UPS driver enter right through the front door on the street. He had to be a top-flight operator to have gotten by the alarms. Brown baseball cap, wraparound mirrored sunglasses, and a blond beard that was probably fake masked his features.

I watched the intruder on video enter my upstairs loft. He seemed perplexed by all of the boxes stacked everywhere, but in short order went to work installing something in my Sub-Zero refrigerator. It was something that didn't need refrigeration, about as big as a notebook computer but with a shape resembling a butterfly.

A bomb. Unusual looking, but a bomb.

Maybe there wasn't anyone else here after all. Only me. And the butterfly bomb. Mentally I scratched the idea of moving Honey and her mom into my loft.

I logged off the Internet and carefully retraced my steps. The sweet tea I'd left at the top of Ernst Café's stairway was still cold, and I chugged it. I didn't care one whit that I startled a waitress carrying a drink tray when I came out of the stairway door on the ground floor of the bar. I held a finger to my lips, put a twenty-dollar bill in her hand, picked up one of the real drinks from her tray, and walked out.

So much for the theory of the bad guys hurting someone close to us to get us to back off. Honey and I now had contracts on our heads.

CHAPTER EIGHTEEN

I sat with my back against the wall in the pool table room at Dos Jefes Uptown Cigar Bar. I needed something stronger than a cigarillo and was puffing a Honduran maduro torpedo from the bar's large humidor. Lieutenant Eric Mondrian, supposedly NOPD's *former* CIA liaison, sat across from me finishing a call on his cell. He terminated the call and then took a long pull on a black-and-tan.

"Good news and bad news. Good news is, the bomb didn't go boom. Your building is unscathed. Bad news is, the bomb squad boys had to cut through both sides of your Sub-Zero refrigerator. And those things ain't cheap."

"What was the explosive?"

"They think it's some kind of advanced land mine."

"Land mine?"

He nodded.

"Let me guess—a prototype," I said.

"Yeah, they texted me a photo; take a look."

Mondrian's cell-phone screen showed a photo of a jar of Dijon mustard, a quarter bottle of Piper-Heidsieck Brut, and a land mine. He took another quaff, like he was in a hurry, as I studied the picture, then used Bluetooth to copy the photo to my cell. The land mine resembled some kind of plastic, olive drab butterfly.

"I got some other good news, some strange news, and some more bad news."

"Give me the strange news," I said.

"The bomb wasn't rigged to explode."

I studied his face as I thought about that. "A real bomb but not armed. So they're sending me a message, after all."

"Not necessarily. Maybe the perp knew you were coming back and had to beat feet before he could rig it."

"He didn't know I was coming back."

"You only missed him by five minutes. They probably had people watching you."

"I don't think so."

"Don't be so sure. Cockiness can be terminal."

He was right about that. "What's the good news?"

"The Agency wants you alive and kicking."

"Bullshit."

"Bless you. I'm just the messenger. I thought you had some bad blood with them, but they say no."

"You know how it is, you're just another no-good prick . . . until they need you. I can't take anything the CIA does around here too seriously."

"Well, here's the bad news: a Chinese hit team. You're the target. I was told the local spooks rolled them up at the airport when they got off a commercial flight out at Louis Armstrong. They were carrying what appeared to be some exotic poisons, okay? So to be brutally honest, the reason I'm guzzling my drink is because I don't want to be near you right now. Is that serious enough for you?"

"Twee Siu's still the CIA station chief, right? She tell you all this?" I had a pretty intense history with Twee Siu. I trusted her as far as I could throw a brick.

"Shut up and listen." Mondrian slid a house key toward me on the table. "Here's the key to a safe house, the location of which I'm told you already know. I was also told you seldom need a key to get in anywhere, but what the hell, give your lock picks a day off. Stay away from your dojo, your home, Pravda, and your friends, including Detective Baybee. There's a black Suburban parked over on Annunciation. Armored. Weapons in a case in back. Here." He slid a Chevy key toward me. "The Agency folks are looking for the local contact the hit team would have rendezvoused with."

"Tan Chu and Ding Tong. I can give you the address in Harahan."

"But actually, that's secondary, because the other hit team, I'm told, is more problematic."

"*Other* team?"

"Russian. Just what did you do to piss these people off, anyway?"

"Beats me."

"If I were you, I'd take a long vacation. But since I know you won't, just make sure you shoot straight and have enough ammo."

"What's being done for Detective Baybee?"

"The contract is on you, not her."

"Negative. They broke into her house, took pictures, planted bugs—"

"That was FBI CI-3, not a wet team. They're unhappy with you guys, but they won't kill you. Of course, after the way you had their surveillance team detained, maybe they will come for you."

"That surveillance team was not FBI."

"Technically that's true. They're CI-3 assets. Not sworn agents."

"I don't appreciate the distinction. CI-3 is not on our side. They're in bed with some very bad people."

"Saint James, don't be a complete idiot; at least try to keep it to a part-time basis. The CI-3 people like to catch spies, which is a good thing. They got families, mortgages, credit-card debt. So you think maybe they have to obey orders and sometimes do things they don't like to do? Like babysit Tan Chu?"

"If they mess with somebody's family, they need to be slapped."

"I won't argue that point. I'm suggesting you consider tempering your judgment of them."

"I'll take that under advisement." I slid the keys back to him. "Tell Twee I need to see her. Immediately, if not sooner."

I stood and took a few steps toward the side door.

"You might have been clocked coming in here. Go out the other side, onto the patio. Jump the fence, cut through some yards, and stay off Tchoupitoulas."

"You trying to make me paranoid, Eric?"

"Far be it from me to do that, just because people are trying to kill your ass."

"Assign some coppers to Honey. Good people. Can you do that?"

"I'll make it happen. I'd offer you a protective detail, but I know you won't take it."

I exhaled bluish smoke and set the torpedo butt in an ashtray. "I'd feel bad if somebody got hurt. But I mean it, I want to talk to Twee, face-to-face."

I rented an armored white GMC Yukon from Billy Burke who runs PSD details for Hollywood celebs when they come slumming for dirty long weekends. I had an Omni parking valet retrieve my Bronco from the street near Ernst Café and take it back to the hotel garage.

Honey and I had spoken on our encrypted cells as I took a spin on I-10, and we quickly filled each other in, keeping the call short in case someone was tracking my signal. She'd seized all the shipping records from TDF and had been trying to sort through them at her desk on Broad Street when the two main FBI CI-3 boys showed up. Her daily briefing to them consisted of three screamed words: "Kiss my ass!" She knocked one of them down with a hard right, and other detectives jumped in to restrain her as she went after the second FBI agent. She told them in no uncertain terms what she would do if they ever broke into her house or talked to her mother again. I so wished I had it on video.

After heading back into the city, I retrieved the GIDEON sample from where I'd stashed it in the abandoned warehouse, then drove to Scrap Brothers' closed yard and hid it among tons of assorted scrap-metal items. Breaux's laptop had already been hidden safely away in a false wall at Pravda after I'd copied all the files the morning I'd seen Kerry Broussard.

I had Kendall retrieve a shopping list of items I might need from the Bronco. He used my circuitous passages out of the Omni Hotel to make sure he wasn't followed, and then he joined me at Scrap Brothers. Since the yard was out of business for the foreseeable future, it seemed as good a place as any to lie low. At least I knew the air-con ran cold.

I remembered the bottle of cheap brandy next to the old phone book and poured myself half a tumbler as Kendall watched. I sat down with my feet up on an old steel desk.

"That rotgut gonna rot your brain and your gut, Coach."

I inwardly cringed at "Coach," embarrassed that I'd stopped being a role model for Kendall or anybody else. "You got that right," I said. I pushed the drink away from me.

We sat there in silence and my mind wandered. I thought about Del Breaux. Each member of the Buyer's Club—Clayton Brandt, Nassir Haddad, Grigory Pelkov, and Tan Chu—had his reasons to want Breaux dead, plus the manpower and resources to make it happen. And as Breaux's lover and confidant, it made sense that Ty Parks would have been taken out, too. Alibis meant nothing, since these principal suspects would not have been at the crime scene but would have been very visible elsewhere.

Then there was Danforth. How convenient to have an out-of-town alibi. But if he were so frightened, why even return to New Orleans?

I'd found him rather easily. Why couldn't the Buyer's Club do the same, if they wanted to? Or the Feds? If Pelkov would kill over shorted merchandise, then he'd have to kill Danforth as well as Breaux. Perhaps Danforth had indeed been located, but the killers were waiting for the right opportunity to do their worst.

Then add the murders of Leroy and Jimmy Jefferson and their employee Herbert into the mix. Tan Chu was the obvious suspect. Or anyone who wanted to keep the brothers from saying the wrong thing in a National Security Investigation. Someone like Clayton Brandt?

Which brought me to the sealed silver container that used to sit about fifty yards from where I now lounged. Decon had said that the container was already sealed when he came to work at Scrap Brothers about eight months ago. There had to be some extremely sensitive contraband in that container. If I'd only put a GPS tracker on both containers, I might have my killers.

"Kendall, we still have signals from the GPS trackers?"

"They done stopped. Late this mornin'. I sent you a text."

"If we don't have the GPS signals, that means Customs must have found the ones I placed in the weapons crates, and Chu's people found the one I put on top of the green cargo container."

"Chu ain't left his warehouse since he seen Brandt. He layin' low."

"That makes two of us. Here, take a look at this." I took the SIM card out of my phone, then powered it up and showed him the photo I'd gotten from Mondrian. "This is the bomb that was in my fridge."

As Kendall studied the photo, I kept thinking about the fact that the bomb hadn't been armed. Maybe Mondrian had been right: the bomber had to bolt before he had time to arm the device. Anyone performing even cursory due diligence would learn that I wasn't the type of guy who backed down, so why fool around with a "message?" As to who had access to a prototype explosive not currently fielded by our military, well, I knew a whole bunch of folks who fit the bill, all of whom I had seriously pissed off in the last forty-eight hours.

"We're playing with fire here. You want to walk away, I understand."

"I ain't goin' nowhere."

"Maybe I should just close this whole thing down. If the Feds want to sell weapons and technology and don't care about people getting murdered, why should I? I should be worried about my own friends and not dead dirtbags like Del Breaux." I rubbed my eyes. One of Kendall's cousins had been killed doing surveillance for me on a case just six months ago. I didn't want to see anything like that happen again.

Kendall stayed silent, and my mind kicked into gear again. If Eric Mondrian were to be believed, a Russian wet team was trying to make my acquaintance. A Chinese team sent by Chu, a Russian team sent by Pelkov. Which begged the question: Why would the CIA expend resources to protect me? Twee Siu, the NOLA CIA station chief and I had history—some good, some bad. We'd briefly been lovers, and I'd tracked down and brought to justice her father's killer. I'd even saved her life. But I had also been paid handsomely for my trouble, and ultimately I'd represented a potential liability to her clandestine operations in the region. I couldn't imagine she felt she owed me anything or cared whether I lived or died.

I kept coming back to Del Breaux's laptop and the GIDEON sample. I had both. And suddenly, the world was coming to my door.

Maybe I looked like I had the weight of the world on my shoulders, maybe he misunderstood my musings, because Kendall brought up something I'd put from my mind, at least temporarily, anyway.

"You know, I sparred with the dead man. Bobby Perdue."

"You're kidding," I said surprised.

"Said he wanted to spar, and I had the L.A. fight comin' so I needed a tune-up. You was busy on some case, so I drove to the North Shore. Slidell. Didn't even finish round one, but I stop the show. Jawboned him 'bout not knowin' how to pull a punch."

"You stopped the round? The first round?"

"Hell yes! I didn't go for no full-boogie fight with a heavyweight. He try to make fun of me, but I say till I seen his sorry ass fightin' in the UFC like me, he be lucky I let him hold my towel."

"You left the cage?"

"For sure."

I stared at the wall behind Kendall for a long beat. "Wish I had done that."

"No, sir. What you done was right. I had a big fight comin'. If I didn't, I'd'a beat his pimply white ass down. Smacked him, same like you did. Don't you know why we all respect you, Coach? 'Cause you ain't afraid to fuckin' fight. Hell, you didn't kill that boy; he killed hisself."

Round two opened up with more of the same: wild punches from Perdue, followed up by what struck me as reckless kicks. Normally, when you throw a round kick at another body, you do it carefully, so as to minimize possible injury to yourself. With Bobby Perdue there was none of that. So I changed my strategy to aggressive checking. I'd be damned if I was going to get injured by this careless fighter. I'd always understood the difference between being hurt and being injured.

When my checking started to annoy him, he stopped with the kicks and went back to the hands. At this point, I decided to keep him away with my foot jab, in hopes I could survive the round. Quickly though, I realized how adept he was at countering my foot jabs and then striking at strange angles.

I was getting tired of his immature game and needed to pull something out of my toolbox, but I wasn't sure what tool it should be.

A sound in the dark startled me awake. All the lights in the Scrap Brothers office were out. My laptop screen had also gone dark. I'd been going over the computer files from Brandt's offices and must have started drifting. Before he left, Kendall had inadvertently made me face what I was trying to duck, a judgment on my guilt or my innocence and what that meant to my life.

But right now there was nothing to think about except the location of the 1911A, because an intruder stood in the room near me. I'd set the piece on the desktop, and my fingers found the cool steel in the blackness, curling into their proper positions as I slowly raised the barrel.

The silhouette stood just inside the door and took a small quiet step forward. As my finger tightened on the trigger . . .

"Easy now. Hope I didn't scare you, if you know what I mean." A pause. "Even though I owe you one."

The thing about falling asleep in a place where you have never slept before is that it's easy to wake up disoriented. Especially if you wake up from being startled by a sound or a touch or maybe just a bad feeling.

I'd completely forgotten I'd called Decon and told him to meet me at Scrap Brothers. I wanted him with me tonight, not Honey, because he was the best B&E guy I'd ever seen. I expected serious security systems at Michoud Building J-19 and figured Decon was the one guy who might be able to get past them.

Building J-19 was a remote, stand-alone structure at the edge of the swamp in the sprawling facility in New Orleans East. We parked just off Old Gentilly Road and jumped the chain-link and barbed-wire fence. We had to slog a couple hundred yards through swampy overgrown bottomland until we emerged at the dead end of Pluto Drive. We stood sweating, mosquitoes dining on our blood, as I checked my battered old Garmin GPS handheld unit.

"That's the building right there," I said, staring at the moonlit cinderblock structure with a flat roof. The building had to be more than fifty years old and didn't look well kept. I removed a special monocular from my backpack and scanned the area. The device would indicate the presence of cameras, even very small lenses. "Don't see any security cameras, either."

"Nonexistent lighting, no sentries," considered Decon, out loud.

"Motion sensors?" I wondered.

We both used night-vision monoculars to carefully study the building and the expanse of open ground surrounding it. We took our time and performed a 360-degree sweep. One end of the structure served as the shipping area. A small forklift and a couple of pallet jacks sat out in the open. Amazingly, the double steel doors near the forklift stood wide open.

"What do you make of the open doors?" I asked.

"This is either a setup or you got some bad information, if you catch my meaning. On the other hand, it could merely be a reflection of the poor work ethic instilled in the federal work force. These people are well paid, get generous pensions and benefits, but they can't be bothered to lock the frigging door when they leave. Do you know how many paid holidays a federal employee—"

"Setup doesn't make sense. This is the right building, though. Look at those big-rig tire tracks in the dirt where a driver went off the pavement while backing up. And the forklift and pallet jacks confirm it."

"Then after you," said Decon.

I slowly walked up to the building and right in through the open double doors with Decon a few steps behind me. I used my SureFire to light up the large windowless room, packed to the rafters with weapons, ammunition, electronics, and other military gear whose function I couldn't determine.

"Close those doors in case a security patrol wanders by."

As Decon secured the doors, I checked the stock. I saw cases of experimental ammunition. There were super-small drones—the type deployed at platoon level. How could these be surplus? I knew them to be in short supply for army units on the ground in Central Asia. I kept looking. There were racks and racks of exotic electronics. I saw rugged communications sets, laptop computers in hard cases. Stacked in a corner were shallow wooden crates with rope handles on the ends. They held land mines. Mines that resembled butterflies, identical to the one found in my refrigerator. I helped myself to one of the deadly devices and stashed it in my backpack.

I continued a cursory search and found boxes of gadgets that looked like pagers, but I didn't dare press any buttons.

"Hey, I got some strange-looking grenades over here. In rainbow colors, like Baskin-Robbins."

"What do you make of these ink pens?" I held up a black ink pen from a cigar-box-sized steel case. It was identical to the pens I had seen in the Jefferson brothers' file cabinet.

"Exploding ink pen. I wouldn't mess with that, if you know what I mean."

"How would you know what they are?"

He walked over and joined me. "Just kidding man. But think about it: what the hell else would it be? This ain't Office Depot, this is an ammo depot, if you get my drift. Careful with the pen. Who knows what it will do?"

I put the pen back, and we entered a big adjoining room full of folding chairs and tables. Samples of all the items we had just seen in the stockroom were carefully displayed on the folding tables that ringed the room. Brochures accompanied some of the items. I found the black-ink-pen display and, sure enough, it was an explosive device. Twist the cap, and if it's not twisted back in thirty seconds, it will explode with the capacity to kill every human being in a ten-by-twelve-foot room. I took one and dropped it into a cargo pocket of my 5.11's.

I checked the area. These two rooms and some restrooms comprised the entire building.

"Some black-bag job this is; we could have brown-bagged it. We could have brought snacks and played Parcheesi, know what I'm saying?"

"So this is where they hold the actual auction," I said. "They display the items, customers can look and touch, read a brochure, then Brandt or an underling starts the bidding. The orders are filled in the warehouse room, trucks probably standing by to haul the stuff away. I still can't get over those doors being wide open just now."

"I was in the military, once upon a time," said Decon. He paused for a moment to appreciate the surprise that must have shown on my face. "I've seen this kind of thing before, especially with Special Operations. Many times. It's an arrogance. An attitude. Michoud is a secure federal facility. They know local crooks like me won't trudge through the swamp like you just made me do. So the guys running this yard sale here, they just got lazy. They think they're above it all, anyway, if you know what I'm insinuating. They're so special, nothing can happen to them."

"We'll see about that."

It took me about twenty-five minutes to plant a few pinhole video cams with audio in both of the rooms, then Decon and I beat feet. We trudged back toward the white Yukon and stopped at the chain-link fence.

"You told me once that you had been incarcerated, but not by law enforcement. 'A prisoner of conscience,' you said. Was that when you were in the military?"

"Yes, sir. I spent quite a bit of time in the brig. Then I was given a medical discharge, but you won't find any record of that."

"Why not?"

"It's been expunged. All of my records have been purged. You see, I don't exist. Never have, if you can appreciate the contradiction in that remark."

I couldn't.

"Did you have a chance to talk with any of those Chinese TDF drivers?" I asked. Computer software had recorded the calls Decon had made on the cell I gave him, and I'd carefully listened to those calls, so I knew if he'd be lying to me.

"I planted the seeds, just as you ordered, cap. I pretended to be in a hurry to move the merchandise, and I hinted I might take a bus to Houston to visit the Russian, German, and French consulates to solicit their interest. The Chinese have the number of the cell phone you gave me. Let's see what happens."

What he'd just described was exactly what he'd done. I didn't completely trust Decon—he was a crook, after all—but I had virtually eliminated him from my murder-suspect list. I suspected Harding had taken Decon's rabble-rousing threats too literally. Decon was a burglar and thief; few such criminals ever became physically violent. I handed him a hundred-dollar bill. "For your time."

"I didn't do a thing tonight, no locks or alarms. I almost feel bad taking this."

I reached to take the hundred back, but Decon stuffed it into his pants pocket.

"I *almost* feel bad," he said, with a smile, "but I know that you *do* feel bad." His face turned serious. "You're hurting, I can see it. But I said this before: redemption is within your grasp. Find a mirror tonight, look into it, and tell yourself that you forgive yourself. Look into your own eyes, and see what happens. Maybe even tell yourself that you love yourself. Say it out loud."

"Thanks for your concern, but that sounds like some woo-woo hippie shit. That doesn't sound like the guy who was talking to me the other night about the necessary application of extrajudicial extreme prejudice against your garden-variety dirtbag."

"I'm a complex guy, full of dichotomies, if you can appreciate the incongruity."

"What branch of the service were you in, the namby-pamby navy? You suffer from PTSD due to some bad liberty in Thailand, sailor?

Maybe the chilies were a little too hot, and when you took a dump your ass burned so you put in for a Purple Heart? Let's delete any future discussions of my personal life so I don't have to rip you a new dirt chute, okay?"

"Yes, sir, macho man. So how you dealing with the emotional roller coaster? Couple of extra whiskeys every night? Maybe you should try absinthe. It opens up a whole new world."

"If I ever start sleeping in a tomb, I promise I'll take up absinthe."

CHAPTER NINETEEN

The 8 A.M. meeting Honey summoned me to in the office of NOPD Police Chief Harold Pointer marked the first time I'd ever been invited into the hallowed chamber. And hopefully the last. Ask any police officer in any big-city department and you will learn that usually the brass don't climb the ladder because they were good street cops or well liked by the rank and file or even remotely competent at basic managerial skills demanded in the private sector.

The brass primarily become brass due to favoritism, blackmail, brownnosing, political connections, nepotism, large campaign donations (as in a sheriff's department), and by having avoided making career-gutting gaffes, decisions, and comments—meaning most of them were spineless sycophants who could only be relied upon to put a knife in your back in order to cover their asses, but not to watch your back when the chips were down. This didn't apply to all the captains and lieutenants at NOPD, but generally it was a good rule of thumb for higher-ranking officers in many police departments.

Sometimes a person, male or female, who had clawed the way to the top truly understood how to wield power, truly understood what the outer limits were at having an armed mobile force at his or her beck and call, and was truly a son of a bitch/bastard/whore whose finely honed sense of survival cut every which way, including loose. And such persons, knowing their days were numbered, numbered with small figures not large ones, could be a spectacle in action. Chief Pointer was now such an individual.

I was the last one into his office and looked like a turd on a plate: I still had scabbed cuts and bruises on my face from my original alter- cation with Ding Tong; I wore yesterday's clothes and hadn't show- ered or shaved; dark half-moons hung under my eyes from lack of sleep. I sat down next to Honey. At least she could use makeup to semimask her fatigue. Honey and I had caught up over the phone early this morning and brought each other up to speed. The big news item for me being that the TDF Shipping offices had burned down over- night in a suspected arson fire. One body found inside was thought to be that of the owner, Eddie Liu, since his car was in the parking lot. Nightshift detectives were still on the scene. If Chu was eliminating potential witnesses, he was doing a pretty good job.

Honey and I both held paper cups of nasty coffee as the chief read a report on his desk that Honey had just turned in. She'd been briefing him several times a day, which was highly unusual even on a Five Alarm high-profile case, as they were known. He'd granted her special status in the Homicide Section, which I knew was causing some prob- lems with her immediate superiors and coworkers. Pointer had taken her under his wing, ordered her to report directly to him, and that was that. But I'd advised her to copy reports to and seek advice from her supervisors in Homicide—Detectives Mackie and Kruger—as a mat- ter of courtesy and to try to mitigate blowback. Since just before she'd made detective six months ago, she'd brought nothing but good press to the department, the most recent being the young quadruple mur- derer she corralled in his FEMA trailer. She was a golden goose, and Pointer made it clear to all and sundry that you don't mess with his golden goose. It behooved him to give Honey what she needed, be- cause he was fully expecting another golden egg.

The two FBI CI-3 guys sat silently on the opposite side of Pointer's desk from us. The shorter one had a black eye, recently installed by my cuddle-buddy. They both looked like their hemorrhoids were acting up. Pointer's two bodyguards, huge black plainclothes officers in nice threads, leaned casually on either side of the closed door. The fact that the chief had his personal muscle in the room for this meeting suggested fireworks might be expected. In spite of my long war with the chief, I liked both of his bodyguards and had known them for years.

Everyone waited for the chief to finish reading the report. Pointer was an average-looking black man of average height and average weight. He had average intelligence and had been an average detective when he first befriended and covered up for a local politico who would later become mayor, a man with a penchant for high school girls. That friendship was eventually rewarded by the position the chief now held. That the relationship had frayed badly was merely a testament to the finite quantity of loyalty one can expect to get in this town, especially when the winds shift.

"Saint James," said Chief Pointer, "the FBI CI-3 gentlemen here, Agents Minniear and Gibbs, have just threatened me with losing federal funding for the department if I don't turn over the murder investigation of five local citizens to them, along with all of the evidence, including the two point five million dollars you and Detective Baybee found in Del Breaux's home. They're claiming some national security bullshit. What do you say to that?"

"I think their investigation will be the cover-up, Chief."

"Don't they know that TDF burned down with Eddie Liu inside? Shouldn't it be six murders they're trying to cover up?" asked Honey.

"All right, I've had enough of this crap." Agent Minniear, the one with the black eye, stood up in high dudgeon. "You were supposed to give us the two and a half million yesterday, Chief. You're screwing with us, so DC is going to crawl up your ass."

"Sit down, agent; you're not going anywhere yet," said the chief.

Minniear reluctantly sat back down.

"We need your case notes and all the evidence you haven't turned in, and, yes, that's for six murders, to include all the documents you got from TDF yesterday, Detective Baybee," said Gibbs to Honey and me. "We especially want Del Breaux's DOD-issued laptop and a certain item that you have eight-by-ten photos of."

"That item was in Tan Chu's green cargo container at the port. Customs locked it back into Chu's container, which Chu now has possession of. You guys know this, because you're his security detail. I'm just a consultant," I said.

"Bullshit," said Minniear.

"Saint James, do you have the items they're talking about?" asked the chief.

"The lab and the evidence warehouse have everything we developed on the case," said Honey, answering for me. "Sir, you already have all of my paperwork, the reports, appropriate forms, my personal notes."

This time both FBI agents stood and took steps toward the door. "Your officers are lying," said Minniear to the chief. "And they'll be going down, just like you."

"Gentlemen—"

"We're finished here," snapped Gibbs. "If there's any problem at the evidence room, I'll get a federal warrant."

"I said sit your sorry white asses down!"

The chief's two bodyguards blocked the door with about seven hundred pounds of muscle and bone. Minniear apparently was unlucky or not too bright. He tried to force his way out and got shoved so hard he stumbled back and almost crashed into the chief's desk.

Gibbs looked like he was ready to pull his gun. "Who the hell do you think you are, with your crooked little police department down here in Shitsville! I'll put you in a federal—"

"No, who the hell do you carpet bagging pricks think *you* are, coming into my town and threatening me, because you made a mess with your crooked, illegal, gun-running spy shit!" yelled the chief, pounding his fist on his desk. "You take a crap in my backyard and then you come here and try and rub my nose in it? And threaten my funding? Uh-uh! No. You rolling tape, Saint James?"

"Um, yes, sir, Chief."

"Good."

"That's illegal!"

"Not in Louisiana," I said. "One-party consent to record a conversation, and I'm the one consenting party."

"Now you listen to me, *agents.* Detectives Baybee and Saint James are off the case. And his tape won't go public. You get custody of any physical evidence as it exists and the six case files. And in return, my funding doesn't get pulled, it gets *doubled. Doubled.* Starting now!" roared Pointer.

"You have to be kidding. Is it something in the water down here? Is it too much gumbo? The only thing that will get doubled, Chief, is the amount of time you will do in a federal pen," said Gibbs.

"You know, Chief," I said, "all of those TDF semitrucks pulling out of Michoud and going to the port, I bet there are all kinds of violations going on with that. Improper placarding, forged driver's logs, equipment violations, mislabeling of cargo. Maybe some officers could look into that. You know, set up rolling checkpoints. A thorough search of every last truck that leaves Michoud. Be something if arms smuggling through the port went public, wouldn't it?"

"That's right," added Honey. "Some of the documents I took yesterday from the shipping company office? TDF picked up 'crates of eggs' from Michoud two weeks ago. Those 'eggs' were sent, unrefrigerated, by ship to Caracas. Then freight-forwarded on to Lima. Then to Singapore. Finally to Tianjin, China."

"There must be a big demand in China for rotten Louisiana eggs," I said.

"You didn't know Michoud has a chicken ranch?" Honey asked.

Gibbs and Minniear stared hard at Honey and me.

"Even if my officer's interdictions didn't go public, any illicit cargo would get impounded and stored in our evidence warehouse for who knows how long," added Chief Pointer, going along with Honey and me. "And we all know how much evidence disappears out of that warehouse. Or maybe you're not aware of that, agents."

The two FBI men looked at each other.

"Chief, I hope you're not suggesting that the money seized at Del Breaux's house—money that you were supposed to hand over to federal custody this morning—has gone missing."

"I'm not suggesting that; I'm stating it. Perhaps you are unaware of this, but since the Storm destroyed our evidence room, we have been leasing a warehouse on the South Peters Street Wharf to use as temporary evidence storage. There are huge holes in the roof of that building; there's no air-conditioning; it's overrun with rats. And the Evidence Unit shares that building with the quartermaster, as well as with commercial vendors. *Civilians.* We don't even have secure control of who goes in and what comes out. As of this moment, we can't locate the bag with the two point five million. If the federal government had granted us funding to purchase a secure building to house our evidence room, we wouldn't have this problem. Of course, if the federal government had fixed the levees right in the first place—"

"Well, maybe we need to open an investigation into where that money went, Chief." Minniear practically spat as he spoke.

"Be my guest. My police department has no budget for security cameras, scanners, or even locks for all of the doors at the evidence warehouse. The place is a sieve. Cash, drugs, and property have gone missing. And the city owes over one hundred thousand dollars in back rent for the building. I suggest you focus your investigation on the sweet old Uptown white lady landlord who justifiably wants her rent money. She has already threatened in writing to seize collateral in terms of what we have stored there."

"Holy fucking shit. New Orleans," said Gibbs, shaking his head and pulling out his cell phone. "The shakedown begins as soon as you cross the parish line and never ends. Doubled funding, huh?"

"You're not going to recommend he gets it?" asked Minniear.

"What do you care? It's not your money," Gibbs retorted.

I sat there in semi-awe. I'd never seen the exercise of such raw political power. Chief Pointer, who had held a vendetta against me and had essentially destroyed my law-enforcement career, showed none of the old utter hate for me. He simply very neutrally used me as a tool in his reverse shakedown of the Feds.

The chief had essentially just told the FBI to its face that he was stealing the two and a half million and that they could go take a long walk on a short pier. Plus they were doubling his funding. One had to admire his *cojones*. He knows he'll be out on the street soon, so he's cashing in while he can.

It only took seven minutes for Gibbs to get the word that the funding would be doubled. They didn't mention the Breaux money again, but they got in a parting shot at me.

"Impersonating an FBI agent, I hear," said Gibbs.

"Why would I insult myself like that?" I countered.

"He's not even a real detective," said Minniear.

"Oh, yes, he is," said Honey.

I turned in time to catch a gold badge, a detective's shield, tossed at me by the chief. "Saint James has been officially recommissioned."

I wasn't sure what the chief was up to, but I knew it was a gag, part of the show, so I played along.

"Hey guys, before you go away mad, do you know what FBI stands for?" I asked.

"Eat shit," said Minniear.

"No, it doesn't stand for that, although I understand you had to eat some yesterday when my partner decked you. It stands for 'Fucked-up Beyond Imagination.'"

The two agents eye-fucked me for a second, the human wall of bodyguards parted, and they left. I took a sip of now-lukewarm coffee and leaned forward to hand the gold badge back to the chief.

"You owe me sixty dollars for the shield," he said.

My jaw dropped. Then I realized he was just screwing with me. But wait . . . why was Honey smiling? She wouldn't go in on a joke like that. She knew how much getting a gold shield had meant to me when I was on the force. That I'd been denied it was the main reason I resigned.

"Well, are you in or not? You and I have a lot of water under the bridge, but I'm willing to wipe the slate clean. Are you?"

What a question. This was not what I thought I'd be dealing with this morning. Wipe the slate clean? It was a big-ass slate he referred to, covering most of five years. The hate I held on to for the chief had almost become a physical object, it was so real. I knew it wasn't healthy, but what was I supposed to do, forgive him?

I flashed on a hokey e-mail I'd gotten recently, supposedly composed by some ninety-year-old lady in Iowa who had written down her rules to live by. I usually don't read that kind of dippy crap sent by well-meaning friends, but I'd needed a distraction from thinking about Bobby Perdue, so I'd read the old lady's list. Two things simply jumped out at me. The first was "Use the good china today." I liked that and immediately popped open a cold bottle of French champagne I'd been saving for a holiday and dug out a crystal champagne coupe from a box, stemware I'd bought but never used because it was supposed to be for a special occasion. Well, the old lady had taught me that the special occasion was being alive that day. The other thing she wrote that hit me was "Forgive everyone, everything." What a concept.

As I stood there with Honey and the chief staring at me, I remembered a Japanese judo instructor I'd had when I was a teenager. He had told me that to "forgive and forget" was bullshit. He'd said it was important to "Forgive but *remember*." What the hell . . . I knew that holding on to the old anger wasn't helping me any.

"Sure, clean slate," I said.

"I don't want you back full-time; you're not in the rotation. I just want you for the Five Alarm cases, working with Detective Baybee. The high-profile, high-publicity cases: a dead prominent citizen, a dismembered child, a murder scene with more than three stiffs—that kind of thing. And of course, you have to deliver. A new chief comes in and might very well pull the plug on this arrangement, so it could be very short-lived. The rest of the Homicide Section will resent you, try to sabotage you, so get used to it. Does that work for you?"

"Yes. I'm in."

"Good. I don't like it that you were trying to help us out and somebody put a bomb in your house. If you were a real cop, they might not have done that. And I don't like it that those assholes went to Detective Baybee's mom's house and spooked her. So to hell with them.

"But don't make the mistake of thinking that I'm backing you two up. I'm not. I'm giving you a little more rope. You can either hang yourselves or hang a killer. You are both officially off the case. I will swear up and down to everyone from the governor to a newspaper boy on the street that I ordered you off the case. But unofficially, I want you to deliver me a headline-grabbing homicide arrest in the next forty-eight hours. I'm expecting it, is that clear? Your continued tenure in the department depends on it, Detective Saint James. That badge has a two-day expiration date on it unless you close the case."

"Yes, sir," Honey and I said at the same time.

"Sign here on the dotted line. We'll take care of the rest of your processing-in paperwork and equipment issues after you apprehend the killers."

I signed. I was officially NOPD again. I turned and took a step toward the door.

"Saint James, are you forgetting something?"

I looked to Honey, then the chief.

"My money?"

"Oh, yeah." I counted out sixty bucks but thought better about asking for a receipt.

"You're behind this." I stood in front of Honey in the dreary ground-floor hallway of Broad Street headquarters, dull brown linoleum under our feet. The building had been badly damaged by the Storm, and repairs were still underway, one year later.

"I need a partner flashing a badge, not a piece of paper." She couldn't stop grinning. "Besides, Pointer's desperate. So don't let it go to your head."

I looked at the shield in my hand and felt complete neutrality. I had so coveted obtaining a detective's badge when I was an officer. Now I had one, via an instant recommissioning, and I felt nothing. The situation was an anomaly and surely wouldn't last. I held little confidence we could solve the case in forty-eight hours. And to be honest, I wasn't sure I wanted to be NOPD. Even part-time. But since the badge might help me solve this case, I'd use it for all it was worth.

Honey handed me a leather badge holder from her purse. I attached the gold shield, hooked it to my belt, and covered it with my shirttails. She smiled like she'd just given me an engagement ring and I'd said yes.

"I'm afraid the shield might cramp my style. I've gotten used to operating in a much more gray area than when I was on the force, if you know what I'm saying." I stopped myself. "Damn, I need to stop hanging with Decon, I'm starting to sound like him."

"We've got two days, so don't change your MO. Okay, hard charger? In fact, we need to go balls to the wall."

"Exactly. So screw being in hiding. I'm not convinced there's any hit team after me."

"The bomb was pretty convincing."

"It wasn't armed. I'm thinking it was a ploy, immediately followed up by unsolicited contact from our old CIA buddy, Twee Siu, using Eric Mondrian as the conduit."

"You think the CIA is in on the arms smuggling, too?"

"Knowing Twee, how could we rule it out?"

Honey nodded. "We should rule it in." She checked a small spiral notebook. "When is the next auction at Michoud?"

"The last auction you mean? Tomorrow night, according to the appointment book I copied from Brandt's executive secretary. They have a big dinner at Restaurant August every Saturday night and then caravan out to Michoud for the auction. I checked with the restaurant, and the usual private dining room is booked by Clayton Brandt. Dinner for thirty-five people."

"A moving sale. Everything must go."

"What we want is a going-out-of-business sale. We need to stop this crap or they'll just set up shop someplace like Galveston or Mobile."

"I'm seeing a judge right now. Try to get a warrant for Tan Chu's place. Facts are thin, but it might fly."

I nodded. "Honey, not to change the subject, but . . . thanks. You're the best thing that's ever happened to me," I blurted out without thinking.

She bit her lower lip as she looked at me. As her eyes started to moisten, she spun away and hurried off down the hallway.

Honey showing emotion again? What was the world coming to? She must have sold the chief quite a bill of goods to convince him to reinstate me. She had seriously jeopardized her own career in an effort to give me something that had once meant the world to me but that had been denied. And she wanted to help me heal. She was singlehandedly trying to evict Bobby Perdue from my aura and risking her life to do it. For that reason alone—Honey's safety—I wanted to wrap this case ASAP. I had some errands to run, and it occurred to me I needed to go back to my loft to get my body armor. Like Mondrian said, it doesn't pay to be cocky.

CHAPTER TWENTY

I dropped by my loft to retrieve my body armor, careful to log on to the Internet and remotely check my security video for an intruder before even stepping out of the rented white Yukon. Upstairs I saw that the bomb squad had made a mess in my kitchen, but considering the way the place looked anyway, it wasn't that different. I've been neat all of my life, a way of rebelling against a slovenly mother. Only in the last month had I gone frat house.

The big stainless steel fridge, now missing sections of both sides, was running; I could hear the compressor. The bomb boys hadn't unplugged it. As I stood there wondering if the Sub-Zero could be repaired and donated somewhere, I caught sight of a moving reflection in the shiny stainless steel door. I instantly dropped to the floor, and three shots rang out, the rounds puncturing the fridge I'd just stood in front of. No time to think, I crouched, shielded by the massive kitchen island, and squeezed off two rounds from the 1911A over the black granite countertop. Unaimed covering fire was better than none, then I scrambled to the other side of the island, peeked around the corner, and saw a shadowy figure open fire—I saw the muzzle flash—and the bullet creased my temple and skull above the left ear; I didn't feel anything, but sticky red blood oozed onto my face as I squeezed off two more rounds, the booming .45 sounding like a how-itzer within the confines of my walls as the smell of nitrate filled my nostrils. My shots were half aimed this time, trying to find the figure that disappeared amid stacks of unopened moving boxes.

So much for my theory of no hit team. A bomb yesterday, a gunfight in the house today; I was coming around to the concept that some-body wanted me dead. They had to be serious pros since they beat the alarms and the video cams.

Focus, I told myself. *Four caps busted. Six had been in the stick and one up the pipe, so three more rounds for the cannon. Plus two mags holding six each in the paddle holder. Plus seven in the backup Glock.* If I needed more than my remaining twenty-two rounds, I was in deep shit. *Extra mags and ammo in my locked safe room. A Ruger 9mm in the main living area in a cigar box on the table behind the couch, if the killer hasn't already found it.*

Check that, *killers,* as several shotgun blasts from a different direc-tion tore into the kitchen island where I crouched, sending slivers of granite countertop spraying into the side of my face.

I pulled my cell, put it on speaker, and speed-dialed a number that rang in central dispatch. I set the phone down and pulled a spare magazine.

"Dispatch."

"Officer needs help, Six-zero-two South Peters Street, upstairs," I said loudly. "This is Detective Saint James, badge eight eighty-eight. Shots fired—"

The killer with the shotgun must have had a semiauto breakdown, because a nonstop stream of pellets demolished my kitchen, and I caught a few in my left thigh. I heard myself moan as circles of red im-mediately appeared in my jeans. I figured the first shooter was closing in from the other side of the island while his partner laid down cover-ing fire, so I fast-crawled that way and sprang to my feet, firing. The first two rounds missed the short, stocky blond guy—*Russian,* my mind told me in an instant—I could see his eyes were blue and he hadn't shaved this morning. It occurred to me that perhaps it was superstition on his part, not to shave on the day he carried out a wet assignment.

Funny, I could hear myself think, but I couldn't seem to hear anything else anymore, except the Sub-Zero compressor, laboring behind me. The blond guy squeezed off a round from what looked like a 9mm, but I couldn't hear the shot. He stumbled on a box on the floor, causing his torso to lurch left, disrupting his aim as he continued to fire and catapulting him into the trajectory of the third and last round from my weapon.

The blue-eyed guy went down, and I knew he would never be getting up. I did a combat reload on the run, charging toward the shotgun operator, who had ducked behind the wall also to reload. I saw the black barrel sticking out from the edge of the wall and emptied the new magazine, sending all six high-capacity rounds into the red bricks as I ran forward, at the same time reaching for my last mag.

I say "on the run," but my feet felt like I wore iron boots as I seemed to move slower than a disgruntled DMV employee. I'd practically made it to the wall as I ejected the spent mag and swung the new one toward the pistol butt.

Then the operator stepped into the open and swung the long gun. I hesitated, shocked for good reason by the visage I stared at, and only just had time to raise my right hand to block the barrel arcing toward my head. The front sight ripped open a deep cut on my hand and the hard hit knocked the 1911A from my grasp.

She was on me like a cat, going for my elbow. I jerked right and kicked her below the knee. It was a weak kick but still had to hurt her, since I wear steel-toed boots. I swung, using the magazine as a striking tool, but she sprang back out of harm's way.

Jeez, she was beautiful. Stark black hair, pale skin now flushed, and eyes almost the same color green as mine. We both stood at just under six feet, nose to nose. A blade flashed. I momentarily grasped her knife-hand forearm, but she spun free. She had significant upper body strength and muscular thighs like she'd spent a lifetime running slaloms. The upper body of a tennis pro, the legs of a downhill gold medalist, the face of a fashion model. I'd be in heaven were it not for the fact she intended to send me to hell.

I backpedaled and pulled my Benchmade automatic folder, opening the blade without looking, as she came at me. She knew how to knife-fight. We feinted and parried in an incredibly fast series of moves, as if we'd choreographed them and practiced for months. I operated on pure instinct now; I'd entered a zone of perception that was something akin to pure consciousness, but in a reactive, purely defensive mode.

We both took serious, significant cuts on our forearms as the death dance moved back toward the kitchen area. A new noise impinged on my consciousness. A tinny, high-frequency, plaintive sound. Imploring voices from my cell phone, disjointed and not understood. Immaterial now, as every grain of my focus had to remain on the big, buff, green-eyed brunette with a fine ass and huge breasts who was trying to give me the Big Shank.

She spun and caught me with a lucky foot strike, her heavy boot breaking some fingers and knocking the knife from my already cut and banged-up right hand. She lunged before I could recover, and we locked handgrips, the six-inch-blade tanto knife she held inching toward my neck. I couldn't grip her knife hand well because of my busted fingers, giving her a distinct advantage. My weak-side hand battled for control with her weak-side hand as she used her powerful thighs to wedge my hips firmly against the kitchen island.

Kind of ironic that the Russian chick used a knife made by Cold Steel, an American company that itself used Japanese steel for the blades. A good tanto is a nasty thing, and when the point entered a human neck, it was like the last period in a biography.

She kneed me, trying for my groin but missing as I gauged my options. That didn't take long because I couldn't think of any. Her knife hand, which I could only grip with two functioning fingers, felt like it was attached to a pneumatic arm, she was so strong. I slowly ceded ground in the death grasp.

My weak-side hand and hers were also locked in battle, so there was no way I could reach behind me for the Glock in my waistband. I should have pulled it earlier instead of indulging in the edged-weapons battle, but 20/20 hindsight is only instructive as an after-action learning tool. She used her weight to force me farther back over the counter, making a head butt on my part out of the question. And I couldn't risk kicking her without losing balance.

For a moment I felt lost in her beautiful emerald eyes, tranquil as a Caribbean lagoon, weakening my will to survive. I thought maybe I deserved what she was trying to give me. But that was my negative ego talking, and I instantly cast that thought aside. I didn't want to die, but for some reason, I didn't want to kill her, either. An untenable position that I needed to rectify in the next few seconds.

I remembered the karambit in my front waistband. My weak-side hand was stronger than hers, so I brought our hands down toward my belt. Her eyes flashed a recognition that I was up to something as the tanto edged closer to my neck. All I needed was to get my index finger into the hole on the karambit's handle and then pull up sharply. The blade would automatically open and slice right into her belly. I could gut her.

I felt the tip of the tanto touch my skin. This was a slow-motion race now. *Fuck you Bobby Perdue, you son of a bitch. You asshole. What did I ever do to you?* One month ago, I would have already put this killer down. Instead, because I had let myself go to seed, because my thinking was clouded, because my reaction times slowed, because I now second-guessed my use of violence, even to defend myself, she was about to win the race.

My left hand touched the karambit, but I felt the tanto pierce my skin. Damn, I'd lost. I could only spit in her face as a statement of contempt for her and everything she stood for.

Then a puff of red exploded from her forehead, her green eyes rolled up in her head, and she slowly slid down to the floor.

Behind her stood a slender Vietnamese-American woman in diamonds and a black cocktail dress, an LBD, actually, that hugged her perfectly proportioned form like a long-lost lover. Her makeup, silky hair, and nails were perfect, as usual. She looked like a million dollars but was actually worth thirty. Using a black gloved-hand, she held a revolver with a sound suppressor, smoke spiraling out from the business end. Conventional wisdom states that revolvers can't be silenced, but the KGB and the CIA had long ago done just that, with a special design to prevent the sound-causing exploding gasses from escaping the cylinder. It was bad form, after all, to leave spent shell casings on the ground, as semiautos did, if one could avoid it.

I teetered against the half-demolished kitchen island, a disoriented, light-headed, bloody, broken mess, shot in a couple of places and bleeding heavily from knife wounds in several more, but all I could manage to say in a whisper was "Thanks for stopping by."

"I heard you want to talk to me. Make it quick; I'm busy," said New Orleans CIA Station Chief Twee Siu.

I had plenty of questions for Twee, but instead of quizzing her, I collapsed to the floor.

It's embarrassing passing out in front of a beautiful woman before exchanging contact information, but so be it. I woke up surrounded by coppers in the ER at Touro, still the only functioning hospital for adults in the city of New Orleans one year after the killer Storm came to town. There was no sign of Twee. Honey held my hand as they wheeled me into surgery, and I could see that she'd been crying.

I was actually in fair shape. I'd lost a good bit of blood, so I got a few units. Just before the anesthesiologist, who was listening to techno pop on his MP3 player, put me under, I reminded them I wasn't there for a sex change or a vasectomy. That got a smile from the head surgeon, who said he was going to remove four shotgun pellets from my thigh, one a bit too close to the groin for any man's liking. I'd also lost a small chunk of meat from my left calf—a round from the blond guy I hadn't realized I'd taken. The doc said he would stitch up the deeper knife wounds, bandage the others, tape my broken fingers onto splints, pull the fléchettes of granite out of my face. The neck wound wasn't very deep and somehow hadn't hit anything vital, so he said I was one lucky SOB. I told him not to bandage the graze on my scalp because it might interfere with my social life. I had more instructions for him, but they put me under just to shut me up.

I eventually found myself in a private room requesting a whiskey and a smoke from a pretty, shapely black nurse who'd brought in my personal effects. I'd asked for her cell-phone number too, but before she could respond, Honey barged in and the nurse departed.

Honey pretended she hadn't been worried about me. "I'm not sure if you're worth all the trouble you cause."

"I'm definitely not worth it. Do we know if there are more of these people?" I asked.

"We don't."

"Russians?"

"Russians. The chief is pissed. You were shot in the line of duty. Meaning he can't fire you. No one can. Ever. It's a free lifetime pass. And you're a hero."

"I'm no hero. I got my ass handed to me."

"Your call to dispatch? It was recorded; all incoming calls are. They rebroadcast it on the police frequency. Fifty squad cars from all over the city were racing to your loft while they listened to the shootout. Word spread fast you took out two professional assassins."

I started to say something about Twee killing the woman, then stopped myself. "Was I found with a silenced pistol in my hand?"

"Well, yeah. You took it from her and shot her, right?"

I hesitated answering. I couldn't lie to Honey, but I had a problem here. Twee Siu had saved my life. She must have put the gun in my hand after I passed out to keep her participation unknown. So if I told what I knew, I'd be ratting her out. I'd saved her life once, and now she'd returned the favor. It wasn't for personal glory, for trying to take credit for killing *two* assassins; I simply couldn't dime Twee out.

Practical matters also needed to be considered. Since I sought her help, why piss her off?

And in a larger sense, I owed her, even before the events of today. Twee had entered my life when I was practically destitute in the wake of the Storm. Even though she had used me like a dishrag, the result of our association had created the new Cliff St. James. I'd become the most sought-after private investigator in New Orleans and had earned a ton of money. Twee Siu had been the catalyst for it all.

"I don't have any memory of shooting the Russian woman." I could parse words with the best of them, if given the chance. I wasn't lying to Honey by saying this, I simply withheld pertinent facts.

"They cut a hole in your roof with a chainsaw to get in. They were waiting for you. You don't remember anything?"

"I remember plenty, but I was bleeding out, I was disoriented. I have no memory of shooting her." I hated misleading Honey; I'd tell her the truth eventually. "Who's handling the crime scene?"

"Lieutenant Carondolet handles all officer-involved shootings, but the chief—"

Honey and I were distracted by a commotion just outside the door to my room, as the unmistakable voice of Kendall Bullard seemed to be arguing with the police guard. Honey crossed to the door, gestured that it was okay for Kendall to enter, and the UFC fighter hurried into the room holding a laptop.

"I know you too mean to die, Coach, so I weren't worried 'bout that. But this, you gots to hear now."

"What is it?"

"From Brandt's office, those boys who work for him, 'bout fifteen minutes ago."

"The bugged computers of his staff, yeah?"

Kendall nodded, then clicked on an audio file on the laptop, and we all listened.

"Things are getting too weird around here, Mario. I mean, I didn't sign on for this."

"Why, what just happened?"

"I was in the general's office to have him sign these contracts, when he got a call on the encrypted line. Pelkov demanded the general give him five hundred thousand dollars' worth of credit because two of his people had just been killed by Saint James."

"What?"

"No kidding. The general told him to piss off and train better assassins next time."

"Jerry, you need to forget you heard that."

"I need a new job, is what I need."

Kendall clicked off the recording.

"That settles it." I swung my legs over the side of the bed. The deep cuts hurt the worst, like I could still feel the blade slicing through me. "I need some clothes."

"You're in no condition to—"

"I need my truck, too. The big one, not the Bronco."

"Hey cowboy," came a voice from the doorway.

Detectives Mackie and Kruger entered the room.

"I don't even want to ask where you got that recording. But you're not in this alone. Every homicide dick in the city has been in fifth gear for the last three hours," said Mackie. "Even the night-shift crew came in."

"The shooters were checked into the Embassy Suites. Posed as a vacationing couple from Poland. Flew in yesterday. We ran their prints, and they had a couple local arrests up in New York City," said Kruger.

"Remember all the New York cops who were down here after the Storm helping us out?" asked Mackie.

"Yeah, there were hundreds of them. They stayed for a couple months," I said. "The department issued a special patch in honor of that."

"Well, I got to be good buddies with a detective from their Russian-mob unit in Brooklyn. I called him and told him these perps tried to take out one of our guys. Turns out there's a secret grand jury up there that had authorized a wiretap on a Russian-mob nightclub owner. The mobster got a call two days ago from Grigory Pelkov requesting two 'units' be sent down here to mop up a spill. Pelkov specifically requested 'Nati.'"

"'Nati' is the nickname of the Amazon you capped," said Kruger.

"Gentlemen," I said, "and Detective Baybee, it's time for an unfriendly drink with a fat-ass Ukrainian."

CHAPTER TWENTY-ONE

It violated procedure that I wasn't sitting at a desk shuffling paper-work until the officer-involved shooting investigation finished, but everyone, including the crime-scene ramrod Lieutenant Carondolet knew Honey and I were on special assignment reporting directly to the chief, so screw procedure. Honey wanted me to stay in the hospital, of course, but hospitals aren't places to get well, they're places to get fixed, and I done got fixed good enough.

I took a peek through a window, watching as the chief held a press conference on the front steps of Touro, announcing that an NOPD detective had been seriously wounded while taking two highly dangerous killers from out of town off the streets. He adroitly spun my near-death into another triumph for the department. Pointer will have a career in PR waiting for him somewhere, whenever he finally gets the boot.

Meantime, a convoy formed up in the rear of the hospital. A uniform delivered my special-occasion truck to one of Touro's back doors. Painted in the black and gold of the New Orleans Saints, the Ford F-350 dually featured a five-inch lift, long bed, extended cab, over-sized tires, custom heavy-duty bumpers, and a massive wraparound front grill guard. It was a monster and I felt mean.

Kendall had gone ahead to reconnoiter with high-powered binoculars and checked in with two pieces of information: a moving van was loading up furniture, and Pelkov had a special guest for a late lunch in the sunroom.

Honey and I hit the front gates to Grigory Pelkov's Uptown mansion at about thirty-five miles per hour. I disliked having to scratch the paint on my truck, but I enjoyed the look on the face of the Russian security guy as he leapt clear of my charging behemoth, trailed by eight PD units. A couple of movers carrying an antique chest out of the house did a double take as I veered off the curved flagstone drive and drove right for the converted atrium. I guess I was pioneering a new take on the no-knock warrant we had been given.

I'd cased Pelkov's house well the day I broke in; I knew where he'd be sitting for his lunch, so I had a good idea of what I had to do. And that meant pedal to the metal, right into a corner of his damn sunroom. Glass, wood, and red brick showered one end of the room as I powered the big diesel rig indoors, crushing tables and chairs underfoot.

Pelkov and Nassir Haddad reacted as I'd anticipated: the big flinch as we crashed through the flimsy wall and drove into the room, followed by frozen shock as Honey and I hurtled out of the truck holding pistols, one gun pointing at each of their heads. I tried not to limp as I approached their table.

"Gentlemen, mind if we join you?"

I sat uninvited across from the two men, just as three bodyguards, including the bald Neanderthal Sasha ran into the room.

"Tell them to drop their weapons, turn around, and lace their fingers behind their heads."

Grigory thought about it, then gestured, and the men complied. As Honey confiscated their guns, a couple of uniforms entered the room, cuffed the three men, and took them away. When Mackie and Kruger entered, Honey patted down Pelkov, removing his cell phone, watch, wallet, and other items. We all observed as she used a pocket-size

SIM-card copier to download the contents of his phone, including deleted texts, to a USB drive.

Cell phones had been found on the two dead assassins, and Honey wanted to try to make some connections with the Buyer's Club. She repeated the process with Haddad.

"I don't think you—"

"Shut the fuck up unless I ask you a question," I said to Pelkov.

Haddad had the sweat-beads thing going on his upper lip again. And his blinking-eye thing kicked in. Using my left hand, since my right was too banged up, I kept the Glock aimed at Pelkov's forehead as I reached over to grab his champagne coupe.

"Celebrating?" I asked.

"Yes, we get to leave this toilet-bowl city."

"No, you don't, because I haven't flushed you into the sewer yet."

"What can you do to—"

I flung the champagne into Pelkov's face, and for the first time he dropped his mask of invincibility.

"I said shut up unless I ask you a question."

I nodded to Honey, and she disappeared with Mackie and Kruger to search the house and seize whatever evidence would reasonably fit within the scope of the warrant, especially the one million in cash in his desk. Two uniforms stepped into the room and took up positions in the doorway. It was understood by every officer in the department that I was given a free pass to get in some licks on Pelkov. And I just might, depending on how the interrogation went.

I slid passport photos of the two dead Russians over to Pelkov. Detectives had found passports and other items in the hotel room the assassins had checked into. He examined the pictures dispassionately.

"Know them?"

"No. But girl is hot."

"I can arrange a meeting. You can have the roll-out tray right next to hers in the autopsy room. I have to admit, she's a good-looking corpse. Her breasts are real, not fake. And big nipples, big as a casino chip."

It was in his eyes. A flash of something. Pelkov did his best to remain stoic, but something had changed, as if his inner dialogue was processing potential eventualities. And he was angry. I liked that.

"Now what's this I hear about you arranging for a Russian hit team to kill me? I thought we were pals." I poured myself some bubbly and took a sip.

He looked askance at the mess in the room and at my looming, parked truck. "Why you don't just knock?"

"Don't make me remind you again that when I ask you a question, you need to answer it." I said it slowly and with a distinct lethality.

"We not in Saint Petersburg. I don't know about hit team." He looked away.

"You're not the best liar Ukraine has to offer, are you? You told me you weren't buying weapons here in New Orleans, but you've been buying them every Saturday night for the last year out at Michoud. That's why you moved into this house. You're making too much money; you can't afford to leave. Did you and Chu have a bet as to which of your goons would knock me off first?"

The hint of a smile appeared on his lips. "Not bad idea. But until two minute ago when you drive into my house and point gun at me, why I want to kill you?"

"I'm shining a light on you maggots. I'm shutting you down."

Grigory laughed heartily, long and hard. "God, I love innocence. I wish I had some. So does Nassir, is why he like young boy and girls. He wants their innocence."

Nassir's eyes drilled into Pelkov, but he said nothing. Pelkov looked at me.

"You think you will shut down American defense industry selling its merchandise?"

"Of course not. I'm simply herding the jackals out of my town. But a few like you will stay here and get stuffed and mounted for display."

Pelkov seemed to be working hard at keeping his cool now. Time to make my move.

I slid him a photo of the GIDEON sample. He studied it, then handed it to Nassir, whose hand shook as he held the photo.

"Tell me about this."

"Some kind of metal or something," said Pelkov. "I don't know this. Nassir?"

Nassir shook his head and handed the picture back to me.

"Come on, you're a smart guy; you know what it is," I stated, never taking my eyes off Pelkov.

"Okay, you investigate murder of Del, so I see maybe now. Del was material guy. Engineer. Still work on some secret project. Okay, maybe now I understand. This some espionage. This spy stuff. This something he sell?"

"You tell me. He certainly had plenty to sell. I'm guessing he bought some things, too. Including from you. Why else would he have a roomful of Soviet bloc weapons stashed away?"

Pelkov looked over to Nassir. The Egyptian said, "Barter. When Del had clients who wanted low-tech goods, I traded with him. Kalashnikovs for computers or boots for burst-transmission radio sets."

"You keep military goods on your ship?"

Nassir shrugged, but I caught his eye with a hard look. "Yes, I do," he said, with his crisp British-accented English.

"So you swapped out weapons and ammunition and war matériel you had in stock on your ship for items Breaux had, the higher-end stuff."

Nassir nodded. "Yes, we've all covered each other, at one time or another. Except for Chu. He's not really an arms dealer. He simply buys goods for China. Period."

"Kind of like you, Pelkov. Think I don't know you're full-blown

GRU? Samples of everything you buy here finds its way to the Russian Defense Ministry in Moscow. But go ahead and keep lying. You're going to rot in a shithole. You won't be traded for an American agent, because you're being arrested by the NOPD, and we don't make swaps."

Pelkov stayed silent. His usual smug look transformed into a scowl.

I handed one more photo to Pelkov. "Last picture."

Pelkov grunted. "I wanted to buy these land mines. Nassir too. Even Breaux. But Chu outbid us every time. Where you find this?"

"In my refrigerator."

"Good reason to eat out."

"Speaking of a fine dining experience, ever try prison food?"

"Never."

"You'll have to let me know how you like it. Because you're under arrest for conspiracy to commit murder."

"But I—"

"You called your Russian-mob buddy in Brooklyn, the ex-KGB guy with the nightclub you like to party at up there."

"I not hire hit team!"

"You specifically requested the girl. 'Nati.' Did you have plans with her for later tonight, after she waxed me? They were both naturalized U.S. citizens, which makes a good argument for tightening up our immigration policies, don't you think?"

"I never pay for hit team. Clayton Brandt pay for—"

Grigory Pelkov's head exploded right in front of me, and the force of the sniper's round knocked him and his chair over backward. I lunged forward, grabbed Haddad, and pulled him to the floor. I heard one of the uniforms on his portable radio calling in the shooting. Haddad had fainted, and Pelkov, well, he turned out to be a dead end.

CHAPTER TWENTY-TWO

The sniper had fired from a seldom-used sundeck at a classic old apartment building that had gone condo one block away. The police found it easily because the shooter had left the Russian Dragunov SVD sniper rifle there, still perched upright on its bipod. The shooter had made one hell of a shot. And curiously it had happened just as Pelkov was naming Clayton Brandt as the money guy behind the wet team sent to kill me.

Pelkov's sunroom wasn't bugged, so Honey and I operated on the suspicion that a hacker had compromised his cell phone and turned it into a listening device. This was a technique gaining in popularity, used mainly by the Feds, and I wanted to add it to my list of tricks.

Honey cut me loose from the crime scene, and I drove out of the demolished sunroom with Haddad next to me in my big Ford. I took River Road all the way to a St. Rose dock on the Mississippi River. Oceangoing cargo ships could navigate far north into Louisiana on the Mississippi, but it struck me as unusual that Haddad docked here, since most of the ships were off-loading gravel from Africa or standing by to load up with massive tonnage of American grains. We caught a slow skiff to his faded, black-hulled cargo vessel—its name *El Fazlin* emblazoned across the stern—sitting high in the water. Sweat bees gave chase, skimming the surface of the warm, glassy current as large lumbering flies buzzed us. Even the river seemed to lag due to the brutal heat. I had no warrant, but Haddad didn't make a fuss and gave me the VIP tour of his ship, which had now been docked in NOLA for ten months but was clearly undergoing preparation to get under way. Soon.

I saw his holds, mostly empty but some fat with weapons. Interestingly, I saw crates of Dragunov SVD sniper rifles. A crate of pistols was open, and I reached in to grab one: a Steyr M9, in scratched, used condition. There were dozens more like it in the crate. They all looked exactly like the murder weapon found next to Del Breaux's hand.

"You sell used weapons?" I asked Haddad.

"Reconditioned. I have many clients on a budget who aren't so choosy."

"I'm going to have to keep this one as part of my investigation."

Haddad didn't seem fazed. "Consider it a gift."

The tour resumed, and he showed me his ultraplush, oversized accommodations that would seem more appropriate on a yacht than an old rust-bucket cargo ship. Two teenage girls, possibly over the age of consent, lounged in the master suite listening to hip-hop and drinking Jäger Bombs when Haddad and I walked in. I was out of my jurisdiction, but even if I wasn't, I wouldn't collar him on a contributing-to-the-delinquency charge.

He waved the girls off and sank heavily into a velour chair. He looked burned out. Even his blinking had slowed down. But he still looked frightened. A Filipino valet brought us Turkish coffees and baklava.

"This has gone far beyond anything I want to be involved in. No amount of money is worth this. I just want to leave America."

"You'll have to stay for at least another twenty-four hours. The Harbor Police will make sure of that. You're free on bail for the drug charge, but I'll hold you as long as I can."

"In that case I won't be leaving my ship."

"So who just shot Pelkov?"

"It doesn't make sense. Your government wouldn't shoot a Russian agent on American soil. It's a gross violation of rules. They don't want a U.S. agent killed in retaliation. Maybe it was Chu."

"Tan Chu?"

"Yes. He was very upset with Grigory."

"Doesn't sound like the Buyer's Club was much of a fraternity. Why was Chu upset with Pelkov?"

Haddad sighed and wiped his brow. "Del joined us for lunch last Friday at Grigory's house. It was me, Chu, Grigory, and Del. Without any warning, Del offered to sell the GIDEON secrets and sample to the highest bidder."

About an hour ago Haddad had denied knowing anything about the GIDEON sample. Funny how seeing an associate get his brains blown out right next to you can jog your memory.

"Del was drunk, but he was serious. He actually had the sample piece with him. He offered to provide the formula, reports, supporting documents—everything. We couldn't believe it. Chu won the impromptu auction, of course. The Red Chinese are the new masters of the universe. The deal was sealed, and an exchange of money for the items set up for the next day, Saturday.

"But later that night, Grigory and I went to Del's house and suggested he cut the sample into three pieces and sell everything to all of us simultaneously. A win-win-win-win scenario. Del would make much more money, Grigory could appease Moscow, and I had my benefactor to consider."

"Benefactor?"

"Please don't ask. Anyway, even though Peter strongly advised against it, Del and Ty thought it was a great idea."

"Peter Danforth was at Breaux and Park's house? Last Friday night?"

"Yes, he was. That was rather typical, actually. I heard he spent a lot of time with Del and Ty." Haddad took a sip of coffee.

"So you're saying that you saw Danforth there yourself?"

Haddad nodded. "Yes, absolutely."

So much for Danforth being in Atlanta the weekend of the murders. Maybe he did fly there and check into a hotel. But he could have flown right back. Then return to Atlanta on Sunday, make a big display of eating in the hotel restaurant and drinking in the lobby bar—Honey had confirmed that—before checking out and returning to New Orleans.

"Okay. So did Chu deliver the money on Saturday to Breaux?"

"Yes, the entire amount, two and a half million. He didn't know Del like we did, or he wouldn't have done that. I imagine he was quite anxious to get his hands on the merchandise. Anyway, Del made an excuse and delayed delivering the sample and other information. He was giving Grigory and me time to come up with cash."

I flashed on the million bucks I'd found in Pelkov's locked desk drawer.

"Okay . . . but, how could you trust him? Wasn't Breaux angry with all of you because he was getting kicked out of the Buyer's Club?"

"He was angry with Clayton Brandt and the U.S. government. And no, Grigory and I didn't trust Del, but our desire to obtain the GIDEON secrets outweighed our misgivings."

"So Chu didn't know what you guys were up to?"

"Correct. He was furious at Del for delaying the delivery. We were all at dinner together at Restaurant August that night. Since Clayton Brandt was there, we couldn't discuss it; Clayton knew nothing about the GIDEON deal. I think if Clayton hadn't been there, Chu would have just kidnapped Del on the spot."

"This was last Saturday night, the night Breaux and Parks were killed."

"Yes."

"So after dinner, everyone went to the auction at Michoud?"

"Yes. Del and Ty both attended the auction. Del bought some electronic nonlethal weapons that night."

"So, just to be clear, who was selling and who was buying?"

"The United States government is the seller. Period. They use a front company, Global Solutions. Clayton Brandt is paid by the Pentagon to facilitate the auctions, to make sure there are no flies in the ointment, so to speak. But he's also an arms dealer who is bidding on lots, competing with the rest of the Buyer's Club as well as with the out-of-town bidders, usually representatives of some foreign military. It's a simple, straightforward auction, made dramatic only by what it is that's being auctioned."

"So Breaux's private selling of the GIDEON secrets had absolutely nothing to do with Global, with the auctions at Michoud?"

"My God, man, if Clayton Brandt knew Breaux was going rogue with GIDEON, he probably would have had him shot."

Maybe he did.

"You said Breaux showed up at a lunch out of the blue and offered to sell the GIDEON secrets. That sounds far-fetched. You guys had been soliciting him, hadn't you? Trying to turn him against his own country."

Haddad paused, then: "That's a fair statement."

No wonder Salerno became suspicious of Del; he knew what a lion's den he'd gotten involved with.

"So Michoud J-19 is just a warehouse, a staging building for matériel that comes from elsewhere?" I asked.

"Yes. Just as in Huntsville and all the cities before New Orleans. Who cares where the weapons are developed or manufactured? We only want to purchase them."

"Can you remember if Breaux had his laptop with him at the auction the night he was killed?"

Haddad popped an entire baklava into his mouth and washed it down with the last of his demitasse of coffee. "He had it. He always had it at the auctions."

"What time did they leave?"

"Maybe eleven, or half past."

The timing worked. Breaux and Parks left the auction and returned to their home in Broadmoor around midnight. The downstairs renters confirmed that. Breaux used his laptop in the toilet off the party room and left it there. Breaux got a call at 12:15 A.M. from someone at the Banks Street Bar, and then for some reason, around 1 A.M. they drove to their rendezvous with fate in a dark parking lot near the old Calliope Projects.

"So Breaux had made the decision to cut the sample into pieces. Do you think he had the sample in his car the night he was killed?"

"I don't know. He hinted he had a safe place to keep it where it was guarded by U.S. soldiers. That made no sense, however; I assumed it was simply drunken bluster."

It made no sense unless you knew that Breaux had warehouse space at the Academy, where armed guards in U.S. military uniforms patrolled the place night and day.

"When he was drinking, Del couldn't keep quiet. He told Chu as we were leaving Restaurant August that Grigory had come up with a good idea to make everybody happy."

"To divide the sample and sell the secrets to all three of you simultaneously. That would have made everyone happy *but* Chu."

"Exactly. Our Chinese friend became even more incensed."

"So Chu was furious with Del Breaux *and* Grigory Pelkov."

"Yes. And Del was dead within a few hours and the sample gone. The next time I heard about it was when you started showing people pictures of it."

Haddad's information felt right. He remained a suspect, of course; he admitted he was guilty of conspiracy to commit espionage. But the Feds didn't seem to be taking that too seriously these days. My take was that he was talking to me in an attempt to save his own hide: he wanted to exit stage right before he could be set up as a fall guy in case Brandt's operation went tits up. But I needed to consider that the murder weapons might have come from his stock, even though he couldn't have been more nonplussed about giving me the Steyr pistol. I wasn't sure if the lab could somehow match the Steyr and Dragunov in NOPD possession with the lots in Haddad's hold. If that could be done, then Haddad had a real problem.

"That crate of Steyr pistols in your hold . . ." Haddad nodded for me to continue. "Did you ever sell or barter any of them to the Buyer's Club? Or anyone else in New Orleans?"

Haddad pursed his lips, thinking. "No."

"What about those Dragunov SVD rifles I saw in there? I'll have to take one of those too."

"No, I never bartered those either."

"And you don't keep the holds locked up?"

"Not really. The ship itself is very secure."

"Have any members of the Buyer's Club been on board your ship?"

"Of course, they all have. Chu and his men, Grigory and his security detail. Brandt and his office staff. Del and Ty. I've had many dinners, many parties here."

Meaning any of my suspects could have lifted the murder weapons from Nassir Haddad's ship.

"You heard what Pelkov said just before he was shot. He said Clayton Brandt had paid for the hit team. And Peter Danforth told me Clayton Brandt was the most dangerous member of the Buyer's Club."

Haddad shrugged. "Clayton was our liaison with the United States government. A powerful, threatening position. But if you don't wield the power . . ."

"What do you mean?"

"For a long time we have watched Clayton and the FBI let local investigators learn too much, first in Charleston, then in Miami, then in Huntsville. Each time the operation became threatened with exposure, we moved to a new city. That's why we came to New Orleans: too many people asking questions in Huntsville. Chu and Grigory think Americans are weak; communists like them would simply kill reporters or local police who asked the wrong questions. And they think the American government is stupid." Haddad set his coffee cup and saucer aside. "I do, too, really. China would never sell such sensitive technology to their enemies. Never. But America is committing suicide by greed."

"A Chinese hit team and a Russian hit team came to New Orleans to kill me. Are you saying Brandt didn't have anything to do with that decision?"

"He might have. He was certainly prepared to frame you. Plant drugs or something like that, is what I heard."

"Really?" That must have been Brandt's Plan B.

"Chu and Grigory categorically decided to eliminate you. The day you met Chu at the port, the decision was made. You have been the biggest threat they have ever faced. They don't want the operation to be exposed. They assumed the U.S. authorities would look the other way if you were killed."

"Business comes first, I understand."

Haddad gave me a Dragunov rifle sample, and I left him aboard his ship. Though I couldn't yet reconcile all of the facts into a cohesive whole, I had made some major connections that I needed to follow up on as quickly as possible.

Back in my pickup I booted up my laptop and checked the software that monitored the cell phone I'd given to Decon. He'd been contacted by the Chinese; they wanted to set a meet to check the authenticity of the GIDEON sample. The sting was going forward.

I dropped off the Steyr M9 and a Dragunov SVD rifle to the lab, feeling like I could fall asleep on my feet. I had to pop a couple of caffeine pills I bought at Walgreens. Maybe it was a result of the anesthetic, maybe I was just getting old before my time, maybe it was an adrenaline comedown from the shootout, but when Harding opened her Mid-City condo door around 6 P.M., I almost asked if I could take a nap on her couch, I felt so tired. I figured by the way Harding gasped when she saw me, I must have resembled an airline crash survivor. I could usually tune out pain, but I kept feeling the Russian's tanto slice me, like it was happening all over again.

"Harding, I could use a cold one."

"Shouldn't you be in the hospital?"

"I don't think they serve Grey Goose."

She looked for a good arm to take—there weren't any—then gestured for me to enter. She closed and locked the door.

"How did you find me?"

"Scent."

I was punchy, and that's when the needle on my smart-ass dial enters red. She took a second to decide whether she was going to be angry that I showed up unannounced, but she must have felt sorry for me and guided me to the sofa. She wore a pink workout-bra top and green short shorts, having been on the treadmill in the corner of her living room when I knocked. Some women don't like to be seen when they're working out and all sweaty with flushed cheeks and no makeup. Maybe it was that. Or maybe she didn't like that I had tracked her down when she had orders to avoid me.

"I heard what happened. I called the hospital to check on you. Martini okay?"

"I like it dirty."

She smiled a coquettish little smile. I admired her goods as she walked into the open-plan kitchen. Sweaty, buff girls kind of rang my chimes. I craned my neck and saw she had a tray set up like a little work table so she could read case files as she ran on the treadmill.

"I heard Chief Pointer ordered you and your partner off the case this morning," she said from the kitchen.

"Was that this morning? Seems like weeks ago." I flashed serious. "Why did that take so long? I figured we would have been dumped days ago."

"Disagreement in Washington. Not all the brass support the Pentagon's cozy arrangement selling to foreign intel agents."

"Really? Maybe there's a little common sense in DC, after all." I watched her pour the liquor. "Say, Harding, you got a first name?"

"Jill," she said, as she mixed the drinks. "What about you; what do like to be called?"

" 'Handsome' works." I stood and joined her in the kitchen area. If I stayed on the couch for any length of time, I'd become part of it.

As she shook the concoction in a stainless-steel shaker, she flashed me a wry smile. "Yeah, you look really suave at the moment. The scabbing on your head is right out of *Details* magazine."

"I try. Gee, if I'd known you make martinis the right way, I would have come a lot sooner."

"I'd prefer if you didn't come too soon," she said.

"Timing *is* everything."

She leaned over and gave me a gentle kiss. "I don't know where to touch you. Is there any part of your body that isn't shot or cut or broken?"

"Well, there's one place."

"Then maybe Nurse Jill better take a look."

Suddenly I didn't feel quite so tired.

The sex was . . . careful. I confirmed my earlier theory that Harding liked a man who could take a few licks. My wounds fascinated her, and, well, considering my condition, I pretty much had to let her do all the work. As we reclined in bed nursing our martinis, I brought the conversation around to business and brought her up to speed on the bullet points of the case. I'd always pegged Harding for an ambitious go-getter. Making the arms-smuggling case would have been a sweet résumé builder.

She pursed her lips together like she was thinking about something unpleasant.

"If the public only knew the kinds of things that really go on behind the scenes," she said, looking over to me and lacing her fingers through mine. "When I graduated from Quantico, I was naïve, gung ho, stupidly believing we were going to right wrongs and fix the world, to make America a safer place. But any agent who's posted in DC for any length of time quickly sees the ugly truth. The dirty politics, the backstabbing, desperate career jockeying, the huge rat hole of a broken, thoroughly corrupt system that we have to protect at all costs because it's all about denial.

"I made some enemies and got transferred to a backwater called New Orleans. And until I can make a career change, I need my job. So I have to be semi-careful. But I no longer worry about promotions or scoring points or pissing off people in Washington."

My estimation of Harding just increased tenfold. She wasn't trying to build a résumé with the arms-smuggling case, she just wanted to send some crooks up the river.

"Anything come back on Global Solutions?" I asked.

"They're a front for a front for a front. I can't dig too deep or it will raise red flags."

I nodded. "I have to ask . . . how did you know I was at Pravda when you had the dossiers delivered?"

"Scent."

I deadpanned a "come clean" look.

"I triangulated your cell-phone signal."

"But there's no tracking software on my phone, I wipe it regularly."

"There are other ways. If you're a really bad cop, I'll teach you."

"In that case, assume the position."

CHAPTER TWENTY-THREE

Stopping by Harding's hadn't been intended as a pleasure junket. I needed the local FBI office's assistance for a dustup I hoped to orchestrate tomorrow. In furtherance of that, I had scheduled a late confab with my pirate krewe to take place after I'd met with Harding. We met at Pampy's on North Broad, a Creole soul-food restaurant and bar owned by a former city-hall insider who was currently in a lot of trouble with the federal prosecutor. Something to do with graft, a shocking allegation in New Orleans politics. Shocking in that it was being investigated. Graft or not, I was addicted to the No. 9 Special and had secured us a private room.

Ever adept at multitasking, Kendall worked his laptop with hand and foot casts never seeming to get in the way, while almost simultaneously texting four different girlfriends. Decon lounged casually, nursing a beer and a cigarette. Senior homicide detectives Mackie and Kruger were there, officially as part of the investigation into my attempted murder. Unofficially I wanted to get them pregnant with the bigger picture and hopefully elicit their help. And of course, Honey sat steaming because I was late.

There was no denying the fact that as I entered it was a perp walk, as far as Honey was concerned anyway, especially since I had brought the jezebel FBI agent with me. Maybe there was something to the "scent" thing I'd joked about. Honey said nothing, but her face flushed red and her flashing eyes charged, judged, and sentenced me. Yes, women always seemed to know. I was a man, and that made me guilty, right there. What more evidence was needed?

Introductions were made, drinks served, and my wounds were fawned over by everyone but Honey, who clearly sensed that Harding had already done that. I hadn't wanted to rub Honey's nose in anything by bringing Harding to the meeting, but the local FBI had a key role to play in tomorrow's festivities, and that was that. We would live or die by the result of tomorrow's efforts. All told, we had thirty-six hours to wrap the case in ribbons for Chief Pointer.

"Detective Baybee, I haven't seen you since you were shot at the Hotel Monteleone last winter. I'm glad you're doing well. And congratulations for taking this case a lot further than I was able to." Harding was trying to extend an olive branch of sorts.

"I'm not too happy with the FBI these days, Agent Harding," said Honey coolly.

"I'm not happy with those DC boys, either."

"Honey, we need local bureau assets tomorrow," I said. "NOPD doesn't have an air unit, and we'll need air support."

"All right, calling in an air strike! I haven't done that in years," crowed Decon, getting everyone's attention.

"I'm not so sure about making Decon the centerpiece of your sting," said Harding quietly. "In fact, you have to be kidding."

"There's no choice, really."

"Then we better get to work."

Harding had been ordered off the arms-smuggling case, but she wasn't prohibited from committing resources in a counterespionage operation. So for the next several hours over hot food and cold drinks, we either worked as one large group or broke into smaller groups with constantly shifting configurations as people moved from group to group, planning a series of operations that largely bordered on wishful thinking. If a third of what I wanted to do worked, I'd be shocked.

And as I'd hoped, Mackie and Kruger got caught up in the sheer audacity of it all and provided trenchant counsel and advice.

Decon had kept pretty much to himself, and I crossed to a corner and joined him.

"You're being quiet tonight."

"The hard work is done, if you understand my thinking. Plus, there are too many cops here, so I'm inhibited. Anyway, tonight is chill. Tomorrow's the fun part."

"Tomorrow is the dangerous part."

Decon just shrugged. "I'm okay. It's you I'd be worried about."

"What do you mean?"

"Well, look at you, man. You're the walking frigging wounded, and you're our key guy. A mama gerbil could kick your ass right now, if you comprehend me, no offense intended."

"None taken. You want to bail, you can bail."

"No, colonel, you have inspired your troops. I had to take on a Russian myself once. In Prague. We rolled up a four-man wet team. The last guy, I had to go hand to hand with in a hotel bathroom. Big old bear of a vodka-swilling Bolshevik."

"Decon, that sounds a bit far-fetched. You're a hundred and thirty pounds dripping wet."

"Speaking of dripping, you did the FBI babe, didn't you? And in your condition." He clucked his tongue at me in mock scorn.

I gave Decon my best shut-the-hell-up-or-I'll-kill-you look.

"Your secret is safe with me. All of your secrets."

"All of what secrets?"

He just waved me off and shook his head. I let it go; I was too tired to even think. In short order the meeting broke up and people wandered off till it was just Honey and me.

"The Customs guy won't be calling you anymore," said Honey.

"Because . . . ?"

"Didn't show up for work today. Slit his wrists in a tub of water at home."

I shook my head. "Damn."

"Night-shift detective on the case is a good one. I told her it might be staged. She's on top of it."

"Guess I should feel a little guilty about that, but I'm already on overload."

"He made his own bed."

"Yeah, I guess. Speaking of bed, there's a hole in my roof that hasn't been fixed, courtesy of those Russians. Can I crash at your place? I'm all in."

"Why didn't you ask Harding?"

Ouch. I guess in Honey's mind I deserved that. I tolerated her jealousy because I loved her.

"Never mind, I'll just get a hotel room. See you tomorrow."

I sank into a chair and closed my eyes. What a day. Today had to rank as one of the most intense of my life, starting with the early morning session in Chief Pointer's office and my recommissioning, then the killings in my loft, the hospital surgery, Pelkov getting his head blown off in front of me, the Haddad interrogation, a fling with Harding, and now Honey blowing me off. I couldn't even say I was running on fumes; I was out of those, too.

As my mind flooded with a thousand details, one big one muscled aside all of the others: I had killed again today. And in my own house. But the odd thing was, it didn't bother me. There was no second guessing, no slow-motion replays or recrimination, no pissed-off *Why did this have to happen to me?* inner dialogue. I simply felt numb. Or maybe I was simply getting used to the bloodletting.

But Bobby Perdue hadn't departed just yet.

Round Three. Time to turn the tables. A couple of techniques I know have the potential to bring down a bigger, stronger guy. A low line kick to the common peroneal is awesome with boots on, but Bobby Perdue and I were fighting barefoot. That left my turning back kick, aka "donkey kick," and I elected to go for it. Now, how to bait it?

Based on the way he moved, I figured I could use my right leg kick and straight right hands to get him moving to my left. It started working, and after I unloaded with a solid leg kick, he got annoyed and moved to my left.

In a split second I saw the opening. I let the right hand fly, and he took the bait; he blocked it as I hoped he would, then slid to my left, thinking he had me. He loaded up, ready to throw his own killer right, but I was a step ahead. I planted my left foot, began my spin to the right, picked up my target with peripheral vision as I simultaneously unloaded with my right leg. With my back now to my opponent I was essentially kicking behind me. My head craned so I could watch as my heel slammed into his solar plexus area with a satisfying crunch.

I opened my eyes to see Honey staring at me.

I had no idea what I might have been saying as I recalled the fight with Perdue. I didn't care. I just started talking it out, staring straight through Honey as though she weren't even there.

"He just laid there, in the fetal position. Couldn't speak. I thought I'd knocked the wind out of him. Big Bob counted him out, and the kid's corner man, I mean his buddy, came into the cage, and so did his girlfriend. I turned away. I wasn't trying to gloat or anything. I had knocked his ass down and won the fight; it felt good. I figured he might take a lesson from it.

"It wasn't an alley fight, you know? We wore protective gear: shin and instep guards, sixteen-ounce gloves, headgear, mouthpiece, cup. The guy came at me a hundred percent, but neither of us fought dirty. Anyway, after a few minutes he started making some strange sounds. Sounds I never heard from a guy who got the wind knocked out of him. I asked if the kid was okay. He didn't look okay. Big Bob took a look at him, then looked at me, and I knew it was time to call EMS.

"Paramedics got there quick—six, seven minutes. Nobody had turned off the video camera, so all this was recorded. He was unconscious but alive when they loaded him into the wagon. See, if he hadn't stepped forward after he loaded up, if he hadn't been so damn aggressive, he wouldn't have taken the brunt of the kick. It wasn't designed to hit him full force. To knock him down, yes, but not to damage him. If he hadn't charged me in that half second when I wasn't looking, when I was doing my spin, he'd be alive and healthy today.

"He died at the hospital. I'd fractured his xiphoid process. You know, thoracic trauma. A sharp chunk of bone perforated his internal structures and caused massive bleeding inside his body. I called PD and reported it after EMS took him, and a detective came—in fact, it was Mackie—and took a report. He replayed the video, took it for evidence, interviewed Big Bob. There was no charge or arrest, he just took a report.

"When the kid's girlfriend came the next day looking for the camcorder, she screamed at me and said I'd killed her boyfriend. I wanted to go see the parents, apologize, explain how it was an accident, not my fault. Everybody told me not to go, but I went anyway. I was outside their front door on the porch, and the mother clipped me with a left and cut my chin with her wedding ring. The husband knocked me to the ground. I didn't bother to defend myself. They didn't really hurt me much. They probably would have killed me if they could have, but they were too torn up emotionally. They said they'd sue in civil court for wrongful death, get my dojo from me, get my house and all my money. But the sleaziest ambulance-chasing lawyer wouldn't take the case on consignment because there *was* no case. The kid had signed a release—everybody who fights in my dojo has to—and the whole thing was on tape. Everything was a slam dunk in my favor. The parents just needed to vent and lash out at somebody, and I was obviously the guy.

"I went back a second time, but I didn't let them hit me. They screamed at me, threatened to have me arrested."

My eyes refocused, finding Honey's gaze.

"I've been thinking I might go back sometime when they're more settled down. But what if Bobby's parents read in the paper about what happened in my loft today? They'll just think I'm a stone cold killer. Won't they?"

Honey's eyes never left mine.

I'd never spoken to Honey or anybody else about the events surrounding Bobby Perdue's death. I'd given police the facts, but nothing else.

Decon had been right; this talk felt like a good step.

Honey silently took my hand and led me out of Pampy's.

CHAPTER TWENTY-FOUR

Looking like the sleazy scammer that he was, Decon sat in the patio of Café du Monde on Decatur Street enjoying a café au lait, as my favorite Chinese sparring partner, Ding Tong, sat across from him pointing a Niton gun, an X-ray fluorescence analyzer, at the materials sample stolen by Del Breaux from Project GIDEON. The Niton gun looked a little like a handheld hair dryer with an LED screen, but hair dryers don't cost forty thousand dollars a pop. The state-of-the-art tool was used for metal-alloy testing and identification. Decon had the GIDEON sample stuffed in an drab olive army laundry bag.

Honey and I, pretending to be a tourist couple, watched and listened from the covered rear section of a horse carriage parked across the street. We hadn't bugged Decon or the table, but strategically placed super-sensitive unidirectional shotgun mikes in the patio and ran the sound input through an instantaneous filtering software so we heard everything Decon and Tong said. I used a camera's zoom lens to monitor the action while pretending to take pictures of Honey. Harding, Kendall, and a local FBI team handled video surveillance and provided a security perimeter in case Tong tried to pull a fast one, but I didn't expect him to.

The meet today was for Tong to confirm that Decon had the real goods, and for Decon to agree to a price. A second meeting would then be arranged to do the deal, and that's when the bust would come down.

"Okay, is same piece," muttered Tong to Decon through a mouth of swollen lips and missing teeth. I could see now that the SWAT commander had gotten in a great punch.

Tong powered off the Niton gun. It had been Tong, apparently, who had examined the sample when it had been in Del Breaux's possession.

"We do now," Tong said. *"I have money."*

"You have a million bucks in that little bag?" asked Decon. *"Because that's the price, know what I mean?"*

"Five hundred thousand for this."

"Whoa, whoa, whoa," said Decon. *"I said one million."*

"You not have formula, files. Only have this," said Tong.

"Take the money," I urged, even though Decon couldn't hear me. "Tong brought money with him! This wasn't supposed to be the buy."

"We get the exchange on tape? We bust him, it's a wrap," said Honey.

But Decon was having none of it. *"So this formula that you want. Let's see, there wasn't no formula when I broke into that asshole cop's truck. No papers, no formula. But could what you want be in a laptop?"* he asked Tong.

"What's Decon, doing," I asked Honey as we sat in the carriage, listening. "He mentioned the laptop. How does he even know about it? Did you tell him?"

"No," said Honey.

"What laptop?" Tong asked Decon.

"I never seen one like this. In some kind of hard case, if you understand what I mean. On the bottom it said it was property of DOD. This guy Dod important?"

Decon pronounced "Dod" like "God." Nice touch, if a little overdone. I tried to focus the camera lens on Tong's expression but couldn't get a clear look.

"What the hell is he up to? He could blow everything," said Honey.

"You have laptop?" asked Tong.

"I sold it," said Decon. *"But I can get it back. If that means you give me a million for the whole package, you know what I'm saying?"*

"I give you five hundred thousand now and take this metal. Give you five hundred thousand more when you get laptop."

"No, brother. Maybe that cash in your bag is funny money. We met today just for you to take a look; that was the agreement. I don't have one of them special pens to make sure the bills are real and not counterfeit. You know, like the clerks have at the Circle K? Not that I ever have a hundred-dollar bill, if you can feel my pain, but I seen them clerks do it. Even some nice old white lady gives them a hundred-dollar bill, they pull out that special pen, brother."

Tong hesitated. I watched through the camera as he slowly replaced the Niton gun into the oversized shoulder bag. He didn't remove his hand from the bag.

"Damn, what if he's reaching for a gun?" I asked Honey as we watched the action go down. I clicked TALK on my comm unit. "Standby everyone; he might be going for a weapon."

Honey got out of the carriage, ready to run.

"Get laptop," said Tong. *"Then you call me."*

"Okay," said Decon. *"Get the million ready, my Asian brother-man."*

I watched as Tong walked out onto Decatur and hailed a cab that then lurched into traffic.

The fish had gotten a taste of the bait.

Decon waited five minutes, then entered the café's restroom, where I knew two of Harding's local FBI cohorts were waiting to take possession of the real GIDEON sample and supply him with a fake. I wanted the local Feds to have possession of the super-secret piece for a number of reasons, including the fact this was an interagency operation that required mutual trust, even if we were under the official radar of our respective headquarters. FBI CI-3 was to be kept out of the loop, which would allow for the locals, if we could pull this off, to reap the hosannas.

I watched Decon emerge from the bathroom with the fake sample in the laundry bag, then get on a motorcycle I'd provided and roar off.

The day was off to an okay start, but Decon had some explaining to do.

"What are you trying to pull?"

I stood over Decon on Pravda's back patio. We had both surreptitiously entered via different approaches, neither of which involved a door. I was sweating. My skin itched under all the bandages, which felt oppressive due to the heat.

"I thought I did good."

"You know what I mean."

"He squeezed me on the money, so I squeezed back."

"If you had taken the five hundred K, we'd be done, we'd be finished. He wanted to do the deal!"

"Yeah, but I didn't have one of those counterfeit indicating pens."

"Hey, Einstein, we're trying to arrest the guy. If he's paying with phony money, it gives us another beef to hang on him."

"Oh, yeah."

"And how did you know about the laptop?"

"Well, let me ask you this. Why did you endanger me and subject me to interrogation and scrutiny by the counterintelligence boys from Washington with the big bulges and attitudes to match?"

"When did I do that?"

"The CI-3 pricks came to my crypt crib! After we did our little break-in at Michoud. They knocked me around, man, looking for the missing sample and a Defense Department laptop. You telling me you don't have it? You gonna lie to me about that?"

"I didn't dime you to the Feds. And nobody followed us out to Michoud."

"So how did they find me and know my name? They were probably following you when you showed up at the cemetery the night you found me sleeping and scared the piss out of me, if you happen to remember that unfortunate circumstance."

That was entirely possible. And I knew the CI-3 agents had been interviewing practically anyone connected to me and asking about the missing items.

"Why didn't you tell me before that the FBI showed up?"

"What difference would it have made? I cursed you six ways from Sunday to them. Told them you rousted me for the bronze plaque I stole from the old CBD building. They were satisfied I didn't know anything about the missing government stuff."

"All right. But we're not putting any laptop into play, understand? Call Tong back and tell him it's gone, you can't get it back. You do the deal for half a million, period. Tell him to call you at nine o'clock tonight, and that you'll do the exchange in Metairie. When he calls at nine, you'll give him the location in Metairie where we'll do the buy."

I stood over Decon and listened as he made the call to Tong, following my instructions to the letter. Tong agreed, but Decon looked a little dejected as he terminated the call.

"Do I get to keep the money?"

"You get to keep living."

Their names were Jerry and Mario, and the pattern never altered. Building security video showed that every weekday at 11:45 A.M., the two male staff members in Clayton Brandt's company left the office for lunch. I guess it was a holdover military-precision kind of thing. The two young men, both clean-cut, ex–air force and in their late twenties, frequented many different eating establishments near One Canal Place, but they always rode the elevator down to the lobby, and today was no exception. Except today they didn't make it to the lobby.

Kendall got into the elevator with them on the twenty-fourth floor and pushed the button for 15, where Honey and I waited with Detectives Mackie and Kruger. When the doors opened, we flashed our shields and removed Jerry and Mario from the elevator car. I had arranged for the use of a vacant office suite and had video cams set up. We brought the men in for a frank discussion, the kind usually held in an interrogation room downtown.

"Do you want to be sitting at the prosecutor's table or the defense table?" I asked.

"What?" they said simultaneously.

"You are both guilty—you, Jerry, and you, Mario—of being accessories to conspiracy to commit murder. Do you understand that?"

Mario's mouth dropped slightly open, and Jerry's eyes widened.

"And I wonder what might be in your computers," said Honey. "Upstairs? Maybe evidence that Brandt Holdings transshipped weapons illegally to embargoed countries? Countries not under any special waiver provision. Abetting that makes you guilty of a couple more felonies. Federal ones."

Honey and I already knew such evidence existed in those computers, since I had downloaded exactly that.

"Search warrants are a wonderful thing," I said, waving an official-looking document that was actually an extended warranty for my big-screen TV. "Let me refresh your memories. Yesterday, not long after two Russian assassins tried to kill me in my home, you, Jerry, came out of Clayton Brandt's private office and said something to Mario, here. Am I jogging your memory, Jerry?"

"We . . . we . . . are we under arrest?" stammered Mario.

"That can be arranged very quickly," said Honey.

"Unless you cooperate. Unless you do the right thing. I want to help you. I'm willing to give you more of a chance than those killers gave me, but you've got just this one shot at it." I wanted to help them about as much as I wanted to get a proctology exam. Honey and I had sized these two up from the day we first showed up at Brandt's offices; they were simply clerks and weren't going to take a bullet for the boss.

"Maybe we should get a lawyer," said Jerry.

"Maybe you should. But if you ask for one, I can't help you. And even some slick lawyer from DC won't be able to save you from the evidence we have, enough to bury you both. Now you know what I'm talking about, Jerry, what Brandt said on the phone yesterday. And so do you, Mario. You heard what he said, Jerry. And once you hear something like that, you've been exposed."

Jerry and Mario were smart but not street-smart. The hardened thugs of NOLA would never talk to a detective, period. They knew how to work the system too well. Our homeboys would provide no alibi that would cross them up later; they'd make no statements of any kind. The local recidivists understood detectives would lie through their teeth and that it was perfectly legal to do so. They knew we were never interested in helping them, only in sending them to the Big House. So eliciting confessions in New Orleans was nearly impossible, unless you were dealing with rank amateurs. Add in the unwillingness of witnesses to come forward and you have the main reasons the homicide solution rate in the Crescent City ran so low.

"The detectives are now recording this conversation, okay?" I pointed out to Jerry and Mario. I legally had to do this, get it out of the way quick, and then continue my manipulation. "But what you have to realize is I'm offering you a get-out-of-jail-free card. I guarantee no charges will be filed against you if you tell me the truth. I'm just asking for the truth. It's probably something your parents told you to always tell. Tell the truth and you walk. Lie to me, withhold important information, and you're looking at a very unpleasant future."

"Do you know what it's like to do time in a hellhole? Like our state penitentiary in Angola? They still have chain gangs," said Honey.

"So tell me about what you heard, Jerry."

Jerry and Mario looked at each other. "Can I make a call?"

"Yes, if you want me to arrest you first. Then you're entitled to one phone call."

"Tell him Jerry. I didn't sign on for any of this," said Mario sharply.

"You heard him, Jerry," added Honey.

"Okay, okay. We're just employees. We do what we're told. I went into Brandt's office yesterday to have him sign some papers."

"Wait," I said. "What time was this?"

"Ah, about one in the afternoon. He was on the phone. . . ."

He stopped, looking like he was having second thoughts.

"Who was he talking to?" I asked.

"Gee, one o'clock," said Honey. "That was soon after the Russians tried to kill you, Detective Saint James. Maybe we should just charge them with Murder One."

"He was on the phone with Grigory Pelkov."

We all listened as Jerry gave it all up, pretty much matching word for word what I already had on tape. The recording Kendall had made as a result of the software I'd secretly installed in their computers wouldn't have stood up in court, but with living, breathing witnesses whose revelations were now being recorded legally, we had enough to arrest Clayton Brandt, an event I had already scheduled on my calendar. Jerry and Mario sang like birds; they were just hourly employees, after all, and not making the big green. Jerry admitted that he was the phone liaison for the crooked port inspector, Terry Blanchard, and that he and Mario had been dropping off Blanchard's thousand-dollar bribes on a monthly basis. It was Jerry whom Blanchard had called the day Harding and I showed up at the port. Mackie and Kruger could now get a search warrant for Brandt Holdings and legally seize all kinds of damning evidence in the staff computers.

"Jerry, Mario. Who killed Del Breaux and Ty Parks?"

"We started to think it might be you," said Mario.

"Me?"

"We figured it was the only way you could expose and stop the operation."

The statement floored me. Could that really have been the killer's goal in all of the murders? To *shut down* the arms-smuggling operation? If so, it lent credence to Harding's fingering of Decon to me early on. The notion seemed outlandish—I'd removed Decon as a suspect—but the honest truth was, I only knew of one such person who had an ax to grind in terms of shutting down the smuggling operation: Daniel Hawthorne Doakes, aka Decon.

Jerry called Brandt's secretary and said he and Mario had gotten food poisoning from lunch and were both too sick to return to work today; they hung up before she could ask any questions. Then Mackie and Kruger took them into unofficial protective custody. I only needed them on ice until tomorrow.

I couldn't get Decon on the phone. After our meeting at Pravda, Kendall had escorted him to the French Quarter Holiday Inn, where I had rented adjoining rooms. So I called Kendall and he put me on hold. When Kendall came back on the line, he said Decon must have given him the slip; he wasn't in his room. A troubling development to say the least.

Could Decon really be the killer, or at least be complicit? As far-fetched as it seemed, I had to give it more consideration. He alone of all the suspects had no alibi for any of the murders. Then I began to reconsider my previous conclusions that multiple killers had to have carried out the murders. Decon was the quintessential loner. If I asked myself if I could have done the killings without help, the answer was yes. But Decon? I couldn't picture him muscling a big guy like Del Breaux around a parking lot. Still, Decon could have some kind of psychosis, perhaps revenge based, that motivated him to do whatever was necessary to terminate any and all connected with the arms dealing. How else to explain why he was risking life and limb in the sting operation? He was either after some kind of revenge or he was simply crazy enough to cowboy up against the unknown, for no good reason. And that made less and less sense. Trying to solve murders purely based on motive was a weak approach, but the fact was, Decon wanted Brandt's operation shut down—a secret *government* operation—and the murders of the last week were accomplishing exactly that.

Honey and I drove over to Decon's crypt crash pad, but he wasn't around. We conducted a perfunctory search of his belongings, comprised of a lot of dirty, insignificant crap. After fifteen minutes, I motioned for Honey to follow me out of the ungodly chamber.

"We should keep looking for Decon."

"We won't find him if he doesn't want to be found."

"What if the Chinese grabbed him?"

"I doubt that. He's up to something, and I can tell you that it's not good. Why did I ever trust him?"

"We canceling the sting? Because there is no sting without him. He could be setting up his own swap, to try and pass off the fake sample."

"That wouldn't work. Tong will check it again with the Niton gun before he hands over any cash."

"But I wouldn't put it past him to—"

"What do you want me to do?" I snapped at Honey. The Decon turn of events threatened to unravel much of what I had planned. If he had committed the killings out of some obsession with demolishing a smuggling ring that the authorities seemed unable to stop, well, I'd never make a case. Decon knew practically everything I had, while I knew precious little that he had.

I didn't lose my temper often, but when I did it took off at Mach 5. "I've given everything I've got to this investigation: my time, my money, my flesh and my blood, my heart and my soul. I didn't ask you to talk the chief into making me a detective, and I'm not sure I want to keep the job. So I'm really sorry if I can't solve this thing in some ridiculously short time frame and it reflects badly on you. But screw Decon. For all we know he's the damn killer. And if that's the case, don't look for him to turn up anytime soon. If he surfaces, we'll go forward with the sting. If he doesn't, I'll add him to my to-do list, right under the entries: find the killer of Del Breaux, Ty Parks, Leroy and Jimmy Jefferson, Herbert Rondell, Eddie Liu, Terry Blanchard, and Grigory Pelkov."

After my mini blowup, I left Honey standing there and stormed over to my pickup truck. I immediately started to feel bad, but I was too angry to go back and make amends. I was fatigued from lack of sleep and from the events of yesterday. I'd be lying if I said I didn't feel stressed and paranoid about the possibility of more killers tracking me, waiting for the right moment to bust a cap up my ass.

What made everything more frustrating was that I was now second-guessing myself and the whole direction of the investigation. I'd possibly been suckered by a con man named Decon, and on top of that, I absolutely hated deadlines. A deadline on a murder investigation was an asinine concept I should have never agreed to. Tell an electrician the wiring has to be finished by Tuesday afternoon or he won't get paid, and the job will get done. Apply that formula to a homicide detective and what you will have is a lot of vacancies in the Homicide Section. Stupidly, I'd gone along with the idea because of that gold shield I held in my hand. It had meant so much to me, I just couldn't let it go.

But forty-eight hours to solve multiple murders? Hell, we hadn't even gotten back any forensics from the Breaux crime scene yet. Not that forensics made too many homicide cases in New Orleans. Or in the real world. And if by some divine miracle from the goddess of justice I could close this out by tomorrow morning's deadline, the chief would be emboldened to place a deadline on the *next* Five Alarm case I worked. Even if Chief Pointer couldn't fire me because I'd been shot in the line, he could transfer me out of homicide, do a million things to make my life miserable, and cause me to resign. He'd done it before, after all. Aside from everything else, I judged my performance to be pretty lousy so far, and I couldn't even blame Bobby Perdue for that; I could only blame myself.

As I inadvertently ran a stop sign on Dumaine Street, I thought, *Maybe I just need to start cracking heads again. Throw the badge away, crack some heads, find the killer.*

If only it were that simple. I pulled the truck over, parked, and took a deep breath of steamy, magnolia-scented air. All the summer showers had made the city extra green. Fast-moving cotton-ball clouds flew overhead toward Lake Pontchartrain like they were late for an appointment with a rain god. I took another deep breath of heavy, sweet air and consciously hit my stop button on all the mental second-guessing. I needed to stay focused; elaborate plans had been made. I took a moment to visualize how I wanted events to unfold, slid the transmission into drive, and headed toward the French Quarter to prepare for a very special dinner.

CHAPTER TWENTY-FIVE

The elegant Restaurant August on Tchoupitoulas is consistently rated one of the best restaurants in a city rich with great restaurants. While tourists were a scarce summer commodity one year after the killer Storm, the legions of upper-echelon executives from charities and disaster-relief outfits, federal visitors with high GS ratings and expense accounts to match, "prime" FEMA contractors, corporate execs from outfits like Shaw Group and Fluor and James Lee Witt Associates, whose companies suckled on the government-funded recovery tit, and any number of celebrities in town to "show support" for the city by partying their drug-addled brains out with young hookers, kept the booking rate high at the august Restaurant August. Conveniently located right across from the Windsor Court Hotel, where Brandt insisted all out-of-town arms buyers stay, it must have been relatively easy to shepherd the visiting flock from hotel to preauction prix-fixe feast, easing them into a better mood to part with hard cash for cold weapons.

Brandt had kept a standing booking of a large rear private dining room every Saturday night since the restaurant reopened after the hurricane. Tonight was no exception.

About a half dozen FBI CI-3 agents assisted by Brandt's personal security force covered all entrances to the chic *boîte*. Agents Gibbs and Minniear stood guard inside at the closed mahogany doors to the private dining room.

We hit them hard and all at once. Fifteen SWAT officers in full tactical gear, a dozen uniforms, and a dozen detectives. Since this raid was primarily concerned with the attempted murder of a police officer—yours truly—Detectives Mackie and Kruger made sure we brought overwhelming force. Harding and her local FBI team stood by at the offices of Brandt Holdings, where other detectives would be using a search warrant to seize company computers.

The agents and security goons posted outside Restaurant August were easily moved aside. I limped as fast as I could behind the wedge provided by Honey, Mackie, Kruger, and other homicide detectives.

Seeing our approach, Agents Gibbs and Minniear stood shoulder to shoulder—guardians at the gates of hell.

"Arrest warrant for Clayton Brandt for conspiracy to commit murder," said Honey, matter-of-fact. I hadn't apologized to Honey, but in our preraid meeting she acted like nothing had happened.

"Gentlemen, step aside or I'll arrest you for impeding," said Mackie to the FBI men, and he meant it.

Minniear looked ready to rumble, but Gibbs restrained him. "These rubes just don't learn. It's all rigged, they're all on the take, and I guess they think there's more juice in the orange so they're going to keep squeezing."

"You got it bass-ackward, agent," I said. "The real crooks, the thieves of a higher order, are your masters back in DC whose dirty water you carry on a daily basis. The corruption in our little city is chicken feed compared to the sewer you swim in."

Mackie and the other detectives muscled Gibbs and Minniear aside, and we entered the darkened dining room. Clayton Brandt stood behind a small podium at the front of the room, holding a tiny remote in his hand as he cycled through a presentation projected onto a white wall by a mini digital projector. An air force captain stood at ease next to a display table containing brochures and pamphlets. Diners, some in the uniforms of foreign military, sat at tables fat with premium wines and rich fare. Fine white linen, silverware, and crystal augmented the elegant meal of pumpkin soup with blue lump crab, seafood *amuse-bouche* served in an eggshell, and salt-cod ravioli.

Tan Chu and Nassir Haddad were conspicuously absent, as represented by the sole empty table.

"So as you can see, gentlemen, tonight we are offering up an unusual batch of very unconventional explosives—" Brandt stopped midsentence as he noticed our entrance.

Detective Kruger switched on the lights. The sight of our phalanx of hard-looking invaders, including SWAT officers, sent murmurs rippling through the room. Clayton Brandt turned bright red and instinctively looked to the door for his FBI boys but saw nothing but more NOPD officers pile into the room.

"General," I bellowed, grabbing everyone's attention as I tried not to limp too noticeably, moving into the center of the room. "Detective Saint James, New Orleans Police Department, here. I am very happy to interrupt this assembly of death merchants you have so assiduously assembled, and I take great pleasure in announcing that you are under arrest."

Mackie and Kruger moved forward and did the honors. Brandt put up no struggle as they read him his rights and charges and gave him the silver-bracelet treatment. Aside from maintaining his crimson complexion, he said nothing, but if looks could kill, my parents would never have conceived me.

I faced the assembled buyers. "Gentlemen, thank you all for coming, but the dinner is over, the auction is canceled, and you are all invited to get the hell out of New Orleans. You will be photographed by police detectives as you make your way back to your hotel, where you are urged to pack your bags and leave. Now get out!"

Mackie and Kruger stood next to me like onyx bookends to the sad volume of Clayton Brandt. "You want to take him for the perp walk? TV news crews are waiting outside," said Mackie.

"Would you guys mind doing it?" I asked. "I don't want my ugly mug to break the cameras. And guys, great work."

As the room quickly emptied, Honey and I approached the now-befuddled air force officer, Captain Hasse, who looked like a deserter caught in the searchlight of a war wagon.

"What's this all about?" the captain asked.

"Murder," said Honey. "You part of it?"

"Of course not!"

"Let me see your credentials," I said.

Captain Hasse hesitated, then handed me his plastic-coated IDs. This was Honey's cue to spin him around and begin a pat down. With the captain's back to me, I scanned his IDs with a handheld scanner smaller than a paperback book. The scans were immediately transmitted to Kendall, who sat in my brown surveillance van a block away. I pocketed the scanner, then Honey spun the captain around to face me.

"These seem authentic." I handed back his IDs. "Detective Baybee, would you mind taking the captain downtown? But don't place him under arrest unless you hear from me."

"Arrest? Hey, you can't—" said Hasse.

"This is a murder investigation, Captain. Do I have to handcuff you, or will you just cooperate?"

The captain quickly went limp, and Honey gave me a quick look as she led him away, following in Clayton Brandt's footsteps toward a waiting police unit. She didn't know exactly what I was up to, but soon she would be able to guess.

Less than a minute passed when Detective Fred Gaudet from burglary, who had been instrumental in rolling up the CI-3–asset tail vehicles, hurried inside, tossed me a camcorder, and gave me a thumbs-up. I silently turned and made my way to the kitchen, snagged and scarfed down a tiny slice of goat-cheese cheesecake in full view of kitchen staff, then entered the alley. I threaded through a group of coppers and found a just-stolen Harley-Davidson Softail parked beside the brown surveillance van. Yes, I'd stolen the bike earlier, and I was a cop, but devious habits die hard. After tonight's operation it would be anonymously returned to its owner with a cash bonus.

"Without a hitch?" Kendall asked after sliding open the side door of the van.

"I prefer caramel cheesecake, but so far so good," I responded.

Kendall handed me a very official looking fake Michoud ID. He'd cooked it up in minutes on the van's computer based on the template from the scan I sent him.

"Sweet," I said, checking out Kendall's handiwork. "Erase any evidence that you did this, and see you at the rendezvous point."

I eased on a wraparound black motorcycle helmet that nicely scrunched up my few visible features, then gingerly got onto the bike, favoring my leg wounds.

"You okay to ride?" asked Kendall.

"Ride? Don't know what you're talking about. We're fixing a flat under the Crescent City Connection, remember?" I turned the throttle and shot the big loud bike off into the night.

I coasted the sputtering hog to a stop at the NASA Michoud Facility Gate 5 guard shack, where a female rent-a-cop briefly perused my brand-new fake ID, making me almost feel like a scamming teenager again. A gigantic Saturn V, Stage 1 rocket booster, lit up in the dark night and permanently mounted on towering display adjacent to the gate, stood as a mocking reminder of what the United States used to do, of visions it used to hold dear, of might it once wielded wisely. It irked me that almost literally in the shadow of such technological accomplishment, weasels like Brandt and Breaux and others did their best to sell out our accomplishments to agents of governments that were clearly our enemies.

I motored through the base like I owned the place, and in eight minutes I parked the Harley right in the J-19 loading dock. A couple of airmen gave me a look, and I motioned them over to me. I flashed another very nice-looking fake ID, this one from a template courtesy of Harding when she wasn't paying attention.

"FBI CI-3. We have a situation with General Brandt and Captain Hasse. Who's in charge here?" I said with all the arrogance I could muster, keeping the helmet on.

An E-7 stepped forward. "I'm Cline, sir."

"First Sergeant Cline, the general and captain have just been arrested by New Orleans police detectives for conspiracy to commit murder."

Off the two men's shocked looks, I handed the camcorder to Cline and pushed the PLAY button. The two airmen watched wide-eyed as the video taken by Fred Gaudet showed Brandt and Hasse being led out of Restaurant August and put into squad cars.

"This went down about thirty minutes ago, and it's all over the media. I don't want you and your crew getting arrested, too. How many people you have here, Sergeant?"

Cline's eyes searched mine for clarification. "Six, sir. But, I . . . we don't know anything about—"

"Round up your team and get out now! Return to your quarters and wait for new orders. And don't use your cell phones; they're being monitored by NOPD. You got that, Cline? Now move out!"

"Yes, sir!"

Ninety seconds later the airmen had all cleared out in two vehicles. I did a quick walk-through to satisfy myself the place was empty.

Thanks to the Internet, I'd learned how to make a bomb. I'd fashioned it crudely from the butterfly land mine I had lifted from this very building a couple of nights ago. What I was about to do was radical, stupid, dangerous, and highly illegal. I was about to commit a federal offense that could land me in jail for a very long time.

But then, I was at war with the Buyer's Club and the Feds who abetted them, and I intended to win.

In short order I fired up the Harley and powered loudly away from J-19. I cleared security at the front gate and rumbled out onto Old Gentilly Road and into the black uncertain night of the muggy bayou, my sweaty hands nervously gripping the throttle. I held hope but little faith that I had rigged the device correctly, that it would actually blow.

I slowed to a crawl, jinking to keep the heavy beast upright, until suddenly the percussive sound waves of a distant explosion enveloped me like a congratulatory slap on the back. Or maybe it was an admonishing kick in the ass. Secondary explosions kicked in, and I rocketed the bike forward, since there was no turning back now.

CHAPTER TWENTY-SIX

The staging area for the sting was a vacant building in the Fat City area of Metairie, a seedy, past-its-prime, drug-infested, entertainment-district-cum-red-light-strip that was slowly becoming the home of masses of illegal Mexican workers staffing the ongoing post-Storm reconstruction effort. Honey, Harding, and I had decided to stage the actual swap at the food court of the Clearview Mall. We could have the team in place there in minutes, and our operators could easily blend in with the crowds.

I arrived in the staging area rear parking lot in my black-and-gold big Ford following Kendall in the surveillance van. Task-force under-cover vehicles sat parked all around. Kendall and I entered through the back door. It was a typical hurry-up-and-wait kind of deal, with a lot of law-enforcement officers in civvies standing around drinking coffee, waiting to make the move a few blocks away to the big mall.

Honey led an interdivisional team of detectives that included Fred Gaudet. Harding had a strictly local FBI tactical team on hand; one agent held the fake GIDEON sample we would use in the sting. FBI computer-forensic techs were right now going over Brandt Holdings' treasure trove of digital files at FBI headquarters on Leon C. Simon

Drive, files that NOPD detectives had seized in the raid on Brandt Holdings and shared with Harding.

I made a beeline to Honey and Harding, exaggerating my limp slightly in case I needed to play upon their sympathies because I could tell they weren't happy with me.

"No sign of Decon?" I asked.

"No, and where have you been?"

"My truck had a flat. Good thing Kendall was following me, because I'm not too good with a tire iron right now." I'd put a flat tire in the truck bed, just in case they checked.

Harding frowned. I wasn't getting an animosity vibe between her and Honey; it seemed strictly directed at me. Never let two women in your life get together when you're not around.

"I'm getting reports of a massive explosion at Michoud," said Harding. "At Building J-Nineteen, to be exact."

"Sounds like Brandt had a fail-safe mechanism in place. Destroy evidence to wipe out his tracks," I lied, pretty convincingly.

"An FBI agent, or someone pretending to be an FBI agent, on a motorcycle ordered the air force personnel off the premises just before the place cooked off." Harding was definitely ticked, but I could tell she wasn't sure if I had a hand in the blast or not.

I shrugged. "Sounds like your buddies in CI-3. They're in cover-their-ass mode. I suggested to Chief Pointer right in front of them that we station PD checkpoints to jack up every truck leaving Michoud. Perhaps they took that threat seriously. There's no air strip out there. If they thought they couldn't safely and quickly move out the goods, maybe they decided to blow everything in place. Although I'm surprised any of those CI-3 boys know how to ride a motorcycle."

Honey held her tongue. She knew I was lying through my teeth.

"Does any of that have a bearing on us going ahead right now?" I asked Harding.

"Without your boy Decon, who went AWOL earlier today, there's no going anywhere," she said.

I'd tried calling Decon all day, but he hadn't answered. Still, I pulled out my phone as I took a step toward the grimy front windows and peered outside. A small strip club across the street advertised GIRLS G RLS IRLS, according to the neon sign, anyway.

"He knows we were forming up in the minimall at Eighteenth and Edenborn. Give me a minute; let me check across the street."

I hobbled out through the front door, limped across the street, and entered the strip joint. You couldn't fault the owner for lying. The sign hadn't advertised pretty girls, only girls, although referring to the females present as girls was a bit of a stretch. The working ladies were overweight, long in the tooth, and were walking advertisements for plastic surgeons who argued that makeup alone isn't always enough.

I spotted Decon at a small bar with a bountifully chested, tat-covered black female sitting in his lap.

"Yes, baby, I know it's hot outside, but the thing about drinking brandy on ice—" He was smooth-talking her as he stroked her inner thigh. I interrupted by tossing a fifty-dollar bill on the bar and lifting him up by his shirt collar. As I did, he grabbed a small backpack.

"Try answering your phone, asshole," I said, dragging him toward the door. I could feel as I dragged him along that he wore body armor under his shirt.

"Whoa! You said be at the corner of Eighteenth and Edenborn, and I'm here. I even came early, if you know what I'm suggesting. Is it that time, already?"

I hustled him outside and gave him a shove that sent him to one knee. I knew Honey and Harding were watching, and I didn't care.

"What's with the disappearing act? What kind of scam are you running? Did you already sell a fake laptop to Chu?"

"If I'd pulled that off for a half mil, think I would have showed up here?"

"Why did you show up?"

"I thought I was working for you."

"Oh, kiss my ass."

"You said I was on your payroll."

"A good employee wouldn't have disappeared from the comfort of the Holiday Inn and full access to the minibar. After being specifically told to stay put."

"I never represented myself as being a good employee, if you know—"

"I *don't* know what you mean. Why are you even here? What's in it for you?"

"You are the one who asked me to help you, man."

"Where have you been all day, you piece of shit?" I was getting worked up and gave him a shove. "You low-life scumbag. You double-crossing me? There's an FBI tactical team waiting over there! And I'm having a real hard time trying to convince myself that I should ask them to back you the fuck up. You know what I mean, 'Mr. I've Taken out Russian Hit Teams in Hotel Bathrooms'?" I gave him another shove, and he went sprawling on the concrete. "I trusted you!"

"I'm sorry! I had to go out."

"To do what? I parked you in a luxury suite, and you fucked up a baked potato! It's hard to fuck up a baked potato, Decon."

"I have steel plates in my head, man! They put my skull back together. I'm a whole lot of laughs at the X-ray machine at an airport, if you know what—" He stopped himself. He clenched his fists so hard his knuckles turned white. "Things are different. I can't stay in a hotel room. I can't stay cooped up in *any* room, okay? Not for too long. Okay? I can't."

He lasered me with plaintive eyes that seemed to be brimming with pain from traumas I couldn't even imagine. I guessed the traumas were real; I didn't know about the words.

"What you got to knock me down for? You want me to do this tonight, I'll do it. I even got my hands on a bulletproof vest. As to what's in it for me? I was hoping a couple hundred bucks. Is that too much to ask? And . . . it felt good to be part of a team again."

I exhaled, frowning. The continuing riddle of Decon was proving to be as much of a challenge as solving the case. He'd done pretty well with Tong at Café du Monde, so if he didn't have some hidden agenda—like wanting to kill the Chinese—I figured we had half a chance to pull this off. Mostly though, I wanted to go forward because I wanted Chu and Tong, my number-one suspects, detained and exposed. The rats were scattering, and if we didn't take them into custody tonight, they'd be off to the next city.

"What the hell," I said, pulling him to his feet and leading him across the street.

We joined the team in the vacant building. Fred Gaudet quickly attached a transmitting microphone inside Decon's shirt pocket. Before Honey or Harding could get in a word, Decon's cell phone rang. We all went quiet as he answered it on speakerphone.

"Go ahead."

"Drive to Causeway Bridge. Right now. You have four minute get on bridge. I call you fifteen minute."

The Chinese male voice belonged to Ding Tong.

I shook my head *no* to Decon.

"No. Meet me at the food court of the Clearview Mall. I told you we would do the deal in Metairie, man," said Decon into the phone.

The line went dead.

"This is not good," said Honey. "Call him back."

Decon called, but it went unanswered. I gestured and he terminated the call.

"What did he mean we have four minutes to get onto the bridge? Or what happens—the deal is off?" asked Harding.

"He's trying to take control, that's all," said Decon. "I need some water."

"Over there," said Harding.

Decon slouched off toward a table with coffee, snacks, and beverages.

"Can we get the FBI chopper over to the North Shore, Harding?" I asked.

"Sure. It's standing by at Belle Chasse." Harding stole a look over at Decon. "Is he in any kind of shape to do this?"

"Yeah, he's okay."

"I'm not so sure about that," said Honey. "And we have no elements on the North Shore. The whole team is here. We going to string all our assets along a twenty-four-mile-long bridge? I say we abort."

"What do we have to lose? We're not risking the real sample," I countered. "All we're trying to do is get video and audio of these guys handing over money and committing espionage. We get that, and we have their asses behind bars, with a live media feed, and the State Department has to declare Chu and Tong persona non grata. It's not much of a punishment, but it's something. Otherwise they get to keep running amok all over the country."

"We have lives at risk. In case you forgot," fumed Honey.

"The risk is the same regardless of where we do this," I countered.

"We already have video of Tong checking the GIDEON sample with a Niton gun. We have him on tape, talking about the buy. Talking about giving money to get the formula. That's good enough, since we're not trying for a conviction in court," said Honey.

"Yes, we have some video, but it would be much stronger," I said, "if we could take Chu and Tong into custody with money from the Bank of China. That would be incontrovertibly damning."

"It's too dangerous," said Honey.

"Has anyone seen Chu or Tong pull a weapon? Do we have reason to believe they would do that? Decon is wearing a vest. And all of us, backing him up, will be seconds away," I said. I could see Honey wasn't having any of it. "You saw the moving van at Pelkov's; the rats are deserting a sinking ship. And speaking of ships, my people tell me that Haddad has pulled anchor and set sail. We need to take Tong and Chu into custody now. This is our last chance."

"Better decide," said Kendall. "Clock down to two minutes, thirty seconds."

"Agent Harding, this is your show," I said.

All eyes turned to Harding. But before she could speak . . .

"Where did Decon go?" asked Fred Gaudet.

Decon wasn't in the room. I bolted for the back door with every ounce of speed I could muster, ignoring a world of pain shooting up my legs.

Somehow I was first into the rear parking lot and saw the brown surveillance van pulling away. I angled for the parking lot entrance and managed to grab hold of the van's rear door handle and pull myself onto the bumper. As the van turned onto Edenborn, I got the door open and stumbled inside as I heard shouts coming from the parking lot behind me.

CHAPTER TWENTY-SEVEN

Decon ran the light as he hung a screeching right on to West Esplanade. I held on for dear life as he then executed a careening left onto Causeway Boulevard, narrowly avoiding about three collisions.

I pulled the 1911A and carefully crawled up toward the cab. "You've done a little time as a wheel man," I said, pointing the weapon in his general direction.

"I've done a little time as everything."

"The way these things usually work is, a final decision to go is made, and then we depart in an orderly fashion."

"Too much dissension in there. Makes me nervous. If I bolt, you guys follow, the operation goes forward. Wham, bam, thank you, ma'am."

I figured backup was thirty seconds behind. If the approach to the bridge was being monitored, the cavalry wouldn't be obvious. No one was driving Crown Vics or easy-to-identify LE vehicles.

"Thank you for trusting me," he said.

"That comment was made before you stole my van."

We shot past a semitrailer and made it onto the bridge with seven seconds to spare. I glanced out the rear windows and saw something that caused an instant knot in my gut. The semi we had just passed jackknifed, blocking the northbound lanes onto the bridge. Before I could even compute this, another semi performed the same function, blocking the southbound lanes and preventing traffic from exiting or entering the Metairie side of the Causeway Bridge.

Backup had just been cut off.

"Rover One, Homebody, do you copy?" Harding's voice on the radio-set speaker was showing more emotion than Feds usually displayed over the air. I put on a wireless headset with a mike boom.

"Copy, Homebody; we're Code Four here. I saw what just happened. Standby."

I leaned forward into the cab.

"Semi's have blocked off the bridge behind us. Both trestles."

"Impressive," Decon said, pushing the old van along at an even seventy MPH. The Metairie high-rises on the southern banks of Lake Pontchartrain were already shrinking rapidly in the distance.

"We're aborting. You and me."

"Can't believe those Chinese didn't trust me," said Decon.

"I think they trust you have the real deal. And they want it bad. Do a U-turn at the first crossover."

The Lake Pontchartrain Causeway Bridge was a divided-highway bridge that ran two lanes in each direction, supported by nine thousand concrete pilings. The guardrails stood about two feet high, and woozy drivers managed to flip their vehicles over the rails and into the churning waters of the lake on a fairly regular basis. An eighty-foot gap separated the north and southbound lanes, exposing the dark waters below. Technically the Causeway was two distinct bridges—twin spans—sitting side by side. Seven connecting crossovers on the twenty-four-mile span were reserved for disabled cars and trucks and functioned as staging areas for emergency vehicles. The first crossover was seven miles out onto Lake Pontchartrain.

I conferred with Harding and told her we'd be heading back. Her team had secured the Metairie side bridgehead, but both semitruck drivers had escaped on motorcycles. The trucks belonged to TDF, which was no great shock.

I was about to climb into the front with Decon when I started to get a bad feeling.

"If you were the Chinese, would you even want us to get to the North Shore?"

Eyes forward, Decon answered with eerie calm. "I just started thinking the same thing."

"You figure a boat?"

"Could be a combination. Vehicles blocking the lanes up ahead, a boat waiting below. Twenty feet down on a rope ladder in no time."

"Stop the van and throw it into reverse," I said.

"What's that going to solve?"

"Putting your ass on the line with only me backing you up is not an option. You said yourself that a baby hamster could kick my ass."

"I said a mama gerbil. Are you a good shot?"

"Very good, but that's beside the point."

"I dunno. I'd kind of like to take these assholes on, you know? I mean, who the hell do they think they are?"

Who the hell do they think they are, indeed. Decon had once said that he and I had more in common than I realized. Once again, he was proving to be right.

"Rover One, copy."

"Go ahead, Homebody," I said.

"Bridge Police report more semis jackknifing at the eight-mile marker, blocking both north- and southbound lanes."

"Yeah, we figured out we weren't going to see Mandeville tonight."

"Air support should be on scene in ten mikes. Jefferson Parish sheriffs are launching boats right now."

"Roger that. I'm going live with continuous video and audio feed. Out." I flipped some switches that activated the transmitters. "Decon, stop the truck right here."

"That's not you talking, that's your hot partner. She likes me, you know, can't help herself. The FBI babe—I'm not her cup of tea."

"Your microphone is live; they're monitoring this radio traffic."

"Good. Because what I'm saying is true. See I think you and me make good partners. Screw the rules and just get the shit done. That's been my way since forever. And so I was tolerated because I delivered the goods."

"What goods? Tolerated by whom?"

He glanced at me. "If we make it through tonight, I'll tell you all about myself."

"Just stop the truck; do a three-point turn and drive back. We have nothing to sell the Chinese. We left the fake sample back in Fat City."

"Actually, I do have something. And, dude, the crossover is less than a mile ahead. I'll pull a U-ie. We're good."

I somehow doubted that.

"What something do you have to sell?"

"I'm asking you to keep trusting me. You won't regret it."

I shook my head. In for a penny, in for a pound.

"You got a piece?" I asked.

"No."

I wordlessly handed him my 1911A; he stuck it into his rear waistband. I pulled a big Glock 21 from a cabinet and popped a preloaded thirty-round mag brimming with 230-grain Black Hills jacketed hollow points in my preferred caliber of .45. The mag protruded way out from the bottom of the butt and added a lot of weight to the piece, but the high-cap mag made it a nice equalizer. Who needs an MP5 when you can use your sidearm to put thirty high-caliber rounds on target as fast as you can pull the trigger?

The deserted crossover lay just ahead. It was eerie to be on the normally busy bridge but to have no traffic in either direction. It reminded me of the days after the Storm, when the I-10 twin spans over the lake were out of commission—huge sections had collapsed into the water—and the Causeway's southbound lanes were shut but the northbound trestle stayed open for emergency traffic in both directions. The sense that big things were amiss felt palpable then, as they did right now.

"Slow down."

He slowed the van. There was no sign of a boat, vehicle, or living thing in any direction. Heavy chop from stiff winds whipped the salty waters into an undulating malevolence; I wouldn't want to be out on the lake in a small craft tonight. The lights of Mandeville on the North Shore glowed as only a taunting hint on the horizon. Decon was about to start the turn when a tremendous roar enveloped us. Dust and litter blew at the windshield, and the van rocked as wind gusts buffeted the panels.

"Shit, helicopter," I said.

"That's no helicopter."

Decon stopped the van, and a *plane* landed in front of us on the wide crossover in a maelstrom of swirling grit. It was a twin-engine fixed-wing plane, but it landed like a helicopter. I ducked down to stay out of sight but could see that it was a tilt-rotor plane. Not a Harrier jet, but a V-22 Osprey, the problem-plagued VTOL craft—Vertical Take Off and Landing—that the Marines had fought long and hard for. Ospreys can either fly like a helicopter or a fixed-wing turboprop airplane. This one was painted black with no markings of any kind. There was room to spare for the fifty-five-foot-long craft to land on the deserted crossover.

"That's an Osprey, except it's not marked. Civilians don't fly that bird, I can tell you that, if you understand my meaning."

I nodded. "Someone wants the GIDEON goods in a big way."

The crossover was well lit. We were no more than twenty-five yards away, close enough to see the pilot's face in the large cockpit windows. He was Asian. Then Ding Tong appeared in the Osprey's side door holding a Niton gun.

"How the hell did the Chinese get their hands on an Osprey?" asked Decon.

"I'll give you a one-word answer: cash. Last chance. Throw it in reverse. No harm, no foul."

"Oh, hell no." He grabbed his small backpack off the seat and then turned to me. "I'm real sorry I have to do this, but it's for your own safety."

And then he sucker punched me. Hard. I fell back onto the rear floor of the van. My vision clouded over with bright points of light. I blinked, fighting hard to stay conscious. I tried to think, to concentrate, but my head wouldn't stop spinning and I couldn't get up.

CHAPTER TWENTY-EIGHT

Hard to say exactly, I was down for maybe ten seconds when I heard somebody talking over the headset, and it helped me focus. I rolled over and got to my knees. A wave of nausea swept over me, then subsided.

"Rover One, Homebody, copy?"

"Go ahead," I managed to say, adjusting the placement of my headset.

"Be advised, our bird is ETA six mikes."

"Roger." I shook my head, trying to clear my thinking. "Listen, Ospreys can outrun helicopters and have a longer range. You might want to get on the horn to the Louisiana Air National Guard over at Belle Chasse. Out."

Still shaky, I looked at the video screen in the back of the van; no one had come out of the plane except Tong. He held the Niton gun in one hand and a carry bag in the other. He and Decon were just about face-to-face. Decon was up to something; he hadn't just slugged me for my own "safety." And now I was reduced to listening via the microphone he wore and watching on a video screen in the back of the van. I felt isolated from the action and didn't like that at all. The rear doors to the van were angled away from the Osprey. My headset was wireless; I could quietly ease out onto the bridge and listen to the deal go down, poised to intervene.

So I slipped out the back doors and listened via my headset as they shouted in order to be heard above the churning rotors.

"Where is sample?" Tong sounded royally pissed.

"In Metairie, where I said I'd meet you, brother. Doing it out here—this is kinda kooky."

I chanced a peek around the rear bumper. Decon held the backpack in his left hand. Tong mumbled something in Chinese, probably communicating the situation to whomever was inside the Osprey. I assumed that would be Chu.

"You have my money in that bag, right? Because I have something you want."

I watched, listening with the headphones on, as Decon slowly reached into the backpack and pulled out a laptop. From this distance it was hard to tell, but it looked similar to Del Breaux's laptop. What the hell was he doing? I specifically told him to keep the laptop issue out of the equation. Then I saw the brilliance in the move. The Niton gun would have revealed the sample as a fake; it would have pissed Tong off, and we would have had to take him down in a confrontation. That was understood and we had planned for that. But the laptop would have to be vetted later, after a hacker obtained the password. Video and audio were recording the Chinese attempting to commit espionage by taking the computer. Money would change hands, Tong would take possession of the bogus laptop, I would step out with the artillery to make an arrest, and we'd all go home safe. Except Decon had tried to knock me out. Meaning he wasn't on board for my plan or intending to take anyone into custody. I could only assume he was going to kill them.

"This is the same one I got from that cop's truck when I took the metal sample, you know what I mean? I'm betting that formula you want is inside," said Decon to Tong.

I saw Tong quickly examine the laptop, open it, and power up.

"What is password?" asked Tong.

"Brother man, I don't know the password. How am I supposed to know that? You guys are smart; you can figure it out. You want the sample, we got to go back to Metairie. But I do got me one of these here pens, like I told you about, you know, so I can be sure the long green in your bag is the real deal."

Tong handed Decon the money bag, then barked something in Chinese. Two Asian men scrambled out of the Osprey and made for the van, probably to check inside for the GIDEON sample because they thought Decon was lying about its location. When they saw all the electronics in the back of the van, the game would be up.

"Money all there. You count in plane. We go Metairie now."

As I watched, Tong started to pull him toward the plane.

I had to act fast; the two Chinese goons, one of whom who was a good six feet tall, were almost to the van.

I stood and stepped into the open. "Police officer! Stop right there, you're under arrest!" I held the big, ammo-heavy Glock in my weak-side hand, pointing right at them. My banged-up right hand held the gold shield for the bad guys to see.

But damn it if they didn't both go for their guns.

"Stop! Don't move!"

Just before tunnel vision kicked in, I was aware that Decon was watching me confront the goons. He broke away from Tong while clutching the money bag. Tong made a perfect toss of the laptop into the Osprey's doorway, where it was caught by none other than Tan Chu. Tong then bolted after Decon.

I could have just stood there watching, except two thugs were both swinging their pistols toward me from four yards away. I simply could not afford to let them shoot first. And any politically correct idiot who says that a police officer should only shoot to "wing" an assailant is an imbecile who has no concept of what it's like to stand feet away from men who want you dead and are about to achieve their wish. Besides, my trigger finger was broken and my pistol was in the wrong hand. I'd practiced shooting with the weak-side hand—all serious shooters do—but this was the real deal, not practice. So since I didn't want to die tonight, I double-tapped both men, close as I could get to center mass.

I ran toward Decon, who delivered a couple of chops to Tong's throat area, stunning the Chinese agent. *Damn! Decon knows how to fight.* It was a shocking sight, but so was Chu, standing in the Osprey doorway, pointing a long gun at me. I knelt and fired five rounds at him, and he dropped back into the darkness as the plane started to lift off. As the door closed, I put twelve more rounds into the aircraft, then was blinded by swirling dust and groped for a handhold that didn't exist, feeling like I was in a wind tunnel. Harding was saying something over the comm-link, which competed in a jumbled cacophony with the roar of the straining engines and the concussion booms from the .45 still echoing in my brain.

Decon and Tong grappled on the concrete mere feet from me. Three muted shots rang out, muffled only because of my inability to hear well at the moment.

Tong stood up with a gun in his hand, and I instantly did the same. He turned and faced me. I had the Glock, but something made me try another tack. Maybe it was something that I needed to prove to myself. Maybe it was my fighter's instinct. Either way, I was in no condition to rumble, so I put everything I had into one move; a picture-perfect recreation of the turning back-kick I'd used on Bobby Perdue, but this time my intent was to inflict major hurt. I planted, spun right, sighted on Tong as he raised his gun, then I unleashed the right leg, donkey style. My heel crunched his sternum with a sound that reminded me of chomping on a mouthful of Corn Flakes before they had a chance to get soggy.

The force of the blow was such that he fell back against the low guardrail and just kept going over the side. If he were conscious and a long-distance swimmer, he had a slim chance.

I dropped down beside Decon. Even with body armor, being shot at point-blank range can kill you. His vest had stopped two of Ding Tong's rounds, but one had entered his chest just above the top edge of the vest. He was barely conscious. I peeled off my shirt and used it as a compress on the chest wound.

I glanced up as the Osprey's nacelles pivoted forward, the rotors now looking like oversized, slightly droopy prop blades, and the hovering craft shot off into the night sky.

"Homebody, where's that chopper? Man down and we need to medevac him ASAP!" I yelled into my headset.

"You see the way I went toe-to-toe with that dude?" asked Decon weakly.

"Don't talk; we got a bird coming in for you right now."

"We get the money?"

The money bag lay on the concrete within reach, so I grabbed it and placed it next to Decon, put his hand on top of it.

"You got it, man."

"The day I make a million dollars is the day I die. What a bitch, you know what I mean?"

And then he died.

I stood up in a daze. Harding was saying something over the comm-link, but it didn't register. My body hurt everywhere, a walking ball of pain. I felt the Russian killer's tanto knife slicing me all over again. I'd broken open stitches just by doing the one move on Tong and could see the blood seeping into my bandages. My shotgun-pellet wounds hurt my leg like it was on fire, my fingers ached, my head throbbed. And Decon had just died in my arms. I wobbled as I walked to the guardrail and looked down. Tong needn't have worried about being a good swimmer. He bobbed face down in the inky water. He was chum.

I knew I should be doing something, but I couldn't think of what. Then another roar enveloped me, and a MH-6 Little Bird flown by two FBI special agents put down on the crossover. I hobbled under the six spinning rotor blades as soon as it was safe, on the off chance we could track a big black vulture.

It wasn't much of a race, since Ospreys cruise at 460 kilometers per hour and the Little Bird could do maybe 250. The fact we were heading out to sea, in international waters, surprised me; maybe Chu was making a run for Mexico knowing we didn't have the range to follow that far. The chopper's advanced night-vision system and state-of-the-art surveillance optics kept the Osprey in sight, even as we fell far behind. Surveillance, after all, was the prime mission of the FBI's air fleet. Then something strange happened about fifteen miles out into the Gulf. We started to catch up.

The Osprey had slowed in the far distance and was circling to land on what I assumed was an offshore rig. I zoomed-in the mast-mounted optics unit, shocked to see the Osprey setting down . . . on a cargo ship.

And five would get you ten the cargo ship belonged to a certain Mr. Nassir Haddad.

"Can you get us in close enough to read the name on the ship's stern?"

"That shouldn't be a—"

The flash from the explosion caused the copilot to whip his head away from the night-vision sight. I gawked in awe as the watery horizon flickered with bright yellow light, then secondary explosions rocked the cargo ship and it actually lifted out of the water.

The vessel began to break up, but not before we confirmed its name: *El Fazlin.* In short order the broken, burning ship slipped below the choppy, wind-whipped waves and disappeared into the dark bowels of the Gulf.

Just like that, there was nothing left but clumps of floating debris.

Just that quick, souls had been judged and sentences carried out, the obtuse machinations of plotters gone moot. The power of steel and diesel and money and nefarious intent was simply silenced and sealed with a cleansing of salt water, like washing out an ulcerated wound.

The Little Bird's pilot notified the Coast Guard as we circled, checking for survivors. I knew there wouldn't be any, and there weren't.

CHAPTER TWENTY-NINE

My attendance at the packed 8 A.M. press conference was mandatory. Chief Pointer orchestrated the show like a garrulous circus ringmaster who was getting a fat percentage of the gate. Clayton Brandt now resided in New Orleans Parish Prison, under arrest for the attempted-murder conspiracy on the life of an NOPD officer. Honey and I made sure that Detectives Mackie and Kruger took the bow; file that one under good politics in the Homicide Section. In addition, the local FBI office, in the guise of a smiling Agent Harding, had charged Brandt with numerous crimes related to illegal transshipments of weapons to embargoed countries based on files extracted from his office computers and the sworn statements of his former employees Mario and Jerry.

The arms-smuggling case, the chief hinted to the rapturous Fourth Estate members, was related to the murder of one international weapons dealer named Grigory Pelkov, shot in his Uptown home by a sniper. The chief got in a little poke at CI-3 by reminding the press of the recent drug arrest of arms dealer Nassir Haddad, a confidant of Pelkov. He emphasized that it was the hard work of NOPD detectives that broke the case, now in the hands of the FBI for further investigation. Honey took the bow on that one. There was no mention of any U.S. government "sanctioned" weapons sales. Or of the crash of a V-22

Osprey and sinking of a cargo ship in the Gulf of Mexico. Any further questions were referred to FBI CI-3 Agent Minniear, doing the best Pruneface impression I'd seen in years.

As to the dramatic closure of the Causeway Bridge and the subsequent shoot-out that left four men dead at mile marker seven—Jefferson Parrish deputies had recovered Tong's body at dawn—the chief trumpeted a joint NOPD/FBI task force that had stopped cold an attempt by an unnamed foreign power from obtaining super-secret U.S. technology. I'd just moments ago given the chief Del Breaux's laptop, and Pointer now made a showy presentation of the DOD-issued computer into the hands of Harding and Ralph Salerno, who shared the credit with me. CI-3 Agent Gibbs stood off to the side; he and I looked ready to kill each other, but really I just wanted some sleep. I'd been up all night doing the post–lethal-force-shooting debriefing and paperwork dance.

The chief left out the part about one million dollars in sequentially numbered bills from the Bank of China in Beijing being logged into the porous NOPD evidence warehouse as a result of the action on the Causeway Bridge. It was no doubt one of the reasons he looked so happy.

As the press conference neared an end, Chief Pointer deftly directed all follow-up questions to Gibbs and Minniear, since they were now in charge of the "ongoing investigations."

Honey and I had officially missed the forty-eight-hour deadline to solve the murders of Del Breaux, Ty Parks, Leroy and Jimmy Jefferson, and Herbert Rondell. Not to mention Terry Blanchard, Eddie Liu, and Grigory Pelkov. Chief Pointer said nothing to me about the murders or deadline, he just happily shook my hand. I'd again escaped the mandatory post-shooting desk-job assignment; I think he sensed I had another good headline for him if he left me alone. It struck me I was shilling for a sleazeball, but that was the deal I had made.

This was a red-letter day for NOPD, and Chief Pointer mugged for the cameras like the old pro he was. Solving the murders wasn't what he cared about anyway; it was the positive headlines, the perception that NOPD was kicking ass and taking names. So in a sense, Honey and I had made the deadline after all.

That we did it on the back of Decon's corpse was a bitter pill that I had not yet been able to swallow.

Harding and I had spoken briefly before the press conference. Her report and video documentation sent to Washington on the GIDEON espionage activities of Tan Chu and Ding Tong while under the de facto protection of CI-3 was causing major shock waves inside the Beltway. CI-3 had been keeping their efforts to recover the GIDEON items hush-hush, but now that the truth was emerging, well, the long knives were really coming out. She'd be making brutal new enemies and powerful new allies, and isn't that how it usually goes? Harding said she had already given the authentic GIDEON sample to Salerno. That and his acquisition of Breaux's laptop insured his job as Michoud security chief would most likely be preserved; Salerno shook my hand for over thirty seconds after the press conference had finished, and invited me to lunch.

As for Global Solutions Unlimited, no doubt the government's arms-dealing operation was already being set up with a new Pentagon point man in a new U.S. city with new CI-3 agents assigned to keep a lid on things. Business is business, after all.

Just stay out of my town.

After a triple vanilla latte, I wandered up to the Homicide Section offices and found Honey sitting at her battered desk that was covered with case files and paperwork. I sat down across from her.

"You think I'm to blame for Decon's death."

"No. I heard the transmissions. You tried to abort. He wanted to go for it."

I knew Decon hit the nail on the head when we were in the van; Honey had grown fond of the guy, in her own way. Women always seem to fall for the dashing rogues. Even the kind of creepy ones.

"The Buyer's Club is history," I said.

"Seems to be."

"Any chance Haddad wasn't on his ship?"

"If you were him, would you have been?"

I nodded. Honey didn't want to talk. Maybe she just felt empty, like I did. Well, not exactly like me; she hadn't just killed three more people. Maybe she was disappointed with me. I couldn't say, and I knew she wouldn't, so I slowly stood up and moved toward the door.

"Take some time off, okay?"

"Good idea," I said.

"And go to the hospital. Have them check you."

I limped out, knowing my first stop was a place full of people who wouldn't be getting well anytime soon.

It all came back to the laptop. Why did Decon keep bringing a fake laptop into play with the Chinese? In his wildest dreams he knew that he would not have been allowed to keep any of the cash exchanged for either a fake sample or a fake laptop.

On the bridge as the operation went down, I'd thought he'd made a smart move, using the computer, since it couldn't be quickly vetted one way or the other. But where did he come up with a replica DOD-issued laptop so quickly? Had he somehow mocked something up after he disappeared from the Holiday Inn? The unit passed muster with Tong, who seemed to know what he was looking for as he examined the exterior sticker. That made sense, because Breaux always had the laptop with him at the Michoud auctions, and Tong attended the auctions, too. But how would Decon know to duplicate such a laptop?

That he simply took it upon himself to provide better bait in the Chu sting seemed less and less plausible.

Then there was the way he fought with Tong. I'd been muscling Decon around for the better part of the last five days. But he fought Tong better than I fought Tong. And he'd never ceased mouthing off about his background, claiming he'd called in air strikes and taken out wet teams in foreign countries. Had he? He said he served in the military, so his prints should have been on file in those databases, but they weren't. He wouldn't be the first charlatan to claim he served his country when he really hadn't. Decon was as big of a mystery now as he was the first night Honey and I collared him.

And that's why I found myself performing a meticulous search of his crypt crib in Greenwood Cemetery. Honey and I had gone through his stuff yesterday, but now I painstakingly looked for hiding places and stash holds. I checked all of his garments for secret pockets or items that might be sewn into the material. I found six hundred dollars tucked into a padded backpack strap. Taped under the sarcophagus was what had to be a house key. It didn't add up to much, so I drove out to Metairie.

I hobbled along uneven concrete sidewalk slabs in a neighborhood with a helluva lot of more bars than churches, soaked to my skin as a rain shower downpour rinsed the sweat from my arms and face and turned my bandages into soggy lumps. I walked a grid pattern, using the key I'd taken from Decon's pants cuffs the night Honey and I collared him. He'd said it was a gate key, and I was trying it on every apartment security gate in the neighborhood. At the thirty-seventh gate the key worked, and I opened the fake wrought-iron gate to a ten-unit building that needed an exterior makeover.

His was apartment D. The key from under the sarcophagus opened it. Worn carpeting, shabby furniture, dirty dishes in the sink. A large flying cockroach took a pass at me from atop the kitchen cabinets; I swatted it with my finger splints, then crushed it under my boot as I checked the kitchen drawers.

I found cheapie day planners for the last two years, the kind you can get at a ninety-nine-cents store. Every day he had worked for the Jefferson brothers was noted along the lines of: "Scrap Brothers, 7A-5P." I saw no entries indicating any kind of social rendezvous. A key ring held vehicle keys to an Audi sedan and a Ford Explorer parked outside in the lot.

In a shoebox in the living room on the lower shelf of the pressboard coffee table, I found a tattered white envelope stuffed with fading photographs showing a heavier Decon with short hair and no goatee in European and Asian cities, drinking a café crème on the Med, having a Beerlao in an open-air bar with a pretty Asian girl on each arm, standing over a bloody corpse in a narrow street in what looked like Africa.

In dirty fatigues with no insignia I saw him smiling, crouched behind sandbags with the buttstock of a SAW, Squad Automatic Weapon, against his shoulder. Somalia? I saw him geared up for a nighttime high-altitude, low-opening jump in the open doorway of a cargo plane. And I saw him in a team photo: twelve very salty looking operators forming two rows as they held exotic small arms and were loaded for bear like they were ready to overthrow a small country. Decon wore a Special Forces–issue helmet.

A medical discharge, he had said. Steel plates in his head, he had said. Time in the brig as a prisoner of conscience, he had said. I set the photos aside and kept looking.

In the bedroom, in a dirty Whole Foods shopping bag—one of those canvas ones you pay a premium for in an attempt to assuage your guilt at being a consumer—I found a UPS uniform: brown shorts, brown shirt, brown baseball-type cap.

Decon had put the bomb in my refrigerator.

He was the UPS guy on my security video. It made sense that a master burglar like him could get past my locks and alarms. In the bottom of the bag, the presence of a short blond wig and theatrical facial hairpieces confirmed this.

I didn't stop to make assessments; I just kept looking. A mud-caked backpack in the closet contained items from J-19, a half dozen of the black exploding ink pens, several of the pagerlike devices I'd seen, and three odd-looking hand grenades. He hadn't lifted these when he was there with me. A digital camera in the backpack contained photos of the exterior and interior of J-19. The time stamps indicated he had been there earlier the same evening we had gone, so he had made two trips in one night. Maybe he was the guy who had left the doors so conveniently open.

I spotted a cell phone on the nightstand; he'd said he didn't own one. I checked the "dialed numbers" folder and recognized a phone number I hadn't called for about six months.

Suddenly, it was almost as if the room started to spin. I knocked over the bedside lamp as I backed against the wall for support, the scheme clicking into place in my mind's eye, a veil of confusion and misinformation suddenly evaporating.

I'd been set up.

CHAPTER THIRTY

Reduced visibility from the evening's heavy rain worked to my favor. Stabbing pain ripped through my left leg as I ran crouched through the front gate behind the limousine. I rolled right onto the wet grass and sprinted next to the black Lincoln out of the driver's mirror's sight lines. Everything hurt, until I just tuned out the pain, the way I'd always been able to do before. I felt very alive, and more important matters were at hand than physical pain.

The limo pulled under a rear portico of the Uptown mansion. I guessed correctly; the driver ran around the back of the vehicle, and two whacks from an old SR-24 baton knocked him out cold. As I swung open the rear passenger door, I looked into the startled face of Twee Siu.

Two pizza boxes sat in her lap.

We locked eyes and then she glanced at where I held something pointing at her from under my shirttail.

"Cliff, glad you could stop by for pizza. You never met my son, Brandon, did you? Brandon, say hi to my good friend Cliff." Twee was simply one cool customer.

Brandon, who I knew to be about eleven years old now, sat slumped down next to Twee, immersed in a video game on a tablet computer.

Half Asian, half Caucasian, he looked up at me for a microsecond and said, "Hi," then returned to fight the good video fight.

"Well?" asked Twee pointedly.

I gestured for her to get out of the car.

I kept the drop on Twee for twelve minutes while she set Brandon up with his dinner. I figured the limo driver would be out for at least another twenty. We adjourned to the study and she closed the solid mahogany doors. The room was heavy with bamboo, teak, and rattan furnishings and primitive carvings of wooden Buddhas. She had lived in this house with her former husband, Brandon's father, a guy who had shot me once upon a time and who died mysteriously before the FBI and NOPD could arrest him for numerous felonies. But they had raided this house looking for dope, and that's how I knew the location. For whatever reason, Twee hadn't moved out. Oh, yeah, and her ex had been her CIA handler, serving as New Orleans's CIA station chief before Twee.

"Put the gun away; you're not going to shoot me."

"I'll shoot you if I have to."

Twee wore tight jeans and a soft-looking billowy top of a kind now trendy in Tokyo. Her hair and makeup were always done perfectly in a current fashion, and the femininity of her visage belied the tough-as-nails character that I knew resided within.

"Decon liked you. You found his apartment?"

I didn't say anything.

"He wanted you to know, in case he didn't make it. He had a premonition; he told me about it. I wrote it off to drunken absinthe talk."

"So Harding gives me some bullshit story about Decon being a murder suspect, I track down Decon, then he gets me pregnant with the arms dealing."

"You're the best investigator in the whole city."

"The best," I mumbled with contempt. "The most dense, you mean. I was your stalking horse. I ran interference, fleshing out Brandt's operation."

"We knew most of it."

"We?"

"You know my job description."

"Which would seem to put you in bed with everything that was happening."

"Exactly the opposite. Think for a second."

I mentally hit rewind, cycling through key recent events. "Decon said there was one other person who trusted him, someone I knew. He gave me a whole bunch of clues, but I thought he was just full of beans." I pulled the white envelope stuffed with Decon's photos from a cargo pocket.

She shrugged with a knowing smile. "You're like a freight train. Your investigation caused more problems for the Buyer's Club than you can imagine."

"So instead of the CIA shutting down Brandt's operation, you made it out like *I* was shutting it down."

There it was. Twee had manipulated me again, masterfully, like some kind of pint-sized Asian female Machiavellian spymaster. I dropped the white envelope onto the plush Oriental carpet as though it were tainted with E. coli. Decon had played me like a fool from the very first second we met.

And now his handler, a woman who had always elicited conflicted feelings from me, was deigning to explain just what a chump I had been.

"Decon was half crazy and only a shadow of his former self, but he was still the most effective agent I ever ran," said Twee. "He got sheep-dipped in the military; that's why his prints didn't come up for you. Worked for some exotic outfits like ISA."

I didn't say anything as I stared at the wall behind her. Part of me wanted to slug her. I was a wounded, beat-up mess, had almost been killed in her service, and I'm sure that didn't concern her at all. In a city that needed all the unpaid volunteers it could get, I had been one, unknowingly.

"ISA is Intelligence Support Activity."

"I know what it is," I snapped.

As much as I wanted to storm out, catch a flight to someplace fresh and clean, maybe sit at a café table with a smoke and a cold one overlooking a beach with some good jazz playing as I girl-watched with a nice sea breeze blowing, as much as I wanted some simplicity, some beauty, maybe some nurturing even, in other words, as much as I wanted to walk away from New Orleans and Twee Siu's conniving, I wanted more to learn the facts.

"He had a mental breakdown, got a medical discharge."

She was baiting me to continue the debriefing. After a long pause, I took the bait. "Why the breakdown?"

"Why do you think?"

"From what he saw, what he did."

"He was consumed by guilt. Until he learned to sublimate it. After his discharge, he worked as an asset for DEA and got addicted to meth. Cleaned himself up but he was never the same. I mean, what kind of agent creates a cover where you live in a tomb in a cemetery? No other agency would touch him, even as an unofficial asset. But I got him down here to work for me in New Orleans."

"It was no accident he went to work at Scrap Brothers right after the Storm."

"Of course not. The previous forklift driver got a chunk of money and a one-way ticket to Detroit. So Decon showed up looking for work the day the other guy left town."

"Decon was one hell of an undercover operator." I wanted to be angry with the guy, but how could I be? He was dead.

"It might take you a year or two to get that good."

"What are you talking about?"

"You know what I'm talking about."

"Not interested."

"Would you rather keep working for me without realizing you're working for me?"

"I'd rather you left me out of it. The intelligence game is a dirty business."

"So is every case you take on."

"I like being my own boss."

"You're working for Chief Pointer again."

"Part-time."

"You'd be part-time for me after three months at Camp Peary for spy school. You keep the PI agency, keep working the occasional homicide case. I don't want to just use you as an asset; I want you as an NOC, nonofficial cover. That would give you immense protection."

"I say my prayers. Burn incense and sage. Meditate."

"You've already agreed, you just don't realize it yet. We're not so dissimilar."

"We're a bit dissimilar. Better recheck my psych test."

Twee flashed angry. "I have been loosely monitoring this whole enterprise that showed up at my back door right before the Storm hit. CIA was not even informed, can you imagine that? The Pentagon, with CI-3 assistance, brings foreign-intelligence agents into *my* area of operations, and they don't even give me a heads up?"

"So interagency cooperation sucks. What's new?"

"What's new is that I learned that Del Breaux was ready to turn traitor and sell the GIDEON secrets. I'd be damned if I was going to let that happen. But to be honest, I was fed up with Brandt's game and wanted it shut down. How was I supposed to do that in a way that kept the Agency out of the picture? So I had Harding bait you with Decon."

"The assumption being that my nosing around would bring exposure. Brandt would pick up his toys and leave, just like he'd done in Miami and elsewhere."

"It was a good plan. But Breaux's murder was not our doing. That surprised me."

"Really? Decon planted a bomb in my house."

"For two reasons. I knew hit teams had been dispatched. I wasn't sure I could stop them, so I wanted you to get the message to hunker down."

"Second reason?"

"Publicity. CI-3 managed to keep your dope bust of Haddad out of the news, but they couldn't cover up the bomb squad evacuating several blocks of the Warehouse District. At some point, news of the arms dealing had to go viral. Pieces of the truth get out, exposure becomes a real threat, and the dirty business stops for a second or two."

Funny to hear Twee Siu talk about trying to stop dirty business. "And using the butterfly land mine was a way to fuel my anger toward the Buyer's Club suspects."

"Indeed."

"So Harding is one of your assets."

"Not exactly. The Bureau and the Agency don't get along very well, but the 'old girl network' trumps everything. We help each other sometimes."

I shook my head. "You're like some kind of evil force, running around killing people and subverting justice."

"*I* didn't bring Tan Chu and Grigory Pelkov and their minions into town. They set up local intelligence nets. Spy rings. Waitresses at Chinese restaurants, a clerk at a federal building, truck drivers with access to secure facilities, local business owners, a professor at Tulane, scientists at sensitive laboratories. Do I need to go on?"

I forced a chuckle. "You're worried about waitresses?"

"When they're sleeping with socially inept geeks with Top Secret security clearances, yes. Chu was a direct threat to some of my operations. Pelkov too. But they were protected by another arm of the U.S. government. It boggles the mind."

"How protected is Brandt?"

"Now? Not at all. He's an embarrassment who will do hard time for the murder-conspiracy charge. He'll plea on the federal rap, so there will be no trial where juicy details might emerge. He's poison to the Feds; they want him to disappear."

"Why don't you just disappear him like you disappeared Tan Chu and Nassir Haddad and about thirty other people? The laptop your boy Decon was so insistent on selling to the Chinese was a bomb, wasn't it? Let me guess, you had someone on a small boat nearby who triggered it when the Osprey landed. Talk about murder? You're a mass murderer!"

"Wrong again. That was pilot error."

"Bullshit!"

"Are you not aware of how unreliable Ospreys are? How many have crashed due to mechanical failures and pilots making mistakes? The Chinese pilot was attempting a night landing in rough seas and heavy winds, flying a tilt-rotor plane that is not exactly easy to fly. And he was loaded with munitions like those butterfly land mines."

"You wanted Tan Chu dead. And Nassir Haddad."

"I did not!"

"How stupid do you think I am? The laptop was a bomb!"

"Yes, it *was* a bomb! A cyber bomb!"

I blinked. *A cyber bomb. Like the Stuxnet operation in Iran?* Stuxnet was a computer worm introduced into the Iranians nuclear processing facility that, among other things, rendered some of their equipment and centrifuges useless.

"Decon died getting that laptop onto the plane. We could have set back Chinese attempts to militarize space by five years! But he died for *nothing* because of that crash." I had seen it before; Twee Siu was tearing up. "Would you have done the same?"

"After what I've seen the Feds do over the last week, probably not."

"Are you one of those cynical idiots who thinks the whole system is corrupt and worthless? The government is not a monolith. The CIA is not a monolith. There are plenty of good people trying to fight the good fight."

"If you say so."

"Please. It's okay for you to break the rules when you're trying to solve your cases, but it's not okay for your country to do it when we're trying to win at something, is that it?"

"I didn't say that."

"It's okay for you to blow up a federal building—J-19—but it's not okay for me or the CIA to break the rules as we fight the unsung fight, the battles your country has to fight, whether you or any ungrateful citizen likes it or not. Is that how you feel?"

"I always try to do the right thing—"

"As determined by whom? You? I got handed a lemon when Brandt showed up in town, so I tried to make lemonade out of it. But I'll take a few dead Chinese and Russian agents, any day. Does that shock you? Repulse you?"

"Haddad was not an agent."

"He was. For Israel. And if you think I would have anything to do with killing one of the best agents in the Mossad, think again."

I remembered Haddad had told me about his "benefactor." Was he referring to Tel Aviv? Talk about great actors; he and Decon would have to share my vote for the Oscar. But even if he were an Israeli agent, he'd attempted to commit espionage and get the GIDEON secrets along with Chu and Pelkov. And since the Osprey had attempted to rendezvous with Haddad's ship at sea, the Egyptian had obviously cut a side deal with Chu that he neglected to mention to me. A deal that didn't work out too well for him.

"I saw you got some nice press on TV," Twee continued. "Which makes it hurt all the more that a real hero—Danny Doakes—will never get a plaque in the lobby at CIA headquarters for making the ultimate sacrifice."

"Your operation was rogue? Langley didn't know?"

She took a few moments to compose herself. I hoped her grief was genuine. Faking it would place her beyond contempt.

"I couldn't risk it," she said at last. "The politics of money trumps everything. And I have to take orders just like everyone else. I had Del Breaux's house and business wired and learned he was toying with the idea of selling the GIDEON secrets."

"I found two of your bugs. In lamps."

"Then you missed about twenty others. Decon broke into Breaux's house, got his laptop while Del and Ty were asleep; we hacked it and downloaded the files, then returned it before they woke up. I worked behind the scenes with a friend in the Science Directorate. My scientist friend created new files that we put into a duplicate laptop, altering the GIDEON formula in ways that would lead the Chinese, or whomever, down the wrong path and would also unleash a Trojan in their systems."

I nodded slowly. *Exactly like Stuxnet.*

"I didn't take delivery of that duplicate laptop until early last night," Twee continued. "That's why Decon had to sneak out of the Holiday Inn, to meet me. It would have been better if he could have bypassed you and sold it to Chu and Tong directly, but there was no time; they were leaving New Orleans last night."

"But Harding and I were going to take them into custody."

Twee fidgeted just a bit. "You were going to be detained at the staging area in Fat City. There wasn't going to be a sting, just a sale."

Talk about having the rug pulled out from under you. At this point I was ready to hear her say that Honey had been in on it, too.

As angry as I was at Twee Siu right now, though, she had just described the exact kind of reverse sting that I'd hoped the Pentagon had been doing in selling all the high-tech weapons systems. The Pentagon hadn't done so, but Twee had, on her own initiative.

"Who killed Del Breaux, Ty Parks, Leroy and Jimmy Jefferson, Herbert Rondell, Grigory Pelkov, Eddie Liu, and Terry Blanchard?"

"Each of those men were guilty of federal offenses, multiple felonies. No great loss to humanity, and I won't be shedding a tear for any of them. But I only know who killed Pelkov."

"Who?"

She took a long time before answering and looked me right in the eyes. "I did. While you sat across from him in his sunroom."

It took a second for me to digest that. "You murdered him. I was about to arrest him, but you shot him down like a dog!"

"I saved your life, is what I did. He was sending for another hit team to take you out. He wanted you dead from the moment he met you. That was a sanctioned kill I made. Moscow and those old-school Soviet thugs at GRU had to eat it, because their agents are not allowed to order the executions of American police officers, especially while operating in America. We presented the Russians evidence that he had done exactly that. Pelkov was off the reservation; the order was issued, and I executed it."

I stood there reeling, waiting for the next verse in the Book of Revelations, and there was one more.

"I wasn't about to let you get killed."

"Yeah, I mean, puppets like me don't come along every day."

"I've made love to three men in my life. I'd kind of like the third one to stick around."

You could have knocked me over with a feather. Twee Siu had a soft spot for me? I was speechless.

"So maybe you should stop feeling sorry for yourself for a few minutes, man-up, and figure out who the killers are."

Twee stepped up close to me. Even with her heels on I towered over her, so she had to put a hand behind my head to bend it forward so our lips met. It was a tender yet insistent kiss. It spoke of all kinds of possibilities and caught me completely off guard.

"Dawson Hayward," she whispered in my ear. "Decon's real name. From Carbondale, Illinois. It was a privilege to have worked with him."

CHAPTER THIRTY-ONE

I spent two days unpacking all of the boxes in my loft and straightening the place up. I had a new fridge put in and had the hole in my roof fixed, the one the Russians had cut in order to gain access. The kitchen repairs from all the shotgun blasts would have to wait, only because I needed peace and quiet.

I stopped drinking, except for coffee, juice, and lots of water. I spent an afternoon at the Hall of Records, which was still in bad shape from the Storm. My gold shield, badge 888, made some things happen pretty quickly out at Louis Armstrong Airport, things that I needed to have happen. I subpoenaed phone, credit card, and e-mail records, ran background checks that we hadn't run before, did a lot of research on the Internet. Oh, and I confirmed that Dawson Hayward, from Carbondale, Illinois, and one Decon Daniel Hawthorne Doakes were one and the same. At least Twee had told the truth about that.

I holed up for four days, sleeping for only a couple of hours, as I reviewed all the reports, interviews, physical evidence, photos, and crime-scene forensics that had come back, and video- and audiotapes that NOPD still had possession of. Actually, we possessed copies of everything we turned over to FBI CI-3. I reviewed the items of interest I'd taken from Decon's crypt and apartment, and all of my illegally obtained stuff, such as the TDF files: everything Honey and I had gotten from the Scrap Brothers, from Brandt's offices, security video from Breaux's home and office, the files from his laptop. Lastly, I retrieved an impounded white Mercedes S550 that I'd gotten permission from the chief to have Kerry Broussard do some special forensics on.

Honey dropped in from time to time, mostly to brainstorm and to trigger new lines of thinking. We helped nightshift clear the Blanchard death as a suicide. And we administratively cleared Grigory Pelkov's murder by turning it over to the Feds—he was a Russian agent, after all. I invited Mackie and Kruger to drop by for takeout Thai food and Singha beers, to run angles by them and solicit advice I didn't really need on a strategy; I was trying to make nice with guys I'd be working with who might otherwise have reason to pour acid in my coffee due to my special status in the unit. And, yes, I drank a Singha, too; moderation in everything, including moderation.

I felt emotionally numb, having dissociated from all of the recent death and violence that I'd experienced up close and personal; my mind, however, felt razor-sharp, in spite of the dearth of sleep. A jangled anticipation flowed through my veins, energizing me.

We confirmed rumors that Peter Danforth had hired a high-priced criminal attorney and was trying to negotiate a deal with the federal prosecutor, the state, and the DA, granting him blanket immunity from any criminal prosecution in exchange for his cooperation in the pertinent ongoing investigations. I knew that dog wouldn't hunt, so I didn't feel any pressure.

Still, I wanted it over soonest, so seven days after the chief's big press conference, we put the hammer down.

While Mackie and Kruger convinced Danforth to accompany them downtown, ostensibly to identify items we suspected belonged to Del Breaux, Honey and I showed up at the Academy with a large support team.

"Detective Baybee," I said, waving a warrant—a real one this time—in the face of the two beefy guys dressed as swabbie MPs in the main entranceway, "how many times do we have to come back to this crazy place where these assholes think it's Halloween every day?"

"This will be the last time, Detective Saint James."

We used semitrailers to haul away all of the Soviet Bloc matériel Danforth had already showed us, and we found another storeroom that contained Del Breaux's most valuable stash, including the nonlethal-weapons electronics that he bought the night he died. We seized security video files going back twenty-one days, although I suspected they'd been tampered with; we found a few other goodies, and—very important—we took into custody a gentleman who wore a green cloth bracelet on his right hand.

Joey Bales was Danforth's on-and-off-again lover of the last nine years. Danforth had lied to us; Bales lived at the Academy. Barry Morrison had first told me about him the day we had lunch at Jack Dempsey's. Turns out both Bales and Danforth had been given dishonorable discharges way back when from the navy over violating Don't Ask, Don't Tell. Bales started falling apart like a twenty-dollar Hong Kong suit before we even got him downtown. We had to Miranda him in Honey's unit. Bales had multiple arrests for burglary and blabbed that he'd used the Jefferson brothers as fences for goods he'd stolen, but had nothing to do with their murders. He was eager to cut a deal, but we held off.

Honey and I slowly paraded Bales past a big window that looked into the interrogation room where Peter Danforth sat. Danforth's jaw practically hit the table when he saw his old lover. We put Bales on ice, conferred with Mackie and Kruger, then Honey and I entered the interrogation room with a laptop and some show-and-tell aides.

"Peter, thanks for coming in and helping us out," I said, smiling, setting a cardboard file box on a chair next to me. "You'll be happy to know our investigation is almost complete."

Danforth looked at us with contempt.

"I'd like to go now."

"Just a second," said Honey. "You need to look at some things."

"I need my lawyer."

"You can have one anytime you want, but do you really need a lawyer to help you look at some things?" I asked.

"Just hurry up then."

Danforth was being a little bit of a bitch.

"After you were dishonorably discharged from the U.S. Navy for conduct unbecoming, you moved to New Orleans. Ten months ago you bought a building that now houses the Academy, where you get to dress up as a rear admiral every day." I showed him copies of his discharge papers and a copy of the property deed to the Academy building. "You told us 'the owner' rented space to Del Breaux to warehouse his arms. You didn't tell us you were the owner."

"I didn't lie."

"No, you just didn't tell the truth," said Honey. "Right off the bat, just for warehousing the munitions improperly? You got all kinds of legal trouble."

I removed the cigar box of black ink pens with gold trim. Honey and I had just found it in with the Soviet Bloc matériel. I didn't tell him that we knew it had been taken from the Scrap Brothers file-cabinet safe. I simply took one of the pens and doodled on paper. Oh, and I twisted the top as he watched.

It was almost as if his mouth suddenly dried up. He didn't speak as his eyes riveted on the exploding pen.

"Look, I—" He couldn't take his eyes off the pen. I hadn't twisted the top back yet.

"One year ago you joined your sometime-lover Del Breaux in the arms business."

"The goods you showed us? That was your stash. Merchandise you had skimmed," said Honey.

"See, you needed to build up your own stash for when you replaced Breaux, because you didn't have enough working capital yet," I said. "Pelkov and Haddad got furious with Breaux for shorting shipments when there was bartering going on, but you were the guy doing it."

I twisted the cap back twenty-six seconds after first twisting it.

"I . . . ahh . . . don't know what you're talking about." He was sweating.

"And you only got a measly one percent of Breaux's action. You needed to do something about that," said Honey.

"How about a little treason. Hmm?"

I twisted the cap off the pen again.

"I mean if the government didn't care about selling the candy store, why should you or Breaux?" I tapped the pen on the desk; he couldn't take his eyes off it.

"Two and a half million from Tan Chu for the GIDEON sample and formula. That's some walkin'-around money. Was Breaux giving you a piece of that?" asked Honey.

"But then Pelkov had that great idea. I mean, why should Breaux settle for just two point five mil from the commies in Beijing? Why not get the Russkies and ragheads in on the action, right Pete?"

When I clicked the top closed, Danforth audibly exhaled.

"I was in Atlanta that weekend."

"Yeah, for about an hour and a half." I clicked on a laptop video file. "I've edited this copy for brevity, but here you are checking into the Atlanta Hilton with an unknown male; you dip your wick all over the place, don't you, Pete? Here you are both entering your hotel room. Thirty minutes later, here you are in drag—and you make a pretty good-looking bitch—leaving your room. Are you with me, Pete? Now you didn't fly back to New Orleans in drag; I figure you changed clothes in the airport bathroom, but Joey Bales bought a ticket in your name using his credit card, and this shot here shows you coming out of Terminal 2 at Louis Armstrong at about six o'clock Friday night."

"I want to deal. I want witness protection; I told you that from the beginning."

"We've already made a deal. But not with you." Honey stared at him.

We hadn't made any deal yet, but detectives are allowed to lie through their teeth in an interrogation such as this.

Danforth blanched. I twisted the cap on the pen again.

"Did you know today was movie day at Homicide, Detective Bay-bee?"

"I've got my ticket."

"So does Pete. Now take a look at this short subject; it shows men entering the offices of Breaux Enterprises the night Del Breaux and Ty Parks were killed."

"I wasn't there!"

"No, but look at this guy with a green cloth bracelet on. Why I think that's your old buddy, Joey. And here he is again, pretending to be an FBI agent and trying to get into Del Breaux's house to get the two and a half million and the top-secret laptop."

"You are insane."

"He's in the next room, you know. Joey."

I twirled the pen with my fingers, and then he watched me, mesmerized, twist it closed. Danforth looked like he was ready to vomit; the guilty often do that, right in the interrogation room. Honey used her foot to slide a plastic wastebasket on the floor closer to him.

I reached into the white box and retrieved a file. "Don't you love a Mercedes? I mean, I can't afford one, but you have to practically take a weekend seminar just to learn how to use all the gadgets and gizmos they have nowadays."

"Like built-in GPS," said Honey. "And GPS leaves a trail of bread crumbs. Like Hansel and Gretel. Tiny digital tracks. So we can re-create where a vehicle has been."

"Pete, you want to know where Del Breaux and Ty Parks stopped before they drove to the place where they were murdered?" I shoved the file toward him.

"You want to know about the cocaine we found in your room? At the Academy just now. Think it will chemically match the kilo left in the Jefferson brothers' file cabinet?" asked Honey.

"Want to see the FBI report on who drained Breaux's bank ac-counts?" I shoved another file at him. It was bogus, but that wasn't the point.

"Want to see records from Brandt's office showing that Breaux Enterprises secretly smuggled sensitive cargo via helicopter onto Nas-sir Haddad's ship as part of a three-way swap? Think you can't take the fall for that? You were helping to make the arrangements. A file on Breaux's laptop confirms it."

I clicked open the pen, practically holding it in his face.

"On Friday while you were flying to Atlanta, Tan Chu agreed to pay Del Breaux two and half million for the Project GIDEON sample and formula. You left a guy in your Atlanta hotel room ordering room ser-vice for two to make it look like a lover's weekend. But you flew back to NOLA, and on Friday night you were at Breaux's house when Grigory Pelkov and Nassir Haddad showed up with a counteroffer: split the sample three ways and give the formula to all three parties simultane-ously. You were the only one who didn't want Breaux to go for it."

"Because you already had a deal in place with Chu. Certain ar-rangements had already been made," said Honey.

"On Saturday Tan Chu handed over the two and half million, but Breaux stalled him on delivering the goods, because he had to give Pelkov and Haddad time to assemble cash for the secret side deal. But Chu got wind of the double cross that night at Restaurant August. He was furious, but he already had a plan. And you were the linchpin. After returning home from the auction at Michoud Building J-19, Del Breaux got a call from the pay phone at Banks Street Bar. That was you calling, convincing him to meet you at the Academy at one A.M. Breaux and Ty Parks picked up you and Joey Bales in the Mercedes for the drive to that secluded parking lot near the old Calliope Projects, where Tan Chu's boys were waiting."

"You can't—"

"The murder weapon came from Nassir Haddad's ship. Did you get it from him in exchange for giving up some booty?"

"I—"

"Del wasn't going to give you a piece of the GIDEON action; why should he? You'd seen that coming a long time ago. So you made a side deal with Chu. You called him a few times the last few weeks; I have the phone logs. Let me guess: he offered to make you the new Del Breaux of the Buyer's Club; all you had to do, Judas, was to deliver him to that parking lot with the GIDEON sample, the sample you had under lock and key at the Academy. Then you'd get to keep the two point five million, right?"

"You murdered Del Breaux! You shot Ty Parks in the head at point-blank range!" Honey was practically screaming, in his face.

"I did not!"

"Joey's already given you up, man! You're going to Angola for the rest of your sick life, where that sweet little ass of yours will be getting a pretty good workout around the clock by some big bulls, you understand?"

"Click that pen closed! Please!"

I clicked it closed—the bomb squad had disarmed it—just as Danforth turned sideways and tossed his cookies. Thankfully, he delivered them right into the wastebasket. When he sat back upright, his eyes were wet and ringed with red.

"I guess I let things get out of hand."

As understatements went, I thought Danforth's was pretty good.

"You weren't the only one who let things get out of hand. Just tell us what happened in that parking lot," said Honey.

"Tong killed Del and Ty. Chu and two of his other men were there; one of them is a really tall guy. I didn't kill anybody. It didn't occur to me that . . . they would do that."

Honey and I shot each other a look. This was one of those confessions where the guilty party has admitted his guilt, but then tries to spin the scenario in a way to make him seem inculpable.

"I made a deal with Chu. He offered me a half million if I could get Del to that parking lot with the GIDEON material. But I didn't know he was going to kill him. And when he did, what was I supposed to do, protest? Then get shot myself?"

"He wanted you to get the laptop, too, didn't he?"

"Yes. That's why Joey and some of the guys took Del's computer from his office, in case he had the GIDEON formula on his PC. But he didn't. So we tried to get into his house."

"Breaux's renters stopped that."

"Yes."

"And the Jefferson brothers?" asked Honey.

Danforth pursed his lips together.

"You were there, Peter. You supplied the cocaine that went into the file cabinet. And while you were at it, you took the box of exploding ink pens that we just found at the Academy."

"I didn't kill those people, either."

"Why were you even there?"

"Chu and Tong were unbelievably angry that the shipment got intercepted at the port and that the GIDEON sample disappeared. I guess Chu was covering his tracks by killing the Jeffersons. Tong picked me up. Maybe they wanted me to see what they were going to do, as a way to keep me in line down the road. That was my impression, anyway."

"Why put the guys through the shredder?"

"Leroy or Jimmy wouldn't give up the combination to the safe. Chu wanted the money that was inside. He was furious he'd paid two and half million, plus a half million to me, but had gotten nothing. He said he would be in trouble with Beijing if he didn't get something in return."

"Chu had you plant the cocaine to make it look like a drug hit?"

"Yes."

"And he gave you the box of exploding ink pens as a memento, right?"

"He told me to take them. They'd just killed three people, so I wasn't going to refuse them anything."

"Peter, you're doing pretty well, but you're leaving something out."

Danforth looked at me through hollow eyes.

"The silver cargo container?"

But Danforth was done singing. "I want my lawyer. Now."

"We'll get your lawyer right now, Pete, but just one more thought. If you didn't know Chu was going to remove Breaux from the picture, how could you have gotten Joey and your team of boys into mover's uniforms and supplied with replacement computers so they could be at Breaux Enterprises before Del's body was even cold? That kind of sounds premeditated."

Danforth's mouth opened, but the only sound he made was that retching rasp from the dry heaves.

Honey and I had lots more questions, but it didn't matter. It smelled worse than a Bourbon Street urinal in the room, so we called for the lawyer and booked Peter Danforth on multiple felonies, including five counts of murder one.

CHAPTER THIRTY-TWO

Chief Pointer was getting more press than a Hollywood starlet in rehab. Since Honey looked better on camera, I stuck her with the honor
of representing NOPD Homicide to the local newshounds who hung
on every recounted detail of Peter Danforth's treachery.

Of course, Danforth's duplicity paled in comparison to the ruth-
lessness of Tan Chu. The Chinese agent had Breaux and Parks, the
Jefferson brothers, their employee Herbert, and TDF owner Eddie Liu
all scrubbed for the simple reason that dead men tell no tales. Well,
that rule now applied to him as well as Pelkov and Haddad. And with
Clayton Brandt in prison, the Buyer's Club was no more. I should have
felt satisfaction—the murders were solved, the arms-dealing operation
in New Orleans shut down—but instead I couldn't shake the notion
that I'd achieved a *Pyrrhic* victory. I harbored no illusions that the Pentagon would change their ways, nor could I say that I'd want to take on
another case like this anytime soon.

Still, one piece of the puzzle remained, so I cruised with Fred Gaudet
in his unmarked unit over to North White Street and pulled into the
driveway of a corner house, a couple blocks from CC's Coffee House
on Esplanade. This property was number seventeen on my list of

thirty-five. Danforth had told the truth about one thing: he owned a lot of property and was rich on paper.

The shotgun house strangely had a big yard but wasn't much to look at. But then, a whole lot of houses in New Orleans looked more like piles of kindling than they did homes.

We circled around back, dodging an old broken sink and a battered hot-water heater. I was about to cross this property off my list.

And then it caught my eye.

In the ongoing post-Storm recovery, it was still very common to see all kinds of things in people's yards: FEMA trailers, mobile homes and RVs, heavy equipment, piles of construction materials, piles of debris, and portable steel storage containers.

There was a FEMA trailer in the side yard of the corner lot that I hadn't paid much attention to. On the other side of the FEMA trailer, tarps partially covered a steel container. But this wasn't one of the little ten- or twenty-footers so often seen in yards around town. This one was a forty-foot, oceangoing cargo container.

A silver one. With the doors welded shut.

I'd texted Honey to come ASAP with a warrant, had already picked the hockey-puck-type lock, and now we all three stood in front of the big steel box.

"I say we open the gifts now instead of waiting till Christmas morning." And with that, I wrenched up the two levers simultaneously and muscled them to the right. Gaudet had grabbed a tire tool from his trunk, and he wedged it into a door crack.

"One, two, three . . ."

I pulled the handles as he put his weight onto the tool, and the welds broke, the door popped open.

"Imagine that," said Honey, gawking at the contents.

"Holy crap," said Gaudet, wiping sweat from his forehead.

"Funny," I said, shaking my head. "This container has absolutely nothing to do with the murders or the arms dealing."

"Yeah, but this is huge! I recognize some of this stuff. These bronzes were stolen from that famous artist's studio over in Mid-City." Gaudet was a burglary detective, so it was perfect he stood here in front of a treasure trove of loot.

"The Jefferson brothers knew enough not to melt them down."

"The marble-topped table with the gold gilt? Used to be in the lobby at the Fairmont," said Honey.

"The Fairmont was badly looted. Bet some of this other stuff came from there, too." I used my SureFire to light the way. The temperature was sweltering in the trailer, but we were too fascinated to complain. I came across large cartons stuffed with brand new Rolex watches still in their boxes, and small leather cases full of gold and diamond jewelry. "Damn, there's a whole jewelry store in here."

"See those paintings. Looted from Jonathan Murphy, that rich collector Uptown," said Gaudet.

"There has to be ten, maybe fifteen million dollars' worth of merchandise in this container," I said. "Maybe more. Some pretty good junk."

"We need to take photos. Post them on the NOPD Web site. Chief Pointer has sticky fingers," noted Honey.

We found exquisite silver services, artwork of all kinds, gold coin collections, an antique firearms collection that was alone worth over a million. Furniture, crystal, tortoiseshell jewelry boxes brimming with precious stones.

"I get it. Joey Bales fenced high-value stolen items to Leroy and Jimmy after the Storm. He must have gotten a look at what was in this container before it was sealed. He told his boyfriend Danforth about it. Part of Danforth's deal with Chu must have been that he got custody of the silver container."

"But why did the Jeffersons keep the merch? Locked in a container?" asked Honey.

"I know why I would," I said.

Gaudet nodded. "There was so much loot in play after the Storm, prices dropped. If a guy isn't pressed for cash, better to sit on your stash till a later date."

"And better to let the heat die down. This stuff was red hot."

"The Jefferson boys were smarter than we thought," said Honey.

"Yeah." I shrugged. "But look where it got them."

The recovery of stolen goods garnered more ink and TV time than the arrest of Danforth for the five murders. New Orleanians were so used to the overwhelming tide of murder and mayhem that they sometimes tuned it out.

"Another quintuple murder today, darling."

"Really, what's for dinner, steak tartar?"

Due to all the press, for about a week I couldn't buy a drink anywhere in town. I hated it. Better to keep a low profile; you can get away with more. And Twee Siu's words haunted me. Decon had made the ultimate sacrifice, but his deeds would go unsung. I got fifteen minutes of fame just for recovering some stolen property. It's no secret that life isn't fair, but I was currently shedding guilt and not taking any on.

The onslaught of so much good press had strengthened the chief's position to the extent the mayor had to set aside any attempt to force Pointer's resignation. I wasn't sure that was a good development, but it meant I still carried a gold shield.

I returned to my dojo for the first time since I'd killed Bobby Perdue. I was still too banged up to participate, but I climbed back into the fight cage and offered comment and encouragement as Kendall and Big Bob took turns sparring with students.

I asked Honey on a date and she accepted. Over a bottle of pricey Chilean Shiraz I told her I loved her and that I would like us to move in together and become a real couple, complete with sexual intimacy. I told her this would be a big step toward helping me to clarify confusing elements of my personal life. I told her I thought we would make good life partners and would have beautiful children. She said we already were good life partners and quickly changed the subject. I could tell I had made her feel uncomfortable and realized that if we were ever going to become traditional mates, it would happen thanks to her doing and at her pace.

I hadn't yet called Harding, but I knew that day would probably come. I had a serious bone to pick with her. I knew from the get-go that I couldn't count on her to back me in the clutch, but she'd proven more than true to form; she had helped set me up.

As for Twee, I'd always judged her pretty harshly. And damned if I simply couldn't figure whether I was justified in doing so or not. I started to receive copies of classified intelligence reports related to local activities that were delivered to my loft in plain envelopes. I burned after reading and didn't need an astrologer to tell me that a beautiful and mysterious Asian woman was going to play a role in my future.

I kept thinking about Decon. About our talks of violence, redemption, of how I needed to forgive myself. Intellectually, I had gotten to a place where I was comfortable again being who I was, warts and all. Decon and Twee had both been correct: I was indeed more like them than I cared to admit. I repeatedly broke the rules and used illicit means to justify the ends. I could argue gradations, I could hide behind the logic, for example, that I only applied extrajudicial applications of nonlethal force upon those whom I knew to be guilty and who withheld pertinent information necessary to obtain in order to achieve some good. But those were just fancy words that papered over what I really was. I played a dirty game with as much integrity as possible, but I played it. And I knew I would continue to play the dirty game again and again, and let God be my judge, not man.

As for Bobby Perdue, thoughts of him no longer plagued me. Still, I found myself driving with the windows down one beautiful fall afternoon over the I-10 twin spans to Slidell. A new, supposedly hurricane-proof bridge was being built right alongside the old one. It was a sign of progress. Hope for some kind of good future. One took such signs where one could find them in the rubble that was still New Orleans.

I parked in front of Bobby Perdue's parents' home but didn't get out of the Bronco. I simply started to cry. I don't know where it came from or what brought it on so suddenly, but I lost all control and wept openly. I tried to stop it but couldn't; it gushed out. I cried for the souls of those I had killed, for those I'd loved and lost, like my dad and my younger brother, for a dead female friend named Kiesha Taylor, for a failed marriage, for everyone I had ever hurt. I cried for the souls I knew I would be taking in the future. I cried for Decon Daniel Hawthorne Doakes, aka Dawson Hayward, a pretty awesome guy who died in my arms.

But mostly I cried for a little boy. The innocent one I used to be.

I became aware of people watching me. Bobby Perdue's parents stood at the passenger window, looking in. I didn't know how long they had been there, but they held each other.

I reached for my keys and started the engine, ready to pull away as I wiped at my eyes. I didn't want anyone to see me like this, didn't want the Perdues screaming at me right now.

"You've come to our home three times," said Bobby Perdue's father. "The first two times you tried to apologize. You were big enough to do that, and now we are big enough to accept. Please come into our home."

I couldn't speak but I nodded. I wiped away more tears and cleared my throat. I turned off the engine and reached for the door handle. FEMA trailers still sat in many front yards on the block as people slowly facilitated repairs to their storm-damaged homes, most likely the folks who didn't have insurance, and so the self-financed repairs went slowly. Kids played kickball in the street; a couple of boys dueled using slats from a broken picket fence. Two guys up on a roof nailed shingles in the sun. A mom pulled her SUV into a driveway and unloaded bags of groceries. People were rebuilding things, getting on with their lives.

I opened the door to the Bronco and felt pretty damned lucky to be getting on with mine.